HOUSE OF Libra

The Ascendant Series   Book III

Whitney Estenson

Flint Hills Publishing

Flint Hills Publishing
www.flinthillspublishing.com
Topeka, Kansas U.S.A.

ISBN-13: 978-0-9997547-7-1
ISBN-10: 0-9997547-7-7

For my parents.
I love you both.

You will free yourself when you learn to be neutral and follow the instructions of your heart without letting things perturb you. This is the way of Maat.

~ Egyptian Proverbs

Prologue

The sea was angry.

The waves crashed against the cliffs of Awen, their spray reaching for the darkened sky as if it were trying to pluck each star from its grasp. Carefully, I climbed down a rocky hill, following the lit torches that had been left to guide my way onto a hidden beach. Tucked between the two bigger cliffs, the small alcove was safe from the rolling sea, the sand fine and white, looking more like salt in the dark than anything else. My boots sunk into it as I leapt from the rocky edge and onto its soft padding. From down here, the city was hidden from view. The ocean pounded into the nearby cliffs, the waves ricocheting over their peaks, the spray misting my face.

I was the last to arrive.

The Nomarchs stood on the untouched beach, dressed in hooded robes that swept the surface of the sand. I couldn't see their faces, but each robe was colored to represent their element and the jeweled tones flickered in the torch light. I did a quick count.

Eleven. There were only eleven Nomarchs.

One ruby red robe was missing. The Aries Nomarch had yet to arrive in Awen to claim Drake's throne. The new Nomarchs had taken their seats two days ago, during the first night of the full moon. It was a quiet ceremony, one held in the private chambers of the Council Hall. Typically, it would be a large affair—a celebration even. But there was no celebration this time. There was no time for fanfare.

We were at war.

The Nomarchs were situated in a circle, the same order no doubt they sat inside their chambers. Inside the circle of Nomarchs were four large bonfires. Their flames raged toward the sky, their crackling the only sound other than the roar of the sea. In front of them were three others. Grady Dunn, Brynn Hughes, and Roman Sands stood around a podium. They were all dressed in gear similar to mine, their eyes following me as I joined them inside the circle, stepping up to the dais. I kept my eyes trained ahead, avoiding contact with any of them. The pull of Roman's presence tugged at me, demanding I acknowledge him, but I resisted. I couldn't allow anyone to see me recognize him. I wasn't sure if I could hide my feelings so soon to getting him back. So close to the flames now, the strength of my element filled me and I used its power to help me keep my eyes forward. The podium in the middle of the circle was a makeshift stand made from a gnarled piece of driftwood. It was large and flat and atop it sat four silver Kindred daggers, a large silver bowl, and a book I hadn't seen in months.

The Book of Breathings.

Tonight, the four of us would take our vows and join the Guard. While we would be bestowed the powers needed to defeat our enemy through the right to practice magic, the magic came at a cost. The four of us would be bound to each other for life. Bound to obey the will of the Nomarch Council. Forbidden to ever leave the Guard and lead any semblance of a normal life. Forbidden to love.

As soon as I took my place the ceremony began. From the corner of my eye, a glimmering of light appeared in the cliff face. Out of a cave opening that was otherwise hidden, an old woman appeared, hunched over, her back painfully twisted. She held a torch in her hand, briefly illuminating the rock above her. Symbols of the Zodiac were carved into it, proving that the cave wasn't a cave at all but rather a temple. I knew very little about the Guard induction ceremony, only that it was performed by a priestess, a Kindred that still practiced the old ways and worshipped the ancient gods. As I understood it, she was the last of her kind, a final connection to those that remembered when the gods walked the earth. The priestess stepped into the circle, her grey hair shining, and as her eyes landed on me—I flinched, surprised at their clarity. She smiled knowingly at my nervousness before stepping between Grady and Roman to place her hands on the book with loving familiarity.

She began to speak, her words loud and commanding in an

ancient language I didn't understand. As she spoke, the flames behind each of us seemed to grow, as if they were dancing to the tune of her words. She picked up one of the daggers and turned to Grady. He eyed her warily but made no attempt to move. With lightning quickness that should have been impossible for someone her age, the woman snatched Grady's hand, bringing the dagger down over his palm. He hissed in pain, blood pouring out from the wound, dripping into the sand. She pulled his hand over the bowl, letting the blood pool in the basin. As the first drop hit the bowl, Grady's eyes lit a brilliant green. He gasped in shock, as if the power had been pulled from him involuntarily. The flames behind Grady turned a deep green, and the smell of the forest filled my nose as if I were standing in the middle of the Allegheny.

The woman turned to Brynn next, pausing only to switch daggers. She did the same as before, cutting Brynn's hand and dripping her blood into the basin—Brynn's blood mixing with Grady's. The flames behind her crackled with blue sparks before turning the purest azure. The icy blue of Brynn's eyes shone in the darkness. The forest disappeared from my senses, replaced by the bitter taste of salt on my tongue.

Next, she turned to me. I held out my hand, prepared for the sharp bite of the blade. The moment the blade hit my hand, the well of power inside me exploded, bursting out of me. I grit my teeth, trying to control and manipulate the power pouring out. My eyes were a sharp red, and I knew if I turned, the flames would match them. The salt evaporated from my tongue, and I was overwhelmed by the smell of smoke. I held my hand over the basin until the bleeding stopped and the wound healed.

Finally, the woman turned to Roman, the last one left untouched. She brought the blade down, Roman not even so much as flinching at the contact. When the blood entered the bowl, his power surged forward, turning his eyes a molten gold.

The woman returned to the book, placing her hands on either side of it. She finished her incantation, her words swift and nearly undetectable. As she spoke, the brand on my palm sizzled, a circle appearing underneath each line, livid red. One for each of the people I was now bound to for eternity.

The beach went silent, the ancient woman slamming the book closed. The flames returned to normal. She raised her head, not looking to any of us, but to the Nomarchs.

"It is done."

1

The smell of smoke hung heavy in the air, blanketing the city.

It was early, a few hours before dawn, and the city had finally settled into sleep. Torches lined the streets, still lit and illuminating the stone paths that wound past the houses and deep into the heart of Awen. The strength of their flames caressed my arms, filling me with their power and helping me replenish the strength I'd lost during my day's work. I had spent the day, just as I had the last several, at the infirmary, doing my best to help Cassie and the other healers tend to the wounded. I didn't have the knowledge or skills they did, but I could take orders. I did everything I was told to do—wrapping the injuries of the wounded in bandages, cleaning the sick beds, even helping remove the bodies after the injured fell to their wounds. When the work was done, I'd left the infirmary to clean up before heading to the arena at midnight for another funeral.

It'd been over a month since Ezekiel attacked Awen with

his hybrid army and succeeded in releasing the great chaos god, Set. Over a month since Grady had killed Roman, only for me to use my power as a Descendant and his Rafiq to bring him back from the dead. Hundreds of Kindred had been lost in the attack, including four Nomarchs, the oldest of our houses and leaders of our government. Even as time passed, the number of deaths only seemed to be growing. Despite the efforts of the healers, despite all we'd done to help, almost every night for the past several weeks ended in the same place. Tonight had been no different. Two more had died today, succumbing to their wounds suffered during the attack. Two more pyres were lit, adding their smoke and ash to the already hazy sky.

I raised my hood over my head and tucked my hands inside the pockets of my vest, hiding my newly transformed brand. It was unique to those of us in the Guard and others could use it to identify me. Even though the streets were mainly abandoned, I didn't want to run the risk of someone recognizing me. I was too exhausted to deal with it.

The vest I wore was made of a thick, black leather and covered my torso, cutting off at the shoulder, leaving my arms open and mobile. While the heavy material could be sweltering in the dense heat of the island, I wasn't wearing it for style. The leather was part of the new fighting gear I'd been given. Paired with combat pants and boots, the vest was specially designed to be knife resistant while simultaneously allowing me the flexibility needed to fight. My dagger was strapped to my waist, my smaller ring daggers tucked into the scabbard on my ankle. Since recent events, I never went anywhere unless I was dressed in full gear and armed. I had been caught unprepared before. It would never happen again.

Long before Ezekiel and his hybrids invaded, I'd come to Awen in hopes of convincing the Nomarch Council to grant me access to The Book of Breathings, our most coveted and powerful artifact. I was convinced it was the only way to bring back Roman, who had been possessed by a wraith and turned into one of Ezekiel's hybrids. As soon as I stepped foot on the island, I realized it would not be a simple task to convince the Council to give me the book. As the daughter of a woman they deemed a traitor, and the last descendant of the first Aries, the Council saw me as a threat and quickly moved to silence and control me. With no other option, I demanded they reinstate The Blinding of Truth by Falsehood, an ancient and violent challenge between the twelve houses. Only through winning The Blinding could I force the Council to hand over the book. I trained for months to prepare for The Blinding, but on the eve of the competition I was betrayed. Grady Dunn, a man I thought was honorable, a man I thought I could learn to trust, turned on me and watched as Amina—the Scorpio Nomarch—had me arrested, thrown in a dungeon, and then stabbed me. All because I refused to bend to her will. Had it not been for my heritage and superior strength and healing as a Descendant, I would have died before The Blinding even began.

I crossed over the bridge above the river, paying little attention to the water below me. I remembered when I first came to the island, how clear I thought the water was. So blue, I swore I could see the riverbed from the plane still high in the sky. Now, in the middle of the night and with the stars and moon obscured by the ever-present smoke, the water ran black. The arena loomed above me, its broken form a reminder of the hell we'd all been through. I hated the arena. It was where Amina stabbed me. Where I fought for my life in The Blinding and where Ezekiel's army attacked. His hybrids had blasted through the arena wall, cracking the floor right down the middle, tearing open a large fissure and reducing a part of the stadium to rubble. His hybrids poured in over the demolished wall, taking us all by surprise. We did our best to fight back, but hundreds of Kindred died on the sands. Even when it was all over and Ezekiel had released Set, allowing the chaos dod to possess his body right before he vanished with his army, the arena was where we returned.

The dirt crunched under my boots as I stepped around a large chunk of stone that laid against the outer arena wall. It could've been part of the stadium seats, or maybe the dais. Both had been heavily damaged during the attack. There was a dark stain on the jagged edge of the stone, one I knew was blood even before the sharp, metallic scent reached me.

The arena wasn't the only part of the island that had been damaged. As I approached the library, I could see remnants of battle. There were scorch marks in some of the pillars, pieces missing in others. I walked through the front door of the library, my heavy boots echoing off the tile floor. The library was typically closed at this time, but all personnel had been moved to either tending the wounded, rebuilding the city, or defending our borders. No one had time to worry about business hours.

I walked straight through the dark antechamber, directly toward the back of the library where I knew I'd find him. He'd been coming to the library every day for weeks, only leaving when I forced him to. The back corner had become his claimed area, covered in books from all over the world.

As I reached the back of the library, the air changed. The constant heavy heat lifted, replaced by the refreshing cool air that always surrounded me when Roman was near. I rounded the last shelf of books, stopping to lean against it and admire the man in front of me. Part of me still couldn't believe he was back, despite all the evidence to the contrary. He sat humped over a table, completely engrossed in the book in front of him, his back to me. Roman's skin had returned to its normal color, his deep tan obvious even in the minimal torch light. His hair was shorter, trimmed and well kept. He wore gear similar to my own, but instead of cutting off at the shoulder, his was full sleeved, something I knew he did to cover the was-sceptre tattoo on his arm. He hated that tattoo, the one remaining mark of his time as Ezekiel's second in command, but there was nothing he could do to remove it. Just above the collar of his shirt I could see the raised edge of a scar, one that I knew attached to four more just like it, each a perfect match for my fingers, left there from when I brought him back from the dead.

"Your staring is really starting to get creepy."

His voice startled me and I jumped away from the bookshelf. "I wasn't staring," I responded defensively, coming around to sit in the seat next to him. His eyes followed me, a small smirk teasing the edge of his lip as if he were trying not to laugh. "I was admiring," I added.

"Still creepy," he teased.

I punched him lightly in the arm. "Whatever." He laughed, pleased he got a rise out of me. I reached up and lowered my hood, loosened my braid, and shook my hair free. I scanned over the table. It was scattered with books, organized in some way invisible to me. "Find anything new today?" I asked. There was no reply. I turned to look at Roman, but I found him already staring at me. His eyes were shadowed with exhaustion, but the blue shone clear. His gaze moved slowly, following the wave of hair that fell over my back. It had been months since I'd had a haircut and my tresses were wild and almost halfway down my back. Suddenly self-conscious, I raised my hand to pull my hair back, but Roman stopped me, his hand landing lightly on mine.

"Don't," he said quietly. "Leave it down." He lowered our hands, threading our fingers together. An ache bloomed deep in my chest, one that I knew couldn't be fixed. I looked around quickly. It was the middle of the night, but I could never be too careful. Someone could always be watching us. I squeezed his fingers once, a gesture I hoped he would understand. I wished I could hold his hand. I wished I could show the world how much I loved him, but I couldn't. We couldn't. I smiled sadly, then slid my fingers out from between his. His eyes dropped in disappointment.

"I'm sorry," I said quietly, the mood now somber. "You know I wish. . ."

"I know," he cut me off. He took a deep breath and looked me in the eyes again. "Trust me, I know."

I growled, my frustration getting the better of me. "I hate this," I hissed. "It doesn't make any sense. Why can't we just tell everyone we're together?"

"You can't tell anyone. Ever," Roman answered immediately.

"Why not?" I begged. "What is so wrong about us being in love?"

Roman slid his chair my direction, facing me head on. "The Council created the Guard to be their most elite soldiers. Warriors so dedicated to their cause, they would lay down their lives to protect the book. The Guard cannot afford distractions or complications but must be singularly focused on their mission. A soldier in love has a weakness, one that can be exploited by the enemy. Love leaves a warrior vulnerable."

"You don't really believe that, do you?" I asked, my hand instinctively finding his.

"What matters is that the Council believes it. And after what happened with your parents, I'm afraid all it did was prove their point and strengthen their resolve. They cannot find out about us. Ever."

I nodded quietly, his words hitting home. "Two more planes arrived today," I said, changing the subject. "I looked for you on the tarmac. The Guard was expected to greet the last of the Council's army. They each held over a hundred warriors."

Roman shrugged, turning his chair back toward the table. "Unless they give me a direct order, The Council can *expect* whatever they want. The Council's army may be here, but they have no idea where the enemy is. None of us do," Roman added, slamming the book in front of him shut and throwing it angrily on the table. "Did you do more tests today?"

I nodded. "Just a little bit earlier. I have another one tomorrow morning. I think they're starting to give up on me." He shook his head. "I don't know what they think they'll find. I don't know how I did those things any more than they do."

"What did you have to do today?"

"Nothing, really. They just drew more blood. I think they're trying to find what it is about my blood that is different from everybody else's."

"Did they find anything?" he asked.

I shrugged. "If they have, they haven't shared it with me. They're being pretty secretive."

"Not surprising," Roman grumbled.

"Your pile of books seems to be growing," I said, hoping to distract him from his irritation. I nodded toward the mountain of books practically spilling off the table. "How do you keep them all organized?"

"These," he said, pointing at the ones closest to him, "are everything I could find about Set or the was-sceptre. Those in the back are the few I could find pertaining to the Guard, Rafiqs, or any mention of Marius and Davina. Most of that information is locked in special collections." I noticed his personal notebook was included in that stack. I'd never seen inside it, never even asked what was in it. If he included it in that pile, I could only assume it had something to do with the mystery of his parentage.

"And those?" I asked, pointing to another pile.

"Resurrection," he said plainly. "Anything that mentions resurrection rituals or bringing people back from the dead."

"Are you searching for answers of how Ezekiel resurrected Set? Or how I brought you back?"

"Both," he answered simply. "I figured it doesn't hurt for us to do our own research. If we know what spell Ezekiel used, we may be able to reverse it."

"What have you found?" I asked. "Anything about the location of the was-sceptre or Ezekiel-Set—whatever we're calling him. What do we call him, anyway? Is Ezekiel still even technically alive?" It seemed like an odd question to ask, but it had been nagging at me for weeks.

"An ancient god possessed his body. I think it's safe to say

14

that Ezekiel as we knew him is officially dead." I shrugged. Made sense, I guessed. "And to answer your other question, no. I haven't found anything useful. I can't find a single book that makes more than a single mention of Marius or Davina, let alone their descendants. We know what happened to Davina, your dreams showed you that, but there is no mention of Marius, or how he died. It's all locked behind those damn doors. So I'm no closer to piecing together how I'm related to her. Where Set and the sceptre are concerned, Ezekiel was always very secretive of the details of his plan. I never knew where his home base was, let alone what his next steps were after raising Set. So, I've got nothing."

"The Council claims the Kindred don't have the was-sceptre, that it somehow disappeared when Set was killed."

"And you believe them?" Roman asked.

"I never believe them. Have you checked The Book of Breathings?"

Roman shook his head. "Brynn has it. I don't think we'll find anything in it anyway. If the Council is hiding the was-sceptre, I doubt there is any official record of its location. Brynn's been using it to study Ezekiel's hybrid spell. I only managed to get it away from her for about two hours yesterday before she stole it back."

"What about this?" I asked, pointing at a book I recognized on the corner of the table. I grabbed it, pulling it closer. My eyes scanned the familiar drawings. The first one showed a woman sitting atop a throne, her head adorned with an elaborate crown topped off with a feather. She held the was-sceptre in her hand. The second drawing showed the same woman, mid battle and using the was-sceptre to defend herself against some sort of human-animal hybrid. The third and final drawing depicted the hybrid standing victorious over the woman, the was-sceptre now firmly in his hand. There was a series of hieroglyphics underneath all three drawings.

"All I know," Roman said, standing and grabbing another book and plopping it next to the first, "is that this symbol means 'Set.' " He pointed to a symbol in the inscription and then the English translation in the second book. "Which makes the creature in the drawing Set. Which we both already knew."

"Any idea who the woman is?" I asked.

He shook his head. "A pharaoh or goddess of some kind. It's unclear. She's holding the was-sceptre, so my guess is a goddess." He ran his fingers through his hair, scratching the back of his head in frustration. Even without our connection I knew he was exhausted and overworking himself. "What?" he snapped.

I shrugged innocently. "I didn't say anything."

"You don't have to," he replied. "I can feel your emotions. Just say what you're thinking."

I chose to brush off his tone. "You just look tired. I think you need your rest. You can't keep staying here all night."

"You're one to talk." He nodded at my hands, at my broken

and cracked nails, stained red with the blood of others. "Spend the night at the infirmary again?"

I tucked my fingers in, hiding the evidence. "Seemed like the best use of my time. Anytime I try to sleep, I keep getting visions."

"Anything useful yet?" he asked.

I shook my head. "Not so far. I keep seeing the same thing. A dark cave with two tunnels. Torches are posted on either side of the tunnels, lighting the mouth of the cave. I can hear running water, like there's an underground river or waterfall, but anytime I try to move toward one of the tunnels, I'm overcome by this sense of fear and dread. It cripples me, and I never make it into one of the tunnels. I wake up gasping for breath."

He nodded. "I remember." The first time I'd had the dream, I'd been so frightened when I woke up, I wasn't able to calm myself down. I'd gone into a full panic attack. My fear had been so strong, it'd woken Roman up across the island. He ran all the way to my cottage and burst in to find me on the floor hyperventilating. He fell to the ground with me, pulling me into his arms. He'd cradled me, enveloping me in his power and breathing slowly, filling my lungs with oxygen and soothing me until my breaths began to match his and I regained control. That night, he'd carried me back to bed and held me until morning, watching over me in case the nightmare returned.

"I'm sorry."

He looked at me in genuine shock. "What do you have to

apologize for?"

"I know my dreams are stressful and that they—they stress the bond. You shouldn't have to deal with that."

He shook his head, reaching out and running his fingers through my hair, gripping the side of my face, almost as if he couldn't help himself this time. As if he needed to touch me as much as I needed him. No one was around, I told myself. No one could see. I leaned into his hand. "You have nothing to apologize for. After everything that's happened, everything I've put you through. You *never* need to apologize to me."

It broke my heart to hear those words. To hear that he thought it was him that put me through that hell. He was not to blame for what happened to him. Only Ezekiel was. Set might be possessing Ezekiel's body, but I was still going to make him pay.

Roman leaned closer, pulling me to him at the same time. I knew we shouldn't be doing this, that he was right earlier— and that it was risky. I was just about to tell him we should stop when his lips brushed mine and all my resolve melted away. His fingers kneaded the back of my neck and I kissed him again.

A sound pierced the darkness. A door snicking shut somewhere in the library. We jumped apart. I went so far as to leave my chair and go to the other side of the table. We both stood there silently, looking anywhere but at each other as we waited to hear the sound return.

"I should get back to the infirmary," I said, breaking the

tension. "Two more died today."

He nodded. "Yeah, I know. Good idea."

"You should really think about coming to one of the funerals."

He shook his head. "We both know that's not a good idea." He leaned forward on the table. "The people hate me, and I can't even blame them for it. Me showing up at one of the funerals would dishonor the dead."

"Hiding in here isn't doing anything to change their minds. We're in the Guard now. The people will respect you. Revere you." I didn't say it aloud, but I was dealing with a lot of the same issues. The Council had tried to keep it quiet, but some of the other Kindred had learned it was my blood that unlocked Set's cage. Many of them blamed me for what happened. "Don't leave me alone with them," I begged. The other Guard members, Grady and Brynn, were no friends to Roman and me, and frankly I was tired of dealing with them by myself.

Roman huffed, pushing the book in front of him back onto the table. He pinched the bridge of his nose. "We've had this conversation before," he replied tersely. He was right, we had. Several times. Each time went the same way—me insisting that he get out in public, him refusing to do so.

"The people can't see the Guard as just an extension of the Council. We need to separate ourselves from them, show the people that we're on their side."

"I said no, Kyndal." His tone was firm.

I shook my head. It was so typical of us to go from kissing to arguing all in the same conversation. We were always pushing each other, always disagreeing on the best way to do things. "Fine," I said, a plan formulating in my head. "I'll fight you for it."

He sat back in his chair, looking up at me. "Fight for it? You want to fight me?"

"Yes," I replied adamantly. "First to get the kill shot wins, just like before. I win, and you have to stop hiding in the library. No more waiting. Out in public today. You win, and I shut up and never mention it again."

"You remember what happened last time we sparred?"

I did remember. It was months ago, back in Pennsylvania. I'd challenged him when I thought he wasn't doing enough to help me train. He'd beaten me easily, embarrassing me in front of the others. I wasn't the same person I was then. I was stronger, faster, with much more control over my powers. "Scared?" I taunted.

The muscle in his jaw pulsed and I knew I had him. Roman could never back down from a challenge. He gave me a cocky grin. "Fine," he relented. "I'll fight you."

I nodded once, walking around the table and pausing when I reached Roman. "Good. I'll meet you at the training facility after my morning tests."

2

My testing began at dawn. When I'd first come to the island, I'd struggled to keep track of time. With no electricity, there were no digital clocks, and the vortex screwed with any analog devices, so we were left using sundials to tell time. There were large ones positioned throughout the island, and some of the main buildings kept them outside their doors, but I'd learned to keep a general idea of the time without them, using the sun's position in the sky as my guide.

I entered Council Chambers, nodding at the guards at the door on my way through. I immediately headed off to the left and around the main chamber. I wouldn't be meeting in the throne room, but rather in one of the smaller rooms that I had dubbed the conference room. I was a little early, so I sat down on the hallway floor, leaning my head against the wall and closing my eyes. Since I wasn't sleeping well, I was in a constant state of exhaustion. On top of the insomnia, the Council's tests were grueling, and I was barely surviving. I hadn't lied earlier when I told Roman they'd taken more blood, I just hadn't told him the rest. I'd been meeting with Astrid and Maks, two of the Nomarchs, for nearly a month now. Every time I saw them, they put me through a series of physical tests, checking my strength, my speed, my ability to heal. I didn't particularly like being a test subject, but I couldn't do anything to object. As a Guardsmen, I was bound to obey the will of the Council. What I *wanted* didn't matter. And as the first Descendant to work with the Council in thousands of years, they had a lot of questions. For generations, the Council had moved to exterminate those like me, for fear of what we could do.

After Ezekiel used me to unleash Set, I worried that they were right to be scared.

I hadn't realized I'd dozed off until someone kicked my foot. I jolted awake, looking up to see Maks, the Leo Nomarch, standing above me, his dark hair and beard standing out in the early morning sun pouring through the windows above. "Wake up, sunshine," he greeted in his thickly accented voice. Maks was originally from somewhere in Russia, and one of the few Nomarchs I liked. I had saved Maks' life during Ezekiel's invasion, an act Maks had made no qualms about appreciating. He even stood up against Amina for me during a Council meeting. He was the closest thing to an ally I had on the Council.

I jumped to my feet, wiping the sleep from my eyes. "Sorry."

He gave me a wry smile and I followed him into the conference room. Astrid was already there, standing on the opposite side of the table, an unfamiliar woman sitting in front of her. Astrid was the Nomarch for House Cancer and the oldest Nomarch on the Council. She was over 1,000 years old, and according to Sandra's notes, some even believed she had been born during the era of the Vikings. That she was in fact a real life shieldmaiden. Astrid looked tiny and frail, but I knew better. I'd once seen her kill a hybrid by pulling all the water out of his body, mummifying him in seconds.

"If we are boring you Miss Davenport. . ."

"No, no. I'm sorry," I apologized again. "I haven't been sleeping well. It won't happen again." I didn't provide any details on what was keeping me awake at night. The Council knew I could have visions of the past, I'd announced as much, but I'd been lying to them, telling them I hadn't had any visions in weeks.

I only wished that were true.

"Then let's begin," Astrid answered. She stepped behind the seated woman, placing her hands on her shoulders. "This is Yaara. She's going to help us with your final test."

Final. I couldn't help but be excited at the sound of that. If they were stopping the tests, that must mean they found whatever they were looking for. I opened my mouth to ask, when Astrid pulled a dagger from behind her back and ran it across Yaara's neck.

"What are you doing!" I yelled as I tore around the table, dropping to Yaara's side. Blood was pouring from the wound, staining Yaara's white shirt red. "It's okay, Yaara. You'll be all right." I tried my best to soothe her, but Yaara didn't respond. If fact, she didn't move at all, not even to try and stop the bleeding. When I took a closer look, I realized the reason she wasn't moving was because she was handcuffed to the chair. I placed my hand over the wound, trying to stop the bleeding. With unnatural speed, Yaara's head spun, her suddenly sharp teeth snapping at my nearby hand. I stepped out of reach quickly, staring at her in shock. Yaara hissed at me, her eyes turning a bright green at first, then the whites going bloodshot. Black veins began to weave through her cheeks and down her neck, toward the gaping wound, already working to knit it closed. "She's a hybrid!"

"She is your final test," Astrid answered. "I want you to cure her."

"I don't know how!" I protested. Yaara cackled and I glared at her in disgust. Her wound was almost closed, the blood drying on her shirt.

"We managed to capture a few hybrids before Set disappeared. We've been studying them. It seems the wraith dies faster than the body, meaning just before final death, they revert to their original Kindred form." I knew all this. I'd seen it when Roman died. "You have nothing to fear, she is heavily sedated. The problem is that they are too weak, too severely injured to heal themselves. But you can do it."

I shook my head furiously. "I don't know if I can do it again. I don't even know how I did it the first time! She'll die." I sounded hysterical, but I didn't care. This was crazy!

"Possibly. If she does, bring her back."

"I can't!" I yelled again. My eyes cut frantically to Maks, but he stood in the corner, his eyes unyielding despite the sorrow I could see there. "Do something," I demanded.

"It is not up to me," he replied.

Astrid took a step closer. "You brought Roman back from death. Do the same here." Astrid grabbed Yaara by the hair, ripping her head to the side. Then she plunged her dagger into Yaara's heart. Yaara's head ripped back, unleashing a visceral screech, one that immediately reminded me of the terrors I'd seen inside Maat's Hollow. Astrid pulled her dagger out, paying no mind to the blood that dripped off its edge. "Quickly, Kyndal."

I popped my knuckles, shaking my hands out. I grabbed the edge of Yaara's chair, spinning her to face me. Her head was limp, falling back loosely. *Okay, I can do this.* I checked her eyes first, remembering that was the first thing that changed on Roman. The veins were still a bright red, but slowly they began to retreat, clearing until only the green remained. "Okay, Yaara. I'm going to help you, hold on." I placed my hands over her heart, ignoring the wet warmth of the blood that poured from her wound. The black veins were fading on her cheeks and her body spasmed as she let out a wet cough. I closed my eyes and pressed my hands down on her heart. I searched inside me, looking for that kernel of power I'd found before. *Please don't die,* I thought. *Please hang on.* Underneath my hands, I could feel her heartbeat slow, so I pushed harder, demanding my body release that strength I'd found before.

The power that allowed me to save Roman.

No matter where I looked inside myself, no matter how hard I searched, I couldn't find it. "I can't do it!" I yelled, even though I didn't open my eyes.

"Try harder, Kyndal," Astrid urged. "She'll die soon if you don't."

I growled, diving deeper into my power, until I found it. Until I found that hidden part of myself I hadn't known existed until a month ago. It felt different than before, not as strong, not as brilliant, but still I called on it, begging it to come out, willing it to leave me and enter Yaara. My arms grew hot, and I released the power through my hands and into Yaara's heart. "There!" I declared, opening my eyes and lifting my hands from Yaara's chest. "It's done."

I stepped back, even as Astrid and Maks stepped forward. For several moments, no one spoke, all three of us watched Yaara, waiting for her to move. I stared at her still chest, silently demanding her to breathe. But no matter how long I stood there, she never moved. Finally, Maks stepped forward, placing two fingers at the pulse in her throat. He looked up at me, standing in the middle of the room awkwardly, my hands soaked in blood. "She's dead."

When I made it to the training facility, it was nearly afternoon. I'd left Council Chambers in a hurry, Yaara's blood still on my hands. When I'd reached my cottage, I'd scrubbed at them in the hot spring, desperate to remove the memories of what had happened as much as the evidence. It was just like Astrid to do something so extreme, but Maks? Maks had never struck me as someone who would do something so horrible.

The cafeteria was full of Kindred now, more than I'd ever seen, thanks to the visiting warriors. Novices, those still not battle tested, were sprinkled throughout the soldiers from all over the world. They sat wide-eyed as the soldiers told stories of battle and glory, no doubt embellishing some of the details. In my limited experience, I'd never found battle to be glorious—just messy and destructive.

I garnered more than a handful of curious glances as I weaved through the masses of bodies, but most people ignored me. Those that had just arrived were oblivious to who I was. A fact I needed to change if I was going to gain their favor and support in bringing down the Council. It was part of the reason I wanted Roman to meet here. The soldiers needed to see Roman was no longer a threat, but I also wanted to show them our strength.

I noticed Isaac at one of the tables and I gave him a respectful nod as I passed, one that he returned. Our relationship had always been an odd one. He'd proven himself to be loyal more than once, but it always seemed out of more of a sense of duty or obligation than his actual desire to help me. Part of me had always wondered if he only tolerated me because of Roman. Regardless, we were long overdue for a talk. We hadn't even spoken since I brought Roman back. There were many things I needed to thank him for. And I owed him more than one apology.

I hated apologizing.

I entered the gym, which was buzzing with activities. Morning sunlight poured in from the floor-length windows, illuminating the different sparring rings. I walked past the dozens of sparring warriors and headed straight for the armory located in the back of the room.

Across the gym, I caught the eye of Mallory Saenz. She was overseeing a training session, one that from the looks of it was a set of novices. She whispered in the ear of the man next to her and excused herself, jogging my direction.

"Hey," she said, falling into step with me. "I didn't think we were meeting until later." When Roman had been possessed, Mallory had taken over as my trainer. She'd been a teacher in Awen for years and had seen more battles than anyone could count. She was an unforgiving task master and a deadly weaponsmith. She was also one of my best friends.

"We aren't," I answered. Mallory looked at me, but I offered no further information. I pulled open the armory gate and stepped inside. Mallory followed.

"You okay?" she asked.

"Rough morning," I replied. I didn't want to talk about what happened with Yaara. "I saw Cassie last night," I added, changing the subject. Cassie was Mallory's girlfriend. As one of our most skilled healers, Cassie spent most of her time in the infirmary. I knew the two of them had barely had time to see each other. "She looks tired."

"Yeah, I know," Mallory agreed. "I snuck in there this morning before training began. I found her sleeping on one of the cots." Her eyes followed my every move as I unclipped my belt, removing my dagger from my hip. I placed it on the stone counter. I did the same with my ankle sheath and ring daggers. "What are you doing here, Kyndal?" she asked again. At that moment, the air changed, the cooling breeze dancing up my back. I looked up, over Mallory's shoulder, my eyes trained on the entrance. The door opened, and Roman walked in. All activity stopped and the room went silent. Mallory turned around. "Oh," she said quietly, her surprise obvious. "What is he doing here?"

As far as Mallory knew, Roman and I were finished. She didn't know we'd been secretly seeing each other. I hated lying to her, but as Roman reminded me in the library, the punishment for us breaking the law—for us being together—was serious and punishable by death. Mallory would never tolerate me taking such a chance with my life. I shook my head, shrugging nonchalantly. "Just settling a bet," I told her, giving nothing away. Roman moved through the room silently, his steps never faltering, even as every person in the room traced his movement. He was weaponless, just as I knew he would be. He was so concerned that people still saw him as a threat, he refused to carry a weapon on the island.

Mallory and I stepped out of the armory. Roman neared the mat when another Kindred, a large man I'd never seen before stepped in his path. He wasn't as tall as Roman, but he was well built, and had muscular arms that bulged out from under his shirt. "What do you want?" the man demanded, his voice tight with anger. "We don't welcome traitors here." Roman took a strained breath, one I knew was meant to reign in his temper. He took a step, trying to get past the other Kindred, but the man moved too, staying in his path.

"Out of my way," Roman said quietly. Through the connection, I could feel his anger simmering just under the surface. He was doing everything he could to keep a leash on his temper. Trying not to give them another reason to think he was the enemy.

"What are you going to do about it? *Wraith*," the man sneered. Then he shoved Roman in the chest, knocking him back a step. Roman did nothing to stop him, nothing to defend himself. The man shoved him again, and still Roman did not move, even though I knew he was angry. I could feel it.

I was suddenly consumed with fury. I knew it wasn't all mine, that I was projecting some of Roman's as well, but I didn't care. I was pissed. I bolted toward Roman, shoving the other man in the shoulder, pushing him off balance and out of Roman's face. "Back off," I threatened.

The man cackled, cracking his neck to each side and taking a slow step back into my space. His eyes glowed a bright gold. He was an Air User, like Roman. "Who are you?" he drawled. "The bodyguard?" I smiled internally, he had no idea who I was. No idea what kind of shit he'd just stepped in. The others in the gym stood quietly, watching us intently. Two moved closer, closing in the ranks behind the man. I could see Mallory out of the corner of my eye, hand ready on her dagger, prepared to jump in if needed. "Not bad, wraith. She's hot," he added.

"You have no idea," I challenged, calling upon the well of power that waited inside me. Releasing the fire in my blood. After the morning I'd had, the flames ignited the tips of my fingers easily, the flames growing as they spread over my hands, teasing the skin at my wrist. The dormant torches on the walls caught fire simultaneously. The man's eyes grew wide as he stared at the living flames I'd created out of nowhere. I had no doubt he knew exactly who he was messing with now. It was probably overkill but I wanted to make sure he got the point. "You have anything else you need to say?" I pushed.

He raised both hands, backing away slowly. "No. Nothing at all." He turned and walked out of the gym, followed closely by the two others.

I watched them go, not pulling back on my power until they'd slammed the door behind them. The flames dropped instantly and my eyes returned to normal. "What are you staring at?" Mallory shouted. "Get back to work!" Everyone instantly obeyed, resuming their workouts.

I turned to Roman, who I was surprised to see glaring at me. He stomped past me, moving to the final mat. There were four novices there, but with one look from me, all four quickly abandoned it and found somewhere else to workout.

"Are you okay?" I asked. I wanted to reach out, place a comforting hand on his arm, but I refrained.

"I told you this was a bad idea," he whispered harshly. His anger was practically radiating off him in waves.

"What? That guy?" I pointed toward the door. "That guy was a royal douche."

"But he's right," he hissed.

"No, he's not." I snapped back. "And you're going to prove it to everyone. Right now." I stepped back into the armory, ripping two wooden staffs off the wall. I threw one to Roman before dropping into a fighting stance in the center of the sparring mat.

Roman grabbed the staff out of the air. "I don't want to do this."

"Fine," I said nonchalantly. "Then walk out right now. Show everyone exactly how much of a coward you are." I knew I was taking my crappy day out on him, but he was acting like a child and I was tired of it. A jolt of fury flew down the bond, heating my veins. I'd just challenged him in front of everyone. He had no choice but to fight me. I gave him a wicked smile. "You're pissed. Good." I motioned toward the mat. "Fight me."

He stepped fully onto the mat, dropping into a fighting stance that mirrored mine. I didn't give him a moment to think. I struck, my left hand snapping out quickly, my jab catching him in the nose. It was an odd move. He'd expected me to strike with the staff, not my fist. His head snapped back quickly, and a brief moment of shock registered through the bond. He wiped his hand under his nose, the top of it coming away red with blood.

Roman didn't move, so I struck again, this time with a combo. I punched with my left again, then swung the staff directly at Roman's head. He dodged both, moving so fast it was almost hard to see. I wasn't surprised I missed. Roman was rarely caught off guard once. It definitely didn't happen twice. I smiled at him wickedly, thrilled to see when he returned the smile with one of his own. I feigned with my staff, using it to distract him as I wound up a wicked right roundhouse. He saw right through it, blocking my right leg and following it up with a kick of his own directly to my ribs, knocking me backward. I grunted at the impact.

The fight was officially on.

We traded blows back and forth, both of us working at full speed. For every punch I threw, he matched it with one of his own. For every kick of his, I countered with a combination of my own. Our staffs smacked off each other, echoing through the gym with enough force, it caught the attention of the other soldiers. They stood around our sparring mat, watching us in action. I vaguely recognized that Mallory and Isaac were among them, watching with renewed interest as Roman and I tore at each other. We fought long enough that I honestly lost track of time. No matter what we did, neither of us could find an opening. Neither of us could go in for the kill shot. I was coated with sweat, but I refused to quit. Roman needed this. He needed the release fighting provided him and he deserved the opportunity to prove to the others that not only was he restored, but he was strong.

A force to be reckoned with.

I pulled my staff back, preparing to swing a wide sweeping glance under Roman's feet when a gust of wind hit me in the chest, knocking me several feet back and into the wall. I gawked at Roman in shock. Neither one of us had been using our elements, I couldn't believe he'd done it. I glared at him from my invisible prison. He simply shrugged, as if to say, *all's fair in love and war.*

I growled, turning my attention to the staff in his hand, focusing my power there. It took a minute to break through Roman's barrier, but once I did, his staff lit up like a torch. It scalded his hand and he dropped it quickly. He also dropped me. I wasted no time, running straight at him, spearing him to the ground. I rolled through the spear, grabbing my staff from where I'd dropped it when Roman pushed his power at me. I could hear him trying to get back to his feet. I wheeled around, slicing the staff toward Roman, stopping just short of his throat. He froze mid-movement.

"Kill shot," I said triumphantly.

Roman dropped back onto the mat, his back smacking into the ground. I dropped the staff and joined him, laying with my head near his, but not too close. I closed my eyes, taking deep breaths in and out, trying not to wince when my ribs stung. Our connection swirled around us, almost as if it were a real, living thing. So powerful, I don't know how the others couldn't see it. It was calmer now, quieted by the fight and no longer laced with the sharp tang of Roman's anger and fear.

A singular person applauding echoed through the gym, and I snapped my eyes open. I looked around quickly. The gym was almost completely abandoned, save for Mallory and Isaac who both had retreated to the armory. Two other people now stood in the gym. Right on the edge of the sparring mat were none other than Grady Dunn and Brynn Hughes.

Roman and I jumped to our feet, fully facing Grady and Brynn. Roman went deathly still beside me, the momentary relief I'd felt in the bond now replaced by a predatory stillness. I matched him, crossing my arms defiantly. I hadn't seen Grady or Brynn since the Guard ceremony, and every time I saw them, a flood of memories came with it. Brynn had been a part of The Blinding, sent there by Amina to kill me, and Grady had actually succeeded in killing Roman that night in the depths of Maat's Hollow.

I eyed Brynn, sizing her up from head to toe. She wasn't a particularly tall girl, about my height. I remember the first time I'd seen her, I thought she was a living embodiment of hard lines. Her body was lean, the tight muscles ending in sharp points on her shoulders and elbows, evident in the gear she wore. Her cheekbones were pronounced, appearing even sharper than before. She'd cut her hair, replacing her typical braided rows for a shorter look. Her hair was now buzzed against her head, showcasing her beautiful umber skin and deep brown eyes. It was a bold look, one I'd only seen on high fashion models back home. I knew Brynn didn't cut her hair for looks, but rather for practicality. Hair often got in the way during a fight. Not to mention it gave the enemy something to grab a hold of. Standing next to Grady with his light skin and red hair, she was stunning.

As impressive and sharp as her looks were, I never forgot that under the surface rested a mind just as cunning and well-honed as her weapons. Brynn was as smart as she was patient, and that combination made her very dangerous.

"Can we help you?" I snapped at both of them. As much as I didn't want to talk to them, I knew Roman was in no shape for conversation.

"Not at all," Brynn responded, her tone clipped. "We were simply enjoying the show."

"I was hoping you'd give me a turn next," Grady added, his voice dripping with suggestion. He took a miniscule step toward me.

"You touch her and I'll break your hand," Roman growled. He hadn't moved an inch, but his tone brought Grady up short. I could feel the power radiating from him, and I knew if I turned to look, his eyes would be shining a bright gold. Grady turned to him, a cocky smile plastered on his face.

"Down boy. I was only kidding," he responded.

"You act like it'd be a challenge," Brynn added.

Grady shrugged. "True. I've killed him before."

Visions of Roman bleeding out on the floor of Maat's Hollow intermingled with Yaara gasping for breath as she died, but before I could shake them away, a sudden gust of wind filled the room, so fast and so powerful, the bond gave no warning before the wind was pushing Grady against the wall. His head smacked against the stone wall, pinned a foot off the ground. Roman was in Grady's face before I had a chance to react. Brynn made a step toward the men, but I interceded, my eyes a sharp red, a fireball forming in hand. "I wouldn't," I threatened. My eyes cut to Mallory and Isaac. Both of them crept out of the armory, ready to provide backup if we asked.

Grady strained against his invisible prison, but Roman tightened his hold, slowly pulling the air away from Grady. Grady began to cough, his body desperate for oxygen it couldn't find. I could feel the bloodlust in Roman's veins pumping through my own. "I'd be very careful what you say to me," Roman snarled. "My back isn't turned and I'm definitely not in chains anymore. If you ever challenge me like that again, I will end you."

The wind swept out of the room as fast as it had appeared and Grady dropped from the wall, landing in an awkward crouch and grasping at his neck as oxygen returned to his lungs. I stepped to the side, allowing Brynn around me. She ran for Grady, dropping to his side and helping him to his feet.

She glared at Roman and me, now side by side. "The Guard has been summoned to Council Chambers. We're expected at sundown." Then they staggered for the door, leaving the way they came.

3

"That went well."

I shook my head in frustration, walking into the armory. Mallory followed me in, waiting for me to respond. Roman had left almost immediately after Grady and Brynn had, without so much as a glance toward me. I wanted to chase him down, but I knew he was upset and it was best I didn't. Instead, I sent Isaac after him, just in case Grady and Brynn decided to finish what they started in here.

I grabbed my weapons belt off the counter, reattaching it to my hips. "Don't start, Mallory."

She leaned against the gate, blocking the way out. "I'm just saying, first the incident with Dirk, then we had a Guard civil war in the middle of the training facility. Makes for a busy day."

I shoved my ring daggers into my ankle sheath. "Who's Dirk?" I asked, readjusting the pant leg under the sheath.

"The Kindred that confronted Roman. That one you called a royal douche."

"Yeah, well. If the shoe fits."

"Dirk is a dangerous man, Kyndal, you shouldn't dismiss him so easily. There are aspects of Kindred society you still don't understand. Orthodox sects that do not adhere to the traditional governance of our people, that operate outside our laws. Dirk belongs to one of them called the Coterie. He is a dangerous enemy to have."

It was true, I knew nothing of these Kindred sects that Mallory spoke of. In many ways, I was still ignorant of the subtleties inside this world. "What's the Coterie?" I asked her. I may not understand everything, but I was at least smart enough to ask.

"Short answer? A fraternity of misogynistic pigs. They renounce Maat and all that she stood for, instead worshipping only Hermes Trismegistus. They believe he is the only true divinity, and as such they believe only those that walk in his footsteps are the truly blessed. They live, train, and worship together, only venturing out of their walls when it is profitable for them. They don't answer to the Council either, only to their commander."

I was momentarily speechless. The Coterie sounded intense, reminiscent of cults I'd heard of in the regular, human world. One thing I knew about organizations like that—they could justify almost anything through their beliefs. "How is all this possible?" I asked. "How does the Council allow the Coterie to exist if they don't control them?" I had never known the Council to allow *anything* that wasn't under their command.

Mallory pushed off the gate, entering the weapons lock up and leaning on the table in-between us. She lowered her voice. "The Coterie began as an academy hundreds of years ago. Built and orchestrated by the Gemini Nomarch, Cyrus, it was intended to be a school for building leaders. Future Nomarchs, generals of our armies, etc."

"So what happened?"

"There was a mutiny. When Cyrus left the Coterie to live in Awen, his command should have passed to his best pupil, a warrior by the name of Nero. He was a harsh and cruel man. Unbeaten in battle, but with a carelessness for human life, Nero was oftentimes responsible for the deaths of many humans that were unfortunate enough to get caught in-between him and his enemy. As Cyrus is not a cruel man, he passed over Nero, knowing that he would lead the Coterie down a dark path. Instead, he handed command to his favorite student, a soldier that was destined to be Nomarch of House Gemini after him. Angry about his decision, Nero rebelled. He and his men overthrew Cyrus's successor, killing him and all who followed him."

"What did Cyrus do?"

"He went to the Council and begged them to declare war, but as you're well aware, the Council can get lost in diplomacy, more often willing to debate than take action. By the time Cyrus raised his army and returned to the Coterie, it was too late. Nero had already solidified his seat of power. Any men that still followed Cyrus had been killed, and the rest were loyal to Nero. Still, Cyrus and his soldiers tried to take back the Coterie. They waged war for years, but the Coterie is protected by very high, very strong walls. No matter what Cyrus did, he and his men were not able to get past them. Eventually, he was defeated and forced to sign a truce with Nero. From that day, the Coterie has operated outside the Council's reach, allowed to govern itself, and the Council had to swear never to attack again. The treaty still stands and Nero still runs the Coterie."

"He sounds like a monster," I answered honestly.

Mallory raised her eyebrows. "You'd be surprised how many people agree with Nero's way of thinking. The Coterie takes no care of human lives, and its soldiers keep the spoils of whatever they find in battle. Greed is a powerful motivator and his numbers are growing every year."

If Dirk is a part of the Coterie, what is he doing here?" I asked. It seemed it would be dangerous for Nero's men to be found in Awen.

Mallory glanced over her shoulder, making sure no one was within hearing distance. "I don't know," she answered. "But for him to be walking around Awen, the Council has to know he's here. They have to want something from him, which means you can't go around pissing them off all the time," she said, returning to her earlier point.

I stood up straight, fully facing Mallory, letting out an aggravated breath. "What do you expect me to do? Just let him harass Roman like that?"

She shook her head. "No, I just want to make sure you're protecting him for the right reasons."

"What does that mean?"

Mallory crossed her arms, taking a deep breath in. I braced myself. It was never good if Mallory paused before speaking her mind. "You know you and Roman can't be together anymore."

"We're not together," I said quickly. Maybe too quickly.

Mallory raised her eyebrows. "You can't be with anyone. Let alone him. You chose to give that up."

I made sure to keep my face neutral. "I am well aware of the restrictions I'm under. I didn't protect Roman because of whatever feelings you think I have for him. I protected him because he is a Guardsman. People should show him respect not disdain."

"And Grady and Brynn? Do they not also deserve respect?"

"Whose side are you on?" I accused her. "Roman didn't choose what happened to him. Brynn *chose* to enter the Blinding and try to kill me. Grady *chose* to watch as Amina stabbed me. He *chose* killing Roman. Something I seem to remember you repeatedly punching him in the face for. Now you expect me to just forget all of that ever happened?" I couldn't believe her audacity.

Mallory pushed off the gate of the armory and took two steps toward me, getting in my personal space. "I don't expect you to forget, I expect you to *think*. If the Guard is fighting amongst themselves, how can you ever expect the people to follow you? If all you can see is revenge, you'll miss the opportunity to get what you really want."

"And what's that?" I challenged.

"Change," she said simply. "You can't allow your pride to blind you. If you're going to become the leader you want to be, the leader we need you to be, you have to be *more*. You have to look at the bigger picture."

I huffed out a breath. Some part of me deep down recognized that she was right, but I wasn't ready to admit it yet. Forgiveness was not a strong suit of mine and asking me to forgive Brynn and Grady was impossible. It was easier to stay angry. "I hear what you're saying Mallory. I really do. But I can't do it. I won't forgive them. Not ever."

I walked into Council Chambers, just as the sun dropped below the horizon. It was mid-October, the last week of House Libra's reign. In five days the Earth would move into House Scorpio, shifting the island from its current location in the Devil's Sea just east of Japan to just off the coast of Australia. Although the island was changing location with the Houses, the leader of the Council would remain the same. Something that did not bode well for me. The Libra Nomarch had been killed during Ezekiel's attack. Amina, the next Nomarch in line, had stepped in to fill his shoes, gaining control of the Council weeks before her given turn. She was the one that had ordered my testing, the one that had been pulling the strings from the moment I stepped foot in Awen, and with her running the Council, there was no telling what this meeting could be about. What she would expect the four of us to do.

Council Chambers was a strange room. It was large enough to accommodate a large amount of people, as it often did, but it provided no comforts for anyone that would attend. The entire chamber was situated around the center where there were exactly twelve seats. Large stone thrones with high backs and ornate carvings on the armrests, the Nomarch thrones dominated the room, a perfect way for the Nomarchs to set themselves above the rest. The thrones sat empty currently, a fact that didn't surprise me. One thing I knew about the Council was that they did not adhere to standard time constraints. You waited on them. Personally, I thought it was because they liked to make an entrance.

While the Nomarchs weren't present yet, that didn't mean the chamber was empty. The other three Guard members were already there. Grady and Brynn stood in the center of the room, whispering quietly. Roman was on the opposite side, leaning against the wall near one of the large windows. He looked up when I entered the room, watching as I made my way to stand in the same circle as Grady and Brynn. He didn't acknowledge me in any way or move to stand near me as I thought he might have. Instead he lowered his eyes again, returning to his brooding. I sent a shot of curiosity down the bond. *Was he all right after what had happened this morning? Was he mad at me for forcing him to come to the training facility?* I received no response, so it seemed he was ignoring me psychically as well as physically.

The loud groan of a wooden door pulled my attention away from Roman and back to the reason I was here. A private door opened and a set of guards walked through followed by the Council Nomarchs. The guards posted themselves around the circular room with precision, turning as one to face the center of the chamber, their backs ramrod straight, their faces unreadable. One particular guard caught my eye. She had wild, curly black hair, evident even though she tried to tame it by pulling it back tight against her skull. Several curls still escaped near the sides of her face. Her skin was a striking tawny color contrasted by beautiful chocolate eyes. Her beauty was not what grabbed my attention. I'd met her before. She'd been a part of the group when I'd gone cliff diving, and I remembered her talking with Lukas. It was a surprise to see her serving the Council so closely.

The Nomarchs made their way to their seats. Roman pushed off the wall, moving into the center with the rest of us, although I noticed he made sure to maintain his distance from me. As the Nomarchs sat, it was hard not to notice the one empty chair. I caught the eye of Maks as he took his seat on his throne. He gave me a familiar nod, one that I usually would have returned, but not today. What had he done with Yaara's body?

Next to him was Astrid. She sat rigidly on her throne, her stark white hair blanketing her pale shoulders that showed through her silver tunic.

On the other side of her was the Gemini Nomarch, Cyrus. Before this morning, I knew very little about this Nomarch, but now with Mallory's newly explained history, I could see the scars of battle on his arms, the haunting look of a man who had seen too much death.

My eyes traveled around the rest of the wheel, realizing that ten of the Nomarchs had taken their seat, while one remained standing; Amina. I'd taken special care to avoid Amina over the past several weeks. It was one thing to follow her orders from a distance, but I knew that when I finally had to face her, I wouldn't be able to react the way I wanted. I'd pledged myself to the Guard and it was vital that Amina and the other Nomarchs believed I was their loyal servant. I turned to face her fully, knowing anything else would be taken as a slight. I noticed Roman do the same. Amina looked at each of us individually, holding my gaze last, her eyes squinting slightly, her ever-present disapproval clear. I kept my head high, meeting her gaze with strength.

"Five days from now marks the movement from House Libra to House Scorpio. On the eve of the transition, Awen will hold ceremonies to celebrate. A change in House is a time of cleansing and purging. We will purge our island of the death and destruction that has plagued our people and usher in a new era. An era with a united Council and Guard at the helm," said Amina.

"While three Nomarchs have already taken their place on the wheel," added Cyrus, pulling our attention to him, "We have received no word from House Aries, even after several attempts at contact. No recognition of his call to sit on the Council, no correspondence whatsoever."

My eyebrows shot up at the mention of my House.

"That is until yesterday," Amina added. "Late last night, a plane arrived with an emissary for the Nomarch-to-be. He was immediately brought into chambers to deliver his message. It seems the Aries Nomarch-to-be will not be swayed by our letters and pleas for his return. Instead, he demands a personal escort to Awen." I looked to my fellow Guardsmen, each of them wearing the same confused expression I was.

The door to my right opened, and I let loose a low growl as I saw who walked through it. Dirk sauntered through, his large frame filling the doorway, although I noticed his companions were not with him. Subtly, Roman inched closer to me.

He entered the circle, giving Roman and me a cocky grin before turning to address the Nomarchs. "Cyrus, it is a pleasure to see you again. Has the Council considered my master's wishes?" He was taunting him, disrespecting him by not using his title.

Cyrus remained silent as stone, and instead Maks stood, addressing Dirk. "After the attack on the island, and with Set now free," he began, his eyes landing on Roman and lingering, "we cannot afford to spare a large group of soldiers."

"That is a pity," Dirk replied. "My commander is not willing to consider your request without a sign of good faith." The word *commander* sunk into me, and my heart dropped. Dirk was from the Coterie. His master could only be one person, and that meant my new Nomarch could only be. . .

"We didn't say we weren't sending anyone," Amina sniped. "They will go instead." She gestured to the four of us. "You will leave tonight, under the cover of darkness. You will travel to the Coterie with Dirk and his companions. Tell no one where you are going, and when you find Nero, you will retrieve him and bring him safely to the island so he can claim his rightful position. Is this understood?"

"Yes, Nomarch," all four of us replied immediately. As she said his name, the words left a bitter taste in my mouth, confirming what I already dreaded.

"Excuse me, Nomarch," Roman added, surprising me when he spoke up. "You wish us to travel to the Coterie? What of the treaty?"

Astrid jumped to her feet. Her voice was clipped. Cold. "Regardless of obvious *hostilities*, we are at war. The Coterie houses some of the most highly trained and deadly warriors in the world. Forces which will be crucial in the fight ahead. Whether they remember it or not, these soldiers are still Kindred, and Nero, along with his men, *will* be brought into the fold. Now stop asking questions and do as you are commanded." Dirk snickered as Roman was put in his place. I glared at him, eager to finish what started in the training room. "Now I suggest you prepare. You leave for Siberia at midnight."

Did she just say Siberia?

4

By the time I made it back to my cottage, the sun had dipped behind the Hollow, casting Awen in an early shadow. My eyes were heavy and all I wanted was to fall into bed. I had about four hours before I was set to fly out, and I fully intended to spend it napping.

After the Council announced our mission, we'd been immediately escorted down to the basement by three guards to the Council's personal armory. It was the largest on the island, fully stocked with a plethora of weapons, specialized gear camouflaged and reinforced to withstand various climates, and a bounty of medical and healing equipment. We'd each painstakingly packed our duffels, trying to prepare for whatever situation we were getting ourselves into. If Nero was half as bad as Mallory made him out to be, we had to be ready for anything.

I opened my front door, throwing my duffel bag onto the ground. I called to my power, lighting the dozens of candles that populated my cottage; my only light source. It still drove me crazy that Awen didn't believe in electricity. I wandered to my bedroom, kicking off my boots as I went. I made it two steps inside the door when I realized I wasn't alone. Astrid was sitting on my bed. Open on her lap was my mother's journal.

My first inclination was to rip it out her hands, but I hesitated. "Find anything interesting?"

She closed the book slowly, her icy blue eyes meeting mine. "I need to speak with you," she answered.

"I assumed. You could have just knocked." It wasn't smart to get sassy with Astrid, but I was tired of Nomarchs barging their way into my home, and I was even more irritated with this particular Nomarch.

"You remind me of her." The comment caught me off guard.

"Who?" I asked, even though I already knew.

"Not just your appearance, although I see it there as well," she responded as if she read my thoughts. "You have the same spirit. That wild independence that cannot be controlled by anyone." I swallowed nervously, unsure where this conversation was going. I took an unconscious step backward. Astrid laid her hand on the journal softly. "You needn't go anywhere. You have nothing to fear from me, girl." I froze.

"Is that what you told Yaara?" I asked. It was dangerous to pick at Astrid, but I couldn't help it.

"Yaara was a hybrid. I owed her nothing. How many have you killed, girl?"

"That was different," I argued. "They were trying to kill me. You used Yaara as some sort of sick experiment."

"There are hundreds of Kindred still possessed by wraiths, and I am trying to find a way to free them from that hell. If we cannot find a way to cure them, don't think for a second that I will hesitate to kill each and every one of them. One way or another, I will eliminate the hybrid scourge. If you struggle with my tactics, I shudder to think how you will fare in the war ahead. There are many more trials ahead for you to endure. In fact, Amina is testing you right now," she responded bluntly. I didn't react. "You don't seem surprised," she added.

I shrugged. "Not particularly. She is a Nomarch, and you all seem determined to test me. I will do as she asks. I am hers to command." I almost choked on those last words.

Astrid smirked, as if she could see the physical pain those words caused me.

"She does not want this Guard to succeed. Her hands are currently bound, you saw to that when you returned Roman from the dead. The people love and revere you, but their opinions are easily swayed. If this Guard fails, it is all the justification Amina will need to get rid of you and Roman once and for all."

"Why does she hate me so much?" I knew she hated my mother, that she despised Descendants, I just didn't know why.

"Amina has a thirst for power, an ambition that goes beyond the Council. It wouldn't surprise me if she wanted to dismantle it all together."

I pinched the bridge of my nose. "Cassie said Amina is obsessed with tradition. Why would she get rid of the Council?"

"So she could rule by herself. You've already seen how she revels in the power. Imagine if the other Nomarchs weren't there to keep her in check. She is keeping many secrets. Dangerous ones. Purposely withholding information about Nero that could change the outcome of the mission." I crossed my arms, officially interested. "There is the possibility that even once you arrive at the Coterie, Nero will refuse to return to Awen. He is notoriously stubborn and narcissistic. He has himself set up as a king in his remote fortress, why would he return to share the power? But his legion, no matter their unsavory tendencies, *must* be brought to heel. We cannot win this war without them."

"Why are you telling me all of this? And don't pretend it's because you care about me or Roman." Again, my tone was stronger than it should have been, but Astrid made no mention of it. At this point, we'd completely dropped the pretense of rank.

"It is no secret that Amina and I are at odds. Believe it or not, I want what is best for the people, and sometimes that means working with people like Nero. I believe there is only one thing that could convince him to leave the Coterie, one thing that could get Nero to yield. A tightly guarded secret that I would entrust only with someone not under

Amina's thumb."

I feigned surprise. "I serve all the Nomarchs on the Council, including Amina." Even after everything Astrid had said, I still couldn't fully drop the act. There was still a chance this was a trap.

Astrid gave me a wicked smile. "You have no reason to pretend, child. I can see the bloodlust all over your face when you look at her. You'd rather see her dead before you kissed her hand. A sentiment we share."

A surprised laugh escaped my lips before I could stop it. "What is your price for this tightly guarded secret?"

"I need you to get something for me. You can tell no one else what you are doing or who you are giving it to and you must deliver it in person. Tonight. Fail, and there is nothing I can do to help you. You'll be thrown in the Hollow for the rest of your very long life."

"I fly out in four hours." There was no way I could do whatever she needed in such a short amount of time.

"Then I suggest you hurry," she responded quickly.

"Must be quite the secret."

"I assure you, the reward is worth the risk."

I couldn't see where I was going, but I knew I was headed

the right way. The waterfall roared straight ahead of me, and I used that sound like a beacon to find my way to Maat's Hollow. A large, imposing mountain, split in two by a waterfall, the Hollow was our prison, where we locked up the worst of the worst. Embedded with anti-magic wards, the Hollow also served as a tomb for Set. After being defeated by a Kindred Guard led by my ancestor Marius, Set's soul was imprisoned and buried underneath Maat's Hollow, where he was supposed to rot for eternity. Access to the Hollow was severely restricted. No one was allowed in.

Unless you were friends with a guard.

After Astrid left, I spent several minutes crouched in the corner, agonizing over how I'd managed to get tangled up in such a mess. What she had asked of me was nearly impossible. Even with the right connections, I wasn't sure I could pull it off.

I went to Mallory first. She'd been with me that day we cliff jumped, one of the few people I trusted that would know the name of the guard I'd seen today. She'd escorted me to her house, helping me make proper introductions. Her name was Daniela, a Water User from House Pisces. Much like Lukas, she had been quietly opposing the Council for years, waiting for someone to come around with a better opportunity. She worked as the Council's guard and a guard of Maat's Hollow in order to keep an eye on the Council's decisions. She was smart and well connected.

Exactly what I needed.

I'd dismissed Mallory from Daniela's house quickly, even after she protested multiple times, demanding she go with me. She had no idea where I was headed, but she could tell I was headed for trouble. I shook my head, simply explaining that it was something I had to do alone. Instead, I had another, equally important job for her.

I emerged from the trees, standing at the foot of the whirlpool, the spray from the waterfall misting my face. The smell of the water filled my nose, drowning out the ever-present smoke. On the other side of the whirlpool, against the face of the mountain, I could just barely make out the outline of a woman. I unlocked my power, using it to enhance my sight. On the bottom step of the rocky staircase stood Daniela.

I lowered my hood and inclined my head, waiting for her to give me some sort of signal. Both of us were hesitant to speak, in case someone was within hearing distance. Her eyes glowed blue and she nodded at the whirlpool. I looked down at the water, but it still raged and churned, same as it always did. I was really hoping to avoid getting wet, but when I looked at Daniela again, all she did was point to the whirlpool. I groaned internally, then stepped into the water. Right as my foot should have dipped into the water, it landed on something solid. I looked down in surprise. The whirlpool didn't look any different, but I pushed my weight down and the surface held, as solid as walking on the ground. I took another step, now standing directly on top of the water. I smiled slightly. Daniela's magic was keeping me from falling into the whirlpool. I didn't know how long it would hold, so I didn't waste any time. I walked quickly across the water until I joined Daniela on the bottom step. She didn't say anything, just simply turned and started the long trek up the stairs. I followed behind silently, not daring to speak even as she opened the door hidden behind the waterfall, hundreds of feet up the mountain.

I stepped into the mountain and through the anti-magic ward. The ward hit me like a heavy weight pressed down on my chest. I could feel the well of magic that sat inside me, but no matter how I tried, I couldn't reach it. I'd broken through a ward like this before, but when they'd replaced the Hollow's wards, they'd doubled their strength. Being detached from the element that had become such an important part of me was like losing a limb. Also missing was the connection that tethered me to Roman. I hoped Mallory had found him by now and delivered my message. Last thing I needed was him to panic when the cord was cut.

Daniela shut the entrance door behind me, cutting off the minimal light, throwing us into complete darkness. She slid the heavy lock across the door, locking us in the Hollow. Firmly behind the anti-magic ward, she finally dared to speak. "You weren't followed, were you?"

I shook my head even though she couldn't see it. "No. I made sure of it." She grabbed my arm, placing my hand on her shoulder and began the descent through the heart of the mountain. "I appreciate you doing this," I whispered to her. "I know it's a risk."

Her shoulder stiffened. "Well," she started tightly. "Lukas believed in you. He trusted you. That's good enough for me." I could tell that even though she meant the words, she was still nervous about letting me into the Hollow. I couldn't imagine how she would feel knowing a Nomarch sent me here on a covert mission performed behind the rest of the Council's backs.

"I'm sure it was quite a shock when Mallory and I showed up at your door. No one will find out if it makes you feel better."

"It doesn't make me feel any better," she responded quickly.

I followed her down another level, when suddenly I saw the familiar oranges and yellows of firelight flickering against the wall. "I thought there wasn't supposed to be any light in here," I said to Daniela.

She turned partly my way, her curls silhouetted in the torchlight. "It's a necessary evil. We've been working through each level slowly, taking inventory of the prisoners, checking to see if any escaped during the time the wards were down." When Ezekiel had come, he'd crushed through the anti-magic wards, leaving an opportunity for prisoners to escape. "Many of the prisoners have been here so long they refuse to speak or even make a sound. The only way to know they're in their cells is to confirm it visually."

"And are they—accounted for?"

"So far, yes," she responded. "But we still have the bottom four levels to go. It's a tedious process, and the lower we go, the longer it takes."

"Why does it take longer?"

"The lower levels are reserved for our longest standing and most dangerous inmates. Even with the wards back in place, there's still a possibility the cells were compromised. Any one of those inmates could be waiting for the right moment to attack."

I stared at her warily. "You're talking about the bottom four levels that we are getting ready to walk through in complete darkness with no backup?"

She nodded quickly. "It's the only reason the bottom cavern has remained untouched. No one will dare go down there until all levels are cleared. They're scared they'll be killed."

"Awesome," I mumbled under my breath.

I thought of the inmates below us, and the ones we'd already passed. Enemies so dangerous, the Council locked them in the mountain forever. "Do you know where all the inmates are? What level they're housed in?" I asked Daniela.

She nodded. "Why do you ask?"

"Lukas once let me in to see someone. She was my mother's best friend, Sandra Cartwright. What level is she on?"

Daniela hesitated briefly. "She is two levels down."

My heart sunk. It was bad enough Sandra had been unfairly locked in the Hollow, but to hear she'd been placed in a level with the most dangerous of our enemies made it worse. Daniela and I approached the Kindred clearing the cells, several of them taking notice of us. "Wait quietly for me here. Don't say anything."

I nodded, watching as she went up to the men, shaking hands and speaking with them quietly. I leaned against a patch of stone wall and tried to appear nonchalant. Daniela motioned to me several times while talking to the other guards, then walked back my way.

"Let's go."

After that, Daniela and I didn't speak any more. I placed my hand back on her shoulder as we entered the level below and returned to the darkness. I pulled my dagger from its sheath with my free hand. If these levels hadn't been cleared yet, I needed to be ready for anything. When I had been here before, the mountain had been full of sounds. It was a chorus of agonizing screams and desperate wails for light or food. This time was different. The cells were silent, as if the prison was holding its breath. Daniela and I moved slowly, even though she navigated the prison with the same ease Lukas had. I realized she was listening. Searching for anything out of place. I followed suit, listening intently to even the tiniest of sound. At one point, I thought I heard a tapping, like a nail against a cell bar, but when I paused to listen closer, I heard nothing.

With every step I took, I couldn't help but think of Sandra. Wonder if it was her cell we were passing. She'd been locked up for months now. What would she look like? Would she even be able to recognize me? I wished I could stop and speak with her, promise to get her out of that cell as soon as I could, but I knew we had to move quickly. I had a flight to catch.

Finally, Daniela and I made it to the bottom of the mountain, curving through the final tunnel that would bring us to the cavern. Despite her warnings, we made it without incident. "Watch your step," she whispered. "There's rubble here."

I did as she said, shuffling my feet until my toes hit the stones at the entrance of the cavern. Grady was responsible for the rocks at my feet. When Ezekiel made it here, he'd closed the cavern off behind him, using his powers as an Earth User to seal himself in and lock us out. Grady had been the one to take the wall down.

Daniela stepped out of my grasp, walking further into the cavern. I heard the striking of flint, then saw the soft glow of torch light, no doubt left over from Ezekiel's resurrection ritual. Now able to see, I followed Daniela in. She walked the entire cavern, lighting each torch until all darkness was gone. I went straight for the middle. Still drawn on the ground was the diamond Ezekiel had used in his spell, creating a border around the magma chamber that roared at its center. I stepped over its line, trying to ignore the rusty stain on the ground.

"What exactly are you looking for?" Daniela asked from where she walked around the torches, her eyes glued to the ground, jumping from one blood stain to the other. It had been all out war in here, and I could see her piecing the battle together in her head based on the evidence left behind.

I bent down at the mouth of the chamber, drawn there by the glint of something silver. Even without access to my magic, a small part of me could still feel the strength of the magma below. The power that it held. At its edge, exactly where Ezekiel had dropped it, was the silver box that had held Set's soul for thousands of years. It laid there, forgotten in the mayhem. "Set's soul was trapped in this box with some sort of spell." I pulled a small bag out of my vest, placing the box inside it.

"You're going to take it?" Daniella questioned. I knew this could be a problem. Luckily I was prepared.

"The Council wasn't here when Set was released and you said yourself that no one has been down here since that night. As far as anyone knows, Ezekiel took the box with him. This box could be the key to us finding him." What I said was true. The Council wasn't here when everything happened. I had no idea how Astrid even knew the box would be here.

Daniela looked furious. "I agreed to bring you down here, I did not agree to you stealing evidence."

"Shh," I said tersely, cutting her short.

"No," she argued. "I will not be quiet."

"Shut up!" I hissed, moving quickly toward her, covering her mouth with my hand.

Her eyes grew wide, shocked by my boldness. I pinned her

with a stare, then touched my ear before pointing at the entrance. Finally understanding what I meant, Daniela turned her attention to the entrance. She turned her head slightly, listening. I could tell the moment she heard it too. Her posture changed and her back went rigid and straight. Just outside the cavern entrance, we heard a deep scratch, like someone dragging their nails along the stone walls.

We weren't alone.

I slung the bag over my back, freeing my hands. My dagger already out, I grabbed my ring dagger with my left hand, doubling my weapons. Daniela unsheathed her dagger from where she'd hidden it in her boot, and both of us waited.

For a moment, I thought nothing would come. The noise had stopped, nothing but silence came through the cavern entrance. Then, from the mouth of the cavern poured the two most disgusting creatures I had ever seen. Identical to each other, they had stark white skin, pulled tight as if it were made of leather. Their hair was long, falling off their skulls in greasy, tangled strands that almost reached the floor. They jaunted into the cavern, their overgrown, yellowed toenails clicking against the ground with every step. A ripped and dirty gown hung off their bony shoulders. They looked as if they had once been human, maybe even women, but now they were more the things of nightmares.

"What are these things?" I asked Daniela. When I spoke, they turned simultaneously toward me, their eyes milky and unseeing. The closest one sniffed the air then screeched, the shrill sound echoing off the cavern walls.

"They're called the Surori. Romanian sisters, over four hundred years old. No one could ever figure out how to kill them. Our daggers don't work on them."

Awesome.

They moved closer, each moving directly toward us, even though I was pretty sure they were blind. I sheathed my daggers, since apparently, they were useless. I reached out, grabbing the nearby torch and ripping it from the ground.

I dropped into a fighting stance, swinging the torch like a staff and waited for one of them to be in striking distance. I swung right for the ugly thing's head. She ducked, surprisingly quick, and the torch flew over her head. She crouched down and swept at my legs, but I jumped. Her toenails dug into the stone floor as her leg swept under my feet. She flew to her feet, her arms flailing wildly, her sharp fingernails swiping at my face. I stepped back with each advance, keeping just out of range. The heel of my boot knocked into something solid on the ground, and I momentarily lost my balance just as the Surori swung again. I threw my head back, protecting my face, but one of her nails caught me along the side of my neck, slicing into the thin flesh.

I hissed in anger and kicked out with my right leg. I caught the Surori directly in the gut, pushing her back and giving me a moment to regain my balance. I used my advantage, attacking again, this time leading with the torch. I lunged at her, but the Surori was quick, managing to evade almost every advance. Finally, I managed to connect, hitting her in the arm with the flames, spinning her around. The Surori shrieked in pain, grabbing her arm where I'd burnt it.

"Kyndal!" Daniela shouted.

I spared a glance at Daniela. She was locked in battle with the other one. Her arm was ripped and bleeding, but she nodded toward the entrance. Before I could look, the Surori's hand flew up, smacking me across the face, throwing me into the wall. My shoulders smacked into the stone, a sharp piece jabbing me in the soft tissue near my shoulder blade. Sparks from the torch showered down, landing on my arm and scalding my skin. Without access to my magic, I was no longer fireproof. I grunted at the impact, sliding the few feet down to the floor, landing in a crouch. That was when I realized what Daniela was trying to tell me. A third twisted sister had entered the cavern and was headed right for me.

This was not good. We needed to get out of here.

Daniela screamed. The Surori had knocked her down on her back and was moving in for the kill. I grimaced, then ran for Daniela, spearing the Surori to the ground. I rolled through, hanging tight to my torch. I grabbed Daniela's hand, pulling her to her feet.

"Run!" I yelled at her, pushing her toward the entrance. I swung at the approaching Surori, all three of them now moving as one unit. They recoiled, avoiding the flames. I moved slowly backward to the entrance where Daniela was waiting. They followed me closely, practically salivating. I swung the torch again, and the Surori slashed at it, knocking the torch to the ground.

Daniela grabbed my hand and yanked me through the cavern entrance. "Let's go!" she yelled, already starting to run. I turned away from the Surori and we took off into the darkness of the tunnels. We ran at full speed, Daniela never letting go of my hand. The silver box, safe in my bag, bounced off my back as we tore through the tunnels. I could hear the Surori, their shrill screams echoing off the stone walls, chasing us through the lower levels. We didn't slow down, even when we saw the beginning of the light. We'd reached where the others were still working on clearing the cells. Daniela dropped my hand, her arms pumping as fast as they could.

"Surori!" she yelled at the Kindred ahead. "The Surori are free!"

The guards with torches, at least six of them, turned and without a moment's hesitation, sprinted toward us. I expected us to slow down, maybe even turn and fight with the oncoming guards, but Daniela blew right past them, diving onto the stone floor. Her breathing was heavy. Her right hand was pressed tightly against her left arm, trying to stop the bleeding from where the Surori had cut her, but blood poured between her fingers. I soon noticed that wasn't the only place she was bleeding. Three livid red scratches were dug into her neck, bleeding profusely. I dropped down to my knees, pressing my hand against her neck to slow the bleeding. Shrieks and screams roared from the darkness of the tunnel ahead, and I kept my eyes trained on the entrance, prepared to protect Daniela at a moment's notice. I heard a thud, then a guard came flying into our lighted corner, landing hard on his back. A Surori followed, ready to go in for the kill. I lept to my feet. My fist cracked off its cheekbone, but it didn't slow it down. It lashed out, its right arm swinging wide. I ducked underneath and stepped through, now behind it. I grabbed both sides of its head and twisted with all my strength. A crack reverberated off the walls, and the Surori dropped limply to the ground.

"That won't kill it," the guard panted from his spot on the ground.

"It'll keep it down long enough to get it back in its cell," I responded, offering him a hand up. "Where are the others?"

"Finishing off the other two." He nodded to Daniela. "Get her out of here. We can handle the rest."

"No," Daniela argued immediately. "Stay. Help the others."

"If I don't get you outside the Hollow, you're going to bleed to death before you have a chance to heal," I pointed out.

"The Descendant is right," the guard agreed. I looked at him in surprise. I wasn't aware he knew who I was. "We've got this. Get outside the Hollow. Heal yourself."

I helped Daniela up, not giving her a chance to argue any more. We moved as fast as she was able up the remaining levels. We didn't stop until we reached the locked main entrance. I ripped the lock to the side, pulling the door open, and we fell out into the freedom of the clear night.

5

The moment we were outside the Hollow, Daniela passed out. Luckily, I'd had my arm around her and managed to keep her from falling head first into the waterfall. Back outside the wards, I had access to my powers again. My reserves were low, but I tapped into my remaining strength, using it not to heal myself, but to help me lift Daniela into my arms and carry her down the mountain. Unconscious as she was, she wasn't able to heal herself, and her wounds still bled badly, soaking my bare arms in her blood. I had to stop multiple times to adjust my grip and keep her from slipping out of my arms and over the edge of the mountain.

Along with the return of my powers, my connection to Roman also snapped back into place. I was immediately in tune with him, his emotions roaring down the connection, slamming into me. He was scared. Panicking. He was on the move, frantically searching Awen for me. Either Mallory had never found him, or he'd ignored her advice and come looking for me anyway. Knowing him, it was probably the latter.

I could tell the moment he found me, figured out where I was. I pushed back down the connection, forcing his emotions out of the way. *No. Stop. Stay where you are.* I said it over and over. We couldn't actually speak through our bond, but I put all my strength behind the words, hoping he understood. I took a small breath when I felt him quit moving. There was no way I could get him wrapped up in this. I couldn't risk it.

I reached the bottom of the mountain, jumping into the pool below. I sunk under the surface, Daniela's weight pushing me down. Our blood mingled in the water, washing my arms clean. I swam to the top, pushing Daniela ahead of me, refusing to come up until she was floating. I breached the water, gasping for breath. I slowly swam toward shore, pulling Daniela's unconscious body behind me. When I reached the other side of the pool, I crawled out and reached down, grabbing Daniela underneath both arms and yanking her onto the grass. I did a quick check to make sure the box was still strapped to my back, adjusting the strap to make sure it wouldn't slip off. In the minimal light, I couldn't see whether Daniela was still bleeding, so I pressed my fingers to her neck. They came away covered in her blood. She didn't have much time. She needed medical attention. Now.

I hoisted her onto my shoulders and started the trek through the trees. My powers were wide open, pulling on every element around me. Every tree I passed, every blade of grass gave me strength. The wind hit my wet skin, giving me goosebumps, and pushing me forward. I wasn't able to take her to the infirmary, even though I knew that was where she needed to go. Too many questions would be asked. Instead, I went back to my cottage to where I had the medical supplies packed in my bag. Hopefully they would be enough to stitch her up. The front of my cottage was too public and I couldn't risk being seen, so I brought Daniela through the back of my house, sneaking between the trees and through the billowing curtains that separated the hot spring from the wilderness. Immediately, I noticed all the candles in my cottage were lit, even though I hadn't left them that way when I'd gone. Someone else must have done it. I tiptoed past the hot spring, setting Daniela down gently on the ground, out of sight. Whoever was in my house, I couldn't risk them seeing Daniela. I rounded the corner into my living room, and nearly collapsed with relief when I saw Mallory pacing by the front door. It was the first time I was happy someone had let themselves into my house uninvited.

"You shouldn't be here." As happy as I was to see her, I didn't want her getting in trouble.

She wheeled around, surprised to see me. "You're bleeding," she said, doing a quick catalogue of my injuries. I had forgotten about them, but now that I thought about it, my neck did sting where the Surori cut me. "And wet," she added absently.

"I'm fine, but Daniela's hurt. I need your help." I turned around, rushing back into the bathroom. Mallory hurried behind me. She cursed when she saw Daniela's unconscious form on the ground. Her blood was already seeping onto the stone floor. "Help me get her to my bed."

"She needs to go to the infirmary."

"No!" I shouted, louder than I intended. "No infirmary. They'll just ask questions. We have to stop the bleeding ourselves."

Mallory grabbed Daniela's legs and I cradled her underneath her arms, grunting with the effort. We dragged her to my room, laying her on the bed as gently as we could manage. I ran out of the room, toward where I'd left my duffel thrown on the floor. I rummaged through it, grabbing the kit I'd acquired from the Council's armory. I jogged back into my room, pausing to grab towels out of a closet. I threw them at Mallory. "Patch her up. Get her conscious so she can heal herself. I'll be right back."

"What?" Mallory yelled. "Where are you going?"

"There something I need to do," I responded hurriedly. I was running short on time. I had about an hour to deliver the box to Astrid and get to the plane.

"Now?" she shouted incredulously. I winced. It killed me to leave her. I wished I could explain everything to her, but I had no time.

"I have to go," I said , imploring her to understand. I turned away from her again.

"Kyndal!" she shouted and I paused, grimacing. "This is beyond my skill. I need help. I need Cassie."

I huffed a breath. "I'll get her on the way." Unable to wait any longer, I sprinted out of the house.

"On the way to where?" Mallory shouted after me, but I didn't stop to respond.

Astrid lived on the coast. As a Water User, it didn't surprise me that she wanted to be near the ocean. Luckily I would have to pass the infirmary to get to her place, so it wouldn't be difficult to stop and see Cassie. I sprinted through the streets, not caring if anyone stopped to stare. The silver box bounced off my back and I gripped the strap of the bag, reassuring myself it was there. That all of this was worth it. I burst into the infirmary, searching the room for Cassie. I spotted her bright red hair across the room. She was changing the dressing on a soldier's leg. I sprinted to her side, heaving and short of breath. Cassie turned at the commotion, shocked to see me there and in the condition I was in. "I need you," I huffed out. "Now," I added. I grabbed her hand, pulling her away from the wounded soldier. I gave him a quick apologetic glance before dragging her out of the room.

Once we were outside, I bent over, placing my hands on my knees, desperate to get a deep breath. "Kyndal, what's wrong? Why are you all wet? And are you bleeding?" Any other circumstances, I would have smiled at how much she sounded like Mallory. Cassie grabbed my shoulders, yanking me up so she could see my neck. "This cut is deep, you may need stitches."

"I'm fine," I said, pulling my face away. "I need you to go

to my house right now. Mallory is waiting there, and she needs your help."

Cassie's face immediately turned serious. Her grip on my arm tightened, although I don't think she noticed. "What happened? Is she hurt?"

"Mallory is fine," I said quietly. "It's someone else that needs you. She'll explain everything she can. Just go now. I'll meet you there shortly."

"Where are you going?" she asked. So many questions, no good answers.

"I have something I have to do. I'll meet you at my house when I'm finished."

Cassie nodded then ducked back into the infirmary, no doubt to excuse herself so no one would wonder where she disappeared to. I didn't wait for her to come back out. I knew she'd find a way. She'd never leave Mallory alone in a time of need.

I headed down the path, around the infirmary and into the opposite side of the island. I had to move slower than I did before, hiding in the shadows, ducking into alleys when I heard someone coming. This side of the island was much more exclusive. It housed most of the Nomarchs and the high-ranking Kindred warriors. I couldn't go tearing through the streets without causing a scene. There was no excuse that would explain why I was there, so if the wrong person saw me, all this work would be for nothing. As I neared the coast, I started looking for Astrid's house. I looked for a house held up by white pillars with two fountains in front. There were several that fit that description. According to her, I would recognize it because of the large, marbled terrace at the back, overlooking the ocean. Two houses from the end of the street, I came to a large mansion, easily the biggest on the block. The fountains out front were backlit, the crystal blue water easily visible as it cascaded over the carved stone centers, depicting the symbol of House Cancer. I tiptoed down the edge of the house, the soft grass camouflaging my steps as I peeked around the back of the estate and saw a two-tiered, full length terrace made from rose colored marbled stretching from the house to the ocean, the bottom level jutting out over the cliffs. This had to be it.

I returned to the front of the house, took a deep breath, then knocked.

For a solid minute, nothing happened. I looked around suspiciously. Maybe this was a trap. A true test from the Council, and guards would show up to throw me back in the dungeons for stealing evidence. I raised my hand to knock again, when the door pulled open and Astrid's pale figure filled the doorway.

She hurried me into the foyer of her house. I looked around at the opulent entryway, covered in the same marble as the terrace. This room alone was bigger than my entire house. "Did you get it?" she asked. No questions about why I was wet or bleeding, like the others had asked. All she cared about was whether I got the box. I removed the bag from over my shoulder, placing it on the nearby marble table. I opened it, revealing the silver box inside. The top of it was stained red with blood. My blood.

Astrid's eyes gleamed with approval. "I'm impressed," she admitted. She reached for the box, but I grabbed the bag, pulling it from her reach.

"Not so fast." Astrid pinned me with her icy blue stare, but I didn't back down. "You promised me the secret to convincing Nero to return to Awen. Tell me that first, then you can have the box."

Astrid crossed her arms, her slate blue top billowing around her thin arms. "All right then. Nero's weakness is his hubris. He cares about nothing more than his reputation and his legacy. All members of the Coterie pride themselves on their prowess in battle, as well as their impressive bloodlines. You will find that several of the Coterie soldiers were bred into that way of life. The soldiers mate with human women, and when they produce a son, the mother is killed when he comes of age, ensuring his powers manifest. He is then moved into the Coterie, guaranteeing their organization for future generations."

My mouth fell open. "That's the most heinous thing I've ever heard."

"Be that as it may, it is this very fact that gives us leverage over Nero."

"I don't understand," I replied. I didn't know if it was the exhaustion or the blood loss, but I was not following what Astrid was saying.

Astrid smiled. "Nero had a son. Twins, actually, although

he only cared about the boy. One was a girl of flaxen hair and the other, a beautiful, brunette boy. Both with eyes of the bluest topaz." My stomach dropped at the familiar descriptions. *It couldn't be. There was no way.* "Nero believes they were killed before the son could come of age. But in fact," she paused. "Ezekiel intervened and managed to save the boy before he was killed. He took him in, raising him as one of us, away from the Coterie. Now, he is on his way to Nero tonight."

"Roman." I whispered the name.

Astrid nodded slightly. "He may be the only one that can convince his father to join this war."

6

I felt sick to my stomach.

I fell back against the wall, my legs giving out underneath me. "Nero is Roman's father." It was the third time I said it.

"Yes," Astrid said again. It was like she knew I needed it confirmed again.

"Are you sure?" It was a stupid question, but I had to ask it.

She nodded. "We're sure. The Council keeps close watch on specific families and their bloodlines."

"You mean families descended from the Original Twelve." Astrid looked at me in surprise. Drake had explained to me that they tracked the bloodlines, Amina later confirming it when she tried to use my lineage as a pawn in her grasp for political power. I also knew Roman was a descendant of the original Taurus, his ancestor Davina had told me so in one of my visions. "Prove it. Show me the records."

She nodded with approval, not bothering to ask how I knew Roman was from an Original line. "Just like your mother. You know far more than you let on. Amina underestimates you."

"The records, please."

Astrid rounded the corner out of the foyer, ducking into a nearby room. She returned with a book similar to the ones I had seen in the special records section of the library with Drake. I reached out for it, but Astrid pulled it back. "The box first," she said. "If you please."

I thought of Daniela bleeding out back at my cottage. Hopefully Mallory and Cassie had gotten her patched up, but I needed to check on her before I left. I didn't have time to argue with Astrid, let alone read the records now. I'd have to take it with me. I dropped the box on the table and held my hands out impatiently. Astrid obliged, handing over the ancient tome. "You should have told him," I said. "It's not fair to keep that type of information to yourself." I thought of all the research he'd done. The stack of books he'd compiled in the back of the library in a desperate attempt to find out where he came from. No wonder he couldn't figure out who his parents were. To think the Council knew this entire time was heartbreaking.

"I assure you, we did not keep this information to hurt young Roman, but rather to protect him." Astrid said.

I highly doubt that. "You kept it as leverage. You adopted a young, scared boy so that you could one day use him to control his father. The Council hates the Coterie almost as much as it does anyone descended from the Original Twelve, and Roman is both of those things. You toy with people, controlling who knows what, who has access to the information, as if you should be the ones to decide how much they know about themselves. Then you flip it, choosing to exploit that same heritage that you kept from them because it suits your cause."

"You should not presume to understand the will of the Nomarch Council. Not all of us look to exterminate the bloodlines of the Original Twelve." I noticed she didn't deny using Roman to leverage Nero.

"You tried to arrest me the moment we met. But I should assume you don't harbor any ill will toward Roman?" I shook my head. "No. Even if what you claim is true, I refuse to use him as a pawn just so you can get what you want. Now, if you'll excuse me. . ." I turned, but Astrid grabbed my arm, her grip remarkably strong.

"You think you can stand on your moral high ground and judge the actions of others. You cannot even begin to understand the reasons behind my actions, the sacrifices I have made for my people." That was the second time she'd told me I didn't understand. "I have walked this earth for over a millennium, and I will not be condescended to by a girl that is nothing more than a child."

I ripped my arm out of her grip, stomping out of the house.

When I made it back to my house, I had less than twenty minutes until the plane took off. I ripped open my front door, slamming it behind me. I shoved the record book inside my duffel bag quickly before Mallory or Cassie had a chance to see it. I didn't want either of them asking any questions about the book or where it came from. I poked my head inside my bedroom, but no one was there. My bedsheets were disheveled and covered in red stains, and the side table was covered in medical supplies and bloody gauze. "Mallory? Cassie?" I called.

"In here." The response came from the bathroom. I hustled to the bathroom, only to find Mallory and Cassie standing waist deep in my hot spring. Their shoes were thrown haphazardly on the stone floor. Their clothes were wet, sticking to their skin and Cassie's hair was damp. Daniela floated in-between them, held up by the two women. Her eyes were closed and her chest moved up and down in steady breaths. Her wounds were covered in some sort of poultice.

"What are you doing?" I asked.

"We managed to stop the bleeding," Cassie explained. "But she's still very weak. We needed to get her as close to her element as possible to expedite the healing process."

"Has she woken up yet?"

"Briefly," Mallory answered. "But it didn't last long."

"Is she going to make it?"

Cassie nodded. "You're lucky you got to me when you did.

She wouldn't have lasted much longer."

I nodded, satisfied. I don't know what I would have done if Daniela hadn't pulled through. I'd never forgive myself if she died because she chose to help me.

I turned from the bathroom, returning to the living room. I needed to get changed into my gear. I heard the water splash behind me, and then wet steps following me, but I didn't turn. I knew Mallory and Cassie would have questions about what happened tonight, but I didn't have any good answers for them.

"Kyndal, wait," Mallory said. "You owe us some explanations. What went on tonight? Who attacked you and Daniela?"

I shook my head, turning briefly to look at my friend. She was drenched, the water from her clothes dripping onto my floor. "I can't tell you that." I turned back, digging into my duffel bag, careful not to expose the newly acquired book. I pulled out the gear. It was different than what I wore now. Instead of black, it was a combination of whites and greys, no doubt to help me blend into the wintery landscape of Siberia. It was heavier too, necessary for blocking out the cold. Not that it mattered to me. I ducked into my bedroom to change.

"What's all the gear for then?" Mallory asked after me. "Are you going on a mission?"

I reemerged from my room, dressed in my new gear. "I can't tell you that either." I reached back, trying to tame my rat's nest I called hair. The best I managed was a bun.

Mallory threw her arms out, frustrated. "Well, what can you tell us?" she demanded. I ignored her, instead walking back to the bathroom. I needed to wipe the dried blood off my neck so no one would ask questions. I didn't make it far, Mallory stepped in my way. "Answer me, dammit."

I came up short, huffing a quick breath. I hated keeping secrets from Mallory, but I had to. It was too dangerous for her or Cassie to get involved. "I can't," I said again, this time more forcefully. "I wish I could, but I can't. And I need you to be okay with that."

"How am I supposed to be okay with it?" Mallory snapped. "You came to me. You asked for *my* help. And Cassie's. You're the one who brought us into this. I took you to Daniela. If it weren't for me, she wouldn't be lying in that spring, fighting for her life. An explanation is the minimum we are owed."

My shoulders dropped. "I appreciate your help. I really do. But I'm in the Guard now, and there are things I can't talk about. Things that are too dangerous for you to know. I promise you, I'll explain when I can. When it's safe."

"Whatever," Mallory said, brushing me off with her hand. "You're acting just like them. You have all the information, we're just here to do your dirty work and not ask questions."

"Mallory. . ." I began. How could she think that? I was nothing like them. I trusted them both with my life.

"No," she said adamantly, cutting me off. "Don't bother. Just leave, Kyndal. Clearly you have somewhere you need to be. Don't worry, we'll clean up after you." Her tone was cold and bitter. She turned from me, returning to Cassie and Daniela.

I leaned toward the bathroom, wanting nothing more than go after her and explain everything. Just then I felt a tug through the bond. It was Roman, wondering where I was. I grimaced, looking toward my friends once more, before scooping up my duffel bag and heading to the plane.

I was the last one on. I narrowly made it, running up the ramp just before the door was closed. This was not like the plane I'd come here in. It was one of the large cargo planes I had seen soldiers arriving in. There were a few seats toward the front, but the majority of the plane was empty, leaving space for a small army. Clearly Amina intended for us to succeed and come back with Nero and his forces. Brynn and Grady sat next to each other at the front, the row behind them occupied by Dirk and his companions. I promptly ignored them, even as they monitored my every step.

Roman wasn't in any of the seats, but rather sitting on the floor in the back, his head resting on his duffel bag. He looked relaxed, but upon closer inspection, I could tell differently. His jaw was clenched and his right foot tapped slightly. He was worried about me, and angry.

I rushed on, holding my duffel bag over my head. "Cutting it a little close, aren't you?" Grady asked. I ignored him, moving to the back of the plane. Far enough away from Grady and Brynn, but not too close to Roman. I could feel his eyes on me, but I didn't look his direction. I couldn't. He knew I was keeping secrets, and if I looked at him, I wasn't sure I could keep myself from spilling everything. I threw my bag on the floor and propped myself up against it, using it as a makeshift pillow. It wasn't particularly comfortable, but I was dying for some sleep and it was the best I was going to get. A bolt shot through the bond, demanding I recognize him and I lost my resolve. My eyes cut over to Roman, who was giving me a scrutinizing glance.

You okay? He mouthed.

I nodded. He pulled the collar of his gear down, exposing the thin red line there. A shadow of my injury left on him. *Later*, I mouthed back at him. Even though the plane was large, there was no way to speak without being overheard. He nodded curtly in return, then closed his eyes. The bond went silent. He was shutting me out, refusing to acknowledge me until I provided some answers.

The plane started moving, and soon we would be taking off. My stare lingered. He'd been through so much, how was I going to tell him about who his father was? It would break his heart. I reached behind me into my duffel bag and pulled out the record book Astrid had given me. Before I said anything to Roman, I had to make sure what she said was true. I couldn't risk hurting him like that. With six hours until we arrived in Siberia, I dug into the book.

I am back in the cave. *The torches are lit, the roar of water echoes through the tunnels. I lift my foot to step toward a tunnel, and a wave of fear washes over me. I place my foot back where it was, and the fear disappears instantly. Instead of trying again, I decide to do something different. I turn to investigate the rest of the cave. Behind me is the entrance, but it's too dark for me to see anything. There are torches sitting unlit on either side so I call to my power, lighting them instantly. The entrance glows in soft oranges and yellows, illuminating the cave walls. The entrance is rectangular, almost as if someone carved the entrance from the rock to create a doorway. I peek through the opening and find a set of stairs, leading up. Above the doorway, the flames reveal a beautiful painting. The painting is of a woman kneeling on one leg. Her arms are outstretched, and behind them are the most stunning wings I've ever seen. The feathers are painted a collage of blues, golds, reds, and greens. She is wearing a headdress with a singular feather atop it. I instantly recognize her as the woman from the drawing. The goddess who fought Set and was defeated. Her presence here means this isn't just a cave—it's a temple. I grab one of the torches from the wall, swinging the light toward the rest of the wall. Carved into the stone is a series of hieroglyphics, spanning the entire height of the cave. Just looking at them, it's obvious they tell a story, but I have no way of reading it. I study the symbols, trying my best to commit them to memory, when the feeling from before returns. It starts out slow, just a*

creeping feeling on the back of my neck, as if someone is watching me. Then it begins to spread down my neck and over my shoulders, like a blanket smothering me. My breathing turns heavy. I lose the grip on my power and the torches go out, throwing the cave into darkness. A sharp pain rips through my chest and I drop to one knee, clutching at my chest. My hands come away wet, covered in blood. I scream in pain, my voice echoing off the cave walls.

I woke to someone shaking my shoulder. I jolted forward, almost coming off the ground. The book clattered to the floor and I grab it quickly, snapping it shut. Roman was sitting next to me now, his hand on my shoulder, his face full of concern. I took in a sharp breath, leaning forward and placing my head in my hands. *It was only a dream*, I told myself. *It wasn't real.* My heart was racing and my adrenaline was pumping as if I'd just been in a wraith battle. A light sheen of sweat covered my forehead. Roman's hand moved from my shoulder to my back, moving in slow, soothing circles. His power surrounded me, helping to calm my erratic heartbeat. "It was just a dream," he whispered in my ear, repeating my thoughts as if I'd said them aloud. "None of it was real." He'd known what happened without me saying a word.

I sat back against the plane wall, digging my fingers into my brunette tresses. Grady and Brynn were both turned in their seats staring at us. Roman pulled his hand away, as if he didn't want the others to see him touching me. I didn't even have the energy to yell at them and tell them to mind their own business. "I'm fine," I said quietly to Roman.

"Thank you for waking me up, but I'm fine now."

"You were screaming," Grady said. His jaw was set hard, but his eyes were soft, maybe even concerned.

"She said she's fine," Roman snapped at him. "Now turn around." Grady rolled his eyes, but he listened, both he and Brynn now looking away. I had no doubt they were still paying close attention to us though.

"Really, Roman, I'm okay." I set my hand on his knee, imploring him to understand. I couldn't talk about it now. Not with the others around. "Where are we, anyway? How long was I out?"

"You slept most of the flight. We're starting our final descent." Right as he said it, I could feel it. There was a slight drop in the plane, a slight change in the pressure. I stood up, moving to one of the few windows. The clouds were thin, and I could see to the ground below. It was covered in white, the entire landscape blanketed in snow and ice. The majority of it was plains, but off in the distance, there was a snow-covered mountain range. There were trees sporadically placed over the land, some in small clusters, but no real forests that I could see.

"Where's the airport?" I asked.

"We won't be landing at one," Dirk answered. I'd almost forgotten about him and the others. "The compound sits on top of Ozero Lobaz. It's a frozen lake highly secluded in the middle of the frozen tundra. The closest airport is hours away. We'll be landing in a field a few miles out and we'll have to trek the rest of the way."

"Speaking of," Grady interrupted, turning to Dirk, "what can you tell us about the layout of the Coterie?"

Dirk stretched out several maps, detailing the compound. It consisted of several old stone buildings, surrounded by a high-scale retaining wall. There was one gate in the wall, the single point of entry. The surrounding area provided no cover. There were a few small clusters of trees, but nothing large enough to use to cover anyone's approach. It was well fortified. I could see why Cyrus and the Council's forces had been unable to breach its walls.

"What's that?" I asked, pointing to a blank spot on the map.

"None of your business," Dirk answered matter of factly. I snorted in reply. Apparently there was more going on in the Coterie than they were willing to divulge with the rest of the Kindred. "Now it's several miles until we reach Ozero Lobaz. The terrain can be treacherous in places and it is not uncommon for a stray wraith to be hiding outside our walls. We will need to clear the area before we enter the Coterie."

Before leaving the plane, each of us dug into our bags, grabbing as many weapons as we could. I added an additional dagger to my standard one, taking a moment to double check my ring daggers. Roman had another dagger at his hip, one in his boot. Grady strapped a leather double back scabbard onto his back, before sliding a short sword in it. Brynn's dagger hung at her hip, two sais tucked into the back of her belt as well. She slid a fur-lined coat over the top of it, camouflaged in the same whites and greys as our gear. I noticed the others adding layers to their gear as well. Roman added a leather vest, Grady, open finger gloves. He finished gearing up and looked up at me, catching me staring. He gave my gear a cursory glance.

"You're going to need this," he said, then threw me a fur-lined coat similar to the one Brynn wore. I caught the coat, not even looking at it before I threw it onto a nearby seat.

"No I won't." Heat tickled my fingers and soon tiny flames crawled into my palm. Grady looked down at the flames. From the door of the plane, Dirk's eyes cut to my hand, no doubt remembering our introduction at the training room. We may not be able to bring weapons into the Coterie, but that didn't mean we would be unarmed.

"Right. I forgot."

"You good?" Roman asked. His tone was clipped. I nodded once. He checked the other two briefly, satisfied when they nodded as well. "Let's move."

7

The plan was simple. It was two and a half miles to the edge of Ozero Lobaz, and there were a handful of tree clusters between us and the edge of the lake. We had to clear each of those areas of any wraiths as we went. We didn't know how many were out there, so we had to be meticulous. If in fact there were wraiths hiding, we couldn't take the chance of them getting behind us. They already had the high ground and we only had two things on our side.

Surprise and speed.

We moved quickly, Grady and Roman in the lead. Grady was tuned into the earth, feeling for the slightest change in the landscape, while Roman used his power to dampen the sound of our feet crunching on the snow. We moved through the first two clusters of trees without encountering any wraiths. We moved on to the third. Still, nothing. By the fourth, I was beginning to doubt Dirk's warning. Through the bond, I could feel Roman's growing sense of agitation. Although I didn't know if that was because he also thought the mission was a waste of time or if he was irritated I'd shut him out earlier.

By the time we reached the fourth set of trees, the sun had begun to set, even though it was still mid-afternoon. This far north, daytime was short in the fall. We had maybe forty-five minutes until it was completely dark out. We were near the edge of the lake and I could see the compound. From what I could tell, this lake wasn't perfectly circular like the one back home, but rather had a jagged shoreline. It was difficult to tell as the edges blended in the snowy landscape, sometimes making it difficult to tell where the lake began and the safety of the solid ground ended. Currently cast into shadow by the remaining sunlight, the compound itself was a giant, medieval castle that emerged from the center of the icy lake. Made of a dark stone, the main building was at least three stories tall. There was a center turret, flanked by two smaller ones. Cut into the stone were large windows leading out to balconies wrapped in wrought iron. The compound was surrounded by a wall made of the same dark stone. The gate stood out, a set of large, bright white double doors. Upon closer inspection, I realized they were carved from ice. Recalling Dirk's maps, the smaller buildings weren't visible from outside the wall. From where we were, the whole place looked deserted. If it weren't for the braziers lit atop the wall, I would have thought no one was inside.

"Where are your men?" Brynn asked Dirk, her sharp tone cutting through the crisp air. "Aren't they be expecting us?"

"They're watching," Dirk responded.

A branch snapped, cutting him off. Grady froze, holding his hand up, effectively halting our small group. I turned my attention to him and opened my power, trying to sense what he did. He pointed ahead of him, into the trees. My eyes snapped up. The trees ahead of us were large pines, thick with needles and perfect for hiding. I kept my eyes trained up, but reached in my belt scabbard, quietly freeing my dagger. The others did the same, each readying their weapons. The wind had been quiet, nothing more than a light breeze, but suddenly it picked up, shaking the limbs of the trees and kicking up the loose snow. I risked a glance at Roman. A pulse of power flew from him, aimed directly at the nearest tree. It smacked into the trunk, cracking the bark and bending the ancient tree. We braced ourselves, waiting for the hidden wraith to show itself.

Nothing happened.

Roman built his power again, prepared to rock the tree, but I threw my arm out, stopping him. The air had changed, forcing the hairs on the back of my neck to stand at attention. Someone was definitely there, but it was more than that. The feeling was familiar. I could feel the presence of fire and it wasn't coming from the compound.

"Get down!" I shouted, just as a fireball came flying out of the trees. I pushed Roman down, Grady and Brynn following us as we scattered into the snow. Dirk and the others spread out in the opposite direction. The fireball flew over our heads, slamming into the snow, melting it on contact. Before we could stand, another fireball flew from a different tree, this time landing just short of Brynn.

"Hybrids," Grady grunted from where he was sprawled on the ground. I jumped to my feet, launching a fireball of my own at the giant pine. It landed squarely in the center of the tree's mighty trunk. The flames started to extinguish, the bark too wet to catch fire. Next to me, Brynn threw her hand out, siphoning the water from the trunk. I smiled and pushed out my power out again, feeding the flames, forcing them up the trunk and over to the limb. The needles caught fire, acting as kindling to my growing flames. I pulled the flames over, jumping to the other tree, catching it aflame as well. Whoever was hiding up there, I would smoke them out. Roman's power joined mine, creating a wall around the flames and keeping the growing smoke in one place, cutting off their air supply.

Two bodies dropped from the trees, landing in agile crouches. As one, their bodies straightened, bringing them up to their full heights. Dark, inky veins weaved through their exposed arms, necks, and faces. Their eyes glowed a sharp red in the fading sunlight.

The one closest to us smiled, his serrated teeth peeking over his chapped, cracked lips. Absently, I noticed the wassceptre tattoo on his arm. He eyed our small group, his gaze pausing when he reached Roman, his smile growing.

"We thought you were dead." His voice was gravelly and thickly accented. "Set will be pleased when I tell him you have returned."

The wind swirled around us, kicking the snow into a

freezing vortex. "You won't have the chance to tell him anything," Roman replied.

Four more hybrids dropped out of the trees behind the flames, their eyes glowing a variety of colors. "You're outnumbered," the hybrid responded. "You are foolish to..."

Roman didn't wait for him to finish. He sent a burst of air through the trees, blowing the limbs back in a violent show of power, knocking the hybrids into the snow. We took advantage, pressing forward, the fight officially on. Roman took the lead, punching through the first two wraiths, heading straight for the ones in the back. Brynn attacked the wraith closest to us, her sais swinging through the air. I ran for the other fire user, who was staggering back to his feet. Grady flew past us, heading for the remaining two wraiths, the Coterie men hot on his heels.

I jumped a foot away from the hybrid, my right foot barreling into his chest, knocking him back into the burning tree. Embers shook loose from above, showering down on our heads. The hybrid hissed in anger, lashing out with his right hand. I ducked low, avoiding the fist, and came up swinging, catching him under the chin. He wasn't fazed. Instead, he returned the favor, cracking his left fist off my cheekbone. My head whipped to the side. I turned with the momentum, swinging around, retaliating with a brutal backhand. I flipped the dagger in my hand, stabbing directly at his heart. He feinted to the left and the dagger missed, instead burying itself in the tree trunk. Before I could pull it out, the hybrid grabbed me by the shoulders, launching me back into the snow several feet away. I skid along the ground, snow billowing around me, the icy underlayer scraping my skin. I didn't even have time to get up before another hybrid was on me, her foot stomping into my gut. I grunted with pain, doubling in on myself. She pulled her leg back, intending to do it again, but I twisted on the ground, my leg sweeping hers out from underneath her. As she fell, I reached down, releasing a ring dagger from its sheath. I raised it above my head before ramming it into her chest, directly through her heart.

With the nearest threat disposed of, I took a moment to evaluate the battle. Brynn was still battling the Fire User hybrid, although she was down to one sai. The other was lost in the snowy landscape. She was quick, using the terrain to her advantage. She swung her sai, the hilt cracking off the hybrid's cheekbone, then she spun, hiding behind a tree as the hybrid launched a fireball. The flames skid along the side of the tree trunk, then Brynn attacked again, while the hybrid reloaded his power. Behind her, Grady was battling two hybrids—the one I'd fought earlier—and an Air User. Near him, Dirk and his men had surrounded one hybrid and were slowly taking him apart piece by piece. Like cats playing with their food before they killed it.

Grady's nose was bloodied, his russet hair falling wildly in his eyes as he fended off his attackers. His feet suddenly lifted off the ground, the Air User suspending him in the air. Grady thrashed, but no matter what he did, he couldn't break free. I hesitated, waiting for Dirk to help him, but he never turned, even as a Fire User sauntered closer, slowly forming a fireball between his hands. Without even thinking, I pulled on my power, ripping the flames out of the hybrid's hands, launching them at the nearby Air User. They smacked into her shoulder, knocking her down. She lost her grip on Grady, who landed soundly on the ground, and in one smooth move ran his dagger through the chest of the Fire User. I ran to help Grady, throwing one of my ring daggers at the remaining Air User. It buried into her shoulder, distracting her just long enough. She barely had time to grunt with pain before Grady spun, burying his dagger in her heart.

Grady now safe, I turned to find Roman. He was in the middle of the tiny forest, in single combat against an Earth User. He'd originally been fighting two. He must have managed to kill one. The hybrid he fought was strong, ripping entire trees out of the ground and catapulting them through the air, but Roman was amazing. He dodged some, spinning and dipping through the flying limbs. Others he froze in mid-air, using his power to force them back.

I retrieved my daggers, hell-bent on helping Roman when the ground began to shake violently. I braced myself against a nearby pine. "What are you doing?" I shouted at Grady.

"It isn't me!" he yelled back. His eyes searched wildly, desperately trying to find the source of the power. His eyes snapped to the horizon, on the opposite side of the trees. Three more hybrids stood there, their arms outstretched, their eyes glowing green. I watched in horror as seven more hybrids appeared behind them. I had no idea where they came from, but there was no way we could handle this many on our own.

"Run!" I shouted. Brynn and Grady immediately turned, sprinting for the lake. Sprinting for the compound. At the same moment, the hybrids broke, running straight for us. The Coterie men also made a run for it, directly past Roman who was still pinned down by the Earth User. Instead of running to safety, I turned, refusing to leave without him. I ran straight for him, barreling into the hybrid, knocking him off center. Roman lept into the air, coming down with a perfect right cross. The hybrid's head snapped to the side. I kicked out at the back of his knee, dropping him to the snowy ground, then delivered a left cross, rendering him unconscious.

The hybrid had barely hit the ground before I grabbed Roman and pushed him toward the lake. "We have to go."

"He's not dead," he argued, trying his best to get to the unconscious hybrid.

"There's no time," I urged. I could feel the hybrids advancing on our backs. If we didn't get in the compound soon, we'd both be dead. "We have to go now." More hybrids had appeared, bringing their numbers to over fifteen.

Roman looked over my shoulder, finally getting a full view of the approaching hybrids. His eyes widened as he took in their numbers. "We have to go now," he finally said. We sprinted out of the trees, beelining for the frozen lake. Grady and Brynn were at least twenty-five yards ahead of us. They'd reach the gate way before us.

We ran furiously, Roman in the lead. He was naturally faster than me and my legs ached with the effort it took to keep up with him. Even as we crossed the icy surface of Ozero Lobaz, the hybrids gained on us. My foot slipped several times, forcing me to my knees more than once. A fireball flew over our heads, scorching the ground just ahead of us. More landed farther up, aimed at the others. I spun, pausing briefly to launch four fireballs rapidly in retaliation. I didn't pay any attention to whether they hit their mark or not.

When I spun forward again, Grady had reached the icy gate. He pounded on it, yelling to whomever might be inside. Brynn wasn't with him. She knelt in the middle of the lake, her bare palms spread along the lake surface. She raised her head slowly, her eyes now an icy blue. Behind me, directly under the left flank of the attacking hybrids, the ice burst apart, freezing water shooting out of the lake like a geyser. Three hybrids went flying. Another geyser exploded, this time under the right flank. A third one, double the size of the other two, burst through the middle of their ranks, dropping several hybrids into the freezing cold lake, leaving behind a gaping hole in the ice. The edges of it cracked, large chunks falling into the frozen depths below. The crevice grew in all directions, part of it splintering right toward me. The hybrids screamed as they dropped into the water one by one. The ice continued to splinter, dropping one of Dirk's men into the icy water below. I gasped, pushing off toward the compound again, but I only made it a few steps before the ground underneath me broke. I dropped into the water chest high, desperately grasping at the edge of the ice to try and keep myself afloat. My lungs constricted, my breaths coming out in quick bursts, each one like a knife to the chest.

Ahead of me, Roman skid to a halt, immediately turning back and sliding down to the edge of the ice. His hand clasped my arm, yanking me out of the freezing water and onto the ice. There were still a few hybrids left, but now outnumbered and with the lake falling apart, they were retreating back into the trees. Roman pulled me to my feet and we limped together to the gate of the compound.

"Open up!" Grady screamed. He pounded his fist against the icy door, the side of his hand bruised and bloodied from the effort. I heaved forward, losing my grip on Roman and falling to the ground. He lunged at the door, kicking it with all his might. The door shook, but it did not falter. I fell against the stone wall and curled inward, clinging to what little body heat remained. My clothes were frozen stiff and crunched with every movement. My teeth chattered violently as my body tried to generate heat. I focused on the lit braziers atop the wall, trying to pull their heat into me, but nothing happened. I could feel my power inside me, but it was hidden, trapped inside a block of ice. I watched Roman as he repeatedly kicked the ice door. His lips were a slight shade of blue, and his right arm was shivering involuntarily. No doubt effects of my surprise swim rubbing off on him.

Roman prepared to kick again when Dirk stepped in front of him, preventing him from denting the door any more than he already had. "Knock it off," he told him. "There is no use. They will not open the gate until the threat is gone."

Roman shoved him, Dirk bouncing off the double doors. "Get off me," he growled. "They'll open the gate or I'll kick it down myself!" he yelled over the wall.

"That's not doing anything to help," Brynn piped up.

Roman's head snapped her direction. His eyes were a bright gold, his rage pumping through my veins as if it were my own. He pointed directly in Brynn's face. "*You* don't get to speak. You broke the lake apart."

Brynn took a step up. "It worked, didn't it?" she spit. "The hybrids are gone."

"This never should have happened. You were sloppy. You dropped Kyndal in the damn water! The Council made a mistake letting you in the Guard, you don't belong here. Your stupidity is going to get one of us killed."

"Don't. . ." I began, my teeth chattering loudly. It wasn't that I didn't agree with him, it's just that there was no time for any of this. "Don't fight. . ." I tried again, but my breath cut off in a hacking cough.

Roman dropped to my side, peeling off his leather vest and placing it over me. It didn't provide much warmth, but it was at least dry. Without it, he was left vulnerable to the cold. "No," I protested. "You keep it."

"Don't argue with me," he responded with finality. I prepared myself to do just that, when the sound of metal groaning against metal echoed from the wall and the front gate opened.

8

Ten men poured out of the gate, weapons drawn. Even though they looked wildly different than one another, they were all dressed similarly in black tactical gear, blending into the darkness. They split in two, half of them lunging for Grady and Brynn, who were the closest, grabbing them roughly, pushing them face first into the wall. "Hey!" Brynn protested, trying her hardest to push off the wall and escape but with no luck. "Get your hands off me!"

The rest came for Roman and me. Immediately, Roman turned to defend us. He landed a right cross on one of the men before being overtaken by four of them and pushed to the icy ground. "Roman!" I screamed, trying desperately to push myself up the wall, but my muscles weren't cooperating. The remaining man grabbed my arm roughly, yanking me to my feet. Every muscle screamed in agony as he dragged me through the gate. I twisted in his grasp, managing to turn my head just enough to see Roman lifted off the ground and escorted in with the rest of us.

They stripped us of our weapons, throwing us in separate rooms. We'd argued with them the whole way, trying to explain who we were and why we were here, but they didn't seem to care. They simply locked the heavy wooden doors behind us. The room wasn't a cell exactly, but it was empty of all furniture. There were no windows, nothing except a fireplace filled with smoldering embers. I couldn't see the others, but I knew their rooms weren't far away. I could feel Roman nearby.

I crawled to the other side of the room, to the tiny bit of warmth provided by the fireplace. I reached down, grabbing a piece of wood stacked next to the fireplace and threw it on. I sat slowly, my body racked with shivers while I waited for the wood to catch. A small, soft breeze blew past me and under the embers, breathing life into the flames and helping catch the log on fire. I smiled softly. I could feel the power that came with the breeze, and it brought me as much comfort as the heat. Even though he knew I was keeping secrets, Roman was still taking care of me.

I turned to the fireplace where the flames had grown, their warmth seeping into my bones. A tendril of my power unlocked. I grabbed ahold of it, pulling on it, using it to thaw the ice inside me and jumpstart the healing process. As the warmth spread, my eyes fluttered and closed involuntarily, shutting down so that my body could heal quicker.

Just as my body loosened up and my muscles were usable again, the door burst open. A stream of soldiers marched in, filling the room. I hobbled to my feet, standing in as much of a defensive manner as I could manage, my head held high and prepared for anything.

For a moment, nothing happened. Then a large man filled the doorway, his shadow casting all the way to the opposite wall.

Immediately, I knew it was Nero. As much as I wanted to deny Astrid's claim, the evidence was quite literally staring me in the face. He was tall like Roman, his body built in the same lean muscle as his son. His hair was a shade darker, but I could see the resemblance. It wasn't obvious, anyone oblivious to the truth probably wouldn't even notice it, but knowing what I did, it was all I could see. Nero's eyes cut over to me sharply and I almost audibly gasped with relief to see they were a deep brown, so dark it was hard to tell the difference between his iris and his pupil. I don't think I could have handled to see Roman's eyes on a man with such a violent reputation. I stood taller as he sized me up, refusing to show any weakness. The silence stretched on, past the point of comfort. "You just going to stare at me all day? Because if so, I'd really like to sit back down," I snipped.

He didn't smile, not even a little bit. "What is your name?" he asked. His voice was brusque and serious. It seemed to swallow the space in the room, a void that matched the darkness of his eyes.

"Kyndal Davenport of House Aries," I answered, secretly proud of myself when my voice didn't waver.

"An Aries?" his eyebrows raised slightly, the only

indication he was interested in what I said. "You and your friends made quite the spectacle outside our gates."

"Appreciate the backup," I quipped.

"The gates of the Coterie have never been breached, not in hundreds of years. The wraiths posed no threat and I saw no reason to send my men outside the walls."

"Except your people were under attack."

His eyes flashed. "My people? I saw none of my people in danger."

"One of your men died and you could have prevented it had you sent soldiers to help us!"

Nero moved closer. "All I saw was two girls making a mess of everything and men foolish enough to fight with them when they should have cut their losses."

I rolled my eyes, gnashing my teeth at his condescending attitude. Slowly, I crossed my arms, pleased to find they weren't as frigid as before. "What would you have done? Those weren't your typical wraiths. . ."

"I would have let you drown." His reply was immediate. No hesitation. No remorse.

"No honor among the Coterie, I take it." I was liking Nero less and less by the minute.

"There is no honor in weakness," Nero replied. "The Coterie only tolerates the best. The most elite. If you're killed, you were weak. We're better off without you."

I grunted. This was the new leader of my House. "What have you done with my companions?" I asked.

"They are in similar accommodations, awaiting questioning."

"Are we your prisoners?"

He shrugged noncommittally. "For the moment. Until I can determine your intentions."

"Our intentions are simple. You are needed in Awen. The Aries Nomarch was killed. You are the next in line to take his throne."

"So you say."

I scoffed. "Do you think I'm lying? You invited us here. You sent your emissary Dirk to retrieve an envoy of the Council. Bring him in here, he can tell you who we are."

"Dirk is resting after his long travels."

I popped my knuckles, growing increasingly agitated. "The Kindred are at war and your forces have been called to battle."

"Well, which is it?" he drawled.

"What?" I demanded. A spike of power shot down my arm, heat now resting in my palm, waiting to be released.

Nero stepped further into the room, pacing slowly, his arms tucked behind his back. I didn't miss that his eyes traveled up and down my body, no doubt trying to size me up as an adversary. He stepped around me, between my back and the flames. I refused to turn. "First you say I have been called to sit on the Council, next you say you need my soldiers. Which is it?"

"Both!" I yelled. I turned my head, eyeing him. Tiny flames danced on the tips of his fingers. "Do you not know what has been going on?"

"Why should I trust anything you say? How do I know you are not an assassin sent here by the Council to kill me? You look no different to me than the beasts you were fighting on the ice."

I was officially pissed. I hadn't fought my way here and nearly been frozen solid in the lake just to listen to his attitude. "If you think I'm a hybrid, feel free to drive a dagger through my heart to find out. Although you're going to need more than the men you brought." My eyes turned a livid red, my anger fueling my power, allowing it to melt the ice in my veins. The flames behind me crackled in anticipation. Nero eyed them, smiling wickedly.

"Your power does not scare me girl."

I pushed my power out, extinguishing the fireplace, snuffing out the flames Nero held.

"Call me *girl*, one more time," I snarled.

Nero stared at the now smoking fireplace, before dragging his eyes to me. He chuckled, shaking his head as if I was a child that had just done something foolish. "That was stupid of you. You just eliminated the one weapon you had at your disposal."

I turned to fully face him, and this time it was my turn to smile. "Clearly, you underestimate me." I held my arms out and called my power again, allowing the flames to burst out of my palms. Nero jumped back, his eyes wide with surprise and wonder. His mouth dropped open, words escaping him. "Now, I'm only going to say this once, so listen closely. Release me from this room, or I swear I will burn this whole place to the ground."

Nero had no choice but to release me, although I wasn't fooled into thinking I'd scared him. I had no doubt he had always intended on releasing me but had only taken my companions and me into those rooms to shake us—to make it perfectly clear we were no longer under the protection of the Council and that he ran the Coterie. He could do whatever he pleased with us. I'd hoped to be taken to Roman, but there was no such luck. I was escorted to a room of slightly different accommodations. On the third floor of the main house, the room was simple. A cot and dresser on one side, the opposite wall had a small desk which sat underneath a double picture window overlooking the rest of the compound. I peered out the window, taking note of the four smaller buildings within the compound walls, matching them with what was on Dirk's map. I walked over to the fireplace nestled between the bed and window, pausing to light it and bring much needed warmth into the room.

"You are confined to your room. Your personal effects will be recovered from the plane and brought to you. Meals will be brought to you. If you need the bathing room, ask the guard and he'll escort you. He's posted at the end of the hall."

I turned to the guard in the doorway, "How long am I meant to be a prisoner?"

He gave me a cold stare. "Until the Commander decides what to do with you." He left, shutting the door behind him firmly. I tiptoed to it, opening it slightly to peer into the hallway. The soldier stopped at the end of the hallway to address another man, speaking to him briefly and giving him instructions. The man nodded curtly, his eyes sliding to my door. I rolled my eyes and shut the door again.

I paced the room like a caged animal. There was no way I was waiting in this room for Nero to pass judgement. I needed to get out, to get to Roman. I felt for the bond, pulled on the ever-present chord that connected the two of us. He wasn't far. Definitely in the same building, although from what I could tell, he was at least two floors down. A twinge of recognition jumped through the bond. He knew I was searching for him, knew I was worried. A soothing sense of calm filled me, Roman's way of telling me he was okay. Since the door provided no escape, I moved to the window, desperate for any way out of the room. I pulled on the pane, but it didn't budge.

I threw myself back on the bed, frustrated and out of ideas. With no way to get to Roman, I was forced to sit and wait. I kicked my boots off my feet, peeling my socks away next.

Although my power had returned enough to chase away the worst of the cold, it had done nothing to dry my clothes. My socks were soaking wet, and I threw them toward the fire to dry, both of them landing with a wet smack on the stone floor. I still had Roman's leather vest and I wrapped myself in it, curling up on the bed and closing my eyes.

I expected to dream. Maybe of Marius or Davina. It had been weeks since I'd seen either of them in my dreams—or maybe of the mysterious cave—but nothing haunted me. All the visions were suffocated by the intense exhaustion racking my body.

I woke when my door opened, my duffel bag unceremoniously tossed into the room and onto the hard floor. I leapt from the bed, rummaging through its contents. My extra sets of clothes, my medical supplies, even the records book, were all accounted for. The only things missing were my weapons.

I changed quickly, shucking off my old clothes and replacing them with fresh gear; dark grey pants and a white long sleeve. From the bottom of the bag, I dug out a tub of salve, rubbing it in to the scrapes on my hands, the cut on my neck. I could heal the wounds without it, but I needed to reserve as much of my power as I could. Finally, I pulled my feet into a pair of thick socks and picked up the records book. I dragged the chair at the desk over to the hearth, sat down, and began to read.

Three days passed.

Nero never came, no matter how many times I demanded to

see him. Meals were delivered three times a day, each one a variation of the same bland mix of oats and bread, only occasionally mixed with scraps of some sort of unrecognizable wild game. Every time the guard brought it in, he placed it just inside the door on the cold floor, and every time I demanded an audience with Nero, only for it to fall on deaf ears.

I choked the cold food down, knowing it was important to keep up my strength. Between meals, I spent my days alternating reading the records book and watching the men of the Coterie through the window. Nero's men were well trained and highly disciplined, the entire compound running on a seamless schedule without any deviation. It was like watching a military base. Behind the main building was a large courtyard, separating it from the other four buildings. The closest building, the second largest of the outbuildings, was the one that had been unmarked on Dirk's map. I watched it the closest, noticing it didn't get much traffic, just the same man dragging in wild game, only to reemerge hours later, alone, his apron covered in blood. The farthest building, the one nearest the wall and in the shadow of the mountains, was the largest. Men came and went from that building all day, the same men always together, staying for the same amount of time. The traffic only slowed after the sky turned dark.

From my window, I also had a clear view of the wall. Four-man teams worked it, assigned to six-hour shifts. They paced a section of it—their eyes always focused outward, never once turning to the interior—completely unconcerned about what went on behind them. Showing complete faith in their brothers. Every so often, their eyes would turn to one another, a silent message passing between them, a language that could be learned only through time and experience together.

On the fourth day, I woke to the sound of my door opening. Assuming it was the guard with my breakfast, I didn't bother to get up. It wasn't until I felt the breeze on my spine that I sat up. I rubbed my eyes blearily, my power still fuzzy with sleep. There was no light coming through the window. It would still be hours yet before my breakfast would be brought to me. The fire in the hearth had dimmed to smoldering embers, but with a wave of my hand, the flames returned, lighting the room and revealing Roman standing at the foot of my bed.

"What are you doing here?" I whispered.

He raised his finger to his lips, signaling me to be quiet. I obeyed, smoothly rising from the cot, my bare feet silent on the cold floor. Roman turned from me, instead facing the door. I squinted, trying to discern his movements. He held something in one hand, bringing it quickly down on the other, digging it into his palm. I smelled the sharp tang of blood and I hissed in pain as the echo of the wound appeared on my own skin. The wound closed up quickly and moments later, Roman spun back around.

I didn't get a single word out. Roman pulled me to him, enveloping me in a hug. I sunk into it, stealing a moment for myself. His hands traveled up to hold either side of my face, pulling my gaze to his. "Are you all right?" he asked. "When you went into that lake, I thought. . ."

"I'm fine," I said cutting him off. "Good as new." I scoffed, still confused about what was happening. "How did you get in here? What happened to the guard?"

Roman gave a roguish smile. "He's taking a nap at the end of the hall."

My eyes bugged out. "What did you do to him?"

He brushed it off. "It took me a little while to figure out their routine, but he'll be fine. We don't have a lot of time though." He bent down, placing a soft kiss on my lips before leaning his forehead against mine. "You scared me," he whispered. I knew I did. I could feel his fear as if it were a cold chain wrapped around my throat. I closed my eyes and Roman's lips touched mine again, this time stronger, filled with need. I responded, allowing myself this final moment. Then I stepped back.

"We can't." I tapped my ear. The compound was filled with people with supernatural hearing. We couldn't be sure someone wasn't listening.

Roman smiled. "That's not a problem." He leaned against the back of the door. Right by his shoulder, written on the door was some sort of symbol.

I moved closer. "What is that?"

"A spell from The Book of Breathings. A simple one, really. This is the Egyptian symbol for silence. When placed on a door, it soundproofs the room. It burns out quickly though. We have a couple hours, tops."

"Did you write it in blood?!" I gaped at him.

"Gross, I know, but I assumed we could use the privacy."

He'd had such a short time with the book and he was already performing spells. I raised my eyebrows at him. "And what exactly do we need privacy for?" There was no way he could be thinking about *that*. Not at a time like this. But on the other hand, he was a guy. There was a chance he was always thinking about it.

He smiled, knowing exactly where my head was. "That wasn't actually what I had planned, but if you're interested, I could get on board with that."

I stuck my tongue out at him, prompting a laugh. "What *were* you thinking then?"

"You still haven't explained what happened back in Awen, why my neck started bleeding. If the echo was that bad, the real thing had to be pretty deep. What kind of trouble did you get yourself into?"

I huffed. "We really need to learn how to block each other's powers."

"Why?" he asked. "To stop the echoes or to keep me from knowing when you're lying to me?"

"Shouldn't we be trying to find a way to get to Nero?" It wasn't that I didn't want to have this discussion, it just seemed we had other, more pressing matters.

Roman crossed his arms stubbornly, "Explain yourself first. Then we'll worry about Nero."

I paced the room, popping my knuckles individually. Roman remained where he was, still as a statue, patiently waiting for me to spit it out. "Technically, I didn't lie to you," I began.

"Technically, you're not telling me everything either."

I sat on the edge of the bed, rubbing my hands on the front of my pants. "Astrid sent me into the Hollow to retrieve the box that held Set's soul."

Roman's eyes squinted minutely, the muscle in his jaw ticking. His annoyance permeated the air. We were opposites in that way. When I was angry, I yelled, took it out on everyone. Roman went silent. "How did you get in? I doubt Astrid provided an escort."

I shook my head. "The other Nomarchs didn't know she sent me. I had to find my own way in. Mallory hooked me up with a guard, someone sympathetic to our issues with the Council. Not all of the prisoners had been secured since," I hesitated. "Well, since you know when. We were attacked in the cavern and Daniela was severely injured. Mallory and Cassie stitched her up. Even then, she barely made it."

Roman's weight shifted from one foot to the other. "So when you entered the Hollow, the connection snapped. That's why I couldn't find you anywhere and once I *could* feel you, you were panicking."

"I was not panicking," I responded, offended. "I had the situation under control."

"This is a dangerous game, Kyndal. Running covert errands for one Nomarch behind the backs of the rest of the Council. What does Astrid want with the box anyway?"

"She didn't say. I assume that we'll find out at some point though."

Roman nodded. "Next time, don't shut me out. Let me help you. No matter how reckless or stupid your plan is." I nodded, my knee bouncing nervously. "What is it?" he asked.

I took a deep breath. "There's more." Roman crossed his arms, waiting. "The reason I went into the Hollow for Astrid. She said Amina is testing us, trying to make us fail. That she wants to dismantle the Council and rule on her own, but first she has to destroy the Guard. She doesn't expect Nero to return to Awen and when he refuses, she's going to use it as an example of our failure. Justification for getting rid of us. Permanently. Astrid said she knew the one thing that could convince Nero to leave the Coterie—a very old, very well protected secret."

Roman shook his head. "More secrets," he grumbled.

I took another breath. "Astrid said that only Nero's son could convince him to join the war."

Roman's eyebrows pinched together. "Did she explain to you how sons of the Coterie are brought into the organization?"

"Yes," I replied simply.

"So, Astrid thinks his son is already here and she wants us to find him."

"Not exactly." I eyed the book, open on the desktop. "She had the records, Roman. I read them myself." I paused. "You are Nero's son."

9

Roman's spell only lasted an hour. The sigil on the door disappeared, the power along with it. I'd spent the time doing my best to explain to him everything Astrid told me, everything I read in the records book, even showing him the page with his name on it, Nero's name directly above it in the family tree. I spoke quickly, taking advantage of our privacy.

"I've read over most of it. It seems legit."

"If I was Nero's son, I would know. He would have come to find me when my powers emerged."

"Astrid thinks your powers manifested by accident. That whoever died on your birthday wasn't your mother, as Nero had planned it. He didn't know you had been branded. After Ezekiel found you, the Council lied to Nero and told him you'd been killed along with Diana. He doesn't even know you exist."

"It doesn't mention my mother," he responded quietly. He

was right. Next to Nero's name was a blank space. No mention of who Roman's mother was, not a name, not even initials.

Roman sat at the desk, poring over the book by firelight while I laid on the bed. I didn't speak, except to answer his occasional question, allowing him his space while he processed everything. He was focused, clinical almost, but I could feel his emotions swirling through the bond, a heavy mixture of confusion and despair. He might not be able to talk about it, but I knew the hurt was there. Sometimes pain took its time, festering like a wound until the brain finds a way to give it a voice.

Even after the spell wore out, Roman stayed, pushing the limit, only leaving right before breakfast was set to be delivered, sneaking out just as quietly as he came in, even with the book in hand.

That day, my lunch was served with a note. A formal invitation to dinner with the Commander that evening, tucked into a simple box tied with a red ribbon. I opened it slowly, unsure of what Nero would be gifting me. Inside the box was a simple silver chain on the end of which was a charm in the shape of ram horns. The Aries house symbol. It was delicate and beautiful and I had no idea where he'd gotten it from when he lived in the middle of the Siberian tundra.

Promptly at sundown, the guard opened my door, ready to escort me to dinner. I adjusted my gear, making sure the silver pendant was clearly visible. We needed Nero to return to Awen with us—I couldn't risk insulting him by refusing one of his gifts.

Dinner was served in the main dining hall. Three large metal chandeliers hung from the ceiling. Shaped like orbs, flames crackled inside them, simultaneously lighting and heating the room. It seemed Nero enjoyed decorating his compound with as much of his element as possible. Underneath them was the dining table, large enough to sit at least twenty-five people. The table was already full of soldiers, talking and laughing raucously over their dinner plates. It looked like we wouldn't be dining alone. Nero sat at the head of the table, lounging lazily in his chair, a goblet dangling from his hand. A dagger hung at his hip, an extra on his opposite side. A familiar sheath was strapped to his ankle. He'd stolen my ring daggers. Surprisingly, Grady was seated just to Nero's left, speaking quietly to him. From what I could tell, Nero was ignoring him. Brynn was noticeably absent. She'd been attached to Grady's hip ever since joining the Guard. It was odd for her to be missing. Why had Grady and I received invitations but Brynn hadn't? The fire snapped in the fireplace behind Nero, grabbing his attention and announcing my arrival.

The room fell silent, all eyes on me. Nero's gaze immediately zoomed in on the silver pendant that hung around my neck. I scanned the room slowly, gathering as much information as I could in a small time. Each soldier was dressed in fighting gear, fully strapped with weapons, just as Nero was. I stepped into the doorway, moving directly for the seat on Nero's right. My boots echoed off the stone floor. I pulled the seat out, but before I could sit, a voice at the opposite end of the table stopped me.

"Women don't sit at the table."

I paused, not surprised to find the voice came from Dirk. I looked to Nero, my eyebrows raised in silent question. Across from me, Grady completely froze, his eyes trained on me, waiting for me to explode. Nero took a long, lazy drink from his goblet before waving his hand in front of him. "She is here on my invitation."

Dirk jumped to his feet, smacking his hands on the table. The plates around him shook. "This is bullshit!" he yelled.

Nero sat up slowly, placing his goblet on the table in front of him. "Are you challenging me?"

"I'm not sitting at the table with some *girl* that hasn't earned her place." I gritted my teeth. Dirk had brought me here, he'd seen me fight. I wondered what his fellow warriors would think if they knew about how I'd backed him down in the training room. How he'd submitted to me.

I only saw the movement a split second before it happened. Just the smallest flash of silver before one of my ring daggers went flying, embedding itself deep in Dirk's shoulder. Dirk grunted, falling back in his high-backed wooden chair, his hand immediately reaching for the wound. "You will sit," Nero commanded. "Or the next one is in your heart."

Dirk ripped the dagger out of his shoulder, blood dripping down his shirt. He wiped the blade on his sleeve, and for a moment I thought he would throw it back at his commander, but instead he chucked it onto the table. He reached up with his opposite arm, grabbing the turkey leg in front of him, taking a slow, deliberate bite, his eyes glued to me. A silent promise of violent retribution.

Nero turned to me and nodded at the chair. I sat and conversation returned to the room, the challenge of power forgotten.

"Where is the other one?" Nero asked me.

"Which one?" I asked. "We seem to be missing two."

"The Water User is eating in her room. I was referring to the Air User."

"Brynn," Grady piped up, interrupting Nero. "Her name is Brynn."

My eyes shot over to Grady, shocked that he had stood up for Brynn that way. Nero was set to be a Nomarch, it wasn't in Grady to talk back to someone in power—it was nice to see him show some backbone. Nomarch or not, Nero—among other things— was a sexist pig and shouldn't be allowed to get away with it.

Nero shooed his comment aside with a brush of his hand.

"Roman is running a tad behind. He sent his apologies," I lied smoothly. Truth was, Roman was a wreck. His emotions were scattered, barreling down the bond unchecked, the reason for the slight tremble in my left hand. Trying to deal with his emotions left me feeling like I'd drank ten energy drinks. I waited for Nero to mention the guards Roman attacked last night, but he never did. "Why wasn't Brynn invited?" I diverted.

Nero clicked his tongue. "You saw the reaction of my men. Women are not allowed to eat at the table amongst the warriors."

"Clearly exceptions can be made," I retorted.

"It is true, I find you intriguing. For someone of your strength and level of power, I am willing to make an exception. The Water User has no such strength. That pendant looks beautiful on you," he added, switching subjects quickly. "Just as I knew it would." His eyes returned to the necklace, lingering longer than was comfortable.

"I must say, I was surprised at the gesture. It's not often a jailor gives presents to their prisoner."

Nero's smile turned cocky. "Think of it as a peace offering. An apology, even, for locking you in your room."

"Does that mean we are free to roam the compound?" I asked, pushing my luck.

Nero took a lazy drink from his goblet, "That remains to be seen. Dependent on what you and your companions have to offer."

Just then, a cool breeze tickled the back of my neck, marking the arrival of Roman. At first I didn't turn, not wanting to give away the fact I knew he was there. I waited for him to enter the room, but he never did. Finally, I risked a glance and found Roman frozen in place, his eyes glued to Nero. I knew what he was seeing. The familiar stature, the same curve to his jaw. The records Astrid provided indicated Nero was born sometime in the late 1600s and yet he looked no more than ten years older than Roman.

I cleared my throat.

Roman's eyes jumped to mine. I nodded subtly toward the table. Roman took the hint, entering the room and sitting next to me.

Nero refilled his glass, taking another large gulp. From the smell of it, it was some sort of wine. "How kind of you to join us," he quipped. I was beginning to wonder if he was drunk.

"I apologize," Roman answered, fully facing Nero. "I was attempting to contact Awen, hoping to tell them we made it safely to the compound and made contact with you." I smiled internally at his lie. He'd steered the conversation in exactly the direction we needed it to go, while simultaneously making Nero think we had contact with the outside world. Which we hadn't.

Nero eyed Roman for a long moment, taking inventory of his features. I wondered if he could feel it, somehow sense the connection between the two. "I am surprised to see the Council chose you as their envoy. It seems they have stooped to children doing their dirty work."

"We are not children," I retorted.

Nero's eyes slid to me. "Oh, I know you aren't." His tone was slick and full of suggestion. It took everything I had not to shiver in disgust. Roman's fist clenched on his leg, the muscle in his jaw twitching. His eyes cut briefly to me, taking note of the necklace. Rage ran through my veins, whether it was mine or Roman's, I couldn't tell.

"The Kindred are at war," Grady said, bringing Nero's attention to him. "The chaos god Set was released and roams the Earth again. He's inhabiting the body of Ezekiel Sands, former Nomarch of House Capricorn. He has centuries of Kindred intel and an army at his disposal."

"I don't understand why that is my problem," Nero interrupted. "The Coterie does not concern itself with Council affairs. If the Council was stupid enough to let Set escape his cage, they deserve their fate."

"They've already infiltrated Awen and attacked us in our heart," Grady argued. "We need your men to help protect our people."

"Again, not my concern."

"Why even bother sending Dirk if you always intended to refuse your calling?" Roman demanded.

"What's in it for us?" Nero asked, bringing me up short. "My men don't work for free, especially not for Council scum."

"Are you asking for money?" I asked, incredulously. "People are dying. Hundreds have already been lost, and you have the audacity to sit there and negotiate a price?"

"Do you think Set will be satisfied when he takes Awen?" Roman added. "He will not rest until he has destroyed every Kindred in the world. You cannot hide from this war or its horrors behind your high walls. His men are already at your gates. You saw them yourself."

"And I saw them perish on the ice."

"Because a warrior you deem unworthy to even sit at your table dropped them in the freezing water and saved your precious compound," I threw at him.

"The hybrids know we are here, which means Set knows we are here. It won't be long until they come back in greater force," Roman said.

Nero eyed him warily. "What House are you from?" he asked abruptly.

Roman huffed a breath. "House Libra."

Nero pointed at Roman, then me, then Grady. "Libra, Aries, Taurus," he pointed upstairs, to indicate Brynn. "Scorpio. Four warriors, four elements. It seems the Council is desperate indeed if they reinstated the Guard."

I wasn't surprised he figured out who we were. "Then you understand the gravity of the situation," Grady added, confirming our identity.

"I've met Guardsmen before, decades ago. Show me your brands," he ordered. I rolled my eyes and pulled the edge of my sleeve back, revealing the scars on my palm. Nero leaned forward, examining it with mild curiosity. "And the book?"

"What book?" I asked.

His eyes cut up to mine. "Do not play dumb with me. You know exactly of what book I speak. I want to see it."

White hot rage ran through my veins. Of course he would demand from us the most powerful artifact we possess. "Not a chance," I said bluntly.

Roman placed a hand on my arm, the fire instantly reduced to an icy cool. "What Kyndal means is that we don't have the book on us. But we would be more than happy to show it to you, once you have returned to Awen and taken your seat as Nomarch. There are no secrets between the Council and its Guard." I could've kissed him right there. So smooth, not a hint of the lie showing on his face.

Nero crossed his arms. "No."

"Of course," Roman hissed under his breath. He'd apparently figured something out that I still didn't see.

"What do you mean, no?" Grady asked, ignoring Roman.

Nero turned to him. "No, I will not return to Awen. My price is the book. If you wish for my cooperation, the strength of my army, you will provide the book. Otherwise, I will remain here, as will you and your companions."

That is why he sent Dirk. So he could lure us here and demand The Book of Breathings. "You can't keep us here forever," I challenged.

"That is *exactly* what I will do unless you can convince me otherwise," Nero threatened.

"You don't understand how powerful this threat is," Grady

added, trying to smooth over the situation. "They are. . ."

"They are abominations!" Nero screamed, slamming his fist on the table. Every person in the room went still, their eyes pinned to Nero. His eyes were a vibrant red and the flames in the chandeliers above pulsated and cracked in tempo to his anger. Roman's hand was poised on the arm of his chair, every muscle in his body pulled taut like a bow ready to release. Even Grady seemed ready to defend himself. "Everyone out," Nero growled. For a split second, no one moved. "Out!" he bellowed. The soldiers filed out immediately, leaving the three of us alone with Nero.

It wasn't until the final soldier had left the dining hall, pulling the door shut behind him, that the flames above us relaxed, although Nero still sat poised on the edge of his chair, his power still called forward. I pulled on my own power, prepared to snuff out the flames if need be. "You made a mistake coming to the Coterie," he began. "You brought that filth to my gates, and I will not sit here and let you spin your web of lies, adding insult to already grievous injury. I am the commander of this compound and you will do as I wish."

"If you keep us here, the Council will retaliate," I said. I didn't actually know if that was true. They might be happy to let us rot in our icy prison.

"I have already defeated the Council once, I will do it again. I am no more afraid of the Council than I am of Set and his army of the damned."

"Of course you are," I added, leaning forward in my chair.

"You're afraid of both of them. This whole thing is just an act, isn't it? A show you put on for your men. You pretend you aren't scared of the enemy, like your compound isn't vulnerable, but you know the truth. You know exactly what it was at your gates. You are next in line to the Aries throne. Set knows that. He won't stop coming for you until you and your men are destroyed. The enemy is strong, they are organized and well trained, and they are *hungry*. You'd be a fool if you weren't scared."

"We will handle this enemy the same way we always have, with fire and death. Wraith, Kindred, hybrid, it makes no difference to us. The Coterie will not yield."

"And what of the men you'd lose? Your stubbornness puts them at unnecessary risk. How many of them have to die because you refuse to bend to the will of the Council?"

"I believe you saw how willing I am to sacrifice my men." Nero's eyes cut to mine sharply. "We do not yield," he repeated. "If we die, we do so with honor."

I leaned forward. "It isn't just death you face. When they defeat you, every one of you will just be another member of their hybrid army. Another enemy *we* have to cut down."

Nero scoffed, snatching his wine goblet off the table and pushing his chair out. He stalked over to the fireplace, leaning against the hearth and staring at the flames.

"It's excruciating," Roman said to him. It'd been several minutes since he spoke, and now his words were slow and deliberate as if he had to consider each one before speaking. As if it hurt to say them. "Like every nerve, every cell is being cauterized an inch at a time. You're trapped inside your own body. Paralyzed. You scream out, but no one can hear you." My heart stopped. He couldn't be talking about this. He *never* talked about this. Not even to me. "It steals your face, your voice, your memories, everything you hold dear. *Everything* that made you what you once were, and it twists you into something so dark and evil that you can't even recognize yourself anymore." A stab of guilt and self-hate pierced through the bond. A tear escaped, and I hastily brushed it away. Roman's own eyes shone with tears, but his voice remained steady. "All you care about is feeding and the stronger the energy, the more you desire it. Every time you kill, every time you *feed*, another piece of who you used to be disappears, until you no longer remember who that person was and you welcome the day the dagger pierces your heart, because at least you won't have to live in that hell anymore." Across the table, Grady's face was ghastly pale, his eyes wide with shock. "If you keep us here, or if you refuse to come to our aid, *that* is the hell that awaits you." Roman stood from his chair. "If you abandon us in our time of need, it is better than you deserve."

10

I barely slept that night. I tossed and turned in bed, but each time I shut my eyes, all I saw were dark veins and glowing eyes. All I heard were Roman's words as he confessed what he'd been. All I felt was his hatred, for himself and for the man that did it to him. I threw the covers off me, tiptoeing my bare feet to my bag that lay under the window. Dinner had ended abruptly, Nero declaring we had twenty-four hours to agree to hand over the book. While Nero wouldn't allow us to leave the Coterie, he did concede to allowing us to roam the compound. It was no doubt a false gesture, meant to trick us into complacency in hopes we would lead him to the book.

I grabbed a pair of boots and slipped my feet into them. I snuck into the hallway, moving quietly down the steps and out the back door. I could feel the tug of the bond. Roman was awake, somewhere on the opposite side of the compound, even though it was the middle of the night and most everyone was asleep.

I hadn't been outside the main building of the compound since we arrived. The air was still, not a breath of wind, but snow fell from the night sky, covering the ground and camouflaging the thick ice that I knew was under my feet. It amazed me that this entire compound sat atop the lake. I raised my hood, protecting my hair from the snow. Everything about this place was cold. The two times I had ventured to take a shower, the water had been freezing, making it difficult to ever truly banish the cold. I crossed the courtyard, my feet crunching in the fresh powder and drawing the attention of one of the guards. He turned sharply, his gaze lingering for a moment, before he slowly turned back around.

Roman was in the building farthest away. It was larger than the other two, but otherwise unremarkable, giving me no hint to what it was, or why he was there. I entered the building and immediately understood. The familiar sounds of flesh hitting leather echoed against the walls. I paused, taking the time to stomp the snow off my boots and lower my hood.

I entered the training room quietly. The room was dark and cold. The floor was cement, missing the typical padding of the sparring rings. Instead, chalk lines were drawn on the hard floor. There were no windows to speak of, just three skylights spaced evenly down the ceiling that filtered in minimal moonlight. Torches were bolted to the wall but remained unlit. There was a biting chill in the air, somehow colder than outside. Roman was on the opposite side of the room, his back to me. A heavy bag hung in front of him, swinging wildly as if trying to escape his attack. His hair was slicked with sweat, his leather vest thrown into the corner, leaving him in tactical pants and a grey tank. From the looks of it, he'd been working out for a while. He threw a four-punch combination, ending with a spinning back fist. "You're not breathing when you punch," I said, approaching the heavy bag. "You're losing all your power."

He didn't turn to acknowledge me. Another punch reverberated through the bag. "I was the one who taught you that," he replied through gritted teeth. I smiled, pleased he caught my reference, but my smile quickly faded as I watched him. Roman didn't stop pounding the bag. In fact, his punches gained speed, each one landing with more force. There was no technique, no finesse in his moves. He was agitated and punishing the bag for whatever weakness he thought he showed during dinner.

"We can try again tomorrow," I continued, hoping to distract him. Roman still didn't stop his onslaught on the heavy bag. His pace increased again, his fists moving so quickly they were hard to follow. "We aren't giving up. Even if we have to drag Nero out of here by his hair," I added when he didn't say anything. Just then, Roman jumped, landing a perfect spin kick in the middle of the bag, snapping the chains that hung it from the rafters. The bag landed on the cement floor with a thud. I froze. Roman stared down at the defeated bag, his chest heaving with exertion.

I turned and moved to the wash bowl in the corner of the room. I grabbed the towel on the nearby rack and dipped it into the cold water, wringing out the excess. I returned to

Roman, gently grabbing one of his hands. His knuckles were cracked and bleeding, as much from the leather bag as the cold in the air. I dabbed the towel to his hand and he flinched, sucking air through his teeth. "Sorry," I said quietly.

"It's cold," he explained. I nodded, pushing a small amount of power to my hand to warm the towel before I continued. He'd done this for me once before. When I was overwhelmed and struggling, he'd been there for me, understanding that some things were too painful to put into words. I finished his left hand, then moved on to the right, which was in worse shape. He put so much more power behind his right arm, it always took more punishment. "I look like him," he whispered. His voice was small, like a hurt little boy. My heart splintered at the pain in it.

"You don't act like him. That's what matters."

"He disgusts me. He doesn't care about anyone but himself. And the way he treats you—that necklace he gave you—I wanted to rip his throat out right then."

My eyes flicked up to his. He meant what he said, I could see it in his eyes, feel it through the bond. I was suddenly happy I left the pendant back in my room. "You know that gift didn't mean anything to me. I only wore it to gain his favor in hopes he would listen to me. Which obviously didn't work," I grumbled. "Astrid was right. Nero is stubborn."

Roman walked over and grabbed a towel, wiping his face. "That's putting it mildly." He moved the towel around the back of his neck, wiping the sweat there. I watched his movements as I tried to figure out exactly how to say what I was feeling. "Out with it, Kyndal."

I sighed. We *really* needed to learn how to block each other. "You've never talked about it before."

Roman froze, his shoulders tense. He turned partially to face me. "About what?" he asked, stalling. He knew exactly what I was referring to.

"You've never said anything about what it was like when you were possessed. If you even remembered anything."

"I shouldn't have said anything," he said quickly. "It was stupid of me to even bring it up. I tipped my hand and gave Nero unearned intel." His words were biting, not at me but at himself. So, this was why he was mad. This was the mistake he thought he'd made, the weakness he'd shown to Nero.

I walked toward him, placing my hands gently on his shoulders and turning him to face me. His eyes were a soft blue, the color muted with sadness. "Listen to me. You shouldn't be ashamed by what happened to you. It wasn't you that did those things."

Roman barked a laugh, stepping back. His eyes turned feverish. "I wish that were true, Kyndal. I really do. But it was me. Every awful thing that happened was all me." He started to pace the room, agitated.

"It wasn't your fault," I tried reasoning with him.

"Do you think that makes it any better?" he shouted. "You want to know what I remember? I remember everything. The attack on the club where the bouncer was killed. The four hundred and seventeen Kindred I helped turn," his arm flung out, pointing at me, "with the blood I stole from you, after I *bit* you."

"Those were all things Ezekiel made you do," I argued. "I've forgiven you for all of it."

"What about Evan?" Roman challenged. "I rammed my dagger into his chest and watched the light leave his eyes, before he turned to dust under my fingers." His words hit me like a blow. There had been none more innocent than Evan. He didn't deserve the way he died. "Have you forgiven me for that too?"

I fought back tears as I stepped up to Roman. "You think you're the only one that's made mistakes? I've been screwing up since day one." Roman scoffed, turning and punching the speed bag hanging behind him. "I'm the reason Evan was a wraith in the first place! I got Allie kidnapped. I practically handed the book to Ezekiel. Without it, he never would have been able to do that damn spell in the first place. So, if you need someone to blame, start with me."

Roman ran his hands through his sweat-slicked hair. "You couldn't have known the game Ezekiel was playing. There was no way. . ."

I stepped forward, pushing into his space again. "And neither could you."

"I was his second in command," he argued. "I should have seen it."

"There was a Council full of Nomarchs that didn't see his plan for decades. My mother was the only one that did and he killed her for it. We have to stop beating ourselves up over what we should've done, or should've seen, and focus on what we can do now."

"And what about those we hurt along the way?" I thought of Evan, Allie, and Lydia. Drake and the other Nomarchs, the countless number of soldiers killed during the attack on Awen.

"Apologize. Beg for forgiveness. Whatever it takes, and just hope. Hope that one day they can forgive us for all we've done." They were the same words he'd told me once when I was drowning in guilt and self-doubt.

Roman reached out slowly, his fingers playing at the edge of my vest. "Thank you."

I looked up at him in surprise. "For what?"

He gave a shy, sideways smirk, one that had my toes curling in my boots. "For coming in here and yelling at me. Knocking me out of my pity party."

I reached up and placed my hands on his bare shoulders, the corded muscles beneath rippling at the touch. I smiled at him sweetly. "Anytime you need someone to yell at you, I'm your girl."

He chuckled, pulling on my vest so we were chest to chest.

His hands snaked around my sides, resting on my lower back. I wrapped my arms around his neck and angled my head back to look him in the eye. I sometimes forgot exactly how tall he was. "I like the sound of that." He leaned down, kissing me softly. "My girl." I pushed up to my tiptoes, kissing him again. He tasted bitter, the sharp tang of residual anger still overwhelming the bond. I took the kiss deeper, sending my feelings down the bond, soothing his anger until it settled, taking that icy rage that was within him and replacing it with warming thoughts of love. I may not be able to declare to the world how I felt for him, but in moments like this, private moments we stole for ourselves, I would do everything I could to prove to him that I knew exactly who he was and knew exactly how much I loved him.

"We could be caught," Roman whispered against my lips.

"You started it," I teased.

"Someone could walk in and see us," he replied softly.

I kissed him again. "I don't care," I answered, pulling him closer, but Roman's hands fisted in the back of my shirt, and I knew he was reigning himself in, regaining that ever constant control he kept on himself, so I wasn't surprised when a moment later he pulled back. I wasn't offended when he took a full step back, out of my reach. Although, that didn't keep me from giving him a pouty look.

"Don't look at me like that," he teased. "You and I both know where that was heading, and as much as I want to. . ." He looked me up and down, a soft growl escaping. "And I really want to, but this is not the time or place."

I cleared my throat, pulling myself back in. "Right. We have other things to discuss. Like how the hell we get out of here."

We debated for the next hour over what to do, trying to plan for every possibility, every variable. Ideally, we would leave freely with Nero and his men in tow. Amina had made it pretty clear that we weren't to return without him, but short of giving Nero The Book of Breathings, we didn't know how to convince him to join us, and we both agreed there was no way we could give him an artifact that powerful, not when we needed it to stop Set. Roman never brought up Astrid's idea of revealing himself as Nero's son and using the familial connection to sway him to join our cause, and I never pushed. It was not my secret to wield. If Roman chose to keep it to himself, that was exactly what we were going to do.

If Nero couldn't be swayed, we were forced to figure out how exactly we could escape the compound. Better to face the wrath of the Council than to be stuck in Siberia for eternity. Roman had been watching the guards over the last several days, learning their patterns, watching which guards worked during which rotations. He figured out the best time to escape, as well as the most vulnerable part of the wall. His plan was risky, but it was the best we had. Now we had less than twelve hours to organize and execute it.

When I left the training room, the sun had just crested the horizon and the fresh powder atop the western side of the wall sparkled in the sunlight. Torches remained lit, the day not quite bright enough yet to put them out. The sky was clear, although to the north, storm clouds were slowly rolling in over the mountain range. They would be on the compound within the hour. Another obstacle to overcome if we were going to leave tonight. Nero and his men were much more experienced with the harsh environment than we were. We couldn't afford to battle both them and the weather.

I didn't make it far across the courtyard before I was intercepted by Grady. He was fully bundled up in his gear, his fur-lined hood pulled tight over his head, his red hair just peeking through the front. I pulled my own vest tighter, crossing my arms as he approached. "What do you want, Grady?"

"I need to talk to you," he said simply. I leaned back on a heel, expectantly. "Can't we go somewhere warmer?" he asked.

"No."

Grady looked over my head, toward the training building. "Were you just with Roman?" he asked suddenly.

Unprepared for the question, I stumbled over my words. "Why—why would you ask that?"

His eyebrows knit together briefly. "Your power signature is different, changed somehow."

141

I cursed inwardly. I had forgotten about Grady's ability to read magic signatures in the earth. It's what made him a great tracker, but it also allowed him to see who came and went. Who had been together. Thankfully he couldn't read them on people, just the land. Through the bond, I could feel Roman still inside the training building. Silently, I prayed he stayed put. "We were training," I lied. "After being cooped up in our room for days, we needed the exercise. Is this what you came to talk to me about?" I pushed.

He shook his head. "No, it wasn't." He shoved his hands in his pockets, his eyes cast down as he shifted from one foot to the other. *Was he nervous?* "I just wanted to thank you and—and to apologize."

"Apologize for what, exactly?" I interrupted. "You have a lot to choose from."

"I know," he agreed quickly. "You saved my life the other day. Those hybrids had me beat, and you saved me even though you had no reason or cause to keep me alive. And it's just, even though I was following orders. . ."

I scoffed, interrupting him again. "Same old Grady." I dropped my voice lower, doing a poor impression of him. *"Sorry, even though it wasn't really my fault, I was just doing what I was told."*

I pushed past him, moving toward the compound again, but he grabbed my arm, wheeling me around. I ripped my arm from his grasp. "Listen to me," he implored.

"Why should I?" I yelled at him. A burst of concern shot

through the bond. Roman knew I was angry, was worried I needed help. "You just *stood* there. She left me for dead in that cell and you did *nothing*. You're not a soldier. Soldiers fight for the person standing next to them, not for some bureaucrat that wouldn't lift a finger to save them. You're no warrior. You're a drone."

"She had my hands tied, Kyndal. There wasn't anything I could do! And should I remind you that this is the same woman that you pledged your loyalty and eternal allegiance to? Or was that just bullshit?"

I glared at him. We were treading on dangerous territory. I could feel Roman move closer, and out of the corner of my eye, I saw him step just outside the training doors. His leather vest was back on, his blue eyes clear and sharp. No sign of the troubles that plagued him earlier. He hung back, leaning against the wall and watching as I handled the situation, but he made sure he was close enough to intervene if need be.

"I joined the Guard to take down Set. Because I am the *only* one strong enough to see that it is done. Something I wouldn't have had to do if you had just killed Ezekiel when we were inside the Hollow—instead of being blinded by jealousy and revenge and killing the wrong person."

"You should be thanking me for what I did," he shot back. He didn't deny his reasons for doing it. "If I hadn't done it, Roman would still be a hybrid."

I laughed incredulously. "Don't for one *second* pretend you were doing me a favor. You didn't know I could save him.

You got lucky, because if he had died. . ." I let the sentence drop, the threat clear.

Grady stepped toward me. Just past him, Roman pushed off the wall, moving a step closer. "And how exactly did you do that, Kyndal? How did you bring him back? What powers are you hiding?" My power pushed down my arm into my palm and I balled my hand into a fist, containing the flames.

For now.

Grady opened his mouth to speak, but the clouds over the mountains rumbled and the lake beneath our feet shook. The argument forgotten, both of us froze completely still. Before moving to the wall, my eyes cut to Roman who was also on alert—his attention on the guards that were frozen, their daggers drawn. "What the hell was that?" I asked. The words seemed to die in the air, as if whatever chill that moved in had struck them down.

"Do you feel it?" Grady asked quietly. I shook my head. A bitter north wind blew over the wall, pushing the clouds over the compound. "Something is wrong. The earth is trembling."

Just then, a shout rang out from the wall, cut short by the guttural sounds of violence and the harsh thud of a body hitting the ground. I turned just in time to see a guard hit the ground, a spear buried in his chest.

"Hybrids!" Another guard yelled from atop the wall, his voice nearly drowned out by the clap of thunder overhead.

"We're under attack!" Spears sped over the compound wall, dozens of them landing blindly in the lake surface, either bouncing off the compound walls or embedding themselves within the rock. Grady and I both dropped low, sprinting for the nearby training building. We wedged ourselves in under the awning, Roman on my right, Grady on my left. Lightning struck just inside the compound walls, snow spraying in its wake. I felt the bolt in my bones, the sight of it jarring something loose in my mind. Something I couldn't quite place. The shouts of a guard rang out, another body falling from the top of the wall.

"We need to get to an armory," Roman said.

"I need to get to Brynn," Grady countered.

A loud boom reverberated through the compound, the rock wall shaking. The hybrids were trying to knock the wall down. Another bolt of lightning struck, this time directly atop the fractured wall. Rocks tumbled from the top, landing loudly on the frozen lake.

"This ice isn't going to hold much longer," I pointed out. "Not taking that kind of abuse."

"What kind of snow storm has lightning anyway?" Grady said sarcastically.

I shook my head, trying to loosen whatever nagging thought was hidden. Two more lightning strikes hit, one right after the other atop the wall. Each echoed through me. The last time I'd seen lightning strike like that, it'd been—

"It's not a storm," I whispered. Grady and Roman both turned to me.

"What do you mean?" Roman asked.

"The lightning, it's not a storm. I've seen it before, in one of my dreams. It's not a storm," I repeated. Two more bolts hit, cleaving the wall in two. The wall that had stood for hundreds of years. The wall that even the strength of the Nomarch Council could not knock down. Through the fissure stepped a tall figure, his eyes blood red. "It's Set."

11

Set looked different.

It hadn't even been a month since he took over Ezekiel's body, but I could already see the change in him. He wore the same black tactical gear I'd seen him in before, but the material stretched across his chest and over his broad shoulders. His muscles were larger than before, his veins protruding against his skin, weaving a web over his arms, neck, and face, just like the wraiths. Except where a wraith's veins were black, his veins ran red. His hair was still cut short, the buzz cut showing off the sharp angle of his cheekbones, the squareness of his jaw—both harder now than before.

None of that was what drew my eye. Out of those veins seeped a darkness, a black wispy smoke that seemed to billow around him, a living shadow that clung to his skin.

The dread from my dreams immediately returned, my body freezing in fear. Memories flooded my mind, and all I could see was the cavern in the base of Maat's Hollow, the sacrificial ritual that claimed the lives of four Nomarchs and countless Kindred soldiers that fought to try and stop it. All I could feel was the phantom dagger going through my chest, dropping me to the cold floor of my dream world, leaving me to die alone. My breaths came out in short bursts and I swallowed hard, trying to stave off the panic I could feel bubbling in my chest.

Set stood on the edge of the compound with a sort of preternatural stillness that I imagined could only come from a god. The shadows swirled around him, weaving over his arms, caressing the side of his neck. A Coterie soldier barreled out of the back door, headed straight for Set, his dagger raised. Set cocked his head, staring at the soldier with a sort of odd silence. Thunder cracked above, and a bolt of lightning shot from the sky, straight into the chest of the soldier. He flew backward, landing with a sickening thud on the frozen lake, the hole in his chest smoking.

"Holy. . ." I whispered.

"Shit," Roman finished for me.

"I have to get to Brynn," Grady repeated. "She has the book."

"How the hell are we supposed to get past that?" I demanded, my voice laced with panic. Set wasn't directly in-between us and the main building of the compound, but there was no way to cross the courtyard without him seeing us. Even as we stood here, hybrids were stepping over the wall debris to join him. There were at least a dozen of them. I had a brief moment of déjà vu, my brain going to another time, another wall that had been blown to bits, allowing the hybrids to catch us by surprise.

More of Nero's men piled through the back door, drawn to the courtyard by the noise. Attracted to the sounds of battle. They were armed with a variety of weapons—daggers, staffs, axes, even the occasional bow and arrow. Nero led the charge, armed with a brutal short sword made of a dark metal. The hybrids broke rank, intercepting the soldiers before they could reach Set, doing what was necessary to protect their master. The whole courtyard erupted in battle, a chaotic din of clashing weapons and whirling elements. As the others had told me, the Coterie warriors were formidable, as brave as they were strong. Their Air and Earth users took point, their elements the most easily accessible. The torches bolted to the wall now sat cold, extinguished by the north wind that had pushed in the storm. Even with all their strength, the three of us watched as bodies fell on the frozen lake, two Coterie soldiers for every one hybrid. If it kept up this way, the battle wasn't going to last long. "What do we do?" I asked. I'd been in battle before, but nothing like this. This was a slaughter.

"I need a distraction," Grady said, his voice even. *How could he not be freaking out right now?* "I can get to that bench without being seen. Once I do, you draw Set's attention so I can get inside."

I nodded. At least, I think I did, I wasn't sure. My limbs were locking up, my power retreating into that well deep in my stomach. Grady didn't wait. He moved swiftly, keeping his head down as he ran for the bench that was just off the training compound.

Roman turned to me. "You ready?" he asked. I turned to look at him, my hand trembling. He must have read the panic in my eyes, because next thing I knew his hand was cupping my cheek. "Kyndal, look at me." I met his gaze, focusing on the deep blue of his eyes, watching with fascination as they turned gold in front of me. The noise of the battle raging behind me echoed through my skull. "Focus on me, Kyndal." His emotions flooded down the bond—determination, focus, bloodlust. "We need to get to that building," he pointed to the opposite end of the courtyard, at one of the two buildings I hadn't seen yet. "It's their armory. We need weapons. I need you to have my back. Are you with me?"

I took a deep breath, focusing on the gold of his eyes, the feel of his power as it surrounded me, stirring my own power to life and pushing the panic away. I pulled on the tether that always connected me to that internal flame, calling it forward. My eyes turned a sharp red, the shaking in my hands stopped and both now held fireballs. Roman noted the change. "Good. Let's go."

We sprinted for the armory, a building just a touch smaller than the training area. Why they didn't keep weapons in their training facility was beyond me. An oversight I was currently cursing. Our feet pounded into the snow loudly, Roman just ahead of me, the sound drawing the attention of Set. Just like we wanted. The shadows moved first, drawn by our movement, as if they could sense us. Set turned, his movements stiff, as if he didn't quite know how to control the body. As if he didn't quite fit.

He recognized us immediately. He took a step closer, out of the melee. The thunderclap overhead was our only warning. A bolt of lightning struck, zinging past us, scorching the side of the armory. A second followed closely behind. Roman and I pushed harder, our arms pumping as we ran for the armory door. A third lightning bolt whirled past, this one so close I could feel the static as it zipped past my arm. I turned, wildly throwing one of my fireballs at him. Set was closer than he was before, and the fireball went wide, but it gave us the time we needed. Just over his shoulder, I saw Grady pushing through the battle and into the compound. Roman reached the door of the armory, ripping it open. "Let's go!" he yelled. I threw another fireball. Set was slowly walking toward us, an even, determined pursuit, the shadows searching out in front of him. He would be on us in less than twenty steps. I ducked into the armory, slamming the door shut behind us. I didn't fool myself into thinking it would stop him from getting in. It was just an instinct. Seconds later, the floor beneath my feet began to shake, the building faltering with it. I braced myself against the door, squeezing my eyes shut. Even in the heat of battle, I did not forget that we were on top of a frozen lake, and as I learned the hard way, it could crack at any moment, dropping us into the freezing depths below. I had a feeling that if I went in again, I wouldn't make it out this time. No one was that lucky. Around me, the weapons rattled against the walls, clanging loudly as they shook loose, falling to the frozen floor.

Finally the shaking ended, but I still paused a moment

before opening my eyes. When I did, I found so much more than the weapons I'd heard, although there were plenty of those. There were caches of weapons lining three of the walls, a plethora of daggers, swords, spears, axes, even the occasional gun. It was a huge inventory, even with a fraction of them littered along the floor. The back wall was a large garage door, and on the main floor were snowmobiles.

Dozens of them.

It made sense, I supposed. I hadn't really thought about how the men of the Coterie traveled in such harsh conditions. It wasn't as if they hiked or ran to wherever they were going. Of course they used some form of transportation. I weaved through the snowmobiles, desperately grabbing at the daggers on the wall, tucking one into the loop on my pants, gripping the other one tight. Roman had done the same, also adding a sword to the mix so he held a weapon in each hand. We ran back for the front door, hoping we had enough time to get out of the building before Set was on us, but there was no such luck. Just as we reached it, the door was blown open, launching us backward. I felt Roman's power fly out of him before being enveloped in it—as a blanket of air cushioned our fall, saving me from cracking my head on the nose of a snowmobile. I scrambled to my feet, reaffirming my grip on my dagger just as Set's fist cracked off of my jaw. My head snapped to the side, my body flying into the nearby stone wall. I hit the ground, my knees cracking off the stone. A pulse of air blew through the building, punching Set in the chest. He took the hit, not even faltering a step. A deep, twisted laugh rumbled in his chest. "Stupid, Kindred. You are foolish to resist. Soon you will all bow before me."

"Like hell we will." I lunged forward, bringing my dagger down on Set's foot. *Through* his foot. He roared with pain, his head thrown back as if he could see through the ceiling to the storm clouds above. The clouds rumbled in response, thunder booming overhead. Set's other foot came up, kicking me hard in the face, snapping me back into the door. Through it and out into cold. From where I lay prone on the ground I could see Roman lunge for Set, spearing him in the stomach. Set absorbed his weight, his feet sliding backward along the floor. For a moment, I lost Roman in Set's shadows, but they parted just enough for me to see Set bring his arm down hard across Roman's back, breaking his hold before grabbing him around the waist and launching him through the wall and out into the courtyard. He flew past me, landing awkwardly in a heap. Pain blossomed in my shoulder, pain I knew wasn't mine. Set followed him out and I tried to see past him—to see what exactly had happened to Roman—but I wasn't given the opportunity. Set had pulled the dagger out of his foot, dark blood dripping from the tip of the blade. My right arm now almost useless thanks to the echo from Roman's wound. I inched my left hand down reaching for the extra dagger there—bringing it up quickly—intent on stabbing Set again. He hit the dagger out of my hand with little effort, kneeling so we were eye to eye before taking his bloodied dagger and pushing it against my injured shoulder. The tip of the blade punctured my skin and I screamed as he dug it in further, twisting the blade. Ten feet away, Roman's scream joined mine. "It is futile to resist," Set sneered in my face.

He placed his hand over my heart, his mouth close to mine. The shadows snaked over his arm, slithering down to where his hand now rested on my chest. So close to me now, I could see the shadows popped with small sparks of electricity, like living lightning. I knew what he was going to do. I squirmed, trying to escape, but he simply dug the blade in deeper, pinning me to the ground. My panic from earlier returned and my eyes frantically searched for help. Roman was trying to push himself up off the ground, pulling himself toward me as he cradled his right arm to his chest. Even in the state I was in, I could tell his shoulder hung at an odd angle. Most likely his collar bone was broken. The battle still raged behind him, and I caught sight of Nero, blood and gore covering his face. He cut through the hybrids with the most magnificent sword I'd ever seen. The pommel was a deep bloodred, the blade as dark as night. It looked like the kind of sword that had a name. It sliced through the hybrids, a deadly dance that was oddly beautiful to watch. Proof of his deadly reputation.

I could sense Set's power move before I felt it. Like a wild thunderstorm, his shadows engulfed me, dragging me into darkness. They grabbed ahold of my essence and pulled it out of me in every direction. I opened my mouth to scream, but the sound died on my lips. My back bucked off the ground, my nails digging into the ice below me as my power left my body. Not far from me, Roman was screaming again.

I was dying.

Set continued feeding, his power completely overwhelming mine as he pulled every last ounce of my strength from me. My legs squirmed, a final instinct to get away still left inside me. The shadows receded and I turned to Roman. His mouth was moving but I couldn't hear the words. Blood streamed down his face. I strained to say something. To say goodbye, to tell him to run—I didn't know. I just knew that if it was going to end here, I wanted my last effort to be to speak to him. To save *him*.

My vision blurred, my eyelids suddenly heavy. I blinked slowly once, but when I opened them again, I knew I was hallucinating. The air was shimmering, a blanket of multi-colored light coating the sky, settling down to the ground. Screams of pain erupted. First from closer to the compound, and then spreading closer to me, finally ending with Set grabbing his head and falling to the side, screaming in pain. The shadows retreated completely, pulling themselves back to their master. Set continued his roar, clutching at his temples, even though no one was touching him. Moments later, arms were underneath me, lifting me off the ground. The body holding me was unfamiliar, and when I moved my gaze back, my head lolling almost uncontrollably, I caught a glimpse of russet colored hair before my last bit of strength left me and the whole world went black.

The next several hours were a blur. I faded in and out of consciousness, and each time the sunlight broke through my heavy lids, I was only cognizant enough to pick up pieces of what was happening. The same strong arms carrying me. Flying over the landscape. The snow spraying my face. Deep male voices arguing with each other. Some I recognized, some I didn't.

When I finally came to, I was laying on the floor of the plane, a fur coat laid over me, a makeshift pillow shoved under my head. I pushed myself up, grunting quietly in protest as my right arm buckled underneath me. I pushed the coat down with my good arm to find myself shirtless and dressed only in my sports bra from the waist up. My shoulder was wrapped tightly in bandages, the center of them stained red from where Set stabbed me. I searched the plane frantically, desperate to get my bearings.

Roman was laid out not far from me, unconscious. There were deep bruises along his jaw and left cheekbone. He was shirtless, his right shoulder bandaged like mine although his arm was angled across his chest, held there by a sling. It rose and fell steadily as he slept. Beyond him, toward the front of the plane were Nero and his men. At least what was left of them. They sat in the few chairs available, the rest of them huddled behind. Some of them faced forward, but a handful were turned backward, facing the wall across from me, their weapons sitting idly in their laps. I followed their intense stares, surprised to find it was Brynn they were glaring at. Seated next to Grady, she looked utterly relaxed. Her eyes were closed, her legs were sprawled out in front of her, her arms resting comfortably. It wasn't until she rapped her fingers on the object below her that I even knew she was awake and I realized what had them so worried. Her right hand was laying on The Book of Breathings. Grady was next to her, poised on the balls of his feet, twirling his dagger on the tip of its blade. His muscles were taut, his mouth pursed with worry. Even though his eyes were cast down, I could see the sadness that swirled in them.

"What's going on?" I asked him. My voice came out hoarse, burning its way up my throat. It felt like I'd been screaming for hours. Grady's eyes snapped up and I tried to ignore the relief that showed there when he saw I was awake.

That I was alive.

"We're headed back to Awen," he responded.

"How'd we get here?" I asked. "What happened with Set? How'd we get out?" I had so many questions. So many blank spots in my memory.

"You don't remember?" he asked.

I shook my head. "I remember fighting Set. He was. . ." I cut off that train of thought. The empty well of power inside of me told me all I needed to know. "You went inside to get Brynn."

Grady nodded. "Brynn's been studying the book. Translating the spells so we could use them. She got us out."

"I thought that was a dream," I answered, looking to Brynn now. "I saw this bright light covering the sky, filled with

different colors. I thought I imagined it. But it was you."
She opened her eyes slowly. Her mouth lifted in a satisfied
smirk. "What did you do to them?"

"I made them believe their blood was boiling. They feel the
pain as if it were really happening, but no actual physical
damage was done."

My eyes widened, a new appreciation and a new respect for
the woman in front of me. Now I understood why the
Coterie soldiers were staring at her like she was the most
dangerous one on the plane. She glared back at them now,
speaking to the one closest to her. "Try to touch this book,
and I'll do worse to you." The soldier was smart enough to
look worried. Brynn closed her eyes again, as if she were
too tired to keep them open. I wondered how much that
spell cost her. How much power she'd had to use.

Grady pointed to my shoulder. "I did the best I could with
the arm. The wound was deep. You'll need to see a healer
before you can do the rest yourself."

"You bandaged me up?" I asked, not bothering to mention I
couldn't heal myself if I tried. That the power inside me
was completely depleted. "Did you take my shirt off too?"

Grady gave me his signature wolfish grin. "Don't worry. It
was strictly professional." I rolled my eyes, but he tossed a
piece of black cloth at me, a tank top. I took it gratefully,
lifting it gingerly over my head, careful of my wounded
arm.

I looked over to Roman. "Has he woken up?"

Grady shook his head. "Not yet. His collarbone is broken. I've stabilized it for now, but a doctor will need to set it properly. Not to mention the other wound. Did Set stab him too?"

I shook him off, shrugging. "I don't know for sure. I didn't see everything." It was a bold-faced lie, but Grady didn't know anything about echoes and he didn't need to. "How many did we lose?" I asked, diverting his attention.

"Seventeen." Another voice rang from the front of the plane. Nero stood there, his dark hair caked to the edges of his face with blood. Dried blood was also plastered to his fighting gear, crusted into his fingernails. The red pommel of his sword peeked over his shoulder where it was housed in a dark scabbard.

My eyes bugged out. "Seventeen?" I repeated. What a waste of life. Seventeen lives, seventeen fighting men that could have been saved if he'd just swallowed his pride and left the compound when we told him to. "Do you believe us now?" I asked him, unable to stop myself from digging at him.

"I am not to blame for this. *You* brought that filth to our gates. I left my men dead on the frozen ground. They didn't get a warrior's funeral, we left them to rot. So I will not listen to you patronize me. I saw what Set did. He came straight for you. My men died because *you* were there."

"Enough!" Grady yelled, jumping to his feet. "Enough arguing. You were warned of the danger you faced, and you chose not to listen. You chose to remain in your compound. Set knew you were the next Nomarch for House Aries, and he was coming for you no matter what. You cannot return to Ozero Lobaz. Your fortifications have been destroyed, and your men will now scatter all over the world. You have nowhere to go. Unless, when we return to Awen, you take your seat on the Council and together we will do what needs to be done."

As he was speaking, I felt us enter the vortex surrounding Awen, the varying elements entering my body, adding some much-needed strength to my depleted power. Roman, unconscious as he was, stirred in reaction. Nero gave no outward acknowledgement of it, even though I knew he must be feeling it too. "And what needs to be done next?" he sneered at Grady.

"We retaliate."

12

I didn't go to the infirmary with Roman like I wanted to. When the plane touched down, we were met with an envoy from the Council. They carried Roman, still unconscious, on a thin stretcher directly to the healers, along with several of Nero's men who were still nursing their own wounds. Those of his men who weren't injured were taken in the opposite direction, no doubt to be given some form of lodging. Only Grady, Brynn, Nero, and I remained. We were escorted to Council Chambers, unsurprisingly allowed zero time to clean up before we were expected to give our report. I limped along the worn roads, my muscles screaming in protest at every movement. Even with the boost from the vortex, my power was almost completely drained and I had very little strength remaining. My jaw ached and my shoulder throbbed, both wounds that would have to be healed the old fashioned way—with rest and modern medicine. I needed to shower, eat, and I needed to sleep.

For like, three days straight.

The city streets were busy, bustling with more Kindred than I had ever seen in one place. In just the few days we'd been gone, most of the rubble had been cleared from the streets and the arena wall was almost halfway finished. The shops in the heart of the city were reopened, vendors now selling their various weapons, clothing, and food. While the city was repairing, I knew it would take longer for our people to heal. Houses had been destroyed, entire streets demolished in the raid. The scars of the attack would remain long after the streets were cleared.

We reached Council Chambers and I had to practically crawl up the steps. Nero stomped right up them as if he owned the place, Brynn following behind, her head held high, The Book of Breathings tucked under her arm. Grady was a few steps behind, nonchalantly strolling along, trying to pretend like he wasn't keeping an eye on me. He glanced over at me, his hand twitching as if he would reach out to help, but with one glare from me, he wisely pulled his hand back.

We entered the empty chamber, my small group moving to the center of the circle created by the thrones, just as I had done many times before. I posted myself against the wall, just behind the Leo throne. It was near a torch and I hoped the proximity to my element would help with the pain. The side door opened and just as the Nomarchs filed into the room, a bolt of pain shot down the bond, spearing me in my shoulder. I bit down hard on my lip, my hand curling into a fist as I swallowed a scream. Grady eyed me again suspiciously. I waved him off and a moment later, the pain receded. He returned his attention to the Nomarchs and I immediately collapsed against the wall, my breathing heavy.

The Nomarchs took their seats, some lounging lazily, comfortable in their position of power, while the new Nomarchs sat stiffly, lacking the swagger of the others. Their inexperience was obvious, even to the casual observer. Maks sat in front of me, giving me a quick nod of recognition before turning to take his throne. To his left sat Astrid, dressed in her usual pale attire, her silver hair cascading over her shoulders and down her back. She gave me no acknowledgement, not even taking a second glance at my very obvious injuries. It wasn't her I was watching though, it was the man next to her, Cyrus, from House Gemini. I watched him as he entered, his gaze locked on the bloodied Nero, the man that had destroyed the institution he built and turned it into something dark and sinister.

Nero nodded his head once at Cyrus then looked away, the dismissal more condescending than if he had said anything at all. Cyrus took his seat, his fingers twisting over the edge of his throne as if he would dig them through the stone.

Beyond him was Zayna from House Taurus. I knew very little about her, just that she was mostly a silent member of the Council, always siding with the Nomarch in charge, never holding her own opinion. Looking at her, she wasn't built for battle how some of the others were. She was tall and lanky, her dark skin constantly adorned with diamonds, not a single scar to be seen. She wore the diamonds on her hands, ears, and hanging around her neck. Currently, she was wearing a gaudy necklace, five large diamonds hanging from it. It looked heavy. Like it would give her a neck cramp.

The empty Aries seat was next to her. Nero eyed it but made no move to claim it. I wondered what he would do. Would he still argue and refuse to claim his throne? Or now back in Awen, would he succumb to the pressure of the Council?

After Aries came Pisces, the first of the new Nomarchs. Where the old Nomarch had been unremarkable—pale with mousy brown hair and a quiet disposition—the new Nomarch was the opposite. A small man, he had dark skin and bright blue eyes, a startling combination. He was dressed in odd robes, and his eyes were sharp, as if he could see straight through any facade, directly to the truth. I made a mental note to avoid him. Seated next was Elias from House Aquarius. One of the oldest on the Council, he was also one of the kindest. Where Cyrus always jumped to war first, Elias was oftentimes the voice of reason, praising diplomacy over violence. I liked him.

Next was the new Capricorn Nomarch, the second person to take that throne since Ezekiel's betrayal. A blonde female, her hair was buzzed short on the side and longer on top, sweeping over to her right side. The left side of her head was covered in a tattoo that wandered down her neck, disappearing under her shirt. Despite her inexperience on the Council, she was the only new Nomarch that looked confident on her throne. Sagittarius and Scorpio next, my eyes skipped over Haru and Amina and onto the Libra

Nomarch. I hadn't been particularly fond of the old Nomarch, he had been long-winded and obsessed with ceremony. I hoped the new one was nothing like him. He caught my eye as I watched him, giving me a lazy smile and winking. If he'd been anyone else, I would have glared at him, maybe even flipped him off, but I couldn't muster the energy. Next to him, the Virgo Nomarch, Madigan, cleared her throat, finally pulling his attention away. He lifted his eyebrow at her, smiling without an ounce of remorse.

I hung against the wall, satisfied to listen as the others in my group filled the Council in on the happenings in Siberia, but as Grady took the lead, detailing the events that led to the attack on the compound, I was forced to move closer. His report was mainly accurate, but he glossed over details of Nero's stubbornness and unwillingness to join the Council. Instead, he weaved a tale of Nero the warrior, Nero the gracious host that welcomed the Guard, grateful that the Council sent a personal escort to ensure his safety. When he recounted Set's attack, it was Nero's men that led the charge, Nero that distracted Set long enough for Brynn to weave her spell and disable our enemies, ensuring our escape.

As Grady spoke, Nero's demeanor changed. He stood up taller, his arms back as he absorbed the praise and looks of awe and wonder from the new Nomarchs. It didn't matter to him that it wasn't true. That he had refused to leave his compound when we warned him the hybrid army was coming. Stubbornness that cost men their lives. That it was actually Roman and I that took on Set. That it was *us* that nearly died so Grady could get to Brynn. He just stood there, his chest puffed up with pride he didn't deserve to feel. I wondered if he'd be so willing to take the admiration if he knew his son was laying in the infirmary fighting for his life. Brynn added in details, filling in blank spaces in my own memory. She explained how she translated the book, how she used the spell to disable Set and the hybrids. I was surprised as anyone when she explained how we escaped the compound. Apparently, we got out on the snowmobiles Roman and I had seen in the armory, although I had no memory of it.

There was no way I was strong enough to ride a snowmobile on my own. The flash of red from the compound seared through my mind as I glanced at Grady. It hadn't been the same sharp red as Set's eyes, it had been softer, a deeper russet. *Had it been Grady that carried me out?* His eyes cut over to me briefly before returning to the Nomarchs. A knot formed in my gut, one completely unrelated to my injuries.

"Do you have anything to add?" Astrid asked, her sharp voice cutting through the air. It wasn't until her head turned, revealing her pale profile that I realized she was talking to me. All eyes on me now, I stood a little taller, ignoring the ache in my arm.

I wanted to yell. To rage at them that Nero wasn't the hero of the tale like Grady made it seem, but I knew I couldn't. The lies were necessary to complete the mission. To ensure Nero would take his throne. Instead, I said, "Set is vulnerable to injury. I stabbed him through the foot."

"Can he be killed?" Amina asked.

"I don't know," I admitted.

"Anything else?" Astrid snipped.

"He didn't have the was-sceptre. I don't think he knows where it is."

"Why do you think that?" Madigan asked from the other side of the room. Even this far away, I could count the freckles on her nose and cheeks.

"It's been nearly a month since he was freed. If he knew where the sceptre was, he would have gone after it already. He either doesn't know where it is, or he needs something before he can get it."

"If he finds it. . ." Madigan began, but I interrupted.

"Excuse me, ma'am. Do *we* even know where the was-sceptre is?"

All of the Nomarchs went still. Finally, it was Amina that spoke up. "The Kindred are not in possession of it, if that is what you are implying."

My hand tensed. It was the same non-answer they'd fed me before. "How is that possible? Were we not the ones that imprisoned Set? How do we not know what happened to his most dangerous weapon?"

"That is none of your concern," Amina answered tightly.

"With all due respect," *Which isn't much,* I added silently,

"I think it is. We are the ones that went up against Set. The least you can do to help is explain how he was put away the first time. Was it Marius that killed him?" I still knew so little about my history, about what happened to my ancestors.

Astrid stood slowly, her slate blue eyes sharp as diamonds. "You will not mention that name inside these walls again. And you will not question the Nomarch Council again, that is at least if you wish to keep your brand. The Guard does not concern itself with matters such as this. You do as you are told, and you will leave the rest to the Nomarchs. We do not answer to someone such as you."

Nero turned to face me. "What do you know of Set and his plans?" he demanded. It took everything in my power not to roll my eyes at his absurd question. "Set and his hybrids came for you. It was you he fed from."

The air went completely still. Grady hadn't reported that part to the Council. He hadn't been there to see it. But Nero had. He would have seen it all. Would have heard me screaming. My left hand clenched, my eyes hard as they took in the soon-to-be leader of my house. There was no shame in being fed from, not as far as I was concerned. I knew others looked down on it, as something that only happened to those weak enough to be bested by a wraith. But Set wasn't a wraith. He was a damned god. "The hybrids were already outside your gates when we arrived," I reminded him. I ignored Grady and Brynn who were both openly gaping at me, both for what I'm sure were very different reasons.

"No doubt setting a trap for you," Nero argued.

I opened my mouth to object when a crack sounded in my head. I screamed, dropping to my knees, clutching my arm. No one was near me, but still I felt as if my collar bone had been snapped in two. When I looked down, my shoulder had gone completely limp. Grady lunged for me. Even Brynn moved to help. Nomarchs stood quickly, their eyes aglow, searching the room for the invisible threat. Another bolt of pain struck my shoulder, this time opening the wound from Set's blade, fresh blood soaking into my new shirt and down my arm. I bit down on my lip, but the scream escaped anyway. Another crack reverberated through my skull and this time my shoulder popped back in place. There was a moment of relief before my body went limp and I collapsed on the stone floor of Council Chambers.

I wake up on the cave floor. The pain in my arm is gone, and when I pull the edge of my tank top to the side, the stab wound has disappeared as well. The torches are already lit this time, and when I turn around I figure out why. I'm not alone.

Standing in the center of the cave is my mom. Her dark hair is down, falling past her shoulders, her dark eyes reflecting the torchlight. I scramble to my feet. I'd seen her in my dreams before—as a Descendant,. I'm supposed to be able to access all my ancestors' memories, although I hadn't figured out how to do it intentionally yet. Looking at my mom, I am suddenly overcome with emotion. As if she can sense it, she opens her arms and I run to them, hugging her tightly. "My sweet girl," she whispers, stroking my hair like she used to when I was little. "My sweet, brave girl."

"I miss you, Mom," I tell her, pulling back and wiping my cheeks. I didn't remember starting to cry, but my hands come away damp. "I have so much I want to talk to you about." She squeezes my shoulders, then runs her hands down my arms to hold my hands. Her thumb brushes over the newly-changed brand on my palm and I look away. "I—I don't know what to say," I stutter. I couldn't explain it, but I was embarrassed to tell her I was in the Guard. Part of me thought she would be ashamed of me for making the same mistakes she did.

She smiles at me sadly. "It's okay, Kyndal. I already knew."

"How?" I ask.

She looks around. "This place. You wouldn't be here if you weren't in the Guard. It's warded shut. The seal can only be broken by one of us."

"What is this place?" I ask. "Where is it?"

"It was built for the first Guard. A sanctuary for them to train and hone their magic."

I think of the last time I was here, the fear that had overwhelmed me, leaving me crippled on the floor. It was the same feeling I had when Set attacked. "It feels wrong.

Like I'm not welcome here." As *if saying the words manifested it, the dread returns and shadows sweep across the walls, throwing the cave into ever-growing darkness.*

"The gods were cautious when they built this cave. Only those strong enough to face it are allowed entrance." The *shadows creep closer, with them comes an icy chill.*

"Face what?" I *ask my mother. I can barely see her now.* *"My fear?"*

"Something much more difficult than fear," she *responds, and her voice sounds far away—like she's being swept away. Her final words carry to me on the smallest whisper of the wind.* *"You must face your truth."*

I was aware of him before I even opened my eyes. I could hear his breathing—soft and even—like it was when he was deeply asleep. The bond was there, his presence quiet and gentle on the other side of it, like a soft breeze through a window. I opened my eyes slowly. The room was dark, lit only by a few candles and the moonlight streaming through the windows. I wiped the sleep from my eyes, turning my head slowly. I recognized the plain sheets, the rail thin bed and blank walls of the infirmary. In the corner of the room nestled into a chair, his head against the wall, Roman was fast asleep. Surprisingly, Isaac slept on the floor next to him. I smiled softly at the sight of my friends keeping vigil, some of the first people to accept me into the life of a Kindred.

I sat up slowly, trying not to make a sound, in hopes of not waking either of them up. Failing miserably, I grimaced when the bed creaked beneath me. Isaac's eyes shot open, immediately locking on mine. Roman stirred but remained asleep. I held my finger up to my lips, signaling him to stay quiet. To let him sleep.

He pulled his muscular frame off the ground, sitting down gingerly on the edge of my bed. He was dressed casually in sweats and a tank, but I didn't miss the dagger tucked in the scabbard around his leg. "Nice to see you awake," he whispered. "How do you feel?"

I smiled tentatively. "I don't—I don't know." I reached up and under the gown I was in, one that reminded me of the time I went to the hospital to get my appendix removed, and peeled away the fresh bandage around my shoulder. Underneath it, the stab wound was gone, leaving behind a light pink scar I knew would also be gone by the end of the week. I rotated my shoulder, pleasantly surprised when there was no pain. My jaw still ached, but not nearly as much as it had before. I reached inside myself, searching for the well of power that always sat waiting. I smiled when I found it easily, the candles in the room blazing briefly before I returned them to normal.

Isaac smiled, the first genuine smile he'd given me in a long time. "I'll take that as a good sign."

I gave him a smile of my own, but my brow furrowed when I looked to Roman again. "What about him? How is he?"

"When you guys got back, his collarbone was nearly

shattered. His body was trying to heal it before it was set properly. Cassie had to re-break it before she could put it back in place. He woke up in the middle of the whole thing, but he never screamed once, even though it must have hurt like a son of a bitch." I thought of the crack I'd heard, the pain I'd felt as well. It must have come from when Cassie was setting the bone. "He passed out again afterward, even though his body was healing and Cassie couldn't find anything else wrong with him. He woke up two days ago."

"Two days ago?!" I hissed. "How long have I been asleep?"

"Almost four days," he replied bluntly. My jaw dropped. I'd missed four days. I'd only been kidding when I'd thought I needed to sleep for days. "Cassie has been taking care of you. Mallory finally convinced her to go home this morning, although I'm sure she'll be back soon." Isaac turned, looking back at his best friend as the silence stretched out between us. "He told me what you guys dealt with in Siberia. I can't believe you all took on a god and lived. That's some heavy stuff."

I wasn't quite ready to go back down that road, so I said, "I have to admit, I'm surprised to see you here, Isaac."

He shrugged but didn't turn to look at me. "He refuses to leave. Once he woke up, he demanded to know where you were and when he found you, he posted up in that corner and has barely moved since. I had to threaten to kick his ass just so he would take a shower. Yesterday, I started bringing him his meals so he wouldn't starve."

A small chuckle escaped my lips. Roman was so stubborn. I reached out, placing my hand on Isaac's. "I'm sorry."

His head whipped around, looking me up and down quickly. "Something must be wrong with you. I've never heard you say that." The shock on his face was almost comical.

"It was long overdue. I know you and I have always had a rocky relationship, and I never gave you enough credit for everything you do. When I was first branded, I was a mess, still am if I'm being honest. You caught the brunt of that, and I never should have gotten pissed at you for calling me on my crap. I said things I didn't mean, and I'm sorry. You're a hell of a warrior and an even better friend. He's lucky to have someone so loyal."

Isaac took a deep breath, scruffing his fingers through his waves. "If we're being honest, it wasn't all your fault. I was jealous of you. You're so much better at all this than I am. You picked it up so quickly, and then you turned out to be some super special Kindred no one had heard of in hundreds of years. I didn't know how to deal with it."

I smirked, trying to break the tension. "It's not all it's cracked up to be, trust me. I'd trade you places if I could." What I would give to be normal. Well, as normal as any Kindred is.

"I was there," Isaac said, his tone still serious. His eyes glazed over and I could tell he was lost in memory. "I remember you yelling at us to get out of the cavern. The flames were coming for us, bigger and stronger than anything I had the power to stop. But you stepped in front of it. You stopped it." He paused a moment and I was surprised to see his eyes well with tears. "I heard your scream from outside the cavern. I had never heard anything like it before. I remember thinking it sounded like death had swept through the Hollow, and when we went back into that cavern, you were on the ground and Roman was in your arms and there was so much blood." I wiped a tear from my cheek. "I'd never felt more useless than in that moment. I don't have a lot of family. I'm an only child, my dad's always been a drunk, and when my mom died, there wasn't really anyone left. When I was branded, the Kindred took me in. It was Roman that found me and explained to me what I was, what I could do. The Kindred became my family. Roman is the closest thing I've ever had to a brother and when I saw him lying on that cavern floor it was one of the scariest moments of my life. Then you brought him back and it was the most amazing thing I'd ever seen. I felt like a real asshat for being rude to you then." We both laughed at that. "I know you entered the Guard to save him. You sacrificed your freedom to protect him, and he sacrificed his for you. You two are lucky to have each other."

"We. . ." I began to object, to tell him that we didn't have each other. To deny what Isaac was suggesting, but he just gave me a knowing look. After everything he said, I didn't mind Isaac knowing about Roman and me. I knew he was someone I could trust. He would never do anything to hurt Roman, and as I thought about it more, I realized that same loyalty applied to me. He would never do anything to hurt me. "Do the others know?" I asked.

He shook his head. "Mallory and Cassie don't. They think it ended when you both took your vows. Apparently they don't know how much of a pain in the ass you are and how much you hate rules. Lydia suspects."

I snorted. It didn't surprise me that Lydia knew what was going on, even from thousands of miles away. She never did like being kept in the dark. Hell, she'd practically broke into my house to demand what was going on when I was first branded. "I miss her," I admitted.

"Me too."

I leaned forward slowly, mindful of the gown I wore, and wrapped my arms around Isaac in a firm hug. He returned the gesture, albeit kind of awkwardly, before pulling himself back and standing up. "Thank you."

He cleared his throat, reinstating his manly facade. "I'll go find Cassie, let her know you're awake."

I smiled at him, nodding. "Thanks." He'd no sooner left the room than I turned toward Roman. "You can quit pretending."

His eyes opened immediately, his sideways smirk on glorious display. "When did you figure out I was faking it?"

"About the time Isaac called himself an asshat."

His chest shook with quiet laughter. His eyes cast down, a blanket of sadness covering the air. "That was a nice thing you did," he said softly.

"Don't get used to it. I'm sure I'll be back to my typical bad attitude soon enough."

This time I earned a full smile, although he still didn't look up at me. "Good. I prefer you that way."

13

Isaac returned with Cassie not too long later. Roman had stepped out briefly while he'd been gone, giving me an opportunity to change from the gown and into my clothes. I was pulling my boots on when they returned. Cassie's long red hair was wet, braided down her back, and her clothes were freshly pressed. One look at her face though, and I could see the shadows under her eyes, the tight worry lines along her mouth. Mallory was a step behind her, dressed in fighting gear, her caramel colored hair pulled back into a tight ponytail. There was an extra weapons belt and dagger in her left hand.

"Hi," I said brightly, as I finished tying my boot and stood tall. "I was just getting ready to leave."

Cassie smiled at me, and I was relieved to see some of the darkness retreat from her eyes. "I'll be the one that decides that," she admonished playfully. She wasted no time, grabbing the edge of my leather vest and pulling it to the side, checking my shoulder. "Raise your arm," she ordered.

I did as she said. She poked and prodded at my collarbone, looking for any sign of weakness. I kept my eyes trained forward, not daring to look at Roman, who had posted up against the wall.

"That for me?" I asked Mallory, gesturing to the dagger. She didn't respond, just leaned against the door jam. She'd been pretty pissed with me when I left the island, and it was obvious she hadn't gotten over it. "How's Daniela?" I dared to ask.

"She's recovered," Cassie replied.

"She's refusing to talk to either of us, though," Mallory added from the doorway. "Thanks to you." I was relieved to hear Daniela had survived. I still felt bad about leaving her the way I did.

Cassie touched my chin gingerly, turning my head to the side. "You still have a light bruise along your jaw, but it's nothing that won't heal." She stepped back. "What about your power?"

My eyes turned a bright red, my power rushing down my arms to form fireballs. I held them both up, molding them into something smaller, about the size of a softball. I extinguished them both just as quickly. "Good as new."

"So it would seem," Cassie agreed.

"I'm free to go, right?"

"No," Mallory said firmly. "Last time I let you walk out of a room, you left the island and were nearly killed by a chaos god." She crossed her arms. "So sit your ass down because you're not leaving this room until you answer my questions. If—and only if—I like your answers, then you get the dagger."

"We have some questions of our own, too." The voice came from the hallway and my jaw dropped when Grady and Brynn walked into the room.

"What the hell?" I demanded. "Did you invite them here?" I accused Mallory.

"I invited them," Roman said, his quiet voice cutting through the room.

I wheeled around on him. "You did what?"

He pushed off the wall. "We can't keep lying to everyone. Trying to do everything ourselves. We got our asses handed to us in Siberia and we *both* almost died. We need help. Our only chance of defeating Set is if we work together." He looked around the room. "All of us."

Betrayal hit me, more painful than anything Set had done to me. I couldn't believe he brought them in, that he made this decision without even talking to me. "Maybe now isn't the best time," Isaac hedged.

"Thank you! Finally, a reasonable person." I flung my arm out, pointing at Grady and Brynn. "Did you forget? She almost killed me. Twice. He *did* kill you!"

Brynn stepped up. "We both also saved your asses. Without that spell, Set would have sucked you dry. Grady almost took a spear in the gut going back in after you."

So, it had been Grady to carry me out. "If you think that makes up for everything you've done. . ."

"We're not asking you to forget everything that's happened," Roman interrupted.

"We?!" I yelled. "It's *we* now?"

"Yes. Like it or not, the four of us are in the Guard together. We are stuck together, *forever*. So while we can't forget what's happened, we have to start trusting each other. Now do what Mallory said and sit down." I crossed my arms and leaned against the wall, just to be a pain in the ass. Roman glared at me for a moment longer, waiting to see if I had something else smart to say. When I remained quiet, he took that as permission to continue. "You guys are right to think something is going on, although it's not what you think. Kyndal and I share a connection. We're called Rafiq."

"I heard you use that word in Council Chambers. What does it mean?" Cassie asked.

"Two bonded warriors, connected through magic and emotion. I've read about them in the book. No wonder you went down so hard when Set fed from Kyndal," Brynn explained.

"I still don't understand," Cassie admitted.

Roman explained. "Kyndal and I can sense each other, tell when each other is near. We can also sense each other's emotions. In extreme circumstances, when one of us is injured, the other one adopts the injuries too. It's called an echo."

"So, when Set fed from Kyndal it drained your energy as well. Not as quickly, that's why you didn't pass out right away, but you still felt the effects," Brynn filled in.

"Yes," Roman confirmed. "And when Kyndal passed out again, it took me down too."

"That's why I couldn't heal your stab wound. It wasn't yours," Cassie replied, putting the pieces together.

Grady pointed at me. "She dropped in the middle of Council Chambers when you were setting his arm. Watching it, I would've thought someone was breaking her bones," he added. He looked between Roman and me, his brow furrowed, and I could see him making some previously unseen connection.

"Has it always been like this?" Cassie asked. I could see the hurt in her eyes from the secret we kept.

"No," I said simply, my tone clipped.

"You're lying," Mallory accused. "When Deacon took Sandra and Roman captive, I remember you telling Ezekiel you knew he was alive. Injured, but alive. You could sense him, couldn't you?"

"It was new, then. I didn't know what it was."

"You told us you lied to Ezekiel. That you said whatever you needed to in order to get in the bar. Why didn't you just tell us?" Cassie pushed.

"Because I didn't know what was going on!" I yelled, getting defensive. "I didn't know what it was. I was struggling enough being new to my powers, I didn't need to be a freak. And then everything happened with my aunt, and Ezekiel, and Roman being possessed. Everything just got out of hand."

"Well, that's the understatement of the century." Mallory's words were biting. "Did it end there, or could you two still sense each other when he was possessed?" I ground my teeth, refusing to answer. "Holy shit! You could, couldn't you? You have got to be kidding me, Kyndal. The enemy had a GPS tracker on you and you didn't think to mention that to anyone? You didn't think of the danger that put everyone in?"

"Roman isn't the enemy," Isaac interjected, trying his hardest to hold to our new-found loyalty to each other.

"Shut up," Mallory snipped, her eyes turning a bright gold.

"Hey!" I shouted, pushing off the wall. "Don't talk to him that way." I could feel my own eyes changing. Mallory stood up, her feet shifting slightly into a defensive posture. Grady and Brynn stepped back, clearing the path between us.

"Knock it off, both of you." Cassie demanded, her voice stronger than I'd ever heard. Mallory's power pulled back, but her stance stayed rigid. Cassie turned her back to her girlfriend, fully trusting her to heed her words. She took a deep breath and when she spoke again, her voice was soft.

"Bottom line is, you two should have told us as soon as you knew what was going on. You two being connected like this is dangerous, it puts everyone in danger. If one of you goes down in battle and takes the other with you, what happens to the soldiers relying on you to watch their backs?"

"It's not all bad," I argued. "Our powers are stronger around each other, and I'm pretty sure the Rafiq bond is why I was able to bring him back from the dead." Roman looked at me in open exasperation. I hadn't told him that little tidbit of info.

"How do you know that?" Grady asked.

"The Nomarchs have been putting me through a series of tests, trying to find out what's different about Descendant blood. They want to find the limitations to my powers. They brought in a captured hybrid and forced me to try and cure her."

"Kyndal. . ." Roman began, taking a step forward. I cut him off, raising a hand.

"It didn't work. Astrid stabbed her through the heart but there was nothing I could do. She died right in front of me. And the only thing I can think that's different between *that* hybrid and Roman is the bond."

"Still," Cassie reasoned. "You two being connected like this poses a huge risk."

"That's where I'm hoping Brynn can help," Roman jumped in.

"Me?" Brynn asked, the shock clear on her face.

"You've already translated part of The Book of Breathings. I want you to find a spell that will sever the bond."

"You want me to do what?" Brynn asked. She looked over to me. In fact, everyone was staring at me, waiting to see what I would do. Outwardly, I gave no reaction, save for a small catch in my breathing, one I quickly covered by clearing my throat. Inwardly, I was dying. Being stabbed had hurt less than this. Being fed on had hurt less. Roman's words twisted in my chest, digging their way through to my heart. I stared at the floor, my eyes going hazy. The voices in the room started to fade out. "Are you sure?" I heard Brynn ask.

"Yes," Roman responded evenly.

"Kyndal?" Brynn questioned. "Is this what you want?"

I cleared my throat again, bringing my eyes up to meet hers. I nodded stiffly. "Sure—yes. Yes." I said the words with strength and conviction I didn't feel. "You guys are right. The bond is a risk, right? Better to get rid of it." Each word took a piece of me with it, a piece of my happiness. I could feel the emotion burning at the back of my throat. I couldn't break down in front of them. Not in front of Roman. Not anymore. "Are we done here?" I asked tersely. "I'd really like to go home."

I didn't wait for a response. I marched out of the room, pushing right past Mallory. A sharp twist of pain and longing came through the bond. It was brief, almost as if he didn't want me to feel it but couldn't help himself. Behind me, I heard him take a step my direction, as if he would follow. I paused, but didn't turn, and pushed my own emotions back at him, blocking his out. Rage. Betrayal. A silent order to stay where he was. Wisely, he listened.

No one else tried to follow.

I didn't go home. Instead, I wound through the streets of Awen until I found myself in front of a soft blue door. The murmur of voices carried to the front step, not loud enough for me to be able to discern what they were saying, but I could tell there were several people inside. I thought about turning around, but I was determined not to chicken out. I knocked quietly and the voices inside instantly fell silent. I tucked my hands in my pockets and rocked back and forth on my feet, waiting. No one came. I raised my hand to knock again when I heard the soft padding of feet across the floor and the door opened a fraction.

Daniela stood in the doorway, her black curls hanging loose, a few errant strands falling over her forehead. She was dressed casually in sweats and a tank top. I'd clearly caught her on her day off. Her left arm was completely healed, no sign of the wound that had been there before, but three faint scars wrapped themselves around her neck, a shade lighter than the rest of her skin. I could see behind her into the house. Her living room was full of people, at least ten at my initial count. As soon as she laid eyes on me, her posture changed, and she pulled the door closed, cutting off my view of the interior. "What are you doing here?" she asked coolly.

"I—I just wanted to come and check on you, see how you were doing," I answered. As soon as the words left my mouth, I felt stupid for saying them.

Daniela scoffed. "Seriously? You almost get me killed and that's all you can say?"

I took a deep breath. "You're right. I'm sorry. I shouldn't have asked you to do that. It wasn't fair of me and I'm just glad you're okay." I took a step back. "I'll leave you alone now."

She stepped forward onto the front step, leaving the door ajar behind her. "I heard you took on Set, is that true?"

I nodded, laughing ruefully. "Yeah."

"You really think you can put him back in his cage?"

I shrugged. "Honestly, I don't know. He almost killed me and I don't even think he was at full power." I couldn't imagine what he'd be like once he found the was-sceptre. I shuddered to even think about it.

"You fought a god and survived. I doubt there are many people out there that can say that. Don't count yourself out." She gave me a small smile. One I didn't deserve but found myself returning anyway.

"Thanks, Daniela. I appreciate that."

She nodded, and just before I turned to leave, the door

opened fully behind her. A tall man stood there, his blonde hair buzzed close to his head, his blue eyes sparkling with mischief. I recognized him instantly from Maat's Hollow as one of the men that helped fight back the Surori. "Oh, hey," he greeted me. He looked to Daniela. "Did you tell her?"

"Tell me what?" I asked instantly.

Daniela's mouth pursed in frustration and she glared at her friend behind her before turning to me. I knew whatever she had to say was not good. "Kyndal, you remember Travis. He has horrible timing, but since he's already stuck his nose where it doesn't belong, I guess there's no sense in waiting." She took a deep breath. "First of all, I was going to tell you, I really was. We finished the sweeps of the cells. Your friend. . ."

"Sandra Cartwright," I filled in. My heart was in my throat. Had something happened to her? Had one of the Surori gotten to her? Maybe something worse?

She nodded, her eyes screaming with apology. "When we got to her cell, it was empty. Sandra is missing."

14

After Daniela floored me with the news of Sandra's disappearance, I tried to leave immediately. I didn't know exactly where I was going, maybe to Council Chambers to demand a search party, maybe to the tarmac to hop on a plane and go searching for Sandra myself.

"Where would you begin?" Daniela challenged.

"I don't know!" I shouted, throwing my arms out wide. "I have to do *something* though."

"Just come inside," Daniela said, gesturing behind her. "You can't go running around the planet looking for one person. You need a plan. Come inside and *think*. We may be able to help you."

I furrowed my eyebrows in confusion. I knew she was right. It was impulsive and frankly stupid to take off with no idea of where to start, but what did she mean when she said *we* could help? I was going to ask that very question, but Daniela had already disappeared into the cottage, leaving the door wide open in her wake.

Just as I'd initially thought, the cottage was full of people. I did a quick count, finding there were eight people scattered about on the various couches and chairs, another six sitting on the floor. Including Travis and Daniela, that made sixteen people. Most I had never seen before, but a few I thought I recognized. One I knew worked as a guard at Council Chambers, just like Daniela. Another I thought I'd seen working security at the library, a third was a lead instructor at the training facility. Mallory was friends with him. What were they all doing here?

As I entered the room, the hushed voices completely died, over a dozen sets of eyes following me as I stood awkwardly in the middle of the room. Daniela turned toward me, placing her hand on my shoulder. "Everyone, this is Kyndal Davenport. She has a problem and she needs our help solving it." Everyone looked to me expectantly.

I turned to Daniela, my confusion only growing. "I'm sorry, who—who are you people? Why would you help me?"

A soft chuckle went through the room, most of which came from Travis. He was sitting comfortably on the edge of the couch. "Lukas never told you?" he asked, laughing again. "We've been waiting for someone like you for a long time."

Lukas had said those exact words to me once before. I'd climbed up the Hollow steps hoping to see Sandra after she'd been imprisoned. Lukas had recognized me instantly as the Descendant, letting me in to see Sandra even though it was against orders. "I don't understand what you mean."

"You're looking for Sandra Cartwright, a woman that the Council has branded a traitor. You can't go to them for help. They are not interested in rescuing her. In fact, they've already issued an edict declaring for her to be brought in, dead or alive. If you hope to find Sandra before they do, you're going to need people like us. Well connected, well placed people that just happen to hate the Council's rule as much as you do," he answered.

"Who said I hate the Council?" I asked.

"They wanted you to join the Guard, you refused. Instead you challenged them by demanding they reinstate The Blinding of Truth by Falsehood because they denied you the one thing you wanted—The Book of Breathings. They ordered your Rafiq to be killed, and when they succeeded, you defied them by bringing him back. You saved his life again by leveraging the only thing the Council wanted— you in the Guard. Should I go on?"

I shook my head. He'd made his point. "How did you know Roman was my Rafiq?" That little bit of information was not public knowledge.

Daniela answered, "I was in Council Chambers when Roman declared it to Amina." She took a step away, moving toward Travis. "I apologize for the secrecy and confusion. I can imagine this must all seem very sudden, but you must understand, it is vital for people such as us to be careful who we share information with. I had planned to approach you about this differently and with much more subtlety."

"I still don't understand what you mean," I countered, my voice growing tight with agitation. "You said you could help me find Sandra, and instead you're wasting my time with riddles and half-truths. So, get to the point or I'm leaving."

"Lukas and I are not the only ones opposing the Council. In fact, Lukas was a part of a larger organization, one that includes all of us you see here—an underground resistance that is dedicated to restructuring the Kindred government— starting with the overthrow of the Council."

Travis continued, "We've watched for years as the Council made decisions that benefited those on top, oftentimes to the detriment of the rest of us. Too many times the cost of their ignorance is paid in our blood. The blood of the innocent people we were created to protect," he explained. "Lukas had been quietly recruiting for years, placing soldiers like me in key positions inside the infrastructure, so we have eyes and ears everywhere. We do what we can, helping where we can, but we were never truly strong enough to challenge the Council. Not until now. Not until you."

"Me?!" I shook my head. "No, no, you have the wrong person. I have issues with the Council, sure, but I'm not some chosen one." I had my own plans to dismantle the Council, but they weren't anything I was willing to share with this group. Not yet.

Travis laughed. "We are not religious fanatics, but realists. You are the first Descendant in generations. Your powers are no secret among the soldiers. We believe you present the right opportunity," Travis leaned forward, driven by his passion. "You see, it's not enough to dismantle the Council. We have to replace it with a better alternative, a system that represents all of the people. One that gives everyone a voice. It will be you, not the Council, that is strong enough to stop Set. When the soldiers see that, they will follow you in whatever direction you lead them."

"Lukas believed in you," Daniela added. "And so do we, but you cannot do it alone. You need people like us to help you. Which is why we will help you find Sandra as proof that we can be an asset. That we are on your side."

I took a deep breath, popping my knuckles instinctually. I looked around the room, my gaze jumping from one person to the next. They looked back at me expectantly, waiting for me to agree. For me to join their side. My chest tightened, my throat constricting around the words. I couldn't do it. I couldn't agree to be what they needed. I wasn't ready. I looked to Daniela. "Can I speak to you privately?" She nodded, leading me out the back door toward the nearby river. We leaned up against a railing, watching as the blue water traveled underneath us.

"You're going to say no, aren't you?" she said. "You won't help us."

"It's a lot to ask," I responded. "A lot of trust in people I don't really know. I can't agree to help you." I paused. "At least not yet." I turned to Daniela. "We think Set is searching for a weapon called the was-sceptre. The Council claims they have no idea where it is, but I have reason to doubt their story. Do you think you and your people could dig up some information about it? Maybe find out what happened to it?"

"Absolutely," Daniela responded immediately.

"Good," I replied. "Do this, and we'll talk about me joining your cause. If you hear anything, get in contact with Mallory. She knows how to find me."

"We'll see what we can find out," Daniela promised. "And Kyndal, I meant what I said inside, we'll help you find Sandra."

I nodded. "Thank you."

The next morning, I was woken at dawn by a banging on my door. Bleary, I wiped the sleep from my eyes as I staggered to the door. I pulled it open, surprised when I found Astrid standing there, dressed in a large pale cloak, the hood pulled over her signature silver hair. I immediately froze. "Mind letting me in?" she asked bluntly.

I stepped to the side, leaving the doorway clear. She walked through confidently, moving directly to the living room. I shut the door behind her, but only after giving one more look outside. There were no guards, no other Nomarchs.

Astrid was here alone.

I cleared my throat, following her in. She lowered her hood but made no move to sit. Her visit would be brief.

"What are you doing here Astrid?" I asked. I made no move to hide my annoyance or confusion. Astrid and I had long since lost any semblance of formality in our little chats.

She looked around the cottage, her eyes landing on my nearby ring daggers. "I was hoping we could speak privately." She grabbed one of the small blades, handing it to me with a poignant look. I took the dagger, holding her icy gaze for a moment before bringing the blade down on my palm and going to my front door to draw the silence glyph on the back of it. The air became charged with power, the soundproof ward snapping shut around us. "Your wounds are better," she said immediately. "When you fell in chambers, I feared the worst. But it seems you are stronger than anyone thought. It is not just anyone that can recover from being fed on by a god. Do you feel any lasting effects?"

"I'm fine," I responded immediately. I didn't fool myself into thinking she was concerned about my physical well-being. "What are you doing here?" I asked again.

"The Council is convening in the chambers in two hours and the Guard is expected to attend," she began.

"News that a guard could have delivered," I pointed out.

She smiled slightly. "I came here because as strange as it

may seem, I trust you Kyndal. I trust you, and I need you to trust me." I crossed my arms, remaining silent. "In this meeting, you are going to learn things that may upset you and the other Guardsman. I need you to promise me you won't react. That you'll keep the others from doing anything foolish."

"What kind of *things*?" I asked.

"I cannot tell you that. All I can say is that the Council made a deal, one that on the surface is going to look very damaging. But I need you to trust me that there are things going on behind the scenes that you do not see. No matter its appearance, this deal is for the best and everything will make sense very, *very* soon."

"Why should I trust you?" I asked her.

"I told you of Roman's heritage, did I not? Although it seems you did not divulge that particular piece of intelligence."

"Roman knows. It will be his choice if we use it."

"Your loyalty is admirable." She raised her hood, moving to the door.

"What did you do with Set's cage?" I asked her.

She turned, her cold blue eyes startling under her pale hood. "I gave it to a mutual friend of ours. It will be safe with her."

I changed into my gear, giving myself just enough time to stop in the training facility before heading to Council Chambers. The cafeteria was overflowing with people— Nero's men scattered between the Kindred soldiers—some lounging lazily at the tables, others pushing their way through the food lines. Daniela had mentioned that more of Nero's men had been flying in over the last couple of days, called in from wherever they'd been working. She also told me Nero had been formally sworn in as the Aries Nomarch during the time I was unconscious.

A peek into the training room showed me more of them, sparring with some of the male Kindred soldiers. The female warriors were training on the far side of the room, closest to the weapons lock up. I couldn't tell if they were separated by their choice, or if the Coterie soldiers had pushed them that direction, but there was a definite divide among the soldiers. It was dangerous having Nero's men here. Their presence created another divide in our people, when there were already too many. Those that left with Ezekiel, those that followed the Council, the soldiers that followed Nero and only fought for profit, and the quiet underground of rebels waiting for their opportunity to topple the Council.

The question was—where did I fit in among the branches?

I never considered myself loyal to the Council, but I also couldn't see myself fitting in with Daniela and her people. There was a danger to righteous people—their beliefs left them no room to compromise. I caught the eye of Isaac as he exited a sparring ring on the near side of the room. His opponent laid on the mat behind him, doubled over in pain. I raised my eyebrow in approval, which he returned with a satisfied grin.

I managed to grab a quick breakfast, eating on my way to the chambers. I couldn't remember the last time I wasn't eating on the run, or I had the chance to sit down to a home-cooked meal. It wasn't that the food in Awen was bad, I was just homesick for something familiar—like Allie's spaghetti. Or a cheeseburger. Or bacon.

A guard stood in front of the chamber doors, stepping aside as I approached. I took a moment to compose myself. I could already feel Roman on the other side, so I quickly shut my emotions down, shifting my face to one of neutral indifference. I knew exactly where he'd be, leaning against the wall. I could imagine the exact position of his body— one foot posted against the stone, his arms crossed, eyes scanning the room. To anyone else he would look relaxed and non-threatening, but I knew that foot was ready to push him into the action at any moment, that his crossed arms allowed his hand to be closer to his dagger without drawing any attention. These small details were the things I noticed about him, but no one else did. They were the type of thing you only noticed after countless hours watching someone.

When I entered the room, he was exactly where I expected, although surprisingly, he wasn't standing alone. Brynn stood next to him, The Book of Breathings held open in front of them. They were deep in discussion, the soft murmur of their voices carrying over the stone room, reaching me as I entered. It seemed they were wasting no time finding a way to sever the Rafiq bond. He fell silent, his eyes panning up slowly, as if he could no longer ignore my presence. I quickly looked away, ignoring his gaze I could feel following me as I descended into the center of the chambers.

I walked up to Grady who was brazeningly sitting on the arm of Maks's throne. His dagger was out and he twirled it absentmindedly in his left palm. "Any ideas what this is about?" I asked him.

"Nope," he replied, uncharacteristically short. I waited, expecting him to add something sarcastic, but it never came.

"You all right?" I asked.

The dagger went still as he looked up at me. "Does it matter?" His words lacked their usual punch.

I furrowed my brow. It wasn't like Grady to be so openly somber. He always acted like nothing ever bothered him. I entertained the idea of pushing for more information, when the door to the private Nomarch entrance opened, ceasing all conversation. Grady rose to his feet, Brynn and Roman moving to join us in the center of the wheel. I didn't miss the fact that Roman didn't stand next to me, instead allowing Brynn to stand between us. I glared at her out of the side of my eye.

I expected all twelve Nomarchs, so I was confused when only four entered. Amina in the lead, she was followed by Astrid, Madigan, and Elias. Amina sat gracefully on her throne, her black pant suit crisp to match her jet black hair that was pulled back in a tight ponytail. The other three did not sit, but instead stood around Amina. Astrid made no move to acknowledge me, not a single glimmer of our earlier conversation present on her face.

"I see you are back on your feet," Amina directed to me. "Your theatrics from earlier in the week were quite startling."

I ground my molars, her backhanded words making my blood boil. I would never forget what Amina had done to me. As I faced her now, I knew there would come the day when she was no longer Nomarch and I was no longer bound by duty and I would have my revenge. But until that day, I would wait, buying my time, playing the devoted soldier.

"Yes, Nomarch," I said sweetly. "I owe much to our skilled healers for helping me regain my strength."

"Hmm," Amina replied, unimpressed as always. I took a brief moment of joy, knowing how much it bothered her when she couldn't get a rise out of me.

"In light of recent events," Madigan said, taking control of the situation, "there are many things for us to discuss. Never before in our history has such tragedy reached the Nomarch Council. With four new Nomarchs taking their thrones, there has been much discussion and deliberation over territories. New lines have been drawn, new Houses taking control of various parts of the world. Soldiers have already begun deploying, heading to their compounds. Since we do not know where Set and his army are, it is imperative that the Kindred regain a strong presence in the world. We must be ready for war at a moment's notice. I will remain here with a small battalion to protect and maintain the island. And then of course, there has been the discussion of what to do with you."

"What do you mean with us?" Roman asked. I braced myself.

"The last Guard traveled the world freely, often times moving from one compound to the next, all in the name of protecting the book," Elias answered.

"After Sofia's betrayal, and the attack on the Coterie, we simply cannot allow the book to be out of the Council's sight," Madigan added. My power flared. They still blamed my mom for what she did, refusing to recognize she broke the rules in order to keep the book out of Ezekiel's hands. Without her, Ezekiel would have taken the book decades ago. They should be thanking, not blaming her. A calming breeze brushed against my power, trying its best to soothe my anger. I pushed it away. Ignored it.

"The Guard has been reassigned. You will relocate to a territory of our choosing, and report directly to the Nomarch of that area. You will remain there until you are called upon," Amina explained.

"You can't just hide us away," I argued. "We need to be out there hunting Set." Astrid wanted me to trust her, but that didn't mean I wouldn't ask questions. It would be suspicious if I didn't.

"You will go nowhere near Set or his hybrids, not after the

disaster that was Siberia," Amina snipped.

"Disaster?" Roman challenged. "We. . ."

"This is not up for debate," Astrid cut in, her cold voice silencing Roman. "You were defeated and your incompetence cost soldiers their lives and proved that your skills are nowhere near the level necessary to take on Set. You will protect The Book of Breathings. That is all."

From the corner of my eye, I saw Roman's hand move behind his back, his fingers curling into a fist. "Where are you sending us?" Grady asked, doing his best to remain diplomatic.

Amina explained, "For whatever reason, Set has chosen to remain under the radar of the human society. It would appear that he does not yet want his presence to be known, a fact we will use to our advantage."

"What about the sceptre?" I asked. "Wouldn't our time be better served looking for it?" No matter how many times they told me to drop it, I refused to let the issue go.

"We have reason to believe one of our teams has narrowed down its location. The sceptre should be within our reach shortly." I ground my molars at her evasive answer. Amina was the master of talking without actually saying anything.

Elias stepped forward. "You will be returning to a place where Set will be hesitant to go. A place his host body is well known and easily identifiable. It is our belief that he will not willingly show his face there, lest someone identify him."

"Marienville," Grady filled in. The word rang through me, igniting a small spark of excitement. Home. I was going home. "Who is Nomarch of that region now?"

"Nero has offered his services as leader of the area. He, as well as some of his men are boarding a plane as we speak."

"Nomarch. . ." Roman protested. My eyes jumped to Astrid. This was the deal, it had to be. Nero had been given control of the Allegheny, no doubt in exchange for us being sent there. Giving him the Guard meant he also got immediate access to the book, the one thing he wanted. The Council had played directly into his hands. From behind Amina, Astrid gave me the slightest of nods.

I stepped forward, cutting off Roman. "Thank you, Nomarchs," I lowered my head in respect. "We appreciate the opportunity to reinstate your faith in us. We will protect the book with our lives." I could feel the anger permeating out of the others, but I ignored it. I was gambling by putting my trust in Astrid. I hoped I didn't live to regret it.

Astrid stepped forward as well. "I suggest you return to your cottages to prepare. You leave tonight."

"Grady, I need to talk to you!" my voice rang out through the streets of Awen. I continued my trudge forward, chasing after Grady, rounding the corner to his street. Roman and Brynn had scattered after the meeting, no doubt to continue their research into breaking the Rafiq bond.

"Go away, Kyndal!" he yelled over his shoulder.

"Will you slow down?" I begged. "I just want to talk to you. Please, before we return to Marienville. Please."

"I don't know if you've realized, but I've had a pretty rough couple of days and we just got sidelined in the war against Set. If you insist on talking to me, you do so at your own risk." He reached his cottage, leaving the door open as he entered. I took that as an open invitation to follow. His cottage was immaculate, almost twice as big as mine. I'd only been in it once before, when I'd broken in demanding his help. Grady ducked into the bathroom, so I posted myself up against the wall, crossing my arms and waiting him out. I heard him splash water on his face, and I tried to ignore the images that appeared against my will. Daniela floating in my hot spring, fighting for her life. Last night, lying in bed, they had been all I'd seen. Even seeing her at her house alive and well hadn't erased the images. Grady reemerged, rolling his eyes at me standing in his living room. He walked past me, into his bedroom.

"What is your problem?" I shouted toward him. "You've had a bug up your ass all day."

He peeked out his doorway, buckling a weapons belt in place. "Why do you suddenly want to talk to me? You've blown me off every time I've approached you."

"I don't know, you. . ." I stumbled, clenching my hand. I was so bad at this sort of thing. "You just seemed sad. I wanted to make sure you were okay."

He stepped fully into the living room, crossing his arms.

"No, Kyndal, I'm not okay. I'm pissed, actually."

"Why?"

He scoffed, his eyes bugging out. I instantly regretted the question. "Seriously? Let's see, where do I start? How about the Rafiq bond you didn't tell anyone about. Or maybe it was you bowing down in front of the Council just a moment ago, when you should have been asking questions. They just handed Nero the book."

"The bond wasn't anyone else's business," I answered, ignoring the second part of his accusation. Astrid had made it perfectly clear she didn't want me telling the others that she had given me inside information.

"Why did you lie about it?" he pressed. "Is it because you and Roman are still involved?"

I flinched, his words hitting me like a physical blow. "Why would you think that?" I asked, buying myself time.

Grady dug his fingers into his russet colored hair. "You two are always together, your magic signatures have changed to where I can barely tell the two of you apart. I've only ever seen that before with couples who have been together for *years*. So, I'll ask again, are you still together?" he asked again.

"I see you and Brynn together a lot," I diverted. "Are you two together?"

"Answer the question," Grady insisted, refusing to let me distract him.

"No," I lied, making sure my tone was firm. "We're not involved anymore. We haven't been since before he was possessed. That ended a long time ago." I felt a tiny bit guilty lying to him like that. Even after everything that happened, I did believe Grady was on the road to becoming a better person. But that didn't mean I trusted him enough to tell him the truth. Not this time. I took a deep breath, buying myself a moment. I had to tread carefully with what I said next. "He is my Rafiq. We're connected through the bond, but that doesn't mean we're in a relationship." I could see he wasn't buying it. I knew there was only one way to get him to stop asking questions, and I hated to do it. "Maybe when you killed him and I brought him back, that changed our signatures somehow. That has to have a weird effect on them, right?"

His face went white as a sheet. Grady hated when I reminded him of the decision he'd made to kill Roman instead of Ezekiel. I ground my molars when I saw the hurt in his eyes. "Maybe," he said tersely.

"Why do you care so much anyway?" I demanded.

"Because I could have killed you!" he roared. I knew immediately what he meant. I'd seen it the moment Roman explained our connection, but I had ignored it, scared to look too close at what that shadow in Grady's eyes meant. Grady had killed Roman, despite my insistence to wait, despite my pleas for his mercy.

I took a deep steadying breath, turning away to compose myself. When I turned back around, he stood next to the couch, his arms at his side, palms open, his face twisted with worry. I'd only ever seen him this vulnerable once before, when he told me about the girlfriend who'd turned. The one he'd been forced to kill. I sometimes wondered if the Grady everyone else saw, the swaggering bravado and cocky attitude, was a mask. That this was his true face. A quiet young man who believed in doing the right thing, who felt too much, so he pushed people away until he felt nothing.

Almost unconsciously, my fingers reached for my weapons belt, the familiar chill of the dagger metal bringing me comfort. I'd grabbed it and my second set of ring daggers off the bed table this morning. I'd felt naked without them, ever since they were confiscated at the Coterie. "Would it have mattered if you'd known?" I asked honestly. "Would it have changed anything?"

"It would have changed everything," he answered immediately. "I never understood why you protected him so much. Why you stopped me from interrogating him when he was captured. I assumed it was because of whatever relationship you'd had before he turned, that you were blinded by your feelings for him. I never would have guessed that you two were bonded, that you could feel everything he felt, that the pain I was inflicting on him..." He cut off, his hands digging into his hair. "I never would have done what I did, told Amina what I did, if I had known."

I crossed my arms protectively. "You were just following orders, right?" I said, using the excuse he'd given me several times.

"I'm not sure that makes it the right thing to do."

I adjusted my vest. "Careful, Grady. That doesn't sound like something a soldier would say."

"Why do you make this so damn difficult?" he insisted.

"Why should I make it easy?" I threw back. "Just because you say you're sorry doesn't make it any better. It's one thing to throw around words, it's a completely different thing to back it up."

"I already have," he argued. "I saved you at the Coterie."

"And I suppose you expect me to thank you. That we are somehow even now. That's not how it works."

Grady looked at me, his eyes firm. "You know what, just forget it. I said my piece, it's not my fault if you're too damn stubborn to accept my apology." With that he turned and left his cottage, slamming the door behind him.

15

We touched down in Pennsylvania almost thirty-six hours later. The plane ride had been tense, our small plane split in two. One half of the plane was filled with a portion of Nero's men, not the full amount of the Coterie's strength by any means, but enough to protect our town. The second half was made up of our small band of warriors. In addition to the Guard, Mallory, Cassie, and Isaac had been allowed to return to Marienville as well, a parting gift from Astrid. Typically, I would have been happy about that, but currently Isaac was the only one of the three that was willing to talk to me, so being stuck in a small space with them was less than ideal. I'd crammed myself between him and Grady, preferring to be closer to him, even after our argument. I was willing to do anything to keep space between Roman and me.

I hadn't spoken to Roman since the infirmary. In fact, I'd been avoiding him. I'd felt him watching me, but I always made sure to keep myself busy or surrounded by other people. I knew he wouldn't approach me if others were around.

As soon as the plane doors opened, I grabbed my duffel and made for the door, not bothering to wait for the others. It was early morning in Marienville, just after five a.m. On the island it would be night, just after nine o'clock. Even though I'd spent an entire day on a plane, I still got the day back thanks to the time difference. I could see the sun beginning to peek above the eastern horizon, the early purples and blues lightening the sky. The small private airport was surrounded on three sides by forest, and I wasted no time walking directly into the trees. Even though the airport was on the outside of town, nothing in Marienville was out of walking distance, not if you knew how to move through the old growth like we did. From where we were now, it would take me thirty minutes to reach my back porch. It was a Friday, Allie would be waking up soon and heading out for a day in the state park. I heard my name yelled from behind me, but I ignored it. No one would stop me from seeing my aunt.

When I'd left Marienville, it'd been at the height of summer. The trees had been a mosaic of colors, the creeks and rivers running swiftly from the summer rains, leaving the ground a soft bed of green. Now it was fall, just a week short of Thanksgiving, and the air was crisp, a preview of the colder temperatures that would settle in over the next few months. School had started long ago. I wondered if anyone wondered what had happened to me. Did they wonder where I'd disappeared to? Where Roman and Isaac had gone?

Leaves covered the ground, crunching under my feet as I strolled through the Allegheny. I found myself running my fingers along the tree trunks as I passed, allowing the strength of the ancient trees to soak into my bones. There was a different sort of power here than what I experienced in Awen. Awen was built by magic and it permeated out of every part of the island, wild and raw. The strength of these trees came from the centuries it took them to grow, from the hundreds of harsh winters and torrential rains it had experienced. It was a quiet, enduring strength.

My house came into view, just the same as I'd left it. I don't know why I had expected it to be different. Maybe I thought since I'd changed so much, everything else had too. The backyard was freshly raked, the pile of leaves now laying in Allie's compost pile. The backdoor blinds were pulled, allowing me to see into the dark kitchen. In fact, all of the windows were dark. I pulled on a small piece of my power, searching the treeline for the Kindred guards I'd placed here before I left. I didn't find any. I turned my attention to the house, listening for anyone inside. I hadn't been able to get ahold of Allie before we left the island so she had no idea I was coming. There was a chance she wasn't even home, but rather gone on a camping trip. It took some concentrating, but after a moment I picked up on the faint sound of feet shuffling on the wooden floor upstairs. Allie was home. I jogged up the wooden slats of the back porch, pulling gently on the sliding door. The latch gave no resistance and I pulled the sliding door open smoothly, stepping into the kitchen. I set my duffel bag on the kitchen table. "Allie?" I called out. A thud sounded through the ceiling, coming directly from her room.

"Allie!" I hollered as I bounded up the stairs two at a time. "It's Kyndal," I added as I reached for her doorknob pushing my way into her room. Two steps in and I skid to an immediate halt. Allie wasn't in her room, but that didn't mean it was empty. I wish it had been, because some things you just can't unsee. Darius stood in the middle of Allie's bedroom, wearing nothing but his boxers, his T-shirt held awkwardly in front of him trying to cover as much of his bronze skin as he could. I'd clearly caught him in the middle of getting dressed. It took my brain a moment to catch up to what my eyes were seeing. My eyes were round as saucers, and they jumped from him to the rumpled sheets of the bed, then to the clothes strewn about the floor—both his and hers. "Gah!" I yelped, covering my eyes, backing slowly out of the room. "Darius, what are you doing in my aunt's room?!" I shouted. Obviously, I knew the answer, but I was too befuddled to say anything else.

I heard the bathroom door at the end of the hall open. "Kyndal?" Allie asked. "What are you doing home?"

I turned her direction, but kept my eyes covered. "Are you naked? Because I swear if you are, I'm going to gouge my eyes out."

She chuckled and next thing I knew, she had wrapped her arms around me. Her fuzzy, fully robed arms. I pulled my hands down from my face and returned the gesture, squeezing her tight. "You didn't tell me you were coming home," she whispered. "It's so good to see you."

I pulled back and was surprised to see tears welling in her eyes. Her bedroom door cracked open and Darius stood there, now thankfully, fully clothed. I cleared my throat. "Right. So. . ." I turned awkwardly between both of them. "You two clearly need a minute. Meet you downstairs?" I asked Allie.

She nodded, an unrepentant grin on her face.

Ten minutes later, Allie and Darius ambled down the stairs. I eyed them from the kitchen table, where I was currently snacking on a pint of mint chocolate chip ice cream I'd dug out of the back of the freezer. "You have an interesting definition of the word guard," I said to Darius, who at least had the presence of mind to look sheepish.

"Be nice," Allie admonished. "What I do in my private life is none of your business." She turned to Darius, "I'll see you tonight," she said, before she gave him a swift peck on the lips.

"Ew!" I shuddered playfully. "Stop doing that!"

Darius shook his head as he tucked his phone back in his pocket. "It is good to see you Kyndal. There's a briefing in an hour." I nodded, then he ducked out the back door and into the dark forest.

I pointed my spoon after him, eyeing my aunt. "You're going to need to explain that."

Allie fell into the kitchen chair across from me, smiling. "I refuse to be judged by someone who eats ice cream for breakfast."

I took another generous scoop. "It's nighttime in Awen. Not to mention, they didn't have anything like this."

She laughed, but her face quickly grew serious. "What's wrong Kyndal? What are you doing back in Marienville?"

I set the spoon down, eyeing the wood grain of the kitchen table. "Why does something have to be wrong? I can't just want to come home?"

"You know you're always welcome here, and I'm glad to see you, but something tells me this isn't a social call."

I huffed a breath, meeting my aunt's gaze. Her dark hair was a little longer than the last time I'd seen her, falling just past her shoulders now. Her eyes were a dark brown, but I knew if I looked closer, I'd see flecks of honey gold. She looked so different from my dad, it was hard to find a resemblance. It was always in her mannerisms that I found the relation. She had the same smile as him, the same warm hugs. "You're right," I admitted. "There is something wrong."

I went over everything with her from the moment I'd left Marienville. Some of it she'd known, apparently Darius had been keeping her updated on what was happening in Awen. Whenever she didn't know something, she asked a lot of questions to fill in the blanks. I answered them all, holding nothing back.

"So what are you afraid of?" Allie asked, when I finished.

I gaped at her. "Haven't you been listening? There's a lot that's wrong!"

She shook her head, her brown eyes studying me. "That's not what I mean. All *that* is everything that's happening. I'm asking—what is going on with you?"

"I don't understand."

She reached across the table, grabbing my hand gently. She turned it over, revealing the silver scar on my forearm. That had been one of the more difficult things to explain to her. "After I was kidnapped, I couldn't tell the difference between what had happened to me, and who I was anymore. I allowed it to define how I saw myself, and to shape how I acted. I was scared and I allowed that fear to drive me."

"What changed?" I asked her.

"I realized something. Something simple, actually. Bad things happen, and you can't always stop them from happening, but the one thing we can do—the one thing we can always control—is how we react to those things. And just like that, I was free of the fear. It could no longer control me because I chose to be stronger than it. I chose not to let it win. Now, I have no doubt of your bravery, but we are all scared of something. You need to figure out what it is you're afraid of, because only then will you unlock your full power."

Being back at the compound was surreal. I'd spent the walk through the forest digesting what Allie had said. *What was I afraid of?* Several things came to mind—spiders being at the top of that list—but I knew that wasn't what she had meant. She was talking about the deep-seated fear, tucked away so deep inside me, I was unwilling to look for it. Set had almost killed me in Siberia and in the final moments before I'd blacked out, the moments where I truly thought it was over, I hadn't been afraid. It wasn't like I had *wanted* to die, but death didn't frighten me. If anything, death felt like an inevitability. There's a difference between being immortal and invulnerable, and even though I was promised the possibility of an everlasting life, that didn't guarantee it would happen. I was just as vulnerable now as I was before I was branded—probably more so. Back when I was a normal teenager, no one had ever stabbed me. Since then, I'd lost count of how many times someone had tried to kill me.

When I stepped onto the compound grounds, I noticed an immediate difference. The two training rings were freshly outlined in chalk, a middle, larger ring drawn between them, overlapping the smaller ones, creating a sort of violent Venn Diagram. A large hoard of weapons was staked into the ground nearby. The everlasting torch was there, its flame dancing in the light breeze, but it was joined by several unlit torches, ringing the training area. In-between the torches were deep bowls perched on top of pedestals. Two Coterie members were walking the circle, filling the bowls with water. Further past them, directly in-between the main house and Roman's smaller one, there were several wooden practice dummies posted. To my left, lights shone through the back windows of Roman's house. I could feel him in there, the bond instinctively pulling me that direction, but I shoved it down, instead heading toward the main house. I made it as far as the back porch before Isaac came through the back door. "What's all this?" I asked him.

"Skills tests," he responded.

I scrunched my eyebrows. "I thought this was a debriefing."

"Nero has ordered all non-Coterie members tested. Apparently, he wants to see where we measure up to his men." A wicked glint shone in Isaac's dark eyes, no doubt put there by the opportunity to beat on some Coterie soldiers. I couldn't help but return the sentiment.

"You talk to Lydia?" I asked him, changing the subject.

"Not yet. I don't exactly know what to say. She can't come around the compound, at least not while the Coterie is here." I agreed. Knowing the Coterie's violent and abhorrent treatment of women, Lydia needed to stay as far away as possible.

"Don't wait too long. If she knows you're home and you don't say anything, she'll be pissed, and she'll come looking. You need to go to her before that happens."

"I know."

Just then the door opened, everyone marching outside, Coterie and Kindred alike. Grady and Brynn led the group, exiting first. Grady's eyes cut over to mine, Brynn paying me absolutely no mind. They were all dressed in full fighting gear—leather vests, tactical pants, and thick boots. Mallory and Cassie each had their hair braided down their backs, both of them giving me a passing glance as they walked by. Darius came out last, a light blush showing on his dark cheeks. He simply nodded as he walked through. Isaac and I followed them, all of us spreading out to surround the training area, standing just outside of the torches. We all stood silently, hands crossed behind our backs, waiting. Waiting for the commander to appear.

The sliding door on the cottage opened and Roman stepped into the empty space next to me. The sun had just crested the trees, and from the corner of my eye I could see the soft rays highlighting the ends of his hair, bringing out the blonde that was usually hidden. "You've been avoiding me," he whispered, his eyes staying trained ahead.

"I don't have anything to say to you," I responded tightly.

"At least let me explain," he tried.

"I heard everything I need to hear," I said dismissively.

The air changed, and the torch flame jumped, spreading through the air and lighting all the waiting torches just as Nero walked out the back door. He certainly did like to make an entrance. Nero was dressed in fighting gear just like the rest of us with the addition of a silver chest plate buckled around his midsection. His bloodred pommel glinted in the sunlight from where the blade was strapped to his back. His eyes raged a brilliant red, making him a truly formidable sight. He marched through our line, standing directly in the middle of the center circle. He reached above his head, unsheathing his sword. It was the same one I'd seen in Siberia, the blade made of the deepest obsidian, so dark it swallowed the sunlight. Nero pointed the dark blade at Mallory first, then at one of his soldiers, a man I didn't recognize. "Choose your weapons," he ordered.

Neither of them hesitated, both moving to the weapons board. The weapons there were nothing like the one Nero held. Each of them was a typical Kindred silver, although there were a variety of options—daggers, of course—but also swords, axes, staffs, and katanas. The soldier, a large, muscular man, was several inches taller than Mallory. He pushed his way in front of her, plucking a broad ax off the board, twirling the massive weapon in an obvious taunt.

Mallory watched silently, staring daggers at the man, even as he turned his back to her, proving he didn't see her as a threat. Her eyes skipped over his back, landing low and I saw her eyes squint slightly in recognition. I followed her eye line, immediately seeing what caught her attention. There was a slight hitch in the man's step. His knee didn't bend correctly, no doubt from an old injury he hadn't been able to heal properly. Mallory grabbed a small dagger, following the man into the ring. He turned to his brothers, throwing his arms out with a roar. They responded in kind, yelling their own versions of war cries.

Not far from me, Cassie's voice rang out. "You got this!"

"Rules?" Mallory asked Nero.

"Until one of you can't continue," Nero replied roughly.

The man cracked his neck to both sides, his eyes now a bright blue, his mouth twisted into a cocky smile. Mallory simply dropped into a fighting stance, her eyes gold. My blood sang with the power in the air. Mallory was one of my favorite people to watch fight. There were no frills in her technique, just clean precision. She didn't use two maneuvers when one would do, and she never did what her opponent expected.

"Begin," Nero ordered.

Immediately the water in the bowls behind the Coterie soldier rose, flying through the air, headed directly for Mallory. Some people considered water to be the weakest of the offensive elements, but a skilled Water User could push the water inside someone, drowning them, or even extract the water inside a person, leaving them a dried-up husk.

Mallory saw the attack coming, and instead of evading, she ran right at the water, locking a surge of air in front of her, creating an invisible shield. The water bounced right off the shield, dropping harmlessly to the ground. Shouts of disapproval echoed from the other side of the ring, mixing with the yells of encouragement coming from the near side, Roman and Isaac now also cheering on Mallory. Mallory sprinted faster, planting her left foot as she neared her opponent, forcing him to raise his ax to defend himself. But Mallory didn't attack that side. Instead, she feinted, pushing herself to his left side and his now unprotected weak knee. Her right leg flew out, her foot catching the back of his knee, buckling it and bringing the big man down. She twisted as she landed, bringing her dagger up in a sweeping motion, cutting him the length of his back. Blood sprayed after the dagger, her weapon now dripping with it. It was a lot of blood, but only enough to injure, not kill. The Coterie soldier roared with pain, his back bowing and his head thrown back. Mallory flipped the dagger in her hand and brought the hilt of it down hard, squarely on his nose. There was a single, sickening crunch as his nose broke, followed swiftly by the thud of his unconscious body hitting the dirt.

Everyone went silent, the roars of the spectators dying almost instantaneously. Mallory paused only a moment, then wiped the blade on her pant leg and threw the dagger down near her fallen opponent. Without a word, she returned to her position in the outer ring, her power now dormant. The soldiers stared at her a moment longer, and I could feel the mood shift. They had underestimated her, underestimated *us*. They considered themselves to be elite, superior to the other Kindred in every way. Mallory had taken one of them down in under five moves.

I had a feeling they would not underestimate one of us again.

The fights continued, each of us taking our turn, Nero slowly making his way through our line. After Mallory's fight, the Coterie was more cautious, the fights taking longer each time, the outcome less and less guaranteed. Nero's men were well trained, and even those of us that won didn't manage it without injury. By the end of it, there wasn't a single person that wasn't bleeding. After we'd each taken our turn, Nero returned to the middle of the ring. "Guard. Center ring."

All four of us stepped forward, weapons already in hand. Staff for Brynn, short sword for Grady, daggers for Roman and me. My ring daggers were tucked neatly into my scabbard, just as I knew Roman's backup weapon was hidden in his boot. We stood shoulder to shoulder, waiting for Nero to choose which Coterie soldiers we were to fight. He never did. Instead, he pointed at Grady and Roman. "You two first."

Grady looked at him in surprise. "You want us to fight each other?" he asked, trying to understand.

"Not each other," Nero clarified. "Me."

"Sir?" Grady asked again. Next to him, I saw Roman tighten the grip on his dagger, the only hint he gave to his impending attack. Roman lunged, the tip of his dagger headed directly for Nero's chest. Only at the last moment did Nero's blade flash in front of him, countering the move. Grady, not one to be left behind, followed up with several punches, all of which Nero blocked, but Grady managed to land a kick to the back of his leg, buckling it. Roman leapt, his dagger held high, fully intending to bury it in Nero's shoulder. A burst of fire shot out of Nero's hand, knocking into Roman's chest at point blank range. He'd barely managed to get his shield up before it hit, the impact hitting him in the chest so hard, the echo of it took my breath away. He went flying backward, barreling into Grady, knocking them both down in a stunning defeat. The Coterie roared their approval from the opposite side of the ring, their weapons held high in the air.

Nero stood tall, his dark blade hanging at his side. He turned to Brynn and me. "Now you two." I eyed Brynn quickly, a silent understanding passing between us. We wouldn't barrel straight into Nero like Roman and Grady had. Instead, we split his focus, each of us moving to one of his sides. He backed up slowly, keeping us both in his eyeline. When his foot neared the chalk line, he attacked, building a fireball again, throwing it at Brynn. In an impressive show of speed, she pulled the water from the nearby bowls, dousing the fireball midair, leaving behind nothing but harmless steam. While Nero was momentarily distracted by Brynn, I lunged at him, sweeping my dagger toward his left arm. He swiped the blade away with his sword, but the move forced him to reach across his body. Before he could pull his arm back, Brynn landed a beautifully executed left hook to his cheekbone. Powerful as it was, Nero wasn't fazed. He spun, bringing his leg around in a stunning back kick that caught both of us across the face. We staggered backward. Nero pressed his advantage, forming another fireball and throwing it at Brynn. One we were too slow to stop this time. The flame smacked off her left shoulder, knocking her to the ground. Nero turned to me. I backed up slowly, keeping the space between us, allowing me to get my bearings. Nero stalked forward, matching my pace, the whole time his mouth moving quickly, like he was murmuring to himself. As he did, I felt the air change, felt it charge with static electricity. Then, from several feet away, Nero pushed both his hands out, a burst of multicolored light flying from his palms, hitting me in the chest like a freight train. I flew back several feet, landing in an unnatural heap on the ground. I pushed myself up, turning toward Nero in shock. He'd used magic. No one could do that except Guard members. There was no way. . .

And then, in front of my eyes, Nero's body began to shimmer like a mirage, covered in the same multicolored light I'd seen in Siberia. When the light disappeared, it was no longer Nero standing in the ring. It was the same armor, the same sword, but instead of Nero, it was none other than Sandra.

16

***"Don't be angry,"* Sandra said soothingly,** I think for the third time. Or was it the fourth? I couldn't be sure, I was too distracted, busy dealing with the torrent of emotions that were barreling down the bond unchecked, courtesy of the man standing to my right.

After Sandra revealed herself, Nero—the real Nero—had appeared out of the main house, dismissing his men to run patrol through the Allegheny, leaving the rest of us staring stupidly, mouths agape. He brought us inside to the main room, where we all now waited to hear how in the hell it was possible for Sandra to be here.

I sat on the edge of the couch, nervously popping my knuckles as I tried to connect the dots. Sandra had been in the Hollow when Ezekiel attacked. I knew that for a fact. Daniela had said she'd gone missing after that, that her cell was empty. If she hadn't been taken during the raid, how did she escape? And how did she end up in Marienville with the entire Council looking for her?

Roman leaned against the fireplace, his blue eyes sharp, studying every move his adopted mother made, as if he couldn't really believe it was her. Sandra's skin was beautiful and glowing, her blonde hair pulled back, no sign of the withering woman I'd seen inside the Hollow. She removed the scabbard from her back and unbuckled the silver chest plate. "I apologize for misleading you all, but I wanted to see each of you in action without my presence being a distraction."

"That was an impressive spell you cast," Grady said from the couch next to me. "How did you do it? It's like you *were* Nero. You even used his element."

Sandra quickly redid her ponytail, straightening out whatever imaginary bumps she found. "It's called a changeling spell. It allows you to take on the complete persona of a person; looks, voice, element. It is a spell that comes in handy when you do not want to risk discovery. Although, I would caution you from trying it anytime soon. It takes a large amount of power, and if you screw it up, you could get stuck in the form of the other person, unable to return to your proper self."

"How—how did you. . ." I began, when I was hit with another wave of Roman's emotions, knocking off my train of thought. I waded through them, pushing each aside until I could think clearly. First came the relief, he hadn't seen Sandra since the night he was turned into a hybrid, and I knew he thought he'd never see her again. His outward stance might suggest he was relaxed, but I could tell he was dying to run to her, wrap her in his arms and fight off anything that dared come after her again. He wouldn't though, because mixed in with his relief was an intense sadness, a worry that she wouldn't want to see him, that for some reason she wouldn't approve of him after everything he'd done.

Sandra looked at me. "How did I get here?" she asked, finishing my question.

I nodded. "I'd heard you were missing after Ezekiel's raid. Did he take you or did you escape?"

Roman pushed off the fireplace, staring directly at me. "What are you talking about? You knew she was missing?" His voice was rising along with his temper. I tried not to take it personally. I knew he was just worried about Sandra.

"I just found out a couple days ago," I said defensively.

Roman's eyes bugged out. "Days ago?!" he practically bellowed. "You didn't think to tell me?"

I jumped to my feet, losing control of my restraint. "I had just woken up out of a four-day nap! It wasn't exactly the easiest time to talk to you. Besides, you were busy with your own plans," I threw that last bit in his face, along with an arrow of smug satisfaction down the bond. His eyes squinted, the muscle in his jaw ticking. I smiled, knowing I'd gotten to him.

Sandra stepped in, placing her hand on Roman's shoulder. "Don't blame Kyndal. I was never in any danger, and there was nothing you could have done to find me, even if she had told you. We wanted it that way."

"Who's we?" Grady piped up from the couch. *Good question.*

Sandra looked above his head to where Nero was standing strong, as if to indicate him as the answer. Nero crossed his arms, giving nothing away. "There's no way," I cut in, not buying it for a minute. "The guards in the Hollow had been sweeping those cells for weeks. They'd finished before Nero even made it to Awen. There was no way he could have gotten you out. It doesn't fit."

Roman backed up, returning to his spot by the fireplace. Sandra watched him go, her motherly-concern obvious as she watched her son simmer with rage. "A mutual friend freed me."

The words rang in my head, eerily familiar. "Astrid?"

"Astrid wouldn't do that," Brynn replied immediately. Brynn was deeply loyal to the Council. She didn't believe her, and for once I felt inclined to agree.

"Astrid was the one that threw you in the Hollow," I added. "Why would she do that, just to break you out?"

"Because of this," Sandra answered, walking over to the desk in the corner. She opened the bottom drawer, pulling a dark bag from it. A bag I instantly recognized. She peeled the edge of it back, revealing the small, silver box that had held Set's soul. My eyes jumped to Roman, who was already looking at me, a knowing glance passing between us.

"How did you get that?" Grady asked, sitting up to the edge

of the couch. Of course he would recognize it too.

"As I understand it, it was left in the base of the Hollow, forgotten in the aftermath of Set's resurrection." Sandra raised her eyebrows, looking at me. "Kyndal retrieved it, on Astrid's orders."

From the back of the room, Mallory said, "That's why you needed Daniela. She got you into the Hollow. That's the mission you couldn't tell us about."

I turned, nodding slightly.

"Why all the secrecy? Why give the box to you?" Grady asked, ignoring Mallory. "The Council has literally unlimited resources to tackle something like this."

"Astrid thinks the Council is compromised. That if they were given the box, certain Nomarchs would intentionally prevent its use," Sandra answered.

"Astrid is paranoid," Brynn countered.

Sandra turned to her. "Possibly, but there is evidence to suggest otherwise. Ezekiel and his army never should have been able to break through the wards the way they did. Even with their Kindred blood, if those wards were at full power, it should have kept them from entering the vortex. The only way they could've made it through was if the wards were weakened. No one can authorize a change to the wards except a Council member."

Roman crossed his arms. "Ezekiel never mentioned having someone on the inside."

"But he sent you in first," I explained. "You said yourself it was an experiment to see if a hybrid could make it through. The Council knew the island was vulnerable. Even if one of them wasn't working directly with Ezekiel, they might have created the circumstances for his invasion."

"Why would they do that?" Cassie asked.

"War is profitable," Sandra answered. "Power has a tendency to change hands during times like this. The people feel vulnerable and they're looking for anyone that will step up and lead them. There are a lot of people who have something to gain with this war against Set." I thought of Daniela and her resistance. They were looking for an opportunity like this, but I didn't think they would go so far to put Awen at risk. But there was someone else that would.

"It's Amina," I blurted out, interrupting whatever Cassie was saying in response to Sandra. "Astrid told me she thinks Amina wants to dismantle the Council so she can be the sole ruler."

"No," Cassie disagreed. "Amina is a lot of things, but a traitor isn't one of them. She's a literalist, following the letter of our law exactly, and that includes the necessity and rule of the Council. She would never do anything to compromise that."

"She's been undermining our missions from the start. Astrid said she wants us to fail so she can get rid of us and take full control, but she can't do that until she ruins our reputation. Otherwise the people would never follow her. It makes sense, she already tried to kill me once, and she hates Roman."

"Since when do you talk to Astrid?" Roman asked.

I turned to him, trying to ignore the tense set of his shoulders, the sternness of his jaw. "It's not like I'm seeking her out, she just sort of shows up at my house sometimes."

"I agree with Cassie," Brynn said. Her eyes were churning, that sharp brain of hers putting everything together. "Amina would never leave Awen vulnerable intentionally." I raised my eyebrows, not sure I agreed with her.

"The bottom line is the Council cannot be trusted. There are too many of them that benefit from Set's release and the war it created. It is for the benefit of us all that they do not know what we will be doing here," Sandra said.

"Which is what exactly?" I asked.

Sandra placed her hands on top of the box. "This box was made from magic, and only magic will put Set back in it. Astrid entrusted it to me because she knows I'm one of few with the ability to wield magic. Me, and now the four of you. The problem is, Set is too strong for us to take on. Our weapons can wound his vessel, but they do nothing to harm the god living inside it. There is only one thing that can harm him long enough to subdue him while we complete the spell. The was-sceptre."

"We have no idea where it is," Brynn said. "The Council said they have a lead, but. . ."

"They have more than that," Nero cut in. "They've known the whole time where the was-sceptre is. Set was the ruler of the Redlands, so after he was defeated, the sceptre was returned to its rightful owner, Maat. As Goddess of the Blacklands, the Council believes she hid it somewhere within her kingdom. Probably inside a temple of some sort."

I clenched my teeth. *I knew they'd been lying to us.* "So that's it? The Council is going to get the sceptre before us?"

"Not necessarily," Sandra disagreed. "The Blacklands are centered along the banks of the Nile. The ground there is fertile, which is why Egyptians have settled there for thousands of years. There's almost 1,000 miles of river bank in Egypt alone and along it, there were countless temples, countless places the sceptre could have been hidden. It will take the Council some time to narrow it down, even longer if they try to search each temple one by one."

Brynn spoke up. "Not to mention, grave robbers have torn that area apart for thousands of years, raiding every Egyptian tomb, crypt, and pyramid they could find. Chances are, if the sceptre was buried, someone found it already and moved it somewhere else."

"Which is why we think Set hasn't already found it," Sandra added.

Grady raised his hand. "I hate to be the dumb one here, but isn't it a good thing if the Council gets the sceptre before

Set does?"

"Not if there's a mole," Roman pointed out. "If the mole knows where it is, that means it's only a matter of time until Set knows. Then he'll come for it, slaughtering anyone in his way."

"So what do we do?" This time it was Brynn who asked. "How do we find the tomb before anyone else does?"

"It won't be easy," Sandra admitted. "I'm trying to work some old contacts to narrow its location, but I'm hoping we won't need it. Set's cage was forged from the same metal as the was-sceptre, therefore they contain the same magical signature." Sandra's gaze landed on Grady. "I believe we can use the box to track it. And if we find it, we can put Set away. For good this time."

Grady gave her a disbelieving look. "I'm good, but I've never tracked anything over that large of distance before."

"The Book of Breathings contains a spell that will allow you to amplify your power. I can teach you."

"What about him?" Roman questioned, nodding toward Nero. "He's a Nomarch, and yet you speak openly around him. Why should we trust him? What's going to keep him from running right back to the Council with everything he's hearing?"

Nero's cold eyes bored into Roman. "I may be a Nomarch, but I am not under the command of their bureaucracy. I answer to no one. I was the one that brought you this information, don't forget that."

"So you're just here out of the goodness of your heart?" Roman challenged. There was a pause as Roman stared at his father. My eyes cut to Sandra. Did she know the connection between these two men? It was entirely possible that Astrid had explained Roman's heritage, and if she had, Sandra could have told Nero. "How much are you being paid?" Roman pushed.

"Astrid and I came to an arrangement," Nero replied, confirming Roman's suspicions. Nero's loyalty had been purchased behind the rest of the Council's back. "I assure you, my men and I will do our part."

Roman scoffed, "For now. What happens when someone offers you a better price? The only thing you're loyal to is your pocketbook."

Nero took a challenging step forward, Roman standing up a little taller, ready for him to make a move. Before anything could happen, Sandra intervened, her voice hard. "Astrid needed someone connected, someone who wasn't corrupted by the other Nomarchs. Nero was the only new Nomarch we knew could be bought. He took this position to give me an opportunity to leave the island without arousing suspicion. As far as the rest of the Council is concerned, I'm still missing. Now, Nero has just as much reason as we do to kill Set, not to mention an army of men loyal to him. They will protect the area, protect the people here, while I train you to use the spells in the book. Nero will report back to the Council that you are doing as you were ordered, which will keep them off our back and from looking too closely at what we're really doing. Then, when the time is right, we will work together to track the was-sceptre and steal it before Set can get his hands on it."

"Make no mistake about it," Nero added, and I rolled my eyes. He seemed like the type of guy that always had to get the last word. "While Astrid and I may be *business partners*, I work for no one. I am a Nomarch and the Commander of the Coterie. I am the ultimate authority here. None of you will hunt a single wraith or use any magic without my authorization. I do not tolerate rebels or anarchy. You will fall to command, or you will suffer the consequences."

Gee, I thought. *This is going to be fun.*

It was late that night when I was woken by a pebble hitting my window. I sat up slowly, rubbing the sleep from my eyes before walking over to my window and peering out into the yard. Standing there was Isaac, his eyes bright with mischief. I pulled my window open. "What do you want?" I asked. I knew nothing was wrong. If there was, he wouldn't have bothered with a pebble, he would have just burst into my house.

"Get dressed," he shouted. "We're going out."

I ran my fingers through my ratty hair. "I'm tired Isaac. I'm going back to bed." The time change between Awen and Marienville had finally caught up to me and I was struggling to adjust.

"Stop being such an old lady," he taunted. "I'll give you five minutes, then I'm coming in after you."

I groaned, knowing he would do exactly what he said. "Fine." I pointed my finger at him. "But I'm taking more than five minutes and you better not come in here." I slammed the window shut on his laughter.

Fifteen minutes later, I emerged from the backdoor to find Isaac lounging on one of the porch seats, his eyes closed. He was dressed in dark wash jeans and a white shirt with a baby blue design that popped against his ebony skin.

I shut the door behind me and his eyes opened. They traveled over my outfit: black shirt, burgundy skinny jeans, and short boots. I hadn't done much with my hair, just combed it, throwing half of it up while the rest hung wild down my back. "You'll do," he teased, and I flipped him the bird in response. He hopped up from the chair, his eyes catching on the black band around my ankle where my ring daggers were neatly tucked away. "Expecting trouble?" he asked.

I smiled at him sweetly. "Always. Now, where are we going?"

He walked around to the front of the house and I followed closely behind. "For once, can't you just trust someone and go with it?"

I laughed ruefully, "Last time you told me to trust you, you flew me to the top of a mountain and then forced me to jump off of it."

Isaac let loose a genuine laugh and it echoed off the house, the sound so infectious I found myself smiling. "That is a gross over-exaggeration of what happened." He came to a stop near a familiar Jeep. I quickly searched my senses, but I didn't feel Roman anywhere nearby. "I borrowed it," Isaac said, as if he could read my mind. "Now, get in."

I listened, climbing in the passenger side. Isaac and I traveled down the back roads of Marienville, the windows of the Jeep down, allowing the crisp air of fall to reach us. Anyone else, it would have been too cold, but not for us. The cool air stirred my hair, and Isaac turned the music up as we traveled through the dark roads, headed for the small area that made up the town of Marienville. It had been so long since I'd ridden in a vehicle, since I had been able to relax and pretend for just a moment like I wasn't in the middle of an eternal war. I leaned my head back, allowing the music to overtake me. We passed through the town, making our way past the school and town library. When we reached the far side of town, I knew where we were headed. There was only one place to go over here.

Sure enough, just minutes later, we pulled up out front of Sandra's bar. When we'd left for Awen, Sandra had barely gotten it fixed up and operational again. There were only a few vehicles in the parking lot, but I could hear several voices inside, their joyous laughter reaching me all the way in the parking lot. I climbed out of the vehicle, looking at Isaac suspiciously. "What's going on?"

"We're taking the night off," he declared. We walked to the front door, my boots crunching on the gravel parking lot.

"War is coming, but not until the morning. Tonight, we celebrate." I smiled, as a night off sounded perfectly fine to me. Just before we reached the door, it flew open, a tiny blonde figure bursting through it.

"Lydia," I said, the shock clear in my voice. I had no idea she was going to be here. I froze, staring at my friend, unsure what to do. Lydia was dressed in a basic pair of jeans with a T-shirt, her hair pulled into a simple ponytail. It was a subtle look for someone like her, someone who often used fashion to make a statement. I wondered what had her dressing so conservatively. There was a clank, something sharp and breakable hitting the ground and before I knew it, Lydia took two quick steps my direction and wrapped her arms around me tightly. It took me a moment to realize what was happening, even longer for me to respond and hug my friend back. "I'm so sorry," I said, and I didn't think I'd ever meant anything as much as I did in that moment.

Lydia pulled back, smacking me across the arm. "Don't you ever do that to me again, Kyndal Davenport."

"Ow!"

Lydia put her hands on her hips in a familiar gesture. It was one I often saw when I'd done something to piss her off. "First you leave without saying goodbye, then you call out of the blue and give this epic goodbye speech. If you ever pull any crap like that again, I will kick your ass."

I looked at her, my eyebrows scrunched in confusion. "You're not mad at me anymore?"

"Isaac explained everything, and I'm just happy you're safe. And that you're home." She reached down and grabbed the bag of trash she had been carrying, the source of the earlier noise, and threw it over the edge of the dumpster before hooking her arm through mine and leading me into the bar, Isaac trailing behind.

The music was playing, filling the bar, the same country tune as always. Sandra stood behind the bar, pouring a beer for Darius, who carried it over to a nearby table where Allie was waiting for him. He gave her a quick kiss before placing the drink in front of her. The clink of billiards sounded on the other side of the bar where I found Mallory and Grady deep in a game of pool. There was money sitting on the edge of the table, that from the looks of it, Grady was about to claim. Brynn sat on a bar stool nearby, watching the game intently. Cassie was at the jukebox, dancing in place, her red hair swishing as she decided what to listen to next.

Isaac and Lydia moved to the bar, so I went directly to Allie, giving her a tight hug as I joined her and Darius at the table. She smiled up at me. "I was beginning to think you wouldn't join us. You were pretty cashed out."

I laughed. "With the time difference, I'm not even sure what time zone I'm in."

"You fought well today," Darius added in. "You are stronger than when you left for the island."

"Thank you, Darius." I reached over, grabbing a drink from Lydia as she and Isaac joined us at the table. I took a long draw from the beer, aware of my aunt's gaze on me the whole time. "What?" I asked her. "If I'm old enough to fight a chaos god, I think I'm old enough for a drink."

She squinted her eyes, studying me, before slowly lifting her own glass. "Hard to argue with that. But just for tonight," she added. I clinked my glass against hers in agreement.

"Perfect," Lydia giggled, clapping her hands together. "Shots all around!"

Hours later, I stumbled up to the bar, plopping myself onto a stool. Sandra smiled at me from the far side, pouring a glass of water and setting it down in front of me. I took it gratefully. "Thank you."

She smiled knowingly. "It looked like you could use it."

I chuckled, the sound of it echoing strangely in my ears. "Isaac and Darius talked me into playing quarters. You'd think with supernatural senses, I would've been better at it." I cringed a little when my last few words slurred. I took a large gulp of the water.

Sandra smiled. "One thing I've learned is that our supernatural skills do not extend to our decision making. Sometimes we're just as dumb as everyone else."

"A fact your son has proven to be true," I muttered, the words slipping out before I was able to stop them. I set my glass down. "I'm sorry, I shouldn't have said that."

"It's all right," she responded. "I have to admit I've noticed there is some tension between the two of you."

I scoffed. "That's putting it mildly."

"I know I've missed a lot during my time in the Hollow, but you can always talk to me."

I don't know if it was the alcohol buzzing through my system, or the fact that I was just happy to have Sandra home, but I slipped, telling her, "He wants to sever the Rafiq bond."

For a moment, she said nothing, instead only drying the glass in front of her, placing it neatly back on the bar. "Did he explain why?" she asked carefully.

"He thinks I'm a liability."

Sandra scrunched her eyebrows thoughtfully. "I've never known Roman to believe anyone else a liability, if anything there's a good chance it's the opposite."

I took another drink of the water in front of me, relieved to feel the alcohol beginning to leave my system. With our advanced healing, it took a lot for Kindred to get drunk, but tonight I was afraid I overdid it. "He thinks he's the liability?" I clarified.

"I know my son. And if he thinks he's the weak link, he'll do anything to change that. Even at great cost to himself."

"So you agree with him?" I pressed.

She shook her head. "I think the two of you are going to have to figure out what role your bond plays in your lives.

No one else can tell you what to do."

I took another long drink of water, Sandra kindly refilling the glass when I was done. "What do you think of Nero?" I asked her, changing the subject. "Do you trust him?"

Sandra let out an exasperated breath. "From what I can tell of the man, his reputation is well earned. Nero is known for his harsh, often times brutal ruling tactics."

"I saw him bury a dagger in a man's shoulder for disagreeing with him," I interrupted.

"I'm not saying I agree with his tactics, not by any means, but he is the leader of a great army," she continued. "An army we desperately need. War isn't pretty, Kyndal. It's sloppy and horrific and during war you are sometimes asked to make impossible decisions. Right now, we need someone hard like Nero who can make the tough calls."

I knew I was being biased, that my disdain for him mainly came from his relation to Roman and the potential pain he could cause him, but I couldn't help it. "I think he's horrible," I mumbled.

"So is the enemy," Sandra answered, her voice hard as stone. "And sometimes it takes someone willing to do horrible things to defeat them."

I grabbed my water, emptying it as I stood up, Sandra's words settling in. Was Nero a necessary evil? Could he and his men be what tipped the scale in the war to come? The alcohol in my system started to wane, just enough for me to get a hint of the bond that had been muted for the last several hours. Now aware of it, I could feel the cool breeze pulling me outside, to the man I knew was waiting. "Thank you. It's nice to have you back."

"Anytime," she responded. "Tell Roman I expect to speak to him soon."

I nodded, before turning to walk through the bar, past my friends and toward the gravel parking lot. I shut the door tightly behind me, moving slowly over to where Roman leaned against his bike, his head tilted back looking up at the brightly lit moon.

"Nice night for a ride," I said in greeting.

"I wasn't left with much of a choice," he responded. "Isaac stole my Jeep."

I giggled as I came closer, placing my hand on the bike, near his.

His eyes dropped, searching my face, no doubt surprised by how close I stood to him. I'd been avoiding any sort of contact with him for a while. "So, I talked to Sandra," I began, letting the sentence drop, even as I kept my eyes trained down on the bike, tracing the yellow pinstripe as it cut through the onyx paint.

"I heard," he admitted.

I looked up at him, his blue eyes shining in the moonlight. I reached past him, grabbing the helmet off the handlebars. "Let's go for a ride."

"Now?" he asked, surprised.

"Why not?" I teased. "Come on, it's beautiful out." We had a lot to talk about, but I didn't want to talk. Not yet.

"Where do you want to go?"

I shrugged, "I don't know. Take me somewhere new. Take me to your favorite place."

He studied me a moment, then his patented sideways smirk appeared. "All right." He straddled the bike, revving the engine. "But you're going to have to hold on tight, I don't feel like driving the speed limit."

His excitement was contagious, and I found myself smiling back. "Perfect."

17

By the time Roman brought the bike to a stop, we'd been riding for nearly an hour. We'd left Marienville almost immediately, traveling northeast along Route 66, going deeper into the Allegheny. I held tight to Roman as we wound through parts of the forest I'd never seen before. Just as he promised, we were going too fast for me to be able to admire the scenery, but as he slowed, turning on a small dirt road, I caught a glimpse of a wide trail just inside the undergrowth.

I dismounted the bike, unclasped my helmet, and hung it on the peg of the now quiet motorcycle. "This is your favorite place?" I questioned, looking around curiously. The moon was high, but underneath such large old growth trees, its light was muted, only appearing in slivers. I had to pull on a piece of my power to be able to see fully.

Roman took a few steps ahead. "It's a little further still. The trail here is part of the Great Allegheny Passage. It's a series of over 900 miles of trails that connect through the forest." I followed him as he started down the trail, my enhanced hearing picking up on a variety of sounds, including running water.

"I don't know how long we should be gone. The others might come looking for us." It wasn't that I didn't want to be out with Roman, I was just constantly plagued by the fear of us being caught.

"They'll be drinking for several more hours. And if Sandra's pouring, they'll all be too drunk to even notice we're gone. Was that Allie's voice I heard inside the bar tonight?" he asked, changing the subject.

I took a few quick steps to catch up, matching my stride with his. "Yes, she was there with Darius."

"Darius?" he repeated.

I nodded. "Apparently they're a couple now."

"Huh," he replied drolly. "It must be nice to see her again after so many months away. I'm sure you missed her."

"I don't think I realized how much until I got back here. This place is just so different than Awen was. I hated the island. There was too much politics, too much maneuvering. Everyone always wanted something from me, or only pretended to care so they could use my position to their advantage. Allie doesn't care about any of that, in fact if she had her way, she'd prefer I didn't have any involvement with the Kindred. It's nice to have one person who just cares about *me*."

Suddenly, Roman quit walking. He grabbed me by the arm and spun me around. The move caught me off guard and I stumbled forward, falling against his chest. He steadied me, using one arm to hold me in place, while the other hand gently cupped my chin, forcing my head up, and my eyes to reach his. "I don't care about any of that stuff. I never have. Your lineage is of no interest to me, and I've only ever cared about your powers in hopes that that strength will protect you. That it will help you survive because there is no room for weakness in this world. You could drag your dagger across your brand right now and lose every single one of your powers and my feelings wouldn't change."

Momentarily stunned speechless, I slowly tucked a piece of hair behind my ear as my eyes remained fixed to Roman's lips. His words were beautiful, exactly what I wanted to hear from him. But at the same time, I remembered his desire to sever the bond, to be parted from me just as clearly. Roman must have sensed my hesitation, because just as quickly as he pulled me in, he let go of my arm, separating himself from me.

I wavered briefly, having to work to maintain my balance before continuing on and following Roman down the path, this time a little slower as my mind whirled. The words were on the tip of my tongue—it should be easy to ask him why he wanted to break the bond—but I couldn't ask the question. I was too scared to know the answer. Maybe Sandra was wrong and Roman did truly see me as a liability. If that was true, I didn't think I could handle hearing it. We carried on in silence for a while, both of us stuck in our own thoughts, until Roman broke it again.

"Can I ask you something?"

"Okay," I agreed, not sure what it would be. Not after that last speech he'd made.

"Tell me about your visions. You haven't spoken about them in a while, but I know they haven't stopped." Of course he knew. No matter how much distance was between us, he still felt the residual effects of my visions.

"They haven't changed much. I see the same cave, the same two tunnels, and I hear the water running in them, like there are rivers hidden within. Anytime I go near one though, I don't make it very far before I drop to my knees, completely overcome by fear."

"And you don't see any clues to what causes it?"

"I saw an inscription on the wall once, but it was written in hieroglyphics. It could be a warning of some kind, or maybe an explanation—you know—instructions on what to do, but I can't read it. There was a painting above it. I'm pretty sure it was the same goddess I saw fighting Set in that book, but this time she had giant colorful wings."

Roman turned slightly my way. "Colorful wings? Was she seated, one leg tucked under the other?"

I nodded. "Yeah, how'd you know?"

"Many of the ancient gods took on animal forms, but there was really only one goddess that took the form of a bird. Sworn enemy of Set and consort to Hermes Trismegistus, the goddess Maat."

"As in Maat's Hollow?" I asked. "As in Goddess of the Blacklands?"

He nodded. "This could be a very good thing. If your visions are showing you a temple honoring Maat, it's possible it could be the place we're looking for. You need to tell Sandra about your visions."

"All right," I agreed. I had already thought of that. My mother had told me the temple was built for the first Guard. Sandra might be the only living person with any information to add. "Come with me. We'll talk to her together."

Roman shook his head, his eyes not meeting mine. "Do it alone. You don't need me."

I came to a stop in the middle of the path, crossing my arms stubbornly. "Why are you avoiding Sandra? You should be thrilled that she's back."

Roman turned around, his arms falling to his side in defeat. "I am thrilled."

"You're not acting like it," I challenged. "You've barely said two words directly to her. Instead, you've just been hiding in shame."

"I never said I was ashamed," he said defensively.

"Of course you did," I retorted. "You might as well have screamed it, it came so clearly through that bond you hate so much. What is your problem?"

He growled in frustration. "I don't know what to say to her.

She went to Awen and broke her exile because of me. She was thrown into the Hollow because she was trying to help me. If I'd never been possessed in the first place, that never would've happened to her."

"Man, you are annoyingly self-righteous."

His eyes blazed at my words. "Excuse me?"

"Seriously. You can make almost absolutely anything about you. News flash Roman—there are other people out there, and they're allowed to make decisions too." He scoffed, turning and walking away. I followed. "You're doing the same thing trying to sever the bond. Something goes wrong and you find a way to blame yourself, then make a choice that affects everyone under the bullshit pretense that it's for the greater good."

"Is this why you wanted to go for a ride?" he questioned, his voice tight with constrained anger. "So you could yell at me?"

"No, but it worked out didn't it?" I snipped.

He paced a few steps toward the edge of the trail before wheeling back, pointing at me, his voice full of fire. "For the record, I don't hate our bond and it kills me to think of severing it, but I can't take the chance that you being connected to me will be what gets you killed. It's already almost cost you your life."

"That bond is the reason you're alive. You would have died without it."

"A price I would have gladly paid if it meant you were spared."

"You think that makes it better, don't you? As if your death wouldn't affect me if we were no longer bonded. Rafiq or not, you do not get to sacrifice yourself to save me. I won't allow it."

He dug his hands into his hair. "What do you want from me?"

"Quit trying to fix everything by yourself. If you always try to protect me, it's going to end up getting someone else hurt."

He huffed a large breath, staring off into the forest, toward the sound of the water I could hear moving on the other side of the trees. The muscle in his jaw pulsed, and I waited as he chewed on his answer. "Fine. I will do what you want, but only on one condition. If the bond weighs us down again, if it keeps us from protecting people, we find a way to sever it. I don't need it to know how I feel about you."

I moved closer, putting my arms around him. Our first real touch in almost a week. "Deal," I agreed, leaning up on my tiptoes and pressing my lips to his. He returned the gesture, his hands snaking around my waist and pulling me closer, deepening the kiss. The bond swirled around us, a fire-kissed breeze, chasing away the small chill in the air. I pulled away from him slowly, smiling up at him. "Now, where is this special spot of yours?"

He smiled back at me, the first smile of pure joy I'd seen

from him in a while. He nodded over my head, toward the glen of trees behind me. "Behind you." I turned, scanning the area but saw nothing of note. Behind me, Roman wrapped his arms around me. As I continued my search, he chuckled, the deep rumble shaking through his chest. "Not there." He pointed up, into the thick of the tree canopy. "There." I squinted, following his guide. It took a moment, but eventually the outline of a small treehouse took shape, hidden among the boughs of an ancient sycamore. "Want to see it?" he whispered, his breath tickling my ear.

I nodded enthusiastically. "There's no ladder."

Roman grabbed my hand, guiding me to the base of the tree. "Isaac told me you went cliff diving in Awen. Remember how you reached the top?"

The wind was already picking up—my feet coming off the forest floor—a small giggle escaped. Next thing I knew, I was standing on the small deck of the treehouse, Roman's feet landing a heartbeat later. The structure was larger than I originally thought, big enough to seat half a dozen people comfortably, tall enough for Roman to stand without ducking. There were blankets laid out along the opposite wall, a few used candles scattered in the corner. The fourth wall was missing, open to a deck that overlooked a nearby river. I stepped inside, admiring the craftsmanship, the feel of the planks under my fingertips. "This place is beautiful."

"When I was fourteen, Ezekiel and Sandra were fed up with my attitude. Ezekiel was putting me through never-ending drills trying to beat me into submission, but I just kept digging in my heels and pushing back at him. Cassie was living here at that time, so one day, she offered to train me instead. I jumped at the opportunity to get away from Ezekiel, but instead of sparring, she drug me to a nearby hardware store. By the time we left, we'd purchased all the raw materials needed to build this. Then she drove me out here and told me to pick a tree. I still didn't understand what we were doing, so of course I picked the biggest, tallest, oldest one I could find. She unloaded the materials and tools at the foot of the tree, then left me here. She didn't return until the next night."

"She left you out here alone?" I asked. It didn't sound like something Cassie would do.

Roman laughed at my shock. "If you knew me then, you wouldn't blame her for it. I was a real pain in the ass. That night, it rained so hard Cherry Run almost crested its banks. I didn't have as much control of my power then, so I had only managed to get four planks moved up into the canopy before the onslaught. I slept huddled up on them, high in the tree, trying to use the leaves as rain cover."

"What happened when she came back?" I asked, enjoying the peek inside Roman's history.

"She brought me back to the compound, fed me, allowed me to change my sopping wet clothes, then dropped me back here. We kept doing that until I finished the treehouse. Took me almost three weeks. By the time I was done, I was too tired to be angry and Ezekiel had no problem whipping me into shape. I started performing better during training, my elemental control improved, and six months later I started going on missions. Although, I admit I did sneak off to the treehouse every so often, less and less over the years, but I still come here when I'm seeking solace."

"When was the last time you came here?"

"When you used your powers for the first time," he admitted. "After you yelled at me that night, I retreated here, determined to brood alone. Cassie eventually tracked me down, forcing her way into the treehouse, a bottle of liquor tucked in her backpack. She yelled at me for not telling her about you, then got me completely hammered and let me whine about how I'd failed you."

I laughed. "She came to my house the next morning, trying to convince me to forgive you. I was so angry when she said she'd spent all night with you. I thought she was your girlfriend."

Roman's laugh joined mine. "You were jealous."

"I never said that," I defended myself. "You'd just taken me on a date. I thought you were a player."

"It's okay," he teased. "You can admit it. You were crazy about me, even then."

I scoffed, smacking his arm playfully, but he was faster than me. He grabbed my hand, tugging me forward. I didn't resist, instead allowing him to pull me flush to his body. "Careful with the ego, Roman. If your head gets any bigger, you may not fit in the treehouse anymore."

He laughed, the sound echoing in the small space, even as he brought his mouth down slowly, kissing me lazily. I returned the gesture, brushing my tongue lightly over his lips. A groan rumbled in the back of his throat, his hands tightening on my hips. I pulled my hands from around his neck, trailing them down his chest until I reached the edge of his T-shirt. I twisted the soft fabric in my fingers then slowly began to lift. He didn't stop me, his lips breaking contact only long enough for me to remove the shirt. I pushed up onto my tiptoes, placing small butterfly kisses along his neck, over his newly repaired collarbone, ending at the burn marks left from his resurrection.

Too swiftly for me to see it coming, Roman dropped, hooking his arm under my knees, scooping me up into his arms. Three strides later, we'd reached the pile of blankets and he laid me down gently before settling himself next to me. I reached for him, wrapping my hand around his neck and pulling his mouth back to mine. It was slow at first. Sweet. Both of us happy to take our time, knowing this was one of our few opportunities to be together without fear of discovery. It wasn't until I reached forward, hooking my fingers in the loops of his jeans and pulling him to me, that he lost control on whatever leash he'd been keeping on himself. There were two thuds on the wooden floor, he'd kicked his boots off, and I quickly moved to do the same. He climbed up to his knees, holding himself over me as he reached for the edge of my shirt. I sat forward, allowing him to peel it off me. The rest of our clothes soon followed, and we spent the night lost in each other, only the sounds of the forest keeping us company.

Later, much later, when the sky started to turn from black to a light shade of purple, I laid curled under the blankets, my fingers moving idly up and down Roman's naked back. I stared at the candles in the corner, my power calling to them as my hand moved. I lit the wicks as my hand traveled toward his neck, extinguished them as they traced back down his spine, the process repeating until I felt the bond settle into a satisfied slumber. Roman's chest expanded, a deep sigh escaping. Just before sleep claimed him, he whispered, "I love you Kyndal."

I smiled softly, reaching up and kissing his shoulder. "I love you too."

18

We didn't get much sleep. We left while it was still early morning, Roman dropping me off at home before heading back to the compound. The house was still quiet, the kitchen showing no signs of use as I moved through, quickly grabbing a bagel before heading upstairs. I paused outside Allie's door, listening. It wasn't like her to sleep past sunrise, but I could hear her soft breathing, so I cracked the door open to peer inside. She was sprawled out on top her covers, still dressed in the same clothes from the night before. It looked like Roman was right—Sandra's drinks were deadly.

I took a quick shower then dressed in fighting gear, including my leather vest and daggers. I parted my hair, putting it in two French braids, in an effort to keep it out of my way. Today was our first day practicing magic with Sandra, I had no idea what to expect.

When I came back down the stairs, I found Allie sitting at the kitchen table, her coffee mug steaming in front of her.

"Good morning!"

She startled, grabbing the front of her head. "Not so loud," she whined.

I laughed, opening up the nearby cabinet and grabbing a bottle of aspirin. "Rough night?" I teased, setting the medicine in front of her.

"Kindred can really hold their liquor." She shook two pills free then quickly tossed them back. "What happened to you last night?"

"Oh, um," I hesitated. I hadn't thought of what I'd tell everyone yet. "I came home early. I knew we'd be training first thing this morning and wanted to get a good night sleep." I cringed internally at my ridiculously lame excuse.

"All right then. So you're headed to the compound?" Whether she actually believed me, or was just too hungover to push it, I wasn't sure, but I counted my blessings and happily moved on from the subject.

"Sandra is going to teach us to use The Book of Breathings. I'll be gone most of the day." I reached for the back door.

"What about school?" The question brought me up short. I turned toward my aunt who had her hands up defensively. "I'm just asking. You didn't finish your junior credits, and this year has already started. Don't you want to graduate?"

I huffed a breath. I had known this conversation was coming, but I was hoping to avoid it for a little longer. School was a sore subject for me. It was one of the normal things being Kindred had taken away from me. Before my family died, I had plans to go to college and become a writer. Something that was never going to happen. Not anymore. "Of course I want to graduate. The world's just been too crazy. When things settle down, I'll go back. I promise."

"When will that be?" she pushed.

"I don't know," I snapped, my tone harsher than I intended. I took a deep, calming breath. "I don't know," I repeated. "If I survive Set, I'll have plenty of time to go back to school. It's not like I'm getting any older." I ripped open the back door, slamming it shut behind me, bringing an abrupt end to the conversation.

The run through the forest was quick, the path between my house and the compound familiar. My boots crunched on top of the dead leaves blanketing the trail, so I wasn't surprised when the Coterie guards heard me coming, stopping me when I reached the funeral pyres not far from the compound. I intended to walk right past them when one stepped in front of me. It was the soldier Mallory had fought the day before. He was still sporting a sharp cut across the bridge of his nose, courtesy of her dagger hilt. "Where have you been?" he demanded, his voice rough.

I raised an eyebrow at his tone. "Home." My temper was already sharp from my conversation with Allie. I stepped around him.

"You shouldn't be in the forest alone. It isn't safe for little girls like you." The threat in his voice was clear and it was obvious it wasn't wraiths he thought I should be concerned about.

I clenched my fist before turning around, glaring at him. "How's your nose feel? It still looks a little crooked."

His hand reached for his dagger, but the other soldier stepped forward, placing a cautioning hand on his elbow. "We have orders from the Commander," he said quietly.

I gave him a smug smile before flipping him the bird and continuing on to the compound.

When I reached the training rings, Mallory and Isaac were already hard at work. Mallory was using her patented split staff, Isaac, a short sword. I sat down on the bench near the ring to watch. From here, I could feel the bond stronger than ever, almost as if being with Roman last night had strengthened it. There was a moment of recognition on his end, and I knew Roman had just realized I was here. I could tell he was in his house, even tell he was upstairs in the loft. It took all my willpower not to look through the back window to see if I was right. I knew after last night I would have to work extra hard to distance myself from him and keep the others from suspecting we were together. The bond grew stronger, until I no longer needed it to know he was headed outside. The sound of his footsteps hitting the stairs told me he was on his way.

"Making friends again, Davenport?" Isaac asked as he parried an attack from Mallory, effectively pulling me away from the silent conversation with Roman.

I smiled. "You know me, people can't resist my sparkling

personality. Although, that particular brute was Mallory's bestie, not mine."

A wicked smile crossed her lips, even as she continued to do battle with Isaac. "Coterie ego gets them every time." My eyebrows furrowed slightly. From her remark, it sounded like that hadn't been her first encounter with the Coterie. Mallory's left arm lashed out, her staff smacking into the back of Isaac's knees. He fell face up on the sand. Mallory's right arm came down with lightning speed, the other half of the staff now at Isaac's throat in a decisive kill shot. He growled in frustration at being bested, but Mallory only laughed, reveling in her win. She reached down, helping him up before exiting the training ring. I hopped off the bench to join her.

She eyed me suspiciously. "Can I help you?"

"I owe you an apology."

She turned to face me fully, her arms crossed, even as she kept the metal staff in hand. "I'm listening."

"I'm sorry I didn't tell you what was going on in Awen. You are a good friend, and I shouldn't have kept the truth from you."

"Do you think that's all I'm mad at you for?"

Yes, I thought. "No?" I said aloud.

"You put yourself in unnecessary danger insisting you go into the Hollow alone. I'm mad at you because if you wouldn't have kept me from going with you, I could have protected you. I could have kept Daniela from getting hurt."

"Astrid wouldn't let me. . ."

"You didn't trust me," Mallory snipped cutting me off. "I understand you have orders, but you can't just use people for your own gains. You should have trusted me enough to help you."

"I'm sorry," I repeated quietly. "You're right. It won't happen again."

She nodded once. "Good," she said with finality.

"So," I hedged. "Are we good now?"

Mallory raised an eyebrow, a cool trick I wished I could do. "We'll see."

Just then the door to the main house opened and all the others emerged—Nero, Sandra, Grady, Brynn, and Cassie. Grady held The Book of Breathings tightly under his arm, his eyes scanning over me, squinted in concentration. They jumped to Roman's house as I heard the back door open. Grady gave him the same look as he did me, his mouth pursed in annoyance.

"Guard, center ring," Nero commanded. None of us argued, each of us taking position, Roman and I careful to stand apart from one another.

Sandra moved in front of us. "The first thing you must know about the book, is that while overall it operates very similarly to using your elements, there is one startling difference. When we use our elements, we pull from the well of power inside us, and when that well is empty, our powers no longer work. The spells inside The Book of Breathings will begin by syphoning your power, but if you run your power source dry, it will not stop the spell. The magic will find another energy source, any source it can. It will begin to feed on your life force, just as a wraith would. The stronger the spell, or the longer you try to make one last, the more power it will steal from you. Choose a spell over your skill level, or push too hard to maintain one, and the spells will drain you completely, killing you in the process."

"How do we keep that from happening?" Brynn asked.

"By sharing your power with each other," Sandra answered. "The Nomarch Council banned magic centuries ago because the standard soldier can't generate enough energy to sustain the spells, but the Guard is different. You four are bound together through oath and blood. You can share your energy, so when one casts a spell, the others can open their power sources as a conduit and keep those channels open, lending strength to the caster, even in the heat of battle."

"So what do we do?" Roman asked, ever the practical one.

"You begin by thinking of your powers as a muscle, as something you can train to make stronger. You must be able to maintain your own strength before you can expect to link with anyone else. All it takes is the proper motivation." Sandra pointed to the open space in front of her. "Kyndal, step forward." I did as instructed. "Throw a fireball at me."

"Excuse me?" I questioned.

"You heard me," she responded. "Do it."

Hesitantly, I called to my power, creating a small fireball in my right hand. I waited for her to move, to drop down into a defensive stance, or to do something that showed she was prepared to fend off my attack, but she didn't. Instead she stood there casually, her stance loose. I took a deep breath and loosed the fireball. Right on track, it flew for her head, and yet still she didn't budge. Her only movement came from the slight murmuring of her lips and it was then I understood what she was doing. Sure enough, mere inches away from her face, the fireball stopped, bouncing off an invisible forcefield and extinguishing. Where the fireball once was, there was now a slight shimmering of multi-colored light that reflected the sunlight before disappearing again. Sandra had never intended to let the fireball hit her, but rather to give a demonstration.

"What was that?" I asked.

"A shielding spell," she answered to all of us. "One that can be performed to protect yourself or another warrior from elemental attacks. This particular one takes limited energy and can only be used once. The incantation must be repeated if you are to use it again. You are not fighting normal wraiths anymore. When you go up against a hybrid, it's imperative that you can shield yourself from their elemental attacks." Sandra gestured to Grady, taking the book from him as he stepped forward silently. She flipped directly to a page, one no doubt etched in her memory. "This spell will be your first task."

For the next several hours, well into midafternoon, we practiced that spell. We paired off with other fighters, each Guardsman working with someone different. No weapons—only magic to defend ourselves. Mallory had taken up across from me, using this exercise as an opportunity to pay me back for the pain I'd caused her. Even after the apology, it was her way of leveling the score. Mallory was a warrior, taught her whole life to settle things on the battlefield. I didn't hold it against her. I understood how much damage I'd done to our relationship, and if this is what she needed to trust me again, it was something I would gladly endure.

She pushed her power out at me again, just as she had done countless times before. I quickly whispered the words Sandra taught us, and I felt the shield snap around me just before the pressure of her power pushed against it. The shield absorbed the attack, but this time, the strength of her element overwhelmed it, and my feet slid backward in the sand. I held strong to the spell, even as I could feel it draining my power, imagining the shield to be a real thing that I held in front of me, blocking her assault. This type of magic was different than using my element. Fire was wild, often times flying out of me in large bursts of energy. To keep my shield up, to keep it in shape and hold it strong, was a more subtle form of power that required concentration, endurance, and finesse.

And finesse was so not my thing.

With all my focus on the shield, I never saw the strike coming. Mallory moved, feigning to my right, her metal staff drawn. It connected with my side, slamming into my abdomen and knocking all the air out of my lungs. I doubled over, grabbing at what I was pretty sure was a cracked rib. I immediately lost concentration and dropped the shield, leaving myself vulnerable to Mallory's element. The strength of the wind blew me off my feet, dumping me unceremoniously on my ass five feet back.

All activity in the ring stopped immediately. I staggered to my feet, clutching my side as sand poured off my body. I glared at Mallory, who stood there, a smug look on her face that dared me to complain. My eyes flared a livid red, a fireball forming in my hand almost unconsciously. What power wasn't fueling the fire, rushed to my ribs, dulling the pain. A pulse of protectiveness came from across the ring, and from the corner of my eye, Roman took a step closer. "That was a cheap shot," I accused Mallory.

"I wasn't aware there were rules," she countered, her tone daring me to loose the fireball. My power surged down my arm, the fireball growing in response to her taunt.

"Enough!" Sandra shouted. "Stand down both of you." She moved closer, standing in-between the two of us. Slowly I pulled back on my power, the fireball diminishing. Her voice sounded over the sand. "It is not enough to focus on your element during battle. You must be aware of what your magic is doing, while simultaneously protecting yourself from a physical attack. Drop your guard for a *single moment*, and you leave yourself vulnerable. If she had been using a stronger spell, that one moment could've been the difference between life and death." She looked to Mallory. "Well done," she praised, and I gritted my teeth in response to it. Nero stepped into the center of the ring, standing shoulder to shoulder with Sandra. Mallory sauntered past me, pausing to whisper in my ear, "Now we're good."

I bit the inside of my cheek to keep from responding. Leave it to Mallory to find a violent way to level the score. Instead, I eyed Nero and Sandra, Roman's real father and his adoptive mother. How different would Roman be if Nero had raised him in the Coterie. Sandra, even in the short time I'd known her, had always appeared sharp-witted and fiercely loyal, traits Roman shared. Nero was a fierce warrior, I couldn't dispute that, but he held no such loyalty to the people around him. Would he have taught his son to be as cold and unfeeling as he was?

"The Guard is meant to be a single cohesive unit," Nero said, his brusque tone cutting through the air. "Even with your magic, you do not stand a chance of defeating Set unless you learn to fight together. Now, I saw you four fight in Siberia. You are strong individually, but you do not work together, instead you fumble over each other blindly, giving the enemy an unnecessary advantage. You must learn to fight as one, learn to trust the soldier next to you or I guarantee, you will die as individuals."

"This time, you will not shield just yourself from an attack, but each other. A shield made by two is twice as difficult to break through. Grady, Roman, center ring." Sandra ordered.

The men staggered to the center of the sandy ring, each of them visibly drained from the magic they'd been pulling on. Through the bond, I could feel Roman's uncertainty and distrust in the man he'd been paired with. Even after all his speeches about how we needed to work together, he was still just as unsure as I was. Nero gave a quick gesture to one of his men standing by, and he rushed over, handing both men a dagger, just as Nero pulled his sword from the scabbard. It was the same dark blade Sandra had used when pretending to be him. I wondered again at the story behind the unique blade.

With another unspoken signal, four more Coterie soldiers moved into position, flanking their commander on either side, their weapons drawn. A deep pit formed in my stomach. I didn't like the looks of this at all. My eyes cut to Brynn, her fist clenched, ready to move in. I stepped forward to interfere, but Nero turned sharply to both of us. "Do not interfere with the fight in any way. Ignore my command, and I promise, they will suffer for it." I halted my advance, but kept my eyes pinned to the men in center ring, heeding Nero's command, for the moment. *A necessary evil,* I reminded myself.

Grady and Roman both dipped their heads, speaking the simple words Sandra had taught us. Through the bond, I felt Roman's power swirl faintly to life, the strength of it waned after the day's grueling work. My heart twisted, wishing I could do something to help. He adjusted the grip on his dagger, preparing himself for the battle as Nero and his men closed in. I expected the attack to be elemental, for Nero to try and break their shields first, but instead, he drove right at them, sword first. Roman parried the attack, pushing back at his father, a blast of air knocking him back. No sooner did Nero fall back a step, then the other men closed in, two swiping at Grady, the other two at Roman. Metal clanged through the clearing as the men went to war. Grady and Roman for all their strength were no match for the overwhelming numbers stacked against them.

It was Nero that drew first blood, his obsidian blade cutting through the meat of Roman's arm, a growl ripping from behind his lips. The echo of it tore at my own flesh, and I hissed in pain, Brynn's eyes darting to where the fresh wound opened up out of nowhere. The bond pulled taut in pain and I called a piece of my power, healing my own wound, slowing the bleeding to a small dribble. Usually, I would've calmed my power, returning it to my core, but this time I didn't keep it to myself. Instead, I held tight to the bond, sending part of my strength down it, directly to Roman. I wasn't sure exactly what I was doing, but I concentrated on that tether between the two of us, sending every ounce of strength I could muster toward the other end of it. Sandra said the Guard were the only Kindred in the world that could share power. Roman and I were connected in other ways as well, the Rafiq bond forever tethering us to each other. If I could share power with anyone, it had to be him. I pushed my power again, this time until I felt it reach Roman's, the cool touch of his power familiar and soothing even now. As soon as my power made contact with his, it took hold, rushing out of me eagerly to assist him.

There was an instant change in Roman. Where before he had been faltering under the strength of Nero and his men, now he powered forward with renewed energy. His magical shield held strong, protecting both him—and now, combined with my strength—stretching to include Grady. Connected to him in this way, I could feel it as if it were my own, could feel how Roman held it closed tight, not letting a single ounce of outward attack penetrate the shield. It took Grady a moment longer to notice that something was different, that their attacks weren't making it through anymore, but to his credit, he didn't waste a moment of the advantage. His eyes glowing a beautiful earthen green, he gathered his power, uprooting a nearby tree and flinging the giant at his opponents. The trunk slammed into the soldiers, pinning them beneath the bark. Nero was the only one to escape, the only one fast enough to roll out of the way. Now with the advantage, Grady and Roman pressed forward, their daggers flying out at Nero with speed so impressive that without my enhanced senses, I wouldn't haven't been able to follow their movements. Not wanting to be the weak link, I focused on the bond with Roman, making sure it stayed open and my power stayed available to him. I didn't know how much he was taking and honestly didn't care. He could have it all if that's what it took to win this fight.

Nero landed a strong left hook to Grady's face, the hilt of his sword clanging off his cheekbone, dropping Grady to his knees. As Nero turned to defend himself from Roman, he was met with an uppercut boosted with a burst of air. Nero flew up and landed flat on his back.

Slowly, I pulled my power back, not wanting to shock Roman when it disappeared, in case it had an adverse effect on him. As I felt the power return to me, I looked to the men that now stood side by side in the ring, each of them bleeding, their chests heaving with exertion. My heart swelled with pride, not just for the man I loved, but for both of them.

Roman and Grady had won.

19

We were given the rest of the day off. According to Sandra, we had to work up our stamina when using magic and rest was just as important as training was. If we didn't properly hydrate, rest, and restore our bodies, we were more likely to deplete our power sources and screw up a spell. Almost as soon as she'd said it, I heard my stomach growl, demanding sustenance. I thought of the fully stocked fridge just a short distance away inside Roman's house, but when I saw Brynn moving the other direction, I begrudgingly forced my stomach to wait, and followed her.

I caught up quickly, lightly placing my hand on her shoulder. She turned to look at me, subtly moving The Book of Breathings to the other arm as if I might take it from her. "Can I talk to you a moment?" I asked.

She looked at me in clear surprise, a response I couldn't really blame her for. Brynn and I had a rough history to say the least, and now that I thought about it, we'd never had a single private conversation since The Blinding, something that at this point, with everything going on, was long overdue.

She nodded. "Okay." I led her through the tree line, out to the clearing that housed our funeral pyres. It was far enough away from the compound that I knew the others wouldn't be able to hear us. In the distance, I could hear the Coterie soldiers splitting off into their patrols, running the boundary they'd set through the Allegheny. I didn't worry about them, knowing they would pay us no attention. According to Darius, Marienville had been quiet since we returned—quiet for weeks—without a single wraith sighting. Typically when the bad guys went silent, it was because they were planning something. Something big. I felt a small amount of relief knowing the Coterie soldiers were thorough and incessant in their pursuit of the enemy. If there were wraiths out there, they would find them.

I pointed at the book. "You going to do more translating work?"

"Having Sandra here to help has cut through the majority of the work, but there are still some spells her Guard never managed to translate. We've been doing what we can, but the more advanced ones are written partially in what we think is a dead language. It looks similar to Ancient Greek, so we're going to try and translate it to that first, so Sandra and I can read it. Then, we'll be able to translate it to English for the rest of you."

"Anything about how Set was imprisoned?"

She shook her head. "Not yet. We were concerned there

was no record of how it happened, but then Sandra made the point that there has to be a record somewhere. Otherwise, how would Ezekiel have known how to release him?"

A good point.

"How did you get to be so good at all this?" I asked her. I realized as soon as I said it, that I knew very little about Brynn; where she came from, when she was branded, how old she truly was. Brynn chuckled, giving me the first real smile I'd ever seen out of her, and I realized how abrupt my question sounded. I returned the smile with a tentative one of my own. "I'm sorry, it's just how do you know all this stuff about dead languages and spells?"

"I was raised in South London. My father was British, while my mother was born in Nigeria. African. They met while working for the British Museum. My mother was an archaeologist with a love for adventure and my father specialized in preserving and translating ancient tomes. I spent most of my childhood inside that museum, sitting with them through all hours of the night as they worked to decode the newest arrival at the museum. To keep me entertained, my dad would give me pieces of what he was working on to see if I could crack it. Ancient Greek, Arabic, Sanskrit, whatever it was. He started out small with just a word or two, but as I grew older, he started giving me more, until eventually I was working on entire pages of ancient texts on my own. They were like puzzles, codes that needed to be cracked. I would pore over them for hours, sometimes days, insistent that I get them right."

"What happened to them?" I couldn't help but ask it.

Brynn shrugged. "The same thing that always happens. They died." Her words were blunt. "Not too long after, the Kindred found me and brought me to Awen." She took a deep breath, clearing away the memories. "What do you need, Kyndal?"

"I wanted to see if you found anything about the location of the temple we're looking for?"

She gave me a blank stare. "In the two days since we've been working on it? No."

I ignored her tone. I deserved it, asking a stupid question like that. "I want to help. What are we doing to narrow it down?"

"It's a variety of things. Mainly we're just scouring old texts, looking for any references to the sceptre while Grady works on his tracking ability. There's a channeling spell in there that will help him amplify his strength, but he hasn't been able to project far enough to get us a lead." I nodded, my eyes glazing over in thought. "Why all the questions?" Brynn asked me.

I shrugged, unsure. "It's probably nothing. I've been having these dreams, kind of like visions. I wake up underground in what I thought was a cave, but now, thanks to Roman I think it may be a temple. There's a carving of Maat painted above a doorway that leads to a set of ascending stairs. On the wall beside me is a bunch of hieroglyphics, although obviously I don't know what they say. Do you think maybe that could be where the sceptre is?"

"It's possible," she agreed. "Maat was the sworn enemy of Set, his opposite in almost every way. It would make sense for it to be hidden in a temple dedicated to her. One she knew would be protected."

"Does that help narrow it down?" I wasn't a brilliant strategist like Roman or a genius level brainiac like Brynn, but it felt good to help.

Brynn thought for a moment. "Some. But like I said, there were dozens of temples, lots of which have been ruined through the years. It's a starting point though. I found a firsthand account, written by someone who supposedly served in a temple, but it's hard to understand what he's saying. Too bad we can't just ask him."

I had been staring into the trees as she spoke, but at her final words, my head whipped around. "What did you say?"

She furrowed her brow. "I said, it's too bad we can't just ask someone who's been there."

"I can." My words were quiet and thoughtful, as my mind was already working to put together a plan.

Brynn cocked her head to the side. "I don't understand."

I can talk to him, I thought. My ancestor Marius was the first Descendant, and in the Guard. He fought against Set, maybe even helped defeat him. If anyone knew where the temple was, it would be him. I reached out, grabbing

Brynn's arm, my eyes no doubt feverish. I could tell by her reaction she didn't fully understand what was going on, but I didn't stop to explain. Not if this could work. Not if this could be the key to finding the was-sceptre and finally getting ahead of Set. "Thank you," I said sincerely. "Thank you so much." Then I turned and ran back to the compound.

I barrelled through Roman's back door, my eyes quickly scanning the room. I could feel him close by, knew he was somewhere in the house, but I didn't see him anywhere. I heard movement upstairs, heard what I assumed was the shower running, so without thinking I sprinted up the steps, taking them two at a time. It had been months since I'd been in Roman's room. It was a loft, one side overlooking the living room downstairs, a back wall of glass that opened to the forest. His room was simple, minimalist really, a bed and dresser the only real furniture. On the opposite end of the room was his bathroom. The shower turned off, and I heard the curtain pull open across the rod. I waited exactly one minute, then I barged into his bathroom, pulling the door shut behind me and locking it.

A startled Roman wheeled around, keeping a firm grip on the towel wrapped around his waist. "What the hell?"

"Shh, it's just me," I responded quietly.

He waved his hand back and forth in front of him, dissipating some of the steam in the room. "Kyndal, what are you doing in my bathroom?"

I opened my mouth to answer when I got a full look at the man in front of me. With only the towel around him, his chest was on glorious display, water droplets still clinging to his skin and the tips of his hair. My eyes lingered, perusing his body, lingering in some places longer than others, and for a moment I forgot why I was there.

Roman raised his eyebrows, a cocky smirk on his face. "You planning to stand there and ogle me all day?" he asked playfully.

I pursed my lips, shrugging my shoulders dramatically. "I might." I allowed myself one more trip, ending at his lips, the memories of what he did with them the night before still fresh in my mind. He must have read my emotions through the bond and realized what I was thinking about, because he crossed his arms in front of his chest, even as his smile grew. Remembering why I was there, I pulled myself together, refocusing on my task. "We need to talk."

"And it has to happen in my bathroom? Can't you wait for me to get dressed?"

"No," I said quickly, even as I began searching the room. Finding what I was looking for, I grabbed the dagger off the sink. Swiftly, I sliced the edge of my finger, drawing blood. I turned around, drawing the hieroglyphic silence on his door, before turning back around. I waited a moment as I felt the magic of the spell lock in place, sealing us inside the room. "Now we can talk. I think I figured out how to find the temple from my dreams."

"Okay," Roman responded slowly, waiting for me to fill in the blanks.

"I want to ask Marius."

"You want to ask your dead ancestor where the temple from your dreams is?" I could hear the disbelief in his voice, which was precisely why I'd wanted to have this conversation in private.

I took a small step forward in the tiny bathroom, careful not to get too close in case I got distracted again. "Think about it. My mother told me the temple was built for the first Guard. The Guard Marius was a part of! Who else would know if the was-sceptre was hidden there? If I can reach Marius, maybe he can tell me where it is."

"Are you so sure that's what you're seeing?"

I nodded. "What else would it be? Why else would I be getting these dreams if not to find the answer to what we're all so desperately searching for?"

Roman took a deep breath, mulling over the possibility of it. "What do you need from me?"

"I want you to go with me."

"What do you mean?"

"I've never been able to control my dreams before, I think because I haven't been strong enough. But if you came with me, if we combined our powers, I know I could control the dream. I can get us to the temple."

Roman ran his fingers through his still wet hair, a few droplets falling onto his shoulders, catching my eye. "I don't even know if what you're saying is possible."

"It's just like the shield. We connect our powers and when the dream begins, I'll maneuver us to the temple. As long as we hold on to each other, I should be able to bring you with me." At least, theoretically that was how it should work.

"That was you today?" he asked. "I felt this huge rush of power, like I was falling and it lifted me up. I just thought I caught a second wind."

I rolled my eyes. Men and their egos. "I used the Rafiq bond to send you my power, to lend you whatever strength I could. This shouldn't be any different." I was pleading at this point, positive this could work. "Please, Rome. You've seen what happens to me when I go into that cave alone. I'm not strong enough for it. I need you."

"If Nero finds out. . ." he hedged.

"He'll be pissed, I know." I finished for him.

He took a step toward me. "No. He'll be more than pissed. He gave direct orders that no one was to use magic without his permission. He will see this as a violation of rank. Insubordination. He'll punish us."

"If you don't want to help, I understand. I'll go on my own."

"I didn't say I wouldn't help. You just need to know what's

at stake."

"Good. Meet me at the safehouse tonight at eleven. Make sure Brynn and Grady don't see you go. I don't want them to know about this in case it doesn't work."

"Wait, why the safehouse?" he asked quickly. I paused, seeing the pinched look on his face. I smiled softly, understanding why he was hesitant to return there. It was where he'd killed Evan, where he'd bitten me and stolen my blood for the hybrid army.

I moved quickly, giving him a soft kiss on the lips. "It'll be okay," I said quietly. "Trust me." I backed toward the door.

"Where are you going?" he asked, his voice stronger.

"I've got some things to take care of first. I'll see you tonight." I snuck back out the bathroom, quietly closing the door behind me.

Stepping past the silence symbol, outside of its boundary, I was almost overwhelmed by noise as it leaked back into my ears. There was the ever-present clash of metal from outside on the sands, this time coming from Coterie soldiers not on patrol. Closer by was the slamming of cabinets. Someone was downstairs, rummaging through the kitchen. I crept quietly down the steps, knowing if it were the wrong person, it could be incredibly awkward for me to explain what exactly I was doing in Roman's room. As I peeked around the corner into his tiny kitchen, I was relieved to find Isaac standing there, his hand inside a large bag of chips.

As nonchalantly as possible, I rounded the corner, passing Isaac and heading straight for the fridge. His dark eyes followed me the whole way, and I waited, knowing what was coming. I reached into the fridge and grabbed a water bottle, chugging half of it in one gulp. "You guys should be more careful," he advised quietly.

I set my bottle down, stealing the bag of chips from his hand. "We were just talking."

"It doesn't matter. Being alone together is not a good idea for you two. Other people might notice."

"Other people like who?"

"Grady, for one," he responded surprisingly, stealing back his chips. "He watches you, he might put two and two together."

I looked out the back window. "Where is Grady now?"

"He went into the main house with Brynn and Sandra to work on translating a spell. I don't think he saw you come in."

I nodded, relieved. Isaac was right, we did need to be more careful. I looked up as if I could see through the ceiling to where Roman was, a plan forming in my head. "Isaac, can you do me a favor?"

20

It was ten minutes until eleven. Freshly showered and well fed, I sat perched on the edge of the bed in the safehouse, my wet hair dripping down my back. I'd gotten here early, cleaning up as much of the debris as I could. When Roman and I had fought here, we'd done a pretty good job of rearranging the place. In fact, there was still a Kyndal-sized dent in the far wall.

I'd spent some time at home earlier. Dinner with Allie had been awkward, we'd barely spoken, each of us still licking our wounds from the argument that morning. Afterward we'd retreated to our different parts of the house, happy to ignore each other. I'd left her downstairs, studying her maps, preparing for an excursion the next day. I hated to leave with things still bad between us, but I knew what I was attempting was dangerous. Better to keep it away from home. With a quick goodbye, I promised to be back in the morning.

A light breeze blew through the open window, carrying

with it the chill of autumn. Roman was here. He opened the door tentatively, his eyes scanning the room, immediately finding the dent. It didn't take the bond for me to know he was uncomfortable. "Are you sure about this?"

No, I thought about saying. For the past hour I'd been thinking about the gravity of what we were about to attempt. Every time I'd had this dream, I'd woken up in a sweat-dripped panic. If it were my choice, I'd never return to that cave again. But then I thought about Set, and the damage I'd seen him wreak in Siberia. I simply couldn't allow him to reach the sceptre first. "Come sit on the bed," I instructed, ignoring my heart which was now pounding in my chest. I scooched up to the top, leaning against the headboard.

Roman sat on the opposite side, the bed sinking under his weight. "I'm not sure how we do this."

I reached over, grabbing his hand. A small spark jumped from my fingers to his. I let that power swirl inside his palm and he watched with awed fascination, almost as if he could see the power moving across his skin. "You know that feeling you get when you pull on the bond? Like when you're looking for me?" He nodded, his eyes still following my power. "Think of it like a tether, like an actual tangible rope. I'm going to push my power toward you, and when you feel it, grab ahold and don't let go. Hold onto the bond, and when the dream begins, you'll come with me."

He nodded. "All right."

I looked up at him, pushing my power up his arm. He

raised his eyes to meet mine. "Do you trust me?" I asked.

A tiny sideways smirk played at his lips. "That's why I'm here." His voice was strong, sure of his answer.

"Whatever you do, no matter what you see, don't let go of the bond," I reiterated. I laid back on the bed, Roman doing the same. I closed my eyes, digging deep into the well of power inside me. From my left, I felt Roman's power stir as well. My magic moved cautiously at first, unsure of what I wanted from it, but then slowly, I coaxed it toward Roman's. Using the bond between us as a highway, I closed the gap between us. The moment my power touched his, I felt it grasp ahold, pulling me in and intertwining our strength until I couldn't tell what was his and what was mine. Until we were one strength, one power. My heart rate increased, and I let out a gasp at the overwhelming strength of our combined magic. Roman's hand gripped mine tightly, his touch calming me.

At first nothing happened. We laid on the bed, the sounds of the surrounding forest the only things to break the silence. I focused on the temple, on every detail I could remember. The coldness of the cave floor, the consuming darkness when the torches weren't lit. The feel of the rough walls as I ran my fingers over the foreign glyphs. I focused on those senses, on the musty smell of the temple caused by the nearby rivers. As I pulled each detail into me, I felt myself dropping further into sleep, moving slowly toward the temple. I kept pushing, remembering exactly where my mom was standing the first time I'd seen her there. Piece by piece, a picture came into focus, clearly as looking through a window. I was simultaneously aware of my body on the bed, lying next to Roman in the real world, but I could just as easily see the temple. I pushed toward the cave in my mind's eye, bringing us closer, until finally I could hear it. The rush of water. Far off at first, I could have mistaken it for one of the many creeks or rivers in the Allegheny, but it grew louder, and I knew the dream was beginning. I tested my bond with Roman one final time, satisfied when I still felt him on the other end. The rush of the rivers increased, this time accompanied by the smell of smoke from the torches. I felt my surroundings change, and when I opened my eyes, Roman and I stood, hand in hand, inside the cave.

Roman turned, trying to take in the full view of his surroundings. Tentatively, I released his hand, pleased when he didn't disappear. Immediately, he was drawn to the wall of hieroglyphics. He ran his fingers softly over the symbols, his eyes squinting as he tried to derive any meaning from them. "Do you understand any of that?" I asked.

He pointed to the symbol in front of him. "This one I recognize from the wall of Sandra's basement. It means Kindred." He pointed to four more, each in different positions on the wall. "Earth, Air, Water, Fire. These here at the bottom I think mean river, but I'm not sure. Other than that, I don't understand any of it."

"What about her?" I ask, grabbing a torch from the wall and swinging it toward the doorway, toward the painting of the goddess above it. "Is that Maat?"

With barely a cursory glance, Roman nodded. "That's her

all right. Have you tried going up the stairs? It might help us understand where we are."

I shook my head. The temperature in the room shifted, a breeze blowing through that stirred the torch in my hand. I knew we were no longer alone. I turned, unsurprised to see my mother standing there. I smiled. "Hi Mom."

Roman's eyebrows jumped. "This is your mom?" he asked, his voice uncommonly high.

My mom chuckled. "Does that surprise you?"

He cleared his throat, his cheeks turning a slight shade of pink. "N-no. It's an honor to meet you Ms. Sears. I've heard a lot about you."

My mother squinted, sizing up Roman. It was the same look she'd given to any boy I brought home. The same look, I realized, she might give an enemy on the battlefield. "Odd then, that you haven't been mentioned."

"Mom!" I interjected. I couldn't believe she said that. It wasn't like I wasn't dying to tell her about Roman, but we hadn't had much of a chance with her being dead and all. She turned her eyes to me, shrugging unrepentantly. "If you're quite done, we need your help. We need to speak to Marius."

"Marius? What for?" she asked.

"Set is looking for the was-sceptre, and we need to find it before he does," Roman explained. "Marius may be the only one that knows what happened to it."

"He will not be able to tell you where it is," my mom answered.

"What? Why not?" I protested.

"The same magic that allows you to see the memories of your ancestors also prevents us from divulging its secrets. We can only guide you as you discover the information you need on your own."

"Well, that's ridiculously unhelpful," Roman said sarcastically. I nodded in agreement.

My mom looked to Roman, "Duality demands a balance. While Kyndal can see memories of her ancestors, it simply would be too much power for someone to have the collective knowledge of an entire millenia. As her closest blood relative, I am the only one allowed to speak directly to her."

"So how do we find where the was-sceptre is?" I asked my mother, bringing us back on point.

"While you cannot see Marius, the rivers can *show* you him. If you are brave enough to wade through them."

I turned to the tunnels, the rush of the rivers almost overwhelming now, as if the sound was calling me, beckoning me to them. A pit formed in the bottom of my stomach, the same ghastly dread creeping along the back of my neck. "What will I see?" I asked my mother, even as I kept my eyes trained to the tunnel entrance, to the siren call I could hear echoing toward me. I was drawn to it, desperate to feel the cool rush of the water even as the fear climbed over my skin. It was pulling me in two, one part of me dying to move forward, the other part desperate to run away.

"The rivers show you the truth. Nothing else," she responded.

"Have you done it? Have you stepped into the rivers?"

"Never," she said simply.

"Why not?" I asked, but my mother gave no response.

I took a small step forward, but Roman grabbed my arm, pulling me back. "Wait." I turned to him, his strength managing to take a slight edge off the fear that threatened to overwhelm me but doing nothing to satiate my desire to see the rivers. "I don't like this," he whispered in my ear.

"We don't have any other choice," I reminded him. I squeezed his hand once. "Wait for me. And remember— don't let go of the bond."

Moving toward the tunnel, the absurdity of what I was doing wasn't lost on me. Wading through a river in order to see a vision while inside another vision was right up there with the craziest of things I'd done. But considering those other things included throwing fire out of my hand, bringing someone back from the dead, and fighting an Egyptian god, I guessed this plan wasn't exactly out of the realm of possibility.

The walk down the tunnel was short, the edge of the river clearly visible on the other end. As I neared it, I realized the reason it was so clearly seen was because of the skylight that'd been carved into the ceiling of the cave. It was rectangular in shape, far too neat to have been put there by nature. Sunlight streamed through it, illuminating the crystal blue waters as they flowed beneath the rock. I had no need for my torch, so I extinguished it on the cave wall, dropping it to the floor before kneeling down at the water's edge. I peered in, the soft pebble bottom of the river visible through the white caps formed by the much larger boulders upstream. I sunk my feet in, disregarding my shoes and clothes as I waded up to my chest. The water was warm, soothing like a bath that reminded me of the hot springs back in Awen. The current rushed over my shoulders, the pressure of it just strong enough that I had to push against it to stay upright. I took a deep breath and let go, allowing the river to pull me under.

I woke up in darkness. I could still hear the rush of water, but I knew I was no longer in the temple. The sound was familiar, coming not from the river, but from the waterfall that split Maat's Hollow in two. I was inside the mountain, down in the cavern I had hoped never to return to. I scanned the area quickly, searching for threats, but came up empty. I was completely alone.

Then, before my eyes, appearing like a mirage in the center of the cavern was Marius. I could see his face but his eyes were cast down, staring at something on the cavern floor invisible to me. In his hand hung a short sword, the tip of which was stained red, and I tried not to notice the dark liquid that dripped from its end. Marius' entire body was covered in dirt and dried blood. By the looks of him at least part of that blood had to be his own. There was a large cut across his shoulder, a matching one that traveled the length of his chest, the edges of his leather vest hanging loose from the center. His dark hair was a mess, his breaths coming out in ragged bursts. I had no idea how he was still alive. One look at him and I could tell he was exhausted, both physically and magically. He looked like hell.

Or rather, like he'd been *through* hell.

Without warning, the torches in the cavern burst to life. Marius dropped to a knee as if the effort to light them had knocked him down. He placed a palm on the center of the cavern, directly over where I knew the magma chamber was now. He began to chant, his voice hoarse, but I recognized the ancient language that I knew came out of The Book of Breathings. The cavern floor began to quake, splitting beneath his hand, falling in on itself. The orange glow of the magma chamber illuminated his face as he fell back on both knees now. A racking cough broke out of him, and he faltered for a moment, losing his grip on his short sword, the metal clanging to the ground.

I stepped forward, wanting to help, but stopped myself at the last moment. Marius reached over, grabbing his sword again, and I gasped as he brought it down swiftly on his forearm. Blood gushed from the wound, and he grit his teeth together, otherwise showing no signs of pain. He dropped the sword again, this time reaching to his other side, and picking up what I was unable to see before.

The box that held Set's soul.

I could feel him inside it, the wild, raw power bouncing off the sides, desperately looking for an escape. Marius placed the box on his lap then smeared his hand in the blood still flowing freely from his arm. He placed the bloodied hand on top of the box, his lips moving quickly, the chant burning itself into my memory. As he finished, I felt the power rush out of Marius and toward the box, his life force locking it shut for what he hoped would be eternity. With his last act, Marius looked up, locking eyes with me, and for a moment I could tell he saw me. That he knew I was there. A faint smile—one that could only be described as peaceful—appeared on his face as he released the box, letting it fall into the magma chamber below. His mission finished, he fell backward, his body sprawled awkwardly on the cold cavern floor.

Unable to hold myself back, I rushed to the middle of the cavern, dropping down to Marius' side. I scooped him up in my arms, much as I had Roman. I turned his face toward me and let out a terrified scream. It wasn't Marius that looked back at me, it wasn't him that I held. It was me. My cold, bloodied face and lifeless eyes staring back at me.

At that immediate moment, I knew what truth the river was showing me. Marius had sacrificed himself to lock Set away. Something as strong as Set—it took something equally powerful and rare to put him away. Marius had tied his life force—his Descendant blood—to the spell, which is why my blood was able to release him. That also meant only my blood could lock him back up.

If we were going to defeat Set, I had to die.

I don't know how long I sat in that cavern, holding my own lifeless body, but the next thing I remembered, I was back in bed and I was spitting up water.

"That's it, get it all out," a female voice encouraged. I curled over the edge of the bed, coughing and hacking as even more water spewed out of my mouth, splattering on the wooden floor. I inhaled deeply, groaning as my lungs burned in protest. I fell back to the bed, my head landing in a wet squish. I opened my eyes slowly, groaning again for a completely different reason when I saw Sandra standing there, flanked by Roman, Isaac, Brynn, and Grady.

"Well this isn't good," I quipped weakly, pushing myself upright on the bed. I took a moment to look myself over as I realized that I was completely soaked head to toe, as was now the comforter. Besides the wet clothes, I appeared to be unharmed. I looked to Isaac. "You were supposed to keep them busy." I hadn't wanted anyone to know what we were doing, so I'd asked Isaac to make sure everyone stayed at the compound no matter what. That no one came looking for Roman and me.

"Roman called me in a panic," he defended himself.

"I woke up and you weren't breathing," Roman said quietly. "I didn't know what else to do." His eyes slid to Isaac. "Although I didn't think you'd bring *everyone.*"

"You're lucky he called when he did," Sandra admonished.

"When we got here, you were soaking wet and you were drowning. Brynn and I had to pull the water from your lungs, otherwise I'm not sure you would have made it."

Instinctively, my hand went to my throat, where it was still raw from the water pushing its way in. "Thank you," I said sincerely.

"Don't thank me," Sandra began, her tone sharp, "just explain what the hell you two were doing."

"It's not his fault," I started, even as I kicked my wet shoes off my feet, wringing my socks out next. I looked to Roman who stood there completely dry. I didn't want him getting in trouble for this. It was my idea, not his. "He didn't want to do it, I made him."

"Made him do what?" Sandra demanded, each word coming out tight and controlled.

"I was trying to talk to Marius. I thought if I could contact him through one of my visions, I might be able to ask him where the was-sceptre was. But it didn't work, the river didn't show me the answer I was looking for." I thought of my dead body sprawled out on the cavern floor. A chill crept up my spine, one that had nothing to do with the cold water that soaked my skin. "I made Roman combine powers with me, took him into the vision so I could amplify my power. None of this was his fault."

"You combined powers?" Brynn asked, pushing her way in front of Sandra. "How?"

"It was the same as this afternoon during the training

session with the shields. Kyndal did it then, too." Roman explained, looking at Grady. "She's the reason we won."

"Well, not completely," I muttered.

"That was you?" Grady asked. "I could feel it. I thought he'd figured out a way to strengthen his shield. You have to teach me."

"Both of us," Brynn agreed.

I nodded, surprised by their eagerness to have me teach them something. I thought they'd be mad at me for what I did, but they didn't seem to care. And then I looked to Sandra. Her face was twisted in a scowl, one I knew was going to lead to an epic lecture.

"I'm sorry, Sandra. . ." but she held up a hand, silencing me.

My eyes cut to Roman, who glanced at me quickly before studying his adoptive mother. Her eyes were wide, searching through memories unseen. "You said the river didn't show you what you wanted. What do you mean— *river*?"

I pushed off the bed, no longer able to sit there while everyone stood around me. "The visions I've been getting are of a cave, or a temple rather, dedicated to Maat. There are two rivers inside. My mother said if I waded into one, it would show me the truth of what I wanted to know. I was hoping it would show me where the temple was. I figured it had to be where the sceptre is, but I was wrong."

Sandra pinched her nose and loosed a long breath, one weary with years. "You are not seeing a temple, but rather The Hall of Two Truths."

"I've heard of that," Brynn added. "Legends say it was created as a set of trials for the first Guard. They had to pass through the rivers and come out the other side intact. If successful, they would face Maat and Thoth for their hearts to be judged. If they found their hearts to be light, they were granted a gift from the gods."

*Whatever **that** means*, I thought sarcastically.

"Where is this place?" Grady asked.

"It doesn't exist," Sandra said quickly. "Not really. The Hall of Two Truths exists only in the *inbetween*, in the magical realm that lives between this world and the afterlife."

Woah, the afterlife.

"That's why Kyndal sees it in her visions," Roman added. "She's able to move into that realm when she sleeps using the magic that connects her to her ancestors."

Sandra's response was quiet. "So it would seem."

"The gift has to be the sceptre," I said.

"How do we get to it?" Brynn asked, pointing at me. "She can't really bring the sceptre back in a dream." She looked to me. "Can you?" I shook my head.

"There's one entrance in this world," Sandra answered. "I

don't know exactly where, but I do know it's somewhere along the Nile river in Cairo. Most of the time, it's underwater, but as the river levels drop, the doorway becomes visible for a very short amount of time."

"We have to get there," Roman said. "If we can get inside the city, Grady should be able to find it." Grady nodded, agreeing with him.

"The Hall of Two Truths is dangerous. You saw what happened to Kyndal, and she had only projected herself there in a dream. Imagine what could happen if you enter the actual waters. You won't make it," Sandra warned.

"I survived," I argued. "I know the sceptre is there. I've seen it before in my dreams, and I felt the same thing tonight as I did then. Raw power. I can get it, once I make it past the river. I can make it through. I know I can."

"Warriors far more powerful than you have met their end beneath the surface of those waters. Not even a Descendant has enough power."

"Not on my own, but if I combine my power with all three of theirs, they can anchor me to the world of the living long enough for me to make it to the other side and back."

"And if you're wrong the river will take you under and your connection to the others will kill everyone. That's if the visions don't drive you insane first."

"What *did* the river show you?" Isaac asked. My head snapped his direction. I'd almost forgotten he was in the room.

"Nothing," I said quickly, hoping no one noticed the slight lilt in my tone. I'd never been a great liar. Curiosity bloomed in the bond, but I ignored it, very purposefully not looking at Roman. I cleared my throat. "I was only under for a moment. It didn't show me anything," I affirmed, this time managing to keep my voice stronger.

"Of course it didn't," Sandra snipped. "You were foolish to try. You will not try a stunt like that again. We will find another way. Now I'm going to forget you ever mentioned this."

I shook my head. "I don't understand."

From the doorway came a deep voice as Nero walked in to the safehouse. "No, I don't believe you do." A quick peek over his shoulder revealed a dozen soldiers behind him, standing in the grey light of early morning. *Great. Now the sexist asshat is here.* He eyed Roman, who returned the look with equal disdain. He was obviously as pleased as I was that his father had arrived. "You used illicit magic outside the chain of command. You put this entire operation in jeopardy by risking the lives of two Guardsmen. You were not given these powers to do with as you wish. They do not belong to you. You were given them for one purpose only—to defeat Set."

"That's what we were trying to do," I argued.

"And again you failed, almost getting yourself killed in the process," Nero returned, his voice thundering off the walls. "The quicker you learn your place Miss Davenport, the sooner we can all stop cleaning up your messes and return our focus to the war. I had warned you what would happen if you broke rank, but apparently a harsher lesson is necessary. Seize them."

Nero's soldiers burst into the safehouse, weapons drawn. Roman, Isaac, and I closed ranks, quickly dropping into a defensive position. To their credit, even Brynn and Grady turned to defend us. I called to my power, but there was no answer. Whatever I'd been through in the vision, it had completely depleted my power source. I could still feel Roman next to me, but I knew he was just as empty as I was. Dirk stepped up, then a strong burst of air swept through the room, pushing Brynn, Grady, and Isaac against the walls.

With no powers to help us, the fight was over quickly. Nero's men overwhelmed us, throwing Roman and me to the ground, binding our hands behind our backs with vines tied by an Earth User. No amount of strength would be able to break through them. Nero stood by smugly as we were hauled to our feet. Sandra marched up to him, pushing directly into his personal space. "This isn't necessary," she grit through her teeth, her eyes a sharp blue.

Nero drew his cold eyes down to her. "This is *exactly* what is needed. Soldiers must be broken before they can be taught to obey." Nero's eyes cut to the men holding Roman and me. "Take them to the compound."

We were hauled through the forest, my bare feet scraping over branches and rocks, slicing tiny cuts into the soft flesh of my heels. My soaked hair clung to the side of my face, making it difficult to see Roman, even though I could feel him next to me. The others followed behind under armed guard. When we reached the compound, we were unceremoniously dumped into the sand of the center training ring, our ties untwisted long enough for them to be rebound around a large post that had been speared in the ground. The dormant torches roared to life, fueled by the one everlasting flame. For once, they brought me no solace, my magic still sleeping somewhere deep inside me I couldn't reach. "Wake everybody," Nero ordered. His men immediately obeyed, running inside the house. "Tell them to prepare for the gauntlet."

21

I had no idea what the gauntlet was, but it didn't sound good. Roman and I were tied back to back, me facing the main house, him looking into the forest. There was a flurry of activity as Coterie soldiers rushed around, pulling on their gear, grabbing their weapon of choice from the boards. I strained against the vines that tied our hands, their leathery texture cutting into my wrists. Behind me, Roman was oddly calm, staying perfectly still. "What are they going to do to us?" I asked Sandra, who stood not too far away, huddled with Brynn and Grady. They looked as confused as I was.

"I'm sorry," she said simply. "This isn't what I wanted to happen. I would stop it if I could."

I turned as much as I could, desperately trying to see Roman. "I'm so sorry, Roman. I didn't mean for any of this to happen. Please believe me. I didn't want you to get in trouble." He'd warned me, he told me what Nero would do if he caught us and I didn't listen. This was all my fault.

"This isn't your fault," Roman answered. "Everything is going to be all right."

I wanted to believe him, but a horn blasted through the clearing, a single note that sounded ancient and held the promise of blood. The Coterie soldiers converged, forming two lines in the sand, facing each other. Ten soldiers on each side, the twenty men held their weapons in hand, their faces hard, their eyes unseeing. Their Commander walked between them, the red pommeled sword dragging its tip in the sand as he made his way to me. Dirk followed closely behind, a wicked smile twisting his face. They stopped just short of my bare feet.

Nero stared at me, his dark eyes boring into mine. I raised my chin, holding his gaze. Whatever he was getting ready to do to me, I wouldn't give him the satisfaction of seeing me cower. Dirk was practically salivating behind him, eager to see me bleed. Behind me I felt Roman stiffen. "Are you prepared to submit to the will of your Nomarch and Commander?" Nero asked, the words as dead as his eyes.

"Go to hell." I spit at his feet.

Nero smiled, and the gesture was wrong, like it pained him to do it, almost as if the muscles in his face were unfamiliar with the movement. "Perfect." He turned his head, looking to Dirk. "Leave her bound. Take him."

"No!" The word ripped out of me, my arms straining against the vines again. Dirk rounded the post, cutting Roman's hands loose and dragging him around to my side.

From the corner of my eye I saw Brynn and Grady move to intervene, but Sandra held them back. "No," Roman said firmly to them. "It won't help. He'll just do the same to you," he warned them. My heart splintered at the bravery in his voice.

"Take me!" I yelled at Nero. "I'm the one you really want! He didn't do anything wrong!"

Nero knelt down to my level. "It was your decisions that led me to this. Every lash, every cut, every ounce of blood is on your hands. You did this to him." I flinched, his words hitting home.

"You are a monster," I growled at him. "He is your. . " I began.

"Kyndal, don't!" Roman shouted at me, even as Dirk threw him to the beginning of the line. Dirk reached down, ripping Roman's shirt, exposing his chest and the scar he held on his shoulder. A noise of astonishment ripped from Grady, but I didn't turn to look at him, didn't dare tear my eyes away from Roman.

I pressed my mouth shut, obeying Roman's wishes, not saying another word. Nero's eyes narrowed briefly in interest at my newfound silence, but he covered it quickly, pressing to his feet, and turning to address his men.

"We are at war! These two pledged themselves to obey the will of their Commander, a pledge they broke. Their insubordination will not go unpunished. Let each strike serve as a reminder that no man, no soldier is above the law."

"Yes, Commander!" The soldiers shouted as one.

Roman stood slowly, staring squarely at Dirk, the promise of violence clear in his eyes. I could feel the need for retribution coming off him in waves. Dirk was a large man, but Roman was just as tall and he looked the man eye to eye. There were two sides to Roman. The first, the side he allowed others to see, was quiet, polite, always in control. But every now and then he slipped, allowing his temper to show through. Allowing the side of him that revelled in the violence and bloodshed to take hold. As he stood tall and turned to face his fate, to look at me down the gauntlet, I knew he had unleashed that side of him. He would remember every mark put on his skin, every soldier that raised a hand, and he would make damn sure that his father paid for it all.

We both would.

"Begin."

Roman didn't take a single step before the first blow landed. A fist flew out from Roman's right, cracking off his jaw, snapping his head to the side. A tinge landed in the same place on my jaw, the echo of the hit small.

Roman took a step forward, his eyes trained on me. I held his gaze even as a soldier slammed his fist into Roman's ribs, the crack of the bone resonating through the air. Roman growled at the pain, the sound mixing with my own hiss as my rib splintered, but he refused to buckle, trudging forward another step. He passed two more soldiers, each who took their daggers, slicing them deeply across

Roman's biceps, drawing first blood. The heat of the daggers ripped through my skin and I felt wet blood flow openly down my arms. Still I didn't let my eyes drop.

"Stop it!" Grady yelled at Nero. "You're hurting both of them." His eyes turned a rich green and a slight tremor vibrated the sand. Power flowed out of Grady, sliding over the sand toward Roman. None of the others seemed to notice it, the power invisible to their senses, but I could *feel* it. It reached Roman, filling him first, the power boost hitting him just in time for the next attack.

Nero turned slowly, looking upon my wounds with disinterest. I had no idea if he knew this would happen. He'd seen me drop inside Council Chambers when Roman's collarbone was set, but I didn't know if anyone had ever explained to him why that happened. "So be it," he answered Grady, his voice empty. I winced as a shallow cut appeared on my torso, smaller than the others, but still biting. It should've been worse, but Grady's power was shielding us from the worst of it.

Roman continued his march through the gauntlet, taking each hit, each cut of his skin in silence, his eyes glued to mine. The blood dripped down his chest, painting his skin red. I tried to call to my power, desperately wanting to send him my strength, to allow him to heal himself, but each time I came up empty. The vision had drained me completely and I still hadn't had time to recover.

Roman had almost reached the end when Dirk stepped forward, twirling his dagger in his hand. His head twisted, his eyes locking on mine. He gave a sadistic smile before bringing his dagger down hard across the back of Roman's leg. The cut was deep, bringing Roman to his knee as a wail of pain burst from him, the sound a lance directly to my heart. My own scream added to it, as the echo of his wound tore at my flesh. I threw my head back against the post, my breathing ragged as I tried to absorb the pain that came from the various wounds.

When I looked at Roman again, his head was cast down, a hand on his knee as he attempted to push himself up. I could still feel Grady's power pushing out toward Roman, the rich feel reminding me of the smell of the earth after it rained. Roman barely made it to his feet when Nero stepped up, delivering a brutal right hook. Even with the added strength, Roman was unconscious before he hit the ground. My own vision blurred, black spots creeping in from the edge. I blinked hard and tried to pull my hands free again but my limbs suddenly felt very heavy. One more ragged breath stuttered and my head fell loosely, my world going black.

When I woke up, I was back in my room. The windows were thrown wide open, moonlight streaming in, broken only by the variety of candles flickering throughout the room. They were all over the place, all different sizes and colors. I'd never seen a candle anywhere in Allie's house, and I wondered what random closet corner she'd dug them out of.

I sensed Roman's presence nearby, but a quick scan of the room showed that he wasn't in here. However, I wasn't alone. Huddled in the corner were Allie and Mallory, talking quietly. I squinted, straining to hear, but my power was still nowhere to be found. They were an odd pairing, and I didn't think I'd ever seen those two talk directly to each other before. I raised myself up, grimacing at the effort. I pushed the sheets down, noticing I was only dressed in shorts and a tank top, exposing the cuts and bruises that were in various stages of repair. My arms were stiff, the twin cuts on my biceps red and angry. With each breath I took my ribs ached, and I knew if I lifted my shirt, there would be a nice sized bruise over the cracked rib. I shifted my legs, dangling them over the edge of the bed, my bare feet grazing the wood floor. "Don't tell me I slept for four days again," I groaned, my voice scratchy. Both women turned, equal looks of relief on their faces. I stood up, my left leg immediately giving out beneath me. I grunted in pain, dropping back to the mattress. Allie rushed to the side of the bed, Mallory following behind at a slower pace. I pulled my shorts up on my leg, revealing a large white bandage wrapped around my upper thigh. I picked at the edge of the bandage.

"I wouldn't touch that," Mallory warned. "Cassie packed the wound with some herbs that will fight infection and help it heal faster. She won't be happy if you undo her hard work."

I pulled my fingers back from the bandage edge. "Is Cassie with Roman?"

"She's focusing on his wounds, hoping that by healing him, it will heal both of you. Brynn and Sandra are helping her, looking in The Book of Breathings for anything that can speed up the process, or unlock whatever is blocking your powers. Grady, Isaac, and Darius are outside, guarding the perimeter."

I nodded, popping my knuckles to stifle the emotion I could feel building in my chest. Allie reached over, grabbing my hand, putting an end to my nervous tick. "What happened to you?" she asked. Her voice was quiet but steady, no hint of the fear I'd heard months ago whenever I'd mentioned anything Kindred or wraith related.

A tear escaped. I quickly brushed it away, but another followed almost immediately. "I screwed up. I pushed Roman into doing a spell, even though I knew we weren't supposed to and it went horribly wrong. Nero found out and he hurt Roman to punish me. This is all my fault." I looked up at Mallory. "Where were you?" She and Cassie hadn't been at the gauntlet. In fact, I hadn't seen either of them since the sparring session.

"Daniela called. Some of Amina's troops were headed to our airport, stopping by in route to their new outpost in the Blacklands. There's a compound in Helwan, Egypt. Apparently that's where Amina is going to be running her operation from. They were looking for a compound to crash at, but Cassie and I intercepted them. We pushed them toward another compound a few hours away, smoothing out any suspicions or questions they would have had about why they couldn't come to Marienville. We didn't get back until this morning. When we got back to the compound, we couldn't find anyone. It was only Coterie soldiers, so we came here. That's when we saw. . ." She let the sentence drop, but her meaning was clear. That was when she saw what had been done to Roman and me. I readjusted my position on the bed, suddenly uncomfortable. If my wounds were this bad, I knew his had to be worse. "Nero will pay for this, Kyndal. We'll make sure of it," Mallory swore. More tears fell at the conviction in her voice. I'd treated her horribly. I lied to her, kept secrets, pushed her away, and still she was swearing to defend me against those who would see me harmed.

"Thank you, but there is nothing to be done. Not now."

"Kyndal," Allie hedged. "It's okay to be scared."

"Think about what you're saying. He almost killed both of you." Mallory interrupted, her voice mixing in with Allie's, both of them becoming a garbled mess of noise. Allie trying to make me feel better, Mallory trying to convince me to get revenge.

"None of that matters," I shouted, bringing both of them to an abrupt silence. I pushed up to my feet, this time ignoring the sharp pain in my leg. "If we go after Nero now, there's nothing to keep him from telling the rest of the Council what we're doing. And as long as the was-sceptre is still out there, we're all in danger. We have to find it before Set does, or it doesn't matter what we do to Nero. We'll all be dead anyway."

I limped past Mallory, ignoring the anger I could feel

rolling off her. Allie reached after me, but I waved her off, determined to walk on my own. I followed the bond through my room and down the hall to the guest bedroom. This room had never been used as long as I'd lived with Allie, but she still kept it in pristine condition with the bed tightly made and fresh flowers on the dresser.

The windows were open in here, just like my room, the fresh air billowing the sheer curtains softly. Brynn sat in an old rocking chair that I knew once belonged to a great grandmother I'd never met, The Book of Breathings open in her lap. A lamp on the bedside table provided the only light, but it would be enough for her sharp eyesight. Not far from her, Roman slept peacefully on the bed, the covers pulled tightly around his still naked chest. "Has he woken up?"

Her head popped up at the sound of my voice. Her eyes jumped from one wound to the other, no doubt comparing them to what Roman was dealing with. I leaned against the door jam, putting all my weight on my good leg. "No," she answered, and I had to ignore the pity in her tone. I didn't need anyone feeling sorry for us. "He was making some noise earlier, but he hasn't woken up yet." I'd never heard her voice so soft, so caring. That was when I noticed the shadows under her eyes, the fact she was wearing the same clothes from before, even though I'd apparently been unconscious for over a day. "How are you doing?"

"About as can be expected, I imagine," I admitted. The room turned awkward as silence stretched out between us. Brynn and I had made great strides in our relationship, but it was still weird between us. "Where are Sandra and Cassie?"

"They went to the bar. We found a spell that we think might be able to open up the block in your powers, but we need a few ingredients. Sandra thinks she has them in her basement."

"Is that smart? Using another spell without Nero's permission?" That was what landed us in this mess in the first place.

"I don't really give a shit." I raised my eyebrows in surprise. "What he did to you guys wasn't justice. Roman and Grady beat him in the ring, fair and square. He was just waiting for an opportunity to get revenge, and the gauntlet was nothing but payback for being bested in front of his men. I don't know about you, but as far as I'm concerned, we'll do whatever we damn well please."

My mouth twitched. "Thank you, Brynn. For helping him."

"Yeah, well he's a Guardsmen—we have to stick together."

"I don't just mean now. I mean in the ring too." She looked at me in surprise. "I could sense something, a power that smelled like wet earth. That was you, wasn't it?"

"Grady too," she corrected. "I don't know, I was watching what was happening, and it was like it just clicked into place. I felt Grady's power leave him and I threw mine out toward it, wanting to do whatever I could to help. I figure it's the least I could do. I did almost kill you. Twice."

I snorted. "Yeah, you did." I hobbled over to the bed and sat on the edge. The bond intensified as I got closer, a soft breeze that didn't come from the window tickling the back of my neck. It was strong even though I could tell he was completely knocked out cold. I stared at Roman's sleeping form. "Almost seems like a lifetime ago now, doesn't it?"

"I'm not going to apologize for what I did. I want what is best for our people, and when I went into The Blinding, I thought killing you was for the greater good. Amina had told me the story of the Descendants and the danger Kindred like you posed to our safety. I think she knew I wouldn't hesitate to go after you. You see, I will always choose the good of many over the lives of a few, including my own. It's why I joined the Guard."

I turned my head slightly, catching the view of her out of the corner of my eye. "What about now? Do you still think killing me will serve the greater good?" I asked. I still wasn't one hundred percent sure where Brynn and I stood. If she was someone I could trust.

She closed the book and leaned forward, her caramel eyes intense. "No, I don't."

"Why not?" The question popped out before I could stop it. It wasn't that I wanted Brynn to kill me, I just didn't understand the change in attitude.

"All magic runs on duality, on an idea of balance. Whatever binds a spell can also unlock it. Your blood unlocked Set's prison and that only could have worked if it was Descendant blood that locked it." I looked away. "But something tells me you already knew that."

I checked the bond again, making sure that Roman was completely asleep. I couldn't have him overhearing me. Brynn was the strongest of any of us with magic and it didn't surprise me that she understood what it had taken a vision for me to realize. "Marius was the first Descendant and he sacrificed his life to lock Set's cage, binding it with the rarest thing he had—his blood."

"You understand what that means." It wasn't exactly a question, but I nodded anyway.

"You going to try and keep me out of the fight?" I asked. If I died before we were ready to put Set away, there would be no chance of imprisoning him again.

"No, I understand you need to be a part of this. But don't be surprised if they try to stop you." I knew she meant the others, Grady and Roman especially. They would never agree to let me sacrifice myself to trap Set.

"You can't tell them," I answered immediately.

"I won't. As I said, I will always choose the lives of many over the lives of one."

I nodded, pleased with her answer. "I need you to do one more thing for me." I stood up slowly, suddenly completely exhausted and desperate to lie down in my bed. She looked to me expectantly. "I know Roman had you quit searching for a way to sever our Rafiq bond. I want you to start working on it again, quietly. When I die, I don't want him to die with me."

22

When I woke again, I knew he was there before I opened my eyes. I could feel the weight of his body pressing down the bed. I rolled over, pleased when my body ached less than it had before. I blinked sleepily, and it took a moment for him to come into focus. It was daytime, the early morning sun peeking through the now closed window. Roman was perched on the side of the bed, his gaze resting on me. He was freshly showered, his clothes clean. Obviously someone had done a run back to the compound. I sat up as quickly as I could, pushing my messy hair back, suddenly self-conscious. I hadn't cleaned up yet and was still a bloody mess.

"How do you feel?" I asked.

"I'm okay," he assured me. "Cassie forced some sort of herbal brew down my throat. My powers returned and I started healing pretty quickly after that." The aches lingering in my own body told me he wasn't completely healed yet.

I nodded, listening for the others. All I heard was silence. "Where is everyone?"

"They're around. I convinced some of them to sleep after they realized we weren't going to die." I looked toward the closed door, now noticing the silence symbol drawn on it.

"I'm sorry, Roman." The tears from earlier rose up again, and before I knew it, I was crying. "I never should have forced you to help me. What they did to you, it's all my fault." I hastily wiped the tears away. "I'd understand if you never wanted to speak to me again."

Roman lunged forward, pushing himself onto the bed, his knees hitting mine. He dug his hands in my hair, his palms framing my face. "Don't you think like that. Ever. This is not on you. There is only one person to blame for what happened, and you can make damn sure he's going to get paid back in kind."

"But he hurt you to punish me. If I hadn't. . ."

Roman's lips pressed against mine, strong and demanding. He pulled away before I even had the chance to kiss him back. So close our noses touched, he stared directly into my eyes. "Nero did this. Not you. I don't blame you. I never have." Slowly, he leaned over, kissing away the one remaining tear.

"What do we do now?" I whispered. "I don't know how to go back and just pretend like nothing happened." The phone in Roman's pocket buzzed, interrupting the moment. One hand still cradling my neck, he pulled his phone out, reading the text message silently. "What?" I asked.

He tucked the phone back away in his pocket. "Isaac. He said Sandra has called a meeting tonight back at the compound to discuss our plan for getting to Cairo."

"Okay, that sounds like a good thing."

Roman tucked a stray piece of hair behind my ear. "Nero will be there."

I sucked in a breath. "I don't know if I can be around him. After what he did. . ."

"I'm not going to let him hurt you," Roman assured me.

"It's not me I'm worried about. I know he's your father, but he almost killed you. I want to see him and every one of his men bleed. I want to hear them scream as they suffer." I'd said differently when Mallory had demanded justice. I'd told her to stay her hand, to focus on what mattered, but faced with seeing Nero, I wasn't sure I could follow my own advice.

"Nero will get what he deserves. He's had it coming since the first moment he laid eyes on you, but whether we like it or not, he's in a position of power here. If we provoke him, he could do far worse than he already has. He could go straight to the Council and tell them what we are doing. If he blows our cover, it will get a lot of innocent people killed. We have to play this smart."

I growled in frustration. I knew all of this, but that didn't make it easier to do. "Wouldn't it just be easier to punch him in the nose?"

Roman laughed, leaning forward and giving me a soft kiss. "There's that Aries fire I love so much."

I smacked his arm. Hard. "How can you be so calm about this?"

"I don't have a choice," he argued. "If I don't keep it together, if I allow him to get to me, I'll march right into that compound and rip every one of them apart. Consequences be damned. We *have* to keep it in check."

I popped my knuckles in frustration. He was right and I knew it. "So what do we do?" I asked, relenting to his point.

"Exactly what he wants us to do. Let him think he's won. Defer to his command, do absolutely everything he says. Give him no reason to question us."

"Basically, you want me to kiss his ass?"

He pushed off the bed, sporting his signature smirk. "Well, not literally."

I rolled my eyes. *People thought I was the sarcastic one.* "You know that as soon as we find the sceptre, he'll try to steal it for himself."

"I'm working on that. It's a problem for a different day."

I stood up too, my leg giving me only minimal pain. "We should talk to Grady and Brynn, see if they have any ideas of how to keep Nero from getting the sceptre."

Roman's eyebrows shot up in clear surprise. "Really?

Never thought I'd hear you say that."

"They were pissed about the gauntlet. Did you know both of them shared their power, trying to help us? I think the emotions helped them do it, just like when were first branded and our powers were so connected to how we felt. I haven't talked to Grady yet, but I talked with Brynn last night. I think they'll help us."

A small shimmer went through the room, a slight vibration of power I'd come to recognize as magic fading away. Roman and I both turned to the door and watched the silence symbol disappear, taking the spell with it. Without its protection, we could no longer speak freely. Downstairs, I could hear Mallory talking to Grady in the kitchen. Their conversation paused, as if they could feel the spell lift, and were suddenly aware of Roman and me on the floor above.

Roman partly opened the door, his next words for everyone else as much as they were for me. "Get cleaned up. The meeting begins at sundown."

I took the longest shower of my life. The scalding hot water worked its own kind of magic, cleaning away the blood and grime, stinging the still healing cuts on my arms and leg. I threw the clothes I'd been wearing in the trash. There was no amount of detergent in the world that could remove the musty smell of the river. They were a lost cause.

When Roman left, the others cleared away too, returning to the compound on Sandra's orders for some much-needed rest. We were going to have to face Nero soon enough, even though it was tempting to hide out at my house for the rest of our long lives. Only Darius stayed behind, something I knew was more for Allie's benefit than my own. I was glad to have him at the house. My aunt had been thrown into the middle of something she never should have been a part of. She needed someone who could look after her, somebody who wasn't constantly leaving her the way I was. And if my plan succeeded, I knew he would look after her after I was gone.

I slept off and on the rest of the day, replenishing my power. I called Lydia midafternoon. I wasn't surprised that Isaac had already filled her in. She'd wanted to come be with me, but her mom was working double shifts and she had to stay home to babysit her siblings. As much as I loved her, I was happy she hadn't been able to come see me. Lydia was already too deep into the supernatural, and I didn't want her going any further. It felt good to hear her talking about normal things, the mundane parts of life that she should be focused on. Lydia didn't belong in this world of magic and death. She should be thinking about applying to colleges, not whether or not her friends had survived another day.

Allie moved throughout the house all day, but she never came in to check on me and by the time I ventured downstairs to eat something, fully dressed in combat gear and weapons, my aunt was nowhere to be found. I shoveled in some leftover pizza I found in the fridge, not even bothering to warm it up. Out the kitchen window, I caught sight of Darius standing on the yellowing grass, just off the edge of the porch. His eyes scanned the treeline, years of training teaching him to always be on alert. The sun was beginning to drop below the canopy, its' rays splintering through the bare trees. The meeting would begin soon, and I did not want to be the last one to arrive.

I pushed through the back door, standing side by side with the large man. "I've never seen the forest during the fall. Without the leaves, it really opens up. Makes visibility a lot easier. Don't have to worry as much about someone sneaking up on you."

"If you'd been here two weeks sooner, all the leaves were changing color. Some of the brightest oranges and reds I've ever seen. Allie took me on an ATV trip through it. She showed me some parts of the forest even I didn't know existed."

I smiled. Nobody knew the forest like Allie did. "Where is she?"

"Sleeping," he replied simply. "It's been a rough couple of days."

I nodded self-consciously. "I'm leaving for the compound. I wanted to tell you so. . ." I stumbled over my words, "so she wouldn't worry," I finished.

"I'll tell her."

I took a few steps toward the trees, then paused, turning partially to face Darius. "I'm happy she has you. Thank you for taking care of her, when I couldn't."

I didn't wait for him to respond, instead I took off into the trees toward the compound.

Toward Nero.

23

Apparently I got there early. The great room was empty—odd considering it was almost always buzzing with activity. I sat on the edge of the raised stone hearth, the crackle of the wood in the fireplace the only thing at my back. I released a bit of power, the flames behind me jumping in response. One by one everyone filed in. Mallory, Cassie, and Isaac came first, each of them covered in sweat. Clearly they hadn't been resting, but rather training. Brynn and Grady followed shortly after. Without a word, Brynn sat in the corner chair, not far from the fireplace. Surprisingly Grady sat down between us, directly next to me on the hearth. When Roman arrived, he took quick inventory of the arrangement, adding himself to it by not hesitating to stand on my other side, his back against the wall. The power in the room was heavy, the tension thick as each of us anticipated the arrival of Nero.

We waited in silence for five minutes.

Then ten.

Twenty minutes later, I finally heard footsteps sounding down the hall. There were two sets, one lighter than the other. Nero entered first, pausing a step inside the room. Sandra, who had been directly behind him, was forced to stop too. Their eyes scanned the room. The message we were sending was clear. The Guard now stood united, and we would protect each other fiercely. We would not be caught unaware again. As Nero continued to scan the room, Sandra stepped around him, very wisely going to sit in the middle of the room, placing herself in-between Nero and the rest of us. She took the last available chair, leaving Nero to stand on the opposite side of the room.

Alone.

"Well isn't this adorable?" he snipped. His eyes moved from Brynn, to Grady, to me, eventually landing on his son. "I see you finally learned to work as a team." He glared at Roman. "It seems my lesson was well received." A jolt of rage shot out of Roman, straight down the bond. So intense, I was forced to bite down on my lip to suppress a growl. The emotion was powerful but short lived, almost as if he hadn't meant for me to feel it, but it had slipped past his defenses. Intentional or not, the white-hot rage spoke directly to that part of me that demanded revenge, and before I could do anything, the fire behind me popped, sparks flying out of it and landing on the hearth. To his credit, Grady didn't budge, even though the sparks had to be singeing the backs of his arms. I clamped down on the element, extinguishing each little spark. Nero's eyes turned to me, and when they lingered for a moment too long, Roman pushed from the wall, now standing even with me.

"Did you have a problem with my methods?" Nero asked, his tone sharp.

I counted to three before answering, working hard to keep my tone even. "No, Nomarch. It was a lesson worthy of its crime." I curled my toes inside my boot, the discomfort of which was nothing in comparison to how difficult it was to say those words aloud.

Nero looked to Roman. "And you?"

"We have learned the error of our ways and are here to submit to your will and command," he answered, his voice perfectly smooth. I had no idea how he was able to do that, how he could look this man in the face and not try to rip his throat out.

Sandra stood up. "Then let's begin. No matter how ill advised her methods were, Kyndal's dream gave us the location of the was-sceptre. It is hidden in The Hall of Two Truths." She reached behind her, grabbing a map I hadn't noticed her carry in. She spread it out on the table next to her. "Cairo is the largest city in Egypt, and the Nile runs right through the heart of it. The door to The Hall of Two Truths is hidden somewhere along the river banks. We'll fly into the northeastern part of the city, avoiding Amina and her warriors that have taken up residence in the compound at Helwan, just an hour south of Cairo. Once we're there, Nero—you and your men need to get eyes on Amina. If we don't know where her people are, we run the risk of being discovered."

"I can handle that," Roman interrupted.

"How?" Nero demanded. I turned to Roman, trying to hide my own surprise. Whatever he had up his sleeve, I was unaware of it.

Roman stared back at Nero. "Amina will see a Coterie soldier coming from a mile away. We need someone more discreet. Someone that can blend in without drawing attention to themselves. I happen to know someone like that." Roman's eyes flicked to Mallory, who raised her head in silent understanding. It seemed, somehow, she was involved in his plan.

"The Kindred don't have an official compound in Cairo, so we'll have to find our own residence, preferably somewhere close to the Nile," Sandra continued.

"Weapons could be an issue," Mallory added. "Without an armory at our disposal, we'll need to pack pretty heavy."

Grady stood up, taking a step forward. "We have to assume Set will be nearby, possibly with hybrid spies spread throughout the area. If too many of us go, we'll draw attention, which is exactly what we don't want."

"You want my men to stay behind?" Nero contested, matching Grady's step with one of his own.

"A smaller force has a better chance of going unnoticed. It's best if you just let us handle it," Grady retorted.

Nero scoffed. "I'm not leaving this up to a group of incompetent children. If you run into Set, you're going to wish you had my army."

"You're both right," Roman cut in. I looked up at him in shock. "We can't bring a large force into Cairo without drawing attention, but we need the Coterie available at a moment's notice if something goes wrong. Once we get to Cairo, Nero—you and Sandra should take your men to set up just outside the city. Brynn, Grady, Kyndal, Cassie, Mallory, Isaac, and I will find somewhere close to the Nile to use as home base. We'll join our powers so Grady can track the sceptre, then we'll grab it and get out of the city without being seen."

"I'm not waiting on the outside, I'm going with you," Sandra immediately argued.

"You can't," I told her. "By now The Council has publicized your disappearance. Every Kindred will know your face and be looking for you. You need to stay out of sight."

"Not to mention, if this goes south, there needs to be someone left that knows how to use the book," Brynn added.

Sandra's lips pursed in anger. "Fine," she relented tightly.

"Dirk and I will enter the city," Nero added in. "The Coterie cannot be summoned by just anyone. They answer only to their commander. If you are pinned down, I am the only one that can order them to battle."

Roman's hand clenched, his tone matching that of his adoptive mother's. "Fine."

Sandra looked around the room, waiting to see if anyone

else had anything to add. "I want you all to be aware of exactly what you're getting into. With Set and the Council to watch out for, there's a good chance this goes wrong. You're putting your brands on the line if the Council finds you. If Set does, we all know what he'll do. If we don't play this exactly right, we could get caught between two armies that both want us dead. Last chance to back out."

No one moved to object. I scanned the room, a small smile appearing at the bravery of my friends. "All right then. You have eighteen hours to get your things in order. Then we head for Cairo."

Back at home, Allie was awake. The large garage door was thrown open in the backyard, and the hanging lights reached out toward the yard, illuminating the grass. I could hear my aunt inside, rummaging through all her camping gear. I stood in the doorway, watching as she balanced on her tiptoes, reaching for a set of lanterns on a top shelf. "Going on a trip?" I asked her. Allie lost her footing, and one of the lanterns tipped forward, landing on the ground in a loud crash. I cringed, even as she let out an aggravated growl. "Sorry. I didn't mean to scare you."

She bent down, picking up the broken pieces of glass. "It's fine. I just didn't know you were back yet." She sniffled, running her free hand along her cheek quickly.

I turned my head, studying my aunt. "Are you—are you crying?"

She stood up tall, clearing her throat, but her eyes remained cast down. "I'm fine. Are you here to say goodbye?" She threw the broken lantern into the nearby trash can, immediately turning her back on me.

"Allie. . ." I began, but she wheeled around, interrupting me.

"Is it true you're going to Egypt?" she demanded. The tear tracks were clear on her face.

"How did you know about that?" I asked. I hadn't hung around the compound long after our meeting. Just long enough for Roman and me to connect with Mallory and make a plan for her to contact Daniela. Everyone else had gone their separate ways, making the necessary arrangements before we left tomorrow night. I'd been there thirty minutes longer, tops.

"Is it true?" she asked again.

"I was going to tell you. I just found out at the meeting. Did Darius tell you?" I was still trying to connect all the dots of how exactly she'd found this out so quickly. I looked around for Darius, but he was nowhere to be found.

"He got called away, back to the compound. Apparently he'll be in charge since everyone else will be shipping out tomorrow. How could you leave again?" My heart splintered at the pain in her voice.

I took a step toward her, rounding one of the ATVs in-between us. "You knew I wasn't here for long. Set is out there and it's our job to fight him," I responded softly.

"When will you be back?" she asked.

I paused, unable to answer right away. How could I tell her there was a good chance I wouldn't be? Even if we succeeded in getting the was-sceptre, there was no way we could bring it back to Marienville. It was too dangerous. "I don't want to lie to you. . ." I said, letting the sentence drop.

She looked right at me, the tears shining in her dark eyes. In that moment, I knew she understood. "But I just got you back."

I smiled sadly. "I'm sorry, Allie. I wish I could stay, I really do. I know you have all these dreams of what you want me to do, who you wish I was, but I can't change the fact that I'm Kindred."

"I don't want to change you," she disagreed, moving to close the small amount of space left between us. She took a deep breath, pushing the remaining tears away. "I really didn't know my brother. He left so early in my life, we never got a chance to really get to know each other. I never understood why he left us, and my parents would never talk about it. I think it was too painful for them. After they passed, I was all alone for years. Then, when the Sheriff contacted me, told me about what happened to Mark and his family, that I had a niece that had survived and needed a home, all I could think was that you were my second chance. Maybe if I got to know you, it would be like knowing my brother in some small way. And maybe, I would have a chance at a family again."

My own tear rolled down my cheek. "You are my family, Allie. You've given me so much. I never would have known the truth about who I was if you hadn't taken me in. I can never repay you for all you've done for me."

"Bringing you here is what put you in danger. You never would have gone through all of this if I had just left you alone. If I had just let the foster system place you somewhere in Texas. My fear of being alone is what brought you here and ruined your life."

"The Kindred would have found me, no matter where I was. Having you is why I've been able to deal with it all." I looked down to the ATV underneath my hand. "Do you remember my first day of school here?" Allie shook her head slightly. "I came home upset because Paige and her friends had been spreading rumors about me. Telling everyone that I killed my family. I just wanted to come home and hide in my room and cry. You forced me to go on an ATV ride inside the forest. You took me to that lake and told me I wasn't to blame for my family's death. You said you were here for me, whatever I needed. You didn't pretend everything was going to be okay. You saw the pain I was in. You understood it. No one had ever done anything like that for me before. You shouldn't be apologizing to me. I should be thanking you."

I saw it coming—but unlike I would've before—I didn't move to stop it. Allie reached out, enveloping me in a huge hug. I wrapped my arms around her, hugging her just as tightly. "I don't want to let you go," she said.

That sounded just fine to me.

I slept in the next morning. Allie and I had been up most of the night, curled up on the couch, watching some of our favorite movies. After our moment in the garage, we both wanted to spend one final, normal night, just the two of us.

I pushed the deadline, wanting to spend every possible moment at home. Only after I was showered and dressed, I packed my duffel bag with as many useful items as I could; multiple sets of gear, an extra set of boots, the medical supplies Cassie left behind, and of course, my weapons. I had a few stashed around the house, but the rest I would have to get from the compound. I hoisted the bag over my shoulder, taking one more look at my room. When I'd moved here, I never thought I'd be able to see it as home. Now, faced with leaving it again, it was difficult to tear myself away.

My goodbye to Allie was brief. We'd both said everything we needed to the night before. I hugged her tightly, then handed her a sealed envelope. "Give this to Lydia for me."

She nodded. "I'm not giving up on you Kyndal. Go kick Set's ass. I'll be here when you get back."

I laughed. "Thank you, Allie. For everything." With one final hug, I turned away and into the forest.

When I reached the compound, the place was abuzz with activity. The soldiers were loading bags into the vehicles that would take us to the airport. The bond immediately led me to Roman's house, where inside I found he wasn't alone. Mallory and Cassie sat in the living room with him, their heads down, looking at something between them. I closed the door quietly behind me, dropping my bag on the floor. Roman's head popped up, and he greeted me with a smile. The bond filled with love and I found myself smiling back. "What are you looking at?" I asked.

"Cassie found us a place to stay," he explained. I stood between Cassie and Mallory, looking down at what I realized was a map of Cairo.

"I wasn't able to get us directly on the Nile. Everything there is very populated, mainly with apartment buildings or hotels. Not nearly private enough for what we need. I did however, find a villa for rent a few miles east of the river bank. Right about here." Cassie pointed to the map. "It's secluded inside a private neighborhood. It has large, high walls that will make defending it easier, not to mention block the view from any snooping neighbors.

"Where's the airport?" I asked.

Mallory pointed to the top of the map. "Here."

"It's about a fifteen-mile trip," Roman explained, knowing exactly why I was asking.

My eyebrows raised. "That's a long way to travel unseen. What about Set's hybrids?"

"We have the element of surprise," Mallory said. "He may know Kindred are coming to the Blacklands, but he doesn't know exactly where yet. With Amina's troops in Helwan, that may draw their attention. They have a large area to cover, and we're hoping we can slip through the cracks." *Hoping*, I thought. I didn't like the sound of that.

"It's the best plan we have," Roman stated, reading my uncertainty.

I nodded. "I know."

Roman turned to Mallory. "Did you get in touch with our friend?" he asked her cryptically. Any of Nero's men could be listening in, and he didn't trust them not to report to Nero who his spy was. He was so careful, he had yet to share with me who his spy was. Although, seeing that Mallory was his connection, I had a guess who they were working with. While Daniela and her group could be useful, he needed to be careful calling in favors with them. She seemed like the type of person to call in debts.

"Yes," Mallory answered. "She has one asset already on the ground in Helwan. She's sending another over soon. They'll report back to us as soon as we land in Cairo."

"That's good."

Just then, the back door opened and Grady walked in. "It's time to go."

24

Cairo was beautiful. We flew from our private airport, on a plane similar to the one I'd returned to Marienville in. The flight was over fifteen hours long, and my small group of friends had used most of the flight to lay out the finer details on our plan. When we finished planning, we used the rest of the flight to sleep. We knew once we got to Cairo, there would be very little time for rest, and we needed to conserve as much of our energy as possible. I laid on the floor of the plane, wedged between Mallory and Isaac. Roman laid on the other side of Isaac, both of us using him as a buffer. We hadn't had much of a chance to talk since everything happened, not since that moment in my room, but just being near him was enough—the bond wrapped me in a warm blanket of comfort.

Thankfully, my sleep was dream free. Something told me I wouldn't be returning to The Hall of Two Truths through my dreams anymore. It was almost as if it'd shown me what I was supposed to see, and I wouldn't be welcome that way again. I woke as the plane touched down. Rubbing the sleep from my eyes, I looked out one of the few windows the plane had. The sun was beating down, the buildings rising up from the ground in beautiful sand-colored tans and reds. Off in the distance, the pyramids of Giza loomed, their presence a reminder of exactly how ancient this culture was. As the plane rolled to a stop, the back door lowered and Sandra walked down the ramp to talk with a man waiting on the tarmac.

I held up my hand, protecting my eyes from the harsh sun. "Who's that?" I whispered to Mallory.

"Customs agent," she replied. "Mostly likely a contact of Sandra's. She'll pay him off, which will allow us to bypass any inspections. It's how we get our weapons into the country."

I looked closely. Sure enough, Sandra produced a large stack of cash from the bag she was holding. She showed it to the man before shoving it back in the bag and handing it to him. They shook hands before he turned around and returned to the nearby building.

Sandra reboarded the plane. "Let's go."

Nobody hesitated. The Coterie broke off, throwing their bags over their shoulders and marching out into the blazing sun. Sandra gave our small group a final look, her dark eyes sharp, before following the soldiers out.

Nero stood center plane, immediately assuming command. "There are two SUVs waiting for us outside the gate that will take us to the villa. Keep your eyes sharp, hybrids could be anywhere."

We grabbed our things, walking the short distance from the tarmac to the waiting vehicles. As soon as we were outside the airport gates, we were overcome by the sights and sounds of the city. Cairo was a bustling city, with over nineteen million people inside it. The streets were narrow, filled with a variety of cars, busses, even the occasional push cart or donkey-pulled wagon. The sidewalks were just as filled, as people weaved in and out of traffic on their way to work or the corner coffee house.

The SUVs weren't the standard issue black ones I was used to. Instead they were old and dusty, the metal dented in some places, rusted in others. "These are our rides?" Isaac asked. "Can they even *get* us to the villa?"

"We have to blend in," Roman answered as he opened the back hatch, throwing our bags into the vehicle. "Anything too nice, and it would draw attention."

"What's wrong, Isaac?" I teased, even as my eyes scanned the city, looking for anything out of place. "Not cool enough for you?"

He flipped me off, forcing a laugh out of me.

"Isaac—you, Kyndal, and Grady are with me in this one," Mallory ordered as she climbed into the driver's seat of the first SUV.

My eyes flew to Roman's. I didn't like the idea of us being in different vehicles—liked even less him being in the same one as Nero. *It'll be fine*, he mouthed. Reluctantly, I climbed into the first SUV, keeping a keen eye on the rearview mirror. Cassie was driving the other SUV. Nero and Dirk climbed into the middle, leaving Grady and Roman in the very back.

Mallory drove through the streets as fast as she was able. I quickly learned that traffic in Cairo was nothing like what I was used to in the States. The streets were congested, people moving at all different speeds. Pedestrians stepped out into oncoming traffic without seemingly any thought of self-preservation. Mallory weaved through the streets, making sure Cassie was able to keep up behind her. The last thing we needed was to get separated. The SUV was silent, each of us keeping our eyes trained to the streets, looking for anything out of place, the slightest glimpse of dark veins or glowing eyes.

The first several miles went smoothly, our vehicles skating through the traffic with relative ease, then out of nowhere, the vehicle came to an abrupt stop. I braced myself against the seat in front of me while Mallory laid on the horn, yelling at the car in front of us. "Come on!" she shouted. "Move!"

"What's going on?" I asked her.

"I can't tell. The traffic is slowing down. It looks completely stopped up ahead, but I'm going to try to find a way around." She hit the horn again, this time holding it for a solid ten seconds. The car in front of us inched over just enough for us to wiggle past and turn on the next street. We made it another two blocks until the street closed in again and this time we hit a complete gridlock. "Dammit!" Mallory shouted, hitting the steering wheel. "There's no way through. We're going to have to hoof it."

Before I could react, she had pushed the door open and was out in the middle of the street. I scrambled out of the vehicle, following her around to the back. The other SUV was doing the same, each of us grabbing our duffel bags. Horns blared behind us, people sticking their heads out of windows and yelling in a language I didn't understand. "What about the car?" I asked.

"Leave it," Mallory replied quickly. Her eyes were cutting around the area, jumping from one person to the next. We were completely exposed out here on the street, and we were starting to draw attention to ourselves. I skimmed the streets, using my other senses to try and pinpoint a potential enemy.

My eye caught on one person in particular—a woman with tawny skin and jet-black hair. She stood on the corner of the sidewalk, just outside a coffee shop. Dozens of people milled around her, but she didn't move. She simply stood there, staring at our group with a sort of preternatural stillness. "We need to get off the streets. Now," I said, turning to my group. I looked back at where I'd seen the woman, but by then, she had disappeared.

We started walking, trying our best to blend in to the pedestrian traffic that was just as thick as the roads were. Mallory and Cassie took the lead and we pushed our way through throngs of people, careful not to move too quickly. Our goal was to blend in. If we moved too quickly, someone might take notice. "The villa is three miles away," Mallory announced to our group.

Roman moved up to walk next to me. "What'd you notice

back there?" he asked.

I shook my head, unsure. "It might be nothing. There was just this woman, she seemed really interested in what we were doing. I'm probably just being paranoid." We turned off the road, Mallory cutting us through a small alley between restaurants. She took us through three more just like it, until finally the sounds of downtown Cairo faded and we emerged in a part of town lined with large apartment buildings and parking garages. The sidewalks were more narrow and rundown—but for the most part—clear. In fact, our little group was some of the only people on the sidewalk. Up ahead, there were a few people standing against the wall of an apartment building smoking. We all seemed to notice them at the same time. They completely ignored us, but our pace slowed anyway, Roman and Grady adjusting their arms so their hands were closer to the daggers they had hidden inside their gear.

As we moved past them, one man, the one in the middle, looked up, giving me an open view of his eyes. I breathed a sigh of relief when I saw they were clear, absolutely no trace of bloodshot veins. I nodded at the man politely, returning my attention ahead of us. We reached the end of the sidewalk and a strange tingle crossed the back of neck, forcing me to pause. The others continued ahead, only Roman staying behind with me. As slyly as I could, I turned to look behind me. The group of strangers was now casually walking behind us, and the man I'd nodded at froze mid-movement, his hand behind his back. I reached out, blindly grabbing a hold of Roman's arm, turning him around. He followed my gaze, his hand now firmly on the handle of his dagger. The other man smiled, his lips slowly curling to reveal a set of serrated teeth at the same moment the veins in his face darkened into an inky web. From behind his back, he produced a curved silver blade.

"Wraiths!" I shouted to the others, but my warning came too late. From the balcony of an apartment, a host of bodies leapt from above. A mixture of wraiths and hybrids, they landed right in the center of us, knocking Isaac, Cassie, and Grady down in the process. Half a breath later, a Fire User hybrid raised his dagger, bringing it down hard, aiming for the center of Grady's chest. Grady rolled to the side, the blade narrowly missing its mark. He lunged upward, his fist cracking off the hybrid's cheek, buying him enough time to get to his feet and pull his dagger. The others had already pulled their weapons and were fighting off a full-scale attack. The wind kicked up as Mallory and Dirk summoned their element. A growl ripped from my throat as I saw who was in the middle of the melee. It was the woman I'd noticed earlier, the one I thought was suspicious.

I dropped my duffel bag, ripping the dagger I'd hidden in my boot out of its sheath. I wanted to go help the others, to fight off the more obvious attack, but the air changed, and I felt the presence of fire behind me. I turned just in time to see a fireball fly toward my head. Roman's power swelled, and inches from my head, it flew wide, a gust of air pushing it into the nearby wall.

Now, I was pissed.

Bloodlust filled my veins and I called to my power. It rushed to fill me, my eyes changing almost instantly as fire filled my hand. The wraiths' eyes widened with fear as they realized I'd manifested my element on my own.

Good, I thought. *You should be scared.*

I didn't wait for my power to build, I didn't have to. I threw myself at the enemy, my power erupting as I did. I could feel Roman next to me, his shield locking tight around both of us. He would shield me from any magical attacks while I focused on the physical battle.

We cut through the wraiths first. My power had extended outward, now wrapped around my dagger. The fire cut through the air like a living flame, so if the blade didn't kill them, the fire would finish them off.

The clangs of battle echoed off the high walls as my friends and I fought for our lives on the sidewalk. I had no idea how many wraiths there were, whether any of my friends had been injured in the fight behind us. Roman and I focused on the hybrid in front of us, using our joint strength to slowly wear him down. He was strong and well trained, probably way older than Roman and me combined. Since he was a Fire User, my power was no good against him, we had to use physical force. Finally, after several attempts, I managed to land a strong right kick to the hybrid's stomach, doubling him over. Roman took the advantage, throwing his knee upward directly into the hybrid's nose. Blood splattered as his head snapped backward. I grabbed the hybrid by the shirt, throwing him against the wall of the apartment building, holding him there while Roman rammed his dagger through his heart. He held it there a moment, watching as the life left his eyes, only pulling it free when he was sure the enemy was dead.

We didn't pause, not even to wipe the blood and sweat from our faces. We turned, jumping into the fray to help our friends. More hybrids and wraiths were here, although I had no idea where they'd come from. My power thrummed through me, combined with the strength of Roman's shield. The fight had spilled to the street, Grady and Brynn fighting back to back against three hybrids. I could taste the magic in the air, my fellow Guardsmen holding their own shields strong. We barrelled into the hybrids, knocking them off center, and tipping the odds to our favor. I launched a fireball at point blank range, directly through the chest of the nearest hybrid. From my left, a flash of silver caught my eye. One of Brynn's sais cut through the air, and I bent backward, watching as it flew past me, embedding itself in the heart of another hybrid. Before I could thank her, a scream echoed behind me. I wheeled around in just enough time to see Isaac land in a heap on the ground, a hybrid standing over him. I launched a fireball at the hybrid from across the street, hitting her in the shoulder and backing her off my friend and directly into Dirk. Without missing a beat, Dirk wrapped his arm around her neck, driving his dagger through her heart, throwing her body to the ground before her heart could quit beating.

I sprinted across the road, dropping to Isaac's side. His injury was obvious, his chest cut open from hip to collarbone, the wound bleeding profusely. I dropped my dagger on the sidewalk, the battle forgotten. My hands hovered over my friend's bleeding chest. I was shaking with uncertainty. The injury was serious, way too much for

Isaac to try and heal on his own, and I had no idea how to help him. "Cassie!" I shouted over the sound of clashing metal. From several feet away, Cassie turned, her brilliant blue eyes a shock against her bright red hair. Her right arm lashed out, striking the wraith in front of her in the face and knocking him to the ground.

She ran through the melee, dropping at my side. She took a quick assessment of Isaac's wound, of his shallow breathing, and ashen face. "I can't fix this here. If he's going to stand any chance, we have to get him to the safe house."

I looked around at the still raging battle. The first thing I noticed was Nero. He was tackling a wraith, slashing his obsidian blade across his throat. The wraith disintegrated moments later, the ash covering Nero's arms. The sidewalk was littered with bodies, the hybrids not disappearing like the other wraiths did and still we were outnumbered. There was no way we could all get out without the wraiths following us directly to our safe house. "You go," I told her. "Take Nero, Grady, and Brynn. She has the book. The rest of us will fend them off."

"There's too many of them," she argued.

"If you stay, he will die," I growled. "We can't make it out together and we can't leave any of them behind to report to Set that we're here. Now, Mallory knows where the safe house is, she'll get us there, and we can handle ourselves. Go," I ordered.

I didn't wait for her to argue with me, instead I grabbed my dagger and jumped to my feet, running to where Roman and Grady were. Cassie's voice rang out as she called for Nero and Brynn. I jumped in next to Grady, helping him fend off his attacker. "Isaac's injured. Cassie needs your help getting him to the safe house," I explained as I ducked under a wraith's right hook. I countered with a straight right of my own, but the wraith was tough, barely reacting to the hit.

"I'm a little busy here," Grady argued, his dagger slashing out and catching the wraith in the arm.

Not far off, Roman stabbed a wraith, slicing upward until it turned to dust. "I'll go," he offered. Typically, I would have argued, but this was Isaac we were talking about. He and Roman were like brothers. I nodded quickly. Roman took off, helping Nero scoop up Isaac's large frame, the two of them moving as quickly as they could after Brynn and Cassie. Since I watched them leave, I lost track of the fight. I didn't notice the wraith had knocked Grady down, not until his fist was colliding with the side of my head.

Stunned, my head whipped to the side and I growled in pain, my head instantly throbbing. The side of my vision went fuzzy and I had to spare some of my power to heal myself enough to clear up my eyesight. Out of nowhere, the wind kicked up, blowing the loose pieces of my ponytail into my face. From behind me, Mallory sailed the wind, jumping completely over the wraith Grady and I had been fighting, landing behind him. With a flash of her hand, her dagger cut through his midsection. My attention snapped to the street, where Dirk was locked in battle with one final hybrid. I gritted my teeth when I realized it was the same woman that started this whole thing. The one who undoubtedly recognized us on the street and called her evil buddies to help take us out.

I walked toward them slowly, building my power as I went. I sheathed my dagger, concentrating on the hybrid, putting all my focus on her as I felt the power build within me. When it grew to an inferno, when it became too big to contain, I launched my magic at her in one massive push. She caught fire instantaneously, her entire body going up in flames. Dirk leapt backward to avoid the inferno. His head spun my direction, a look that could only be described as awe. The hybrid's screams clawed out of her throat as I pushed the magic harder, forcing the fire to burn hotter. She dropped to her knees, then onto her back when suddenly the screams stopped. I pulled my power back, leaving the fire to consume her body on its own.

Mallory stood next to me, watching the hybrid's body burn in silence. Her breathing was as ragged as mine, her body cut and bleeding. Grady staggered to join us. "Damn," he grunted.

"Let's move."

25

By the time we made it to the villa, the sun was setting. My small group had moved slowly, weighed down by the extra duffel bags and the need to clear each street before we moved on. We even doubled back a few times to make sure we weren't followed. We couldn't take the chance that there were more wraiths that could track us to the safe house.

By the time we reached the large, electronic exterior gate, my power was almost completely drained. Even so, I could feel him, waiting atop the wall for me. The gate buzzed open and just a step through it, Roman dropped from above, landing by my side. He was still covered in dirt and dried blood, having taken no time to clean up. It didn't surprise me. He would never rest. Not until we were back. "How's Isaac?" I asked immediately, dropping my bags to the ground. Dirk and the others walked past us, entering the villa.

"Cassie and Brynn are with him now. It's touch and go."

His voice was quiet and a pang twisted in my chest at the pain in his voice.

"Set knows we're here now," Nero said from the doorway of the villa. I rolled my eyes and turned to face my least favorite Nomarch.

"We were careful. We didn't leave any survivors," I argued. "We don't know for sure they gave away our position. Besides, even if he knows we're in Cairo, the safe house is secure."

"A small victory," he snipped, his arms crossed. His clothes were freshly changed, his skin washed clean. "We need to move quickly. Grady needs to do the spell tonight."

"He's exhausted," I argued. "We all are. If we try to do the spell tonight, there's no way we'll have enough power to find the sceptre. We need to rest and replenish our power."

"Waiting just gives Set more time to find us."

"And doing a spell without the proper strength could kill us," I bit back. "We'll do the spell in the morning."

Nero stepped off the front porch and onto the lawn, slowly swaggering over to stand toe to toe with me. At my side, Roman turned, our shoulders now touching. Nero looked down at me, several inches taller than I was. "Did you just bark at your commanding officer?" he growled.

The memory of blades cutting into Roman's flesh flashed through my memory. The sight of him prone and unconscious on the sands haunted my thoughts. "What are you going to do about it?" I pushed. "Punish us? Your army isn't here, Nero. You'd be dead before your blade spilled a single drop of blood." Anywhere else, it would be dangerous to talk to Nero like this, but not anymore. Here, we had the numbers.

Nero's eyes blazed and he leaned forward. "That sounded dangerously like a threat."

Roman took a step closer to his father, the two men at eye level. "Take it how you want it, but you heard her. We'll do the spell in the morning."

Locked in a staring contest, neither man moved for what felt like forever. My hand inched to my dagger slowly, tensed and ready for the slightest provocation to pull it. From the villa, Mallory's voice echoed out into the front lawn, calling to Roman and me. For half a heartbeat longer, Roman still didn't move. Mallory's voice sounded again, this time closer. Roman broke eye contact from Nero, stepping around the older man and marching into the house. I hesitated a moment longer, glaring at Nero before following Roman inside.

We found Mallory in a back room. Isaac was laid out on the bed, his large frame barely fitting. His shirt lay next to him in tatters, his wound packed full of a dark green poultice. From the edges of the wound, fresh blood dripped out at an even pace. His body was covered in sweat, drops of it beading off his sleeping form. Brynn sat near him, the book open in her lap. She chanted quietly to herself words of healing and health. She looked completely wrecked, as dirty and bloodied as the rest of us, but she chanted tirelessly, her bright blue eyes intent on the words in front of her. Mallory followed my gaze.

"Cassie thinks the blade was laced with some sort of poison that keeps his blood from clotting. Brynn's doing what she can to slow the bleeding, but if she can't get it slowed down soon, he's not going to make it." My stomach dropped. There was no way we could lose Isaac. "That's not all," Mallory added. I pinched the bridge of my nose. *What else could possibly go wrong?*

"I just spoke to Daniela. Amina just gave orders for her forces to split in half. One portion of her soldiers are staying in Helwan. They are going to use the city as a home base while they search areas south of there. Amina and the other half are leaving Helwan tomorrow." I wanted to comment on the fact she'd just confirmed Daniela was their source, but I bit my tongue, saving it for later. I still needed to have that talk with Roman.

"Where are they going?" Roman asked.

Mallory grimaced. "Amina's coming to Cairo."

I growled in frustration. "This is absolutely the last thing we need right now."

"Well, it gets worse," Mallory added. "That fight earlier was in no way discreet. There's a good chance she'll catch wind of it and then she'll know there's an unauthorized Kindred presence in Cairo. Which means she'll send scouts to look for us."

"So, what do we do?" I asked. Next to me, Roman was

silent, and I knew his strategic brain was working on overdrive, already putting together the pieces of things I was too inexperienced to see.

"We have a day, tops, before this city is crawling with Kindred. We have to find The Hall of Two Truths tomorrow before Amina and her warriors get here. Then get out, without being seen," Roman answered.

"That is a tight timeline," I felt compelled to point out. Mallory and Roman nodded in agreement.

"We're going to have to split up," Roman continued. "The Guard has to go, there's no way around that, but Isaac can't be left alone, so at least one of you has to stay behind with him."

I dug my blood-caked nails into my hair. "Nero will never agree to him and Dirk staying back," I said. I threw my hand out. "It has to be you and Cassie," I said to Mallory. "Cassie can tend to Isaac's wounds, while you guard the perimeter of the safe house."

"And if you get pinned down?" Mallory asked. I hadn't thought of that. "Who is going to protect you?"

"Nero can call his men at a moment's notice," Roman answered with confidence I knew he didn't feel. "And if things go sideways and we don't return, you and Cassie get Isaac to the Coterie camp outside of town." I hated to hear him talk like that, but I knew I couldn't deny the fact that what we were doing was risky at best. There was a good chance we'd be found by either Set or the Council, and neither one of those options ended in a bright future for the

Guard. I took a deep, steadying breath, as Roman continued. "We're all too weak to perform the tracking spell tonight. We need to get cleaned up and try to get some rest if we're going to be strong enough by morning. We'll take shifts guarding the house. I'll put Nero and Dirk on the first shift. Are you and Cassie good to attend to Isaac?" he asked. "Kyndal and I can take care of him if you need the rest."

"We're fine, Rome," Cassie answered from the other side of the room. "Go get cleaned up." Her hair was straggly, falling out of her ponytail, and her hands and face were covered in caked blood. I knew as much of it was Isaac's as anyone else's.

"I'll bring you both something to drink before I go to sleep," I told them. It was a small gesture, but the least I could do.

Roman and I left them to tend Isaac, wandering through the safehouse. The house was huge, almost as big as the compound back home. There were at least ten bedrooms, half which had their own bathroom. With Isaac laid out in one, that left plenty of bedrooms for us to choose from. I wished desperately I could share mine with Roman, but we both knew that was impossible. There was no way for us to be alone, not with the others around too. I chose the room upstairs and at the end of the hall, a simple room decorated in reds and golds. The bed was large, and with how exhausted I was, it looked inviting. There were windows all along the back, no doubt meant to be wide open to the city, letting in the view. All the blinds were shut now. It cut us off from everyone else, but it also provided us the privacy we needed.

"I'm going to find the others, let them know the shift schedule. I'll come check on you in a little bit," Roman said quietly from the doorway. "I'll grab your bag too, drop it in here while you get cleaned up."

I nodded. "Thank you."

The bond tightened, our longing for each other pulling me toward him. He paused a moment longer, and I knew he felt it too. With a tight smile, he turned toward the hallway. I was going to let him go. Really, I was. But before I knew it, I crossed the room and grabbed his arm, pulling him into the room with me and hiding behind the wall. I wrapped my arms around his neck, burying my face in his shoulder. He returned the gesture, holding me as tightly as I was him. For what felt like forever, neither of us moved. Slowly, Roman pulled back, lowering his head so his forehead was leaned against mine. I closed my eyes, breathing him in.

A booted foot landed on the bottom step, breaking the moment. When I opened my eyes, he was gone.

I woke up with a start. I sat straight up in bed, my breathing fast and erratic. The room was dark, and I instinctively went for my dagger on the bedside table, scanning the room for unseen threats. As my eyes adjusted, I slowly remembered where I was, and my grip on the weapon relaxed. I pushed my legs off the side of the bed, laying my face down in my hands. I'd been dreaming again. It wasn't The Hall of Two Truths this time. Not exactly. Instead, I'd jumped right back to Marius' last moments, watching as he sacrificed his life to trap Set. Holding him as his body morphed into mine and I was inevitably left watching the life bleed out of my body.

I pulled my boots on, tying my hair back into a quick ponytail. I knew I hadn't been asleep long, as the dark tresses were still damp. I situated my dagger in the combat pants I'd slept in as I went looking for food. Roman had never returned to check on me, or if he had, I didn't remember it. I tiptoed down the steps, peeking in to Isaac's room. He looked exactly as he did before, but this time it was Brynn sitting on the window ledge, not Cassie.

She looked up when a floorboard creaked under my foot. "Need anything?" I whispered. She shook her head in response. "Where's Cassie and Mallory?" I asked.

"Sleeping. We switched shifts about an hour ago," she answered quietly.

From the bed, Isaac's body shook with a racking cough. Brynn pushed off the window ledge, grabbing a washcloth from a nearby bowl and wringing the water from it. She placed it on the side of Isaac's stomach, where his wound had opened up again. Within moments, the white cloth was stained red.

Standing like a fool, I finally jumped into action, grabbing the extra cloths off the nearby dresser and dunking them in the bowl. Hastily, I gave them to Brynn to replace her makeshift bandage. "What can I do?" I asked, my eyes glued to where the blood was starting to slow. "Do you want me to wake Cassie?" I'd never felt more helpless in my whole life. My friend was laying on the bed, dying, and there was nothing I could do to save him.

Brynn shook her head, furiously. "Leave me with him. I need my space to work." I hesitated, not sure I should leave her alone. She tilted her head. "Go."

I shut the door behind me quietly, tiptoeing to the kitchen, remembering why I was up in the first place. The kitchen was as large and opulent as the rest of the house. The cabinets were made of ebony hardwood, the counters of highest quality marble. Whoever had designed this house definitely knew what they were doing, and they had spared no expense. I wondered idly how Cassie had managed to rent it on such short notice. In the center of the kitchen was an oversized island made of the same marble as the rest of the kitchen. And perched on the edge of it, was Grady.

I opened the fridge, squinting at the interior light. The fridge was fully stocked with food and drinks, no doubt another perk of the cush lifestyle this type of house was used to accommodating. I could feel him watching me as I stared at my options. I waited for him to say something, but he never did. Finally, I pulled out a water bottle and a bowl of grapes. I set the bowl down next to him in a silent offer. "Couldn't sleep?" I asked him. He shook his head, avoiding my eyes. He didn't need to explain what kept him awake. A lot was riding on him tomorrow. If he wasn't able to track the sceptre's magic signature, we lost our advantage over the Council and Set. He took a large bite of his food, a sandwich that looked way more delicious than what I had chosen. I popped a few grapes in my mouth, then took a long swig of my water as I leaned against the counter near Grady. A companionable silence stretched out between us, broken only by the sound of Dirk and Nero patrolling the perimeter of the house. "You know, I never thanked you."

At that, he finally did turn, looking at me in confusion. "Thank me for what?"

"For what you did during the gauntlet. I know you tried to help us."

He scoffed. "I didn't do anything. I didn't stop it."

"There was no way you could've. Like Roman said, he would've just done the same thing to you. I appreciate you standing up for us."

Grady shrugged, smiling ruefully. "I owed you one."

I looked out the window once more, searching for Nero. He was on the far side of the villa, out of hearing distance. Even so, I dropped my voice to a whisper. "When we get the sceptre. . ."

"I already spoke with Roman," Grady interrupted, bringing me up short. "Brynn and I are with you. Nero won't touch it."

"What if he orders you to turn it over? You realize you'll be violating command. Violating your oath to the Council."

Grady grabbed my water bottle, taking a long swig. He hopped down from the counter, setting the bottle in front of me. He leaned in close to my ear, his breath tickling my skin.

"Screw the Council."

26

We assembled on the front lawn. The mood was serious, each one of us quiet and lost in our own thoughts. I strapped my dagger to my belt, hiding it in the built-in sheath of my combat pants. I checked the ring daggers at my ankle again, maybe for the third time. I zipped my black vest up, camouflaging the extra dagger I had hidden in a shoulder sheath.

Around me, everyone else was preparing as well. Brynn hid her sais, one in each boot; Grady added a second, then a third dagger. In addition to his standard two daggers, Roman put a third, slim blade up the sleeve of his shirt, flat against his forearm. As I anticipated, Dirk and Nero had insisted on going with us, and they too were readying their weapons. Nero went without his favorite obsidian sword, it was simply too conspicuous. We needed to be armed, but it was important that we blend in as well, meaning that all of our blades had to be hidden into our clothes.

"The spell is pretty straight forward," Brynn began,

stepping up to the oversized map of Cairo flattened out on the ground. Held down by rocks on each corner, I had no clue where she had managed to get such a large map of the city. From the bag behind her, she pulled out the silver box that once held Set's soul. "The four of us combine power, and then Grady will recite the spell while holding on to this. The box will act as a conduit and call out to its counterpart. As long as Grady keeps the box on his person, he'll be able to sense the sceptre's location using this map."

"What do we do?" Dirk asked.

"You're the muscle," she explained. "Once Grady locates the sceptre, we have to maintain the spell if we hope to retrieve it. The closer we get to the sceptre, the stronger the spell becomes, so you two need to keep us covered. Make sure we don't run into any hybrids or wraiths. We can't afford to waste any of our energy on physical fights," Brynn explained.

Nero nodded. "You don't need to worry about us. We'll do our part." I glared at him, confused as to why he was suddenly so eager to help.

"Good," Brynn answered with a bite. "Then let's begin."

Grady stepped forward, grabbing ahold of the small, silver box, his toes on the eastern edge of the map. He closed his eyes briefly, and when he opened them again, they were shining a bright green. Roman, Brynn, and I took our places around the map, each of us representing a cardinal direction. Roman stood on the north side, Brynn across from Grady on the west end, and I took my place on the southern edge of the city.

Brynn was the first to add her strength. It washed over Grady like a wave, and I swore I could smell the salt water of the ocean. I focused on her, on her power. I thought of the ocean crashing into the rocks in Awen, the roar of Maat's Hollow, the creeks and rivers of the Allegheny. I concentrated on it, on the sight and the sounds and the feel of the water until I could feel her power. I called to my own, sending my strength out to hers, encouraging them to join together. My power left me slowly, almost as if the flames could feel Brynn's strength and were frightened of the overwhelming power of the waves. Finally they connected, and the moment my power touched hers, I could feel Grady's too. It was richer than Brynn's, and the combination of the two was like sinking my fingers into damp earth. I held tight to the feel of it, wrapped the warmth of my power around it.

Moments later, Roman's power sailed down the Rafiq bond, instantly filling me with his strength. I took a deep, controlling breath, allowing me to mold Roman's power and encourage it to join Brynn and Grady's. His power clicked into place, completing the circle. We were now one unit, our elements so tightly knitted together I couldn't tell where one ended and another began. The strength of it was a heady thing, and I could see why the Council didn't want all Kindred to have access to magic like this. If I wanted to, I could pull on the others' powers—drain them completely out of each of them if I had the mind to.

Grady readjusted his hold on the box, as if he were getting

a feel for the power that whirled inside him. He closed his eyes as he began the chant. It didn't take long for the spell to take effect, and I could almost instantly feel my power being pulled from my body. It wasn't overwhelming, just a small, nagging pull, reminding me of a small drip from a faucet, just a little bit of power escaping at a time. From the corner of my eye, I saw Mallory fill the doorway of the villa, drawn to what we were doing, even though she was assigned to stay with Cassie and Isaac.

Grady knelt down to one knee, his eyes scanning over the city streets laid out before him. I tried to follow his gaze, tried to see what he saw, but no matter how I tried, the map remained the same.

We stood there for one minute. Five minutes. Then ten. All in silence as Grady studied that map, our power leaking out of us with each passing second. My eyes cut to Roman and Brynn more than once, the same skeptical looks on their faces as I knew I would see on mine.

It wasn't until twenty minutes later that abruptly, Grady pushed to his feet, wrapped the box back up in the bag, swung it onto his back and without a word walked out the front gate to the waiting SUV.

"Apparently we're leaving," Roman quipped.

I punched him on the arm lightly, then pushed him toward the gate.

Dirk climbed into the driver's seat, the rest of us piling in the back. "Head west," was Grady's only direction. Dirk obeyed, driving west, toward the river. The ride was silent, none of us asking Grady what he had seen on the map, each of us keeping an eye out the window, looking for any signs of an ambush. I alternated between checking our surroundings and strengthening the connection to the rest of the Guard. I siphoned strength from the earth around me as we traveled back into downtown Cairo.

Grady only spoke when he ordered Dirk to make a particular turn. Eventually, we rounded a corner, and the Nile came into view. Open to the elements as I was, the power of the mighty river was overwhelming. I looked to Brynn next to me. I noticed a slight trembling of her hand, almost as if the strength of the river was overwhelming her. It reminded me of the first time I'd felt the magma chamber underneath Awen. That close to such a raw source of my element had been intoxicating. Grady pointed at a parking lot across the street. "There. Park there." Dirk did as instructed.

As we got out of the vehicle, I couldn't help but stare at the river and compare it to my dreams. I'd once seen Marius and Davina sit at the river's edge and share a quiet moment together. At the time, I didn't realize what river it was, I was too focused on figuring out who the people were, but standing where I was now, it felt familiar to me, even though it looked completely different.

Where there had once been soft, fertile land, the banks of the river were now supported by cement walls, no doubt to help keep the river from flooding into the city. People walked along the sidewalks, sat with their feet dangling over the wall's edge. Below them, at the river's edge, there were small wooden docks interspersed throughout the river. A surprisingly small amount of boats cruised the water, and what little traffic there was mainly consisted of long, low lying boats giving tours to visitors. It was easy to see why there was little traffic in this stretch of river. The water was cut by several bridges with such low clearance, there was no way a large boat could make it underneath.

A tug on my power pulled me out of my sightseeing and back to the mission at hand. A piece of my strength left me, this time much bigger than before. The spell was getting stronger. I looked to Grady who was searching the area frantically, his eyes seeing a thousand lines of power invisible to the rest of us. "This way." He headed off down the sidewalk, walking alongside the river. We followed closely behind, weaving through the throngs of people. It seemed no matter what time of day it was, Cairo was always jam packed.

We walked for several blocks, following the river's current northward. While keeping myself open to the others, I projected my senses outward, searching for any sign of the wraiths or hybrids we saw yesterday. The river was lined with skyscrapers and hotels, making visibility difficult. "I don't like this. It's almost impossible to sense anything with so many people around," I whispered to Roman.

"We're almost there," Grady announced. We passed another large skyscraper, elbowing our way through the people coming out of the building. As we passed it, the landscape opened up, revealing a building on the other side of the road that was wildly different than anything around it. The first thing I noticed was the high raised, steel fence, the guard shacks built into them every fifty feet or so. Whatever this place was, it required high security. Directly behind it was a large courtyard, landscaped in a variety of green grasses, shrubs, and palm trees, a strange contradiction to the cold steel that caged it in. At the center of it all, a beautiful burnt umber building. Two stories tall, the front of the building was dominated by full length, curved windows. An ivory archway stood at its center, two mahogany doors tucked inside it. Raising out of the rooftop, a large windowed dome reflected the harsh desert sun, reminding me of the library back in Awen. The entire thing was a splash of color in an otherwise sandy city.

"What is that place?" I couldn't help but ask.

"The Museum of Egyptian Antiquities," Brynn answered quickly.

"It's beautiful," I responded.

"Inside is even more impressive. The Egyptian Museum contains the largest collection of Egyptian artifacts in the world. Over 120,000 separate artifacts live inside those walls. They have so much, they had to build underground storage specifically for the items that are not on display." I didn't have to ask how she knew so much about the museum, not after what she'd told me back in Marienville. I imagined Brynn spent a lot of time visiting other museums with her parents.

"It looks like they're having a gala soon, Kyndal, if you would like to go," Nero sneered. "Apparently what we're doing isn't interesting enough for you."

I rolled my eyes. Obviously Nero was still upset about my not so veiled threat earlier. "Bite me," I told him. Even saying that, I couldn't help but notice what drew his eye. A large banner hung off the front of the museum advertising a fundraising event they were holding tomorrow evening. Apparently it was a dance of some sort, and the large mask on the banner made me think it was masquerade themed.

Without warning, Grady turned right, directly into oncoming traffic. A car screeched to a halt, blaring its horn, but Grady didn't notice. He didn't even pause for a moment. Instead he beelined across the road, onto the opposite sidewalk. The rest of us followed behind, crossing the road with more care. We caught back up to him, Dirk huffing in irritation behind me. "You're going the wrong way," he jeered. "The legends say the doorway is at the river's edge, we need to go down to the river, not away from it." Ego dripped from his every word. A sure sign of a man who thought he knew better than everyone else.

There was only a brief warning through the bond before Roman whipped around. "It's not that simple, you dim witted douchebag. The Nile in the legends is from thousands of years ago. Back when the river freely flooded the surrounding area. The Nile hasn't flooded into the city in decades. The door might not be at the water's edge anymore. It could be in the city." I raised my eyebrows at Roman's tone. Not because he snapped at Dirk, but because he did it in defense of Grady.

"Not in," Grady interrupted, promptly ignoring the fact

Roman had just stood up for him. "Under."

I furrowed my eyebrows. "What do you mean, under?"

Grady's head tilted back, eyeballing the mammoth museum that now stood in front of us. "The Hall of Two Truths is under the Egyptian Museum."

I threw my dagger down on the couch of the villa, huffing in annoyance. Brynn, Grady, and Roman followed suit, our various blades clanging off the tables and floor, each of us equally pissy. The sun was setting, the front room of the villa cast into shadow. I stomped over to the kitchen, ripping open the fridge and grabbing a handful of water bottles. I kicked the door shut, rattling the fridge. I tossed the extra water bottles to my Guardsmen. Roman took a long swig from his, then sauntered off to the back of the house, no doubt to check on Isaac. He had no more disappeared from view than Mallory stormed past him, her eyes on fire. "What the hell is all the noise about?" she demanded. "Did you find the sceptre?"

"Oh, we found it all right," I answered angrily.

She threw her arms out, exasperated. "Where is it?"

"Well, let's see," I began. "It's under a building made of stone and marble that is about the size of a damn city block."

Mallory furrowed her eyebrows. "That's not so bad. We'll

just go in at night to get it."

I huffed a laugh. "Did I mention the fact that the building happens to house the world's greatest collection of Egyptian artifacts and because of that fact, it's surrounded with security cameras that we can't evade, metal detectors that will go berserk the second there's a single weapon near them, and armed guards that will shoot us at the drop of a hat?" We'd spent all day trying to find a way into the museum, but there was no way we were going to get in, not strapped with daggers the way we were. Grady had offered to go in defenseless, but we all quickly shut that down. We were left with no choice but to return to the villa to regroup.

"The sceptre is under the Egyptian Museum of Antiquities," Grady translated for her.

Mallory flinched. "Oh," she hesitated. "Shit." Any other time I would have laughed at her ineloquent response. Clearly she was familiar with the place and the challenges it posed.

"Exactly," Roman agreed, returning from Isaac's room. Cassie followed him a step behind. Her eyes were tired, her nails caked in dried blood. She had not gotten any rest since we left.

I looked to Roman expectantly, sending a pulse of curiosity down our bond. He gave me a small nod and a tight smile, despite the worry I could see in his eyes. Isaac was hanging in there. Something tight in my chest eased just a bit. I didn't know what I would do if Isaac didn't pull through.

I flopped down on the couch, throwing my head back on the cushion. Brynn joined me a moment later. Around me, the others were bickering, arguing about the best way to breach the museum. Grady was revisiting his plea to go in unarmed, but just as before, Cassie saw the flaw in his plan. If we were to encounter any hybrids or wraiths, we would be sitting ducks. There was no way we could use our elements inside the building, not without calling a lot of attention to ourselves and potentially ruining millions of dollars in irreplaceable artifacts. Nero called for the alternative approach—sneak in at night and disable the guards, leaving us to roam free. Roman immediately contested his idea, refusing to be a part of anything that hurt civilians. "We're at war, boy," Nero sneered at Roman. "You have to get your hands dirty sometime." *Boy.* I flinched at his use of the word.

Outwardly, Roman was unfazed, but I could feel his anger, simmering just under the surface. "I know the Coterie holds no such morals, but I will not be a part of anything that hurts innocents."

Nero scoffed, shaking his head at Roman in disgust. I waited for him to push, to demand his authority, but he never did. Instead, he and Dirk stomped outside to patrol the villa wall. I breathed a sigh of relief. Nero finally understood we would not bend to his tyranny, no matter how severe the punishment.

I continued to listen to the others, but my body was suddenly overwhelmingly exhausted and I was consumed with the need to shut my eyes and sleep. The spell from this morning had really taken a toll. I reached my power outward, searching for all sources of elemental power I could find. The surrounding air, the earth outside the house, the candles I could feel flickering in Isaac's room. It felt like I had no more than closed my eyes when the floor under me shuddered. I sat forward like a bolt, my back ramrod straight. "Did you guys feel that?" The conversation came to an immediate halt. I stared at Grady. If anyone felt it, it had to be him. He held my stare, and for a solid minute, nobody moved, each of us searching for the tiniest tremor.

Nothing came.

Quietly, walking only on the pads of her feet, Mallory tiptoed over to the window, grabbing one of my daggers from where I'd thrown it. Carefully, she pushed the edge of the curtain aside to peek out into the dying light. "All clear..." she started. Mid-sentence, the window shattered. She turned wildly, using her impressive speed to drop to the floor, covering her face as the shards of glass rained down on top of her. Mere seconds later, a man jumped through the broken window, practically landing on top of Mallory. The intruder was dressed in familiar black garb, a silver dagger glinting in his left hand. He raised the dagger above his head, prepared to bring it down on Mallory. Acting on instinct, I threw my arm out, a fireball ripping from my hand and barreling toward the man. It hit him in his shoulder, spinning him around and into the window frame, giving Mallory just enough time to spin and swipe his feet out from underneath him, knocking him to the floor. She capitalized on her advantage, throwing one solid right hand, knocking him out cold.

Brynn and I now on our feet, we closed ranks with the others, allowing Mallory to stumble behind us. Her caramel colored hair was littered with tiny pieces of glass, and there were small cuts on her face that were already beginning to seal up. More concerning, there was a large shard of glass embedded in her bicep. Mallory promptly ripped it out with a growl, throwing the bloody shard to the floor. Roman looked down at the intruder. "He's Kindred," he announced to the rest of us.

"They found us," Grady added. He didn't need to explain who *they* were. I recognized the man on the floor. He was the same man that'd thrown me in the cell before The Blinding. He was one of Amina's men.

"Where the hell are Nero and Dirk?" I demanded. They had gone out to run patrol. Why hadn't they warned us about the invaders? This villa had been picked for a reason. There was no way someone could sneak up on us, not with our high walls.

Brynn began chanting, a shield snapping into place a moment later. I threw what remained of my power toward her, enlarging the shield to accompany all of us in the house, never taking my eyes off the now busted window.

Waiting.

Waiting for the next assault.

From upstairs, more glass shattered, the thud of footsteps following. They were inside. I looked to Cassie, then both of us turned to Roman, expectantly. "Go," he ordered. Cassie and I took off, sprinting for the stairs, each of us pulling our weapons in the process. I'd left my large daggers downstairs, a fact I was now kicking myself for. Instead, I pulled my twin ring daggers, looping my fingers through them and tucking them into my palms. We didn't bother with stealth, they already knew we were here. Instead we chose brute force. Behind us, I heard the splintering of wood, the large front door of the villa being blown in half as they breached the front of the house. Cassie and I increased our pace, making it to the top floor in no time. I led the way, using my fire as a first line of offense since her element was not readily available. I could hear them at the end of the hall, in the same room I'd slept in the night before. I launched a fireball toward the closed door, blasting it off its hinges, another one loading before the door had hit the back wall.

We ran past the first door, but at the second one, a woman barreled out of the room, knocking me into the wall, my head denting the plaster. My fireball extinguished almost instantly, just before her knuckles ricocheted off my temple in a stinging left hook. A small black cloud appeared at the edge of my vision. I pushed her back violently, lashing out with my ring dagger, satisfied when I felt it slice through soft flesh. It wasn't a kill shot by any means, but it was enough to buy me a moment.

Cassie sprinted past me, her blue eyes shining and her red hair like a living flame, fearlessly jumping into the wave of Kindred pouring out of the end bedroom. It was a flurry of fists and daggers, Cassie sweeping through the area, clearing as many of the intruders as she could. I made quick work of my opponent, knocking her out cold on the bedroom floor. Payback for her cheap shot. I turned to Cassie, ready to help, when a hot pain sliced against my ribs, an echo from Roman. I hissed in anger, my hand rushing to the wound instinctively. My fingers came away slick with blood. I tried to heal it, tried to push my power toward it, but I had none left to give. I was still connected to Brynn, helping her maintain the shield. I had to choose—heal myself or protect the others. I wasn't ready to lose the shield. Not yet. I gritted my teeth, reinforcing my connection to the shield and ignoring the pain in my side as I jumped back in the fight. We worked our way through the Kindred invaders, but it felt like for every one we downed, two more appeared. My power was dwindling, my element surfacing at a slower pace each time I called to it.

Eventually, I was forced to disconnect from Brynn, no longer able to maintain the shield and protect myself. Cassie and I fought back to back inside that bedroom, which now seemed so much smaller than it had the night before. I was knocked into the side of the bed, one of my ring daggers flying in the process. I stumbled sideways, grabbing the nearby vase and smashing it over the head of my opponent. He faltered for a moment, but returned with a blast of air, one that this time I wasn't able to block. I flew backward, my entire body colliding with the wall before I dropped to the ground in a heap.

I coughed raggedly, each breath coming out in a wet gasp. I stared at the bedroom floor, trying to focus my vision, the black dots from before threatening to take over. I pushed myself up, but fell halfway there, dropping on to my hands and knees. I took another deep, racking breath, but my lungs burned for more. The oxygen in the room suddenly absent. The last thing I remember was a pulse through the bond. A final panicked moment.

Then everything went black.

27

I woke up on the floor. Not the same floor I'd been on before, but the hard, cold marble of the main room. I blinked, staring up at the harsh lights that illuminated the grand space. I groaned, rolling to my side. I was met with the sight of Isaac—his unconscious, bleeding form thrown down next to me. I gasped his name, my voice hoarse. I pushed myself up, scooting over to my friend. His wound had opened again and was trickling blood. I searched the room frantically. *Where is everyone?* I thought desperately. My head was still foggy, the edges of my vision not as sharp as they should have been. My power sat empty—exhausted and unreachable. The furniture in the room had been pushed aside, at least what was left of it. Dozens of pieces had been broken, entire tables smashed to bits, laying a mere foot away from what remained of the front door.

"Ahem," a voice cleared their throat behind me. I spun around to find Amina sitting haughtily on the edge of a coffee table. Even dressed in her fighting gear, she still sat with her back straight as a board, her legs crossed, one arm draped over the top knee. Her nails were perfectly manicured, her raven hair braided sharply down the back of her head. The consummate portrait of entitlement. On either side of her were my remaining friends, each on their knees, their wrists in chains, a Kindred soldier standing behind them with a dagger to their throat.

Immediately, my eyes found Roman. Blood dripped from the wound on his torso, the mirror to my own. I felt his pain, the burning he felt with every breath. My body filled with rage at the sight of it and I staggered to my feet, launching myself at the Nomarch poised five feet from me. I only made it a step before two Kindred interfered, their daggers aimed at my throat bringing me up short.

"Even defeated, you still insist on fighting," Amina reprimanded, her voice even.

My eyes skipped over all my friends. Each of them was bloodied and beaten, their powers no doubt as depleted as mine, but I could see in their eyes the desire for revenge. Like caged animals, they were waiting. Waiting for the moment they were given the opportunity to strike.

"Let them go," I said to Amina quietly. It was a task to keep my voice calm. To not yell and scream and roar at her. "They have nothing to do with this." Because this wasn't about the fact that we were here against Council orders. This was personal. It had been ever since I'd survived The Blinding of Truth by Falsehood.

Amina smiled, her red lipstick pulling back behind her

straight white teeth. "I'd be happy to, if you just give me the answers I need."

I scoffed. "What could you possibly want to know?"

"For starters," she said, picking an imaginary piece of lint off the top of her pant leg, "you were ordered to return to Marienville and remain there under the watchful eye of the newly instated Aries Nomarch, Nero. I spoke with him just two days ago and he assured me you were doing just that. Clearly that was a lie."

Outwardly, I made sure to remain still, to make no move that gave away a hint of the fear and concern I could feel spinning inside me. If Amina knew what we had been doing, why we were here and who helped us get here, we were in trouble.

In fact, we were totally screwed.

"I didn't hear a question," I responded, stalling her even though her intent was perfectly clear.

Her eyes thinned, the dark irises switching to blue. The only hint of the slip on her self control. "Who gave the order to come to Cairo?" she said tightly. "Nero never does anything unless it benefits him. He had no reason to maneuver the Guard to Egypt, not unless there was something in it for him. Who paid him to bring you here? Who is he working with?"

I stared at the Nomarch, my brain working as quickly as it could, considering my current state. "It's all true, isn't it?" I asked, because at this point I had nothing left to lose. "You want to disband the Council and rule the Kindred on your own, don't you? I mean, that is why you're doing all of this, right? That's why you're holding soldiers, your own *Guard* as prisoners?"

Amina remained silent, a small flick of her fingernail her only tell. "Give me the name."

I pressed my lips together tightly. She may have questions, but I sure as hell wasn't going to make it easy on her. There were too many lives at stake. Not just those in front of me, but Allie, Lydia, and Sandra too. "Let them go," I countered.

A Kindred guard stepped out from behind Brynn, flipping his dagger in his hand. With deathly speed, the hilt ricocheted off her cheekbone, snapping her head to the side. I lunged forward, straining against the daggers at my throat until they bit at my flesh. Brynn rolled her head back, her eye already cut and bleeding. I grimaced as it started to swell, turning my head to glare at Amina. Brynn belonged to House Scorpio—she was a member of Amina's house and for her Nomarch to strike out at her, through a soldier or otherwise, crossed a line. A deep burning rage ignited inside me, the power that lived deep in my stomach rumbling to life. "I'll ask again. Who gave the order?" she said smoothly.

"Go to hell," I spit. This time it was Grady that felt the pain of my silence. A burly, muscular soldier buried his fist in Grady's stomach. Grady doubled over, coughing uncontrollably.

"When the news reached me yesterday about the fight in Cairo, the hybrid bodies left littering the streets, I had a feeling it might be you," Amina crooned. Another hit. This time to Cassie. "There was no one else I could think of that was stupid enough to defy me. Only you." An elbow to Mallory's nose. Blood gushed down her chin, pooling on her lip. She spit it onto the floor, her teeth stained red. Amina continued, "You see, I left a few of my soldiers in the States to look after my interests there. I sent them to the compound in Marienville. Imagine my surprise when they found it empty. No Nero. No Guard. And now it seems Nero has completely disappeared." She paused. "Tell me who gave the order." The guards next to me reaffirmed their grips on their daggers.

"We both know you won't kill me. You need me alive," I accused, careful not to say too much in front of the others. Because she had to know my death was the key to caging Set.

Her smile turned positively feline. "I wondered when you would figure it out. You were so desperate to save your wraith of a boyfriend, you never stopped to think why I accepted you into the Guard. Why I didn't just kill you both where you stood. You see, I don't have to kill you. You're already dead," she hissed, confirming what I suspected. "Your friends however, there are no such protections for your friends."

The guard on my left stepped away, kneeling down to the still unconscious Isaac. He took the tip of his dagger and dug it into Isaac's sickly flesh, fresh blood gushing from the wound. Isaac stirred, loosing an agonizing groan that ended in a hacking wet cough, blood bubbling onto his lower lip. "Stop it!" I yelled at Amina. "You'll kill him!"

"Tell me who gave the order," Amina pushed. "Which Nomarchs are working against me?"

Suddenly consumed with a blazing ire, my power blasted forward from the depths, filling my body with renewed strength. My eyes snapped to a sharp red. Amina saw the change in me, felt the shift of power in the room, but she wasn't fast enough to stop me. I threw my elbow out, catching my remaining guard by surprise, breaking his nose. With one hand, I grabbed his wrist, my other hand blasting him in the center of his chest, knocking him to the ground and leaving me with his weapon in my hand. "Let them go Amina, or I swear I'll. . ."

Amina stood, "Or you'll what?!" she grit through her teeth.

My brain was whirling, desperately looking for a way out of this situation. We were outnumbered and overpowered. There was no way we could fight our way out. As long as my friends were in chains, Amina held all the leverage. I had nothing she wanted. Nothing except. . .

I flipped the dagger, pointing the tip of it at my own heart. "I'll kill myself."

Amina froze. Everyone did. "Kyndal, no," Brynn pled. "You'll kill us all." She knew better than anybody what was at stake, what I was risking. Slowly, Amina took a step forward.

I kept my eyes focused on Amina, ignoring the crystal blue gaze I could feel staring at me from nearby. He didn't say anything aloud, but I could feel everything as if he had. I knew he was begging me to look at him. That he was desperate for me to explain what was going on. I didn't falter. I knew just one look at him and I'd lose my nerve. "You wouldn't dare," Amina challenged. "You know what would happen. The price your friends would pay for your choice."

My voice was tight, laced with emotion, a few hot tears rolling down my face, which I promptly ignored. "You're going to kill them anyway. What's the difference whether it's you or Set that does it? At least this way, I know I'll have the satisfaction of denying you the glorious victory you have been searching for your entire miserable existence. The Kindred will never allow you to dissolve the Council, not after they hear what happened here. And when I'm gone, and there's no way left to stop Set, at least I'll know that he will find you, and he will end you too."

My heart was pounding. I tightened the grip on the dagger, my muscles flexed as the tip of the weapon dug into my flesh and I prepared to drive it home.

"It was Astrid!" the voice ripped through the room, into my very soul. My arms dropped to my side, the dagger clanging onto the floor. My breathing shuddered as I stared at Roman with wide eyes. He climbed to his feet, his guard allowing him to take a step forward. He turned to Amina. "Astrid sent us here. We found a way to track the was-sceptre to its temple and we were going to retrieve it before

Set and his hybrids had the opportunity to get it for themselves."

"And Nero?" she asked.

Roman didn't hesitate. "His Coterie forces are camped outside the city. He and his second in command accompanied us into Cairo."

"Where is Nero now?"

"He was with us until just moments before you arrived. He must have gone after the sceptre on his own." I grimaced. Of course he had. I had assumed he'd gone back to the camp, but that didn't make sense. Sandra was there and would stop him from going after the sceptre.

Amina simmered with rage, her gaze sliding over to me. "That wasn't so hard, now was it? Tell me where the sceptre is," she demanded of Roman.

"It's not that simple," Roman responded. "Let us help you and we'll tell you where the sceptre is hidden."

Amina turned her head slowly. "Did you miss the part where you are in chains? You have no bargaining power."

Roman didn't waver. "The temple is dangerous. Protected by old magic that only the Guard can withstand. Not to mention, if Nero is going after the sceptre, he has more men than you do, and you don't have time to bring in other soldiers. You need every warrior you can get."

Amina was silent and for a long minute, no one said a word. Her decision would quite literally decide our fate.

"Very well," she said at last. "Release them." Chains dropped to the floor as one by one my friends rose to their feet. Amina's soldiers scooped Isaac up off the floor, hauling him back down the hallway.

"Where are you taking him?" I asked.

"He will remain here, under the careful watch of my soldiers. If you're lying to me, or don't deliver the sceptre directly to my hands, young Isaac will pay with his life."

"He needs medical care," I argued.

"Then I suggest you don't waste any time. Now, the sceptre's location. I will not ask again."

I gritted my teeth. I really hated this woman. "It's in The Hall of Two Truths." I didn't miss the small rise of her eyebrows. Clearly, the temple's legend preceded it. "The doorway to the temple is buried underneath The Egyptian Museum of Antiquities."

Grady stepped up next to me. "It's impossible to get past security with our weapons, and it will take us days to figure out how to disable their system."

"I can get us in faster." I turned to the voice—to Brynn who was standing with her arms crossed, very purposefully not looking at her Nomarch. "We can get in during the gala."

"What gala?" Amina asked. Brynn ignored her, continuing instead to talk to me.

"I've been to events like this before, back when my parents

worked at the British Museum. They're huge fundraising events. Strictly invitation only. Lots of very prominent, very wealthy people will be there. The type of people that have their own security guards and are too important to be checked by metal detectors. They'll most likely have them disabled during the event, allowing us to slip in, our weapons undetected."

"What about invitations?" Roman asked.

Brynn smirked, the right side tightening under her swollen eye. "I can handle that too. There is a woman named Khepri. She is one of the assistant curators and was good friends with my mom. She can get us tickets."

"Just like that?" Grady asked.

Brynn shrugged. "There will be a cost. Khepri doesn't do anything out of the goodness of her heart. We'll owe her a favor. One she won't be scared to collect."

"Good," Amina praised, as if she had been in charge of this operation. As if she had done anything to help at all. "Make the arrangements."

Grady turned to me, that ornery grin on his face. "Looks like you're going to make it to your dance."

I ran my hands over the soft silk of the dress, smoothing it out against my hips. I turned in front of the full-length mirror again, my leg snaking out from the thigh high slit, the soft black material swishing along the floor. A half an inch higher, and the slit would expose the leather sheath I had wrapped around my upper thigh. The one place I could hide my ring daggers.

I tugged on the thin straps of the dress, trying to hike the top of it a little higher. Amina had sent her people out to get us outfits for the gala tonight, apparently not trusting us to do our own shopping. Clearly, this dress had been picked out by a man. It was slinky, the straps of it spaghetti thin. The top plunged low between my breasts, the bodice of the dress conforming to my every curve, leaving absolutely no space for me to hide a full-sized dagger. The back hung low, just kissing the small of my back. I'd swept my hair up in an effort to keep it out of my face, adding some charcoal shadow to my eyelids that I knew would match the black lace mask that was laying on the bed not a foot away.

I stepped into the nude pumps that finished the outfit. "Wow." The whispered voice startled me, and I gasped, my eyes flying up. Roman was reflected in the mirror, standing behind me against the now closed door. My eyes traveled slowly up and down his tall frame, drinking him in. He wore a black tux, the bow tie hanging loosely around his neck. It was a testament to how distracted I'd been by my outfit that I hadn't felt him coming. Now I was overwhelmed by his emotions, by the burning need I could feel pumping through his veins. That now ran through my own.

"You don't look so bad yourself," I responded in a breathy voice that was not mine. Roman took a slow step forward, and I watched him in the mirror as he approached. I hadn't seen him since the night before. Amina had banished us all to separate parts of the villa, the few parts that hadn't been ruined. He was all healed now, each of us given the opportunity to recharge during the day. There were no more hints of the cuts and bruises he'd had the night before, the wound on his torso completely sealed. My eyes skipped to the silence sigil I could now see on the door behind him. "Are you here to yell at me?"

He stood behind me in the mirror, so close I could feel his breath on my ear. "Why would I do that? Because you lied to me about what you saw in the river? Or because you tried to leave me forever last night?" His hand came up slowly, his knuckles sliding down my exposed arm. My breath caught at the touch, my eyes closing briefly in ecstasy as icy fire followed his touch. Roman watched my reaction in the mirror, felt it in my body as I leaned back into his warmth.

"Either," I answered. "Both," I corrected.

He leaned down, pressing the smallest kiss to my shoulder. "I thought about it," he admitted, placing another kiss. "I knew you were keeping something from me the moment you denied seeing anything in the river. You forget I can read your every emotion." Another kiss. "I never dreamed it would have been something this big." He blew out an exasperated breath, one that immediately made me feel guilty for the stress I'd caused him. "Is it true? Is it your blood that seals Set's cage?" I could feel the pain the question caused him.

I turned, looking up at him. At the worry lines along his mouth, the concern haunting his eyes. I'd tried to hide this from him, protect him from the pain of the decision I knew I had to make. "Yes," I admitted.

His shoulders slumped, his body almost collapsing in on itself. "Why would you keep that from me? After everything we've been through." I winced at the betrayal in his voice, even as I thought of the gauntlet, the punishment he'd taken for going into the dream with me.

I cupped his cheek. "You would have been protected. Brynn was going to break the Rafiq bond, so you would be safe if I died. I was trying to protect you. I knew you would kill yourself trying to stop me. That you'd blame yourself when you weren't able to. I couldn't do that to you."

He pulled back, out of reach. "You don't get it. You didn't protect me at all. I could already feel it, Kyndal. I just didn't know what it was. I've never been so scared as I was last night. You pointed a dagger at your heart. And if I hadn't spoken up, you'd be dead right now."

"That's exactly what I'm talking about," I argued. "You put yourself directly in-between two feuding Nomarchs. How do you think Astrid will react when she learns you sold her out to Amina? You've already put yourself in danger trying to save me, and I won't let you take any more unnecessary risks."

"You're doing the same thing!" he hollered. "You're trying to sacrifice yourself!" His eyes were ablaze, the center of the irises turning gold. "And I'm not worried about Astrid.

She clearly knows how important you are. She wouldn't do anything to hurt me."

I shook my head. "I'm trying to *keep* people from getting hurt. This is my destiny, my path I have to walk. The Council kept Descendents from being branded for generations because they knew what our blood could do. The danger someone like me could pose to our people. To the world. And they were right. Just look what's happened since I was branded Kindred. It was my blood that started this, and it'll be my blood that finishes it. Just as Marius did before me."

Roman shook his head, running his fingers through his tousled locks. "I can't just sit back and watch you give up."

I closed the gap between us, my fingers diving into his hair. I pulled his face to mine as I kissed him fiercely. He responded immediately, his mouth hot and insistent against mine, his hand curling along my back, fisting the small bit of fabric there. I pulled away slowly, keeping within a breath's distance. "I have to finish this. My life is no more precious or important than anyone else's."

"It is to me." His voice broke at the end, his head hung in defeat. "Don't ask me to let you die."

"You know I'm right," I said softly. "I will not let Set kill innocents when I have the power to stop him. One life to save thousands. Deep down, you know I'm right."

He didn't answer, instead he pulled me to him, kissing me again. This kiss was different. There was an urgency to it, a desperation that had me wrapping my arms around his neck and pulling him closer. The fist at my back flattened, his fingers kneading at my skin. He turned me, the back of my legs bumping into the bed, even as he never broke the kiss. I laid back, bringing him with me.

I knew this wasn't a good idea. We both did. We were surrounded by people that couldn't know we were together, and we were expected to leave for the gala in less than an hour. None of that stopped us from stealing a few moments for ourselves. From taking the time to show each other how much we loved each other, even if we couldn't always say it out loud. Even if it might be for the last time.

For those few moments, there were no enemies around us, no chaos gods to fight. It was just me and him. Only us.

And for those precious moments, life was perfect.

28

The gala was packed. Amina had arranged for us to arrive by chauffered car, the blacked-out vehicle blending in perfectly with that of the other guests. Brynn had managed to get ahold of Khepri and secured us seven tickets. Enough for the Guard, Amina, Cassie, and Mallory. I hadn't asked her what she'd had to promise in return. I wasn't sure I wanted to know.

Several of Amina's soldiers patrolled the surrounding streets, looking for any sign of Nero and the Coterie, or Set and his hybrids. As the first line of defense, their job was simple—keep the museum clear and give us time to find the sceptre.

My mask firmly in place, I walked up the grand entrance of the museum. The facade had been transformed, the various sections illuminated with red and gold lights. The line to get inside was out the door, and just as Brynn had promised, the attendees were skating past the metal detectors, pausing only to show the man at the door their invitations.

I waited patiently to enter—Cassie and Mallory ahead of me, Brynn and Roman ahead of them. Amina and Grady trailed behind me. I knew we weren't here for the party, but I couldn't help but take a moment to appreciate the beautiful dresses my friends wore. We spent so much time in fighting gear, we rarely had the chance to wear such fine clothing.

Cassie wore a deep green that reminded me of Grady's eyes, her red hair cascading down her back in ringlets that I knew secretly hid the dagger tucked into the back of her dress. Mallory's gown was a shimmering gold with a slit almost as high as mine. The color matched her tawny skin perfectly, making it sparkle. Even Amina I had to give credit to. Her dress was a deep blue, no doubt a nod to her House. Her hair was pulled back in its standard slick ponytail, the end of it falling down her exposed back. As beautiful as they looked, it was Brynn's dress that was the best. She was dressed in a regal, purple gown that fell off her shoulder, the train of it sweeping out around her feet as she walked. Paired with a silver mask, her dark skin, and short hair, the dress was a shock of color—beautiful and daring. A dress only someone as stunning as she could pull off.

The line moved quickly and before I knew it, we were inside the museum. The building was just as impressive inside as it was out. Split into several sections, the central hall spanned the length of the building and was two stories tall. A variety of artifacts were on display, each in pristine condition, kept under glass and away from wandering hands. Patrons mingled in-between them, champagne in hand, waiters weaving in and out of the aisles keeping their customers plied with alcohol and hor d'oeuvres.

On either side of the main corridor, large columns held up the second floor which wrapped around us, intricate bannisters giving us a look into what was housed there. The room was dominated however, by a variety of sculptures of different pharaohs and gods, some life size, others beyond gigantic.

We split up, moving through separate parts of the museum, looking for anything that could lead us to the basement, to where we might find a door. We had to move slowly, careful not to do anything that might draw attention to ourselves.

Cassie and Mallory went directly for the back of the museum. Their steps were confident, and they smiled politely at people as they passed, as if they mingled among these types of people all the time. Grady had moved to the right side of the building, Amina following behind. She wasn't going to let him out of her sight. The Guard had combined powers before we entered, allowing him to channel our strength into tracking the sceptre. It wasn't anything as powerful as what he'd done before with the magnification spell, but connected as we were, we'd all know the second he caught a hint of a trail. There was no way Amina was going to be left out of that loop.

I stepped down the few stairs that brought me onto the main floor, discreetly eyeing Brynn and Roman who had moved to the opposite side corridor. Slightly higher than where I was now, they mingled among the people, pausing intermittently to look at an artifact, to offer a polite smile to someone as they walked past. Only someone who knew what to look for would recognize that they were in fact taking count of security guards, finding the locations of the cameras, so we could avoid detection.

I weaved through the other attendees, moving toward the back of the museum, casting my senses out as I went. I couldn't feel anything strange, nothing that seemed to indicate a wraith or hybrid was nearby. All was completely as it should be. I spied a set of wooden doors at the very back, each adorned with a placard that read *private*. I moved through the room, intent on investigating when I was brought up short. I paused at a pair of sculptures at the rear of the museum, their giant facades demanding my attention. Easily the largest thing in the room, the sculptures rose to the second story, a matching set of a man and a woman sitting, their palms open on their laps. I stared at them, for some reason a sense of familiarity taking root inside me.

Footsteps sounded behind me, light and casual. A man I'd never seen before paused next to me, two flutes of champagne in his hands. "Remarkable, isn't it?" he asked, his voice heavily accented. He offered me a glass and I took it with an easy smile, knowing it would be odd to refuse.

I took the smallest sip. "What is?" I asked him.

He stared up at the statues. "To be surrounded by thousands

of years of history. To know that they once stood where we now stand. Fascinating story, these two. Do you know it?"

"They seem so familiar, almost as if I've seen them before," I admitted.

"They were lovers," he began. "Some say they were the first ones that ever existed. Perfect complements to each other. She was ruthless, the fiercest warrior in history. She believed in truth and justice, and ruled her kingdom with an iron fist. He, on the other hand, did everything he could to disrupt the balance, to bring adventure and mischief to her life. You would think she would despise him for it, but in fact it was the opposite. She loved the turmoil he created. Thrived on being the one to right it again. They were madly in love and for generation upon generation they ruled over the land."

"What happened to them?" I asked the man.

"She betrayed him. He wanted to extend their kingdom, to conquer new lands. So one day, he left to do just that, intent on presenting his conquests to his queen as a gift. But when he returned, he discovered she had been unfaithful and had in fact replaced him with another man. This man whispered lies into her ear, convincing her that her king was evil, that he brought nothing but destruction and chaos to her people. Where she had once seen the beauty in the balance he created, now she only saw destruction. She declared herself sole ruler of the kingdom and cast him out, banishing him for all time. She vilified him, turning her people against him, convincing them he was evil and should be feared, not revered."

"That's awful. What did he do?"

The man shrugged. "She claimed the fertile lands for herself, the ones that were easy to live on, leaving him nothing but desert. But the man was not scared of the difficulty he would face in the endless sand. Instead he embraced the hardship and learned how to channel that strength into one purpose."

"What purpose?" I asked quietly.

The stranger turned to me, his mouth twisting into a smile. "My revenge."

It took a moment for his words to sink in, for me to fully understand the implications of what he was saying. I turned, the champagne flute forgotten as it crashed to the floor. I gaped at the man as his body began to shimmer with the familiar multi-color glow of magic. His form faded away, replaced by one I knew all too well. Dressed just like the other patrons, his black jacket cut across his shoulders, his bow tie neatly placed at his throat, Set smiled down at me. His face was tanned, the veins at the edge of his jaw illuminated the lightest shade of red. His dark eyes disappeared, replaced with glowing red orbs.

"Hello, Kyndal."

"How did you get in here?" I hissed. How had we not felt him? Sensed his presence?

"I am not without my own magic, girl," he responded. "Who do you think taught Maat all those spells? Who do you think helped her write that book of yours?" My hand flashed downward, going for my hidden daggers, but Set was faster. He gripped my hand tightly, pulling me in to whisper in my ear. "I wouldn't, if I were you. I have hybrids all over this museum. One signal from me and they start slaughtering people."

My eyes skipped over the room, to where I could now see who he was talking about. Among the people, there were others that weren't quite mingling, who stood just behind a group of patrons as they made small talk around the thousands of years' worth of artifacts. With effort and concentration, I was able to peel away the glamor, to see the shimmer of magic that coated them.

"What are you going to do?" I asked. "Kill me in front of all of these people?"

His head cocked to the side. "I don't want to kill you." Faster than I could see, his other hand rushed forward, gripping me tightly on the arm. A pulse of pure power shot through me, taking my breath away. I dropped to my knees, my free arm curling in on my stomach in agony. Around me, the other patrons continued to mingle, continued to move around normally, as if they couldn't see me writhing on the floor in pain. I looked up to where I'd seen Roman and Brynn last. Their backs were to me, but as if he could feel me, Roman paused, his head turning slightly and scanning the museum. My heart swelled with hope, right up until his eyes skipped right over where Set and I were. "He can't see you," Set answered, even though I hadn't said a word. "It was simple, really. Just a small cloaking spell and all the power of the Guard becomes worthless. Not even the infamous Rafiq bond can penetrate my magic. The Kindred were stupid for thinking you would ever be strong enough to defeat me."

"We did it before," I grit out. "Marius trapped you. And once we have the sceptre, we'll do it again."

"Ah, yes, the sceptre," Set answered, dragging me to my feet. He gripped my other arm, lifting me off my feet, bringing me face to face with him. "That reminds me. I need you to unlock a door."

"I won't let you into The Hall of Two Truths," I protested.

Set laughed. "Stupid girl. Whatever made you think that was the door I was speaking of?"

I tilted my head in confusion, but before I could respond, thunder cracked in my ear, a wild pulse of power shooting out of Set's center.

Then the room exploded.

29

Glass shattered and marble was reduced to nothing but rubble as I flew through the air. I grunted in pain as my body hit something hard, ricocheting off it, dropping me in an awkward heap on the floor. It took me a moment to collect my senses, for the ringing of my ears to resolve into the collective sound of dozens of screams, and for me to realize that the darkness wasn't because I had been blinded, but because the power had blown out in the explosion.

"Set!" I screamed into the void as I stumbled in the darkness, tripping and falling onto the floor. Now on all fours, I felt blindly around me. My hands slowed as they encountered jagged rock and sharp glass, but I continued to reach out further, until I felt the unmistakable softness of cloth. I gripped harder, realizing it was a person I had a hold of—a woman's smooth leg.

From where I assumed was her head, I heard a wet gasp. "Help me."

"It's going to be all right," I assured her. I crawled up

closer to her when from the darkness, the whip of a backhand hit me across the face, throwing me backward, my shoulder cracking against the cold floor. I groaned in pain, the sound joining the cries of the others. Set had completely demolished the museum. I had no idea how many people he'd hurt or killed, if my Kindred brethren were all right or not. I tried to move, but before I made it too far, my invisible attacker buried a kick in my stomach. I curled inward, my arms folding over my ribs, as a cough wracked my body. My mouth filled with blood, the bitter metallic taste familiar. "That's enough," Set commanded, the sound coming from far away.

I coughed again, spitting the blood onto the floor. Trying to move slowly so I didn't agitate my ribs, I reached for the ring daggers I'd hidden in my leg sheath. I found nothing but the thin leather strap. Whether Set had taken my weapons, or they'd been lost during the explosion, I couldn't be sure.

"What do you want?" I yelled out into the darkness, not exactly sure where Set was. At the same time, I pushed my powers outward. It was too dark to see, but I could use them in other ways. I searched desperately for Roman. The cool breeze on my spine told me he was nearby, but no matter how much I searched with the bond, I couldn't narrow down his position. My body was beat to hell, and I couldn't tell if all the pain belonged to me, or if some were echoes from his injuries. The best I could tell myself—the fact that I was still breathing—told me he was alive.

From behind me, two large hands grabbed my upper arms,

pulling me to my feet. I bucked backward, thrashing wildly against my captor, doing anything I could to fight back. I threw my head back, satisfied when it connected to flesh and I heard the soft crunch of a nose. "Dammit!" a familiar voice growled. Before I could figure out who it belonged to, I was turned around quickly, and a fist blasted me across the face, knocking me out cold.

When I came to, it was quiet. The screams of the museum had faded to the background, and I was only able to hear them if I really strained my senses. I was sitting up, propped against something damp and hard. I opened my eyes slowly, the throbbing in my head forcing me to move slowly. It did me no good, considering wherever I was now was just as dark as the museum had been. I could see nothing, no matter which direction I turned. Blindly, I bumped against something hard, a rock of some kind. I tried to move it, to dislodge it from the ground, but no matter how hard I tried, it didn't budge. I tried calling on my power to help, when a distant sound froze me in my tracks.

Faintly, just far enough away that I could have imagined it, I heard the rushing of water. It was familiar, a sound I would recognize anywhere. I'd been hearing it in my dreams for months. I completely forgot about the rock. Instead, I felt the ground again, realizing this time that what I'd mistaken as rubble from the explosion was in fact something very different. I was underground and the sounds were coming from above.

I raised my hands in the air as I summoned my element. It

reacted slowly, my connection to the rest of the Guard severed. I slammed my palms to the ground, the torches in the cave firing to life around me. Just like in my dreams, I was in the antechamber of The Hall of Two Truths.

I pushed to my feet, ignoring the dust and dirt that now covered my dress. The painting of Maat above the stairs shone in the firelight, the hieroglyphics seeming to shimmer with life. I gasped, when below the writing, I found Cassie and Mallory laying in heaps on the rock floor with twin bruises on their faces. They weren't moving, but I could see their chests rising and falling steadily. They were alive. My heart raced with rage when next to them, the light revealed their captor and the source of my own pain.

Nero.

He stood next to Mallory and Cassie, his hand wrapped around the crimson pommel of his favorite sword. His eyes blazed, his mouth set in a hard line, still covered in dried blood from where I'd headbutted him. He looked every bit the hardened warrior his reputation made him out to be. "You son of a bitch. You betrayed us."

"It is not betrayal to survive. I simply chose the winning side."

"You used us!" I shouted, my voice echoing off the walls. He'd played his part perfectly. He and his men worked with us, learned our strengths, punished us to weaken our physical resolve, all until he got the information he needed. Then he'd run directly to the enemy. "You're going to pay for it with your life," I promised him, summoning my element. The torches blazed, my hands immediately lit up with flames. The tongues of the flames licked up my arms, wrapping themselves around my skin in a deadly caress.

Nero's eyes turned a sharp red. "I am an Aries, girl. Fire cannot harm me."

There was that word again. *Girl*. I was going to burn him alive.

"Your power can only hold for so long. I'd like to find out which of us is stronger."

I'd been so focused on Nero, I hadn't thought to look around the cavern. From behind me, Set's giant voice broke through the space. "And so it is written. Only the master of the elements—the lord of the Earth, the king of the Air, the ruler of the Water, or the keeper of Fire may enter into the river. For if they emerge, they may summon that which is kept beyond its shores. For all others will perish, doomed to wander Duat deaf, dumb and blind, whether human, god, or Kindred," I wheeled around, finding him leaning against the opposite wall, his arms crossed, his stance casual. I strengthened my hold on the fireballs, refusing to relinquish my only weapon. "Nasty little warning, isn't it? I'm paraphrasing, of course. Ancient Egyptian doesn't translate perfectly into English. Still, you get the point. Maat always was a vindictive little bitch. Seemed she wasn't too interested in the Kindred wielding the sceptre. Funny, that she'd deny you the one weapon that could ensure your ultimate victory."

I replayed the words in my head. *Master of the elements. The keeper of Fire.* I looked down to where the fireballs still raged in my palms.

A Descendant.

Only a Descendant was truly the master of their element. It lived within us, as much a part of us as our blood and bone. Sandra had been wrong. I could survive the waters. *Only* I could. "Seems more like you were the one she wanted to keep out," I snipped. "After all, she is the one that left you, wasn't she? I'm assuming that little sob story you told me upstairs was about you and Maat. About how you loved her, but she dumped your ass for Thoth, and when you couldn't handle it, they had to put you down." I dared a step forward, feeling a sense of bravery that was probably ill advised. "I realize you haven't dated in like a millennia, but no one likes a clingy ex. It's pathetic."

The air around me crackled with power. "You forget the part where I tortured them for centuries, turning their precious humans into wraiths, polluting their kingdom with chaos and discord. And when they created the Kindred to combat my strength, I corrupted them too, using their own creation against them. Now I have returned and my children and I will wipe the Kindred from the face of the Earth. Only after she has watched me destroy her most precious creation—then I will come for her and her lover. And I will end them too."

It seemed Sandra hadn't been the only one that was wrong. It wasn't the door into The Hall of Two Truths that Set needed me to open. He needed me to open the door to the other side, to the Inbetween. "I won't get the sceptre for you," I told him. "I'd rather die first," I promised him.

Set's eyes glowed brighter, and I swore inside them I could see the rumbling of storm clouds. "I intend to change your mind."

A scream sounded from behind me, the sound shrill and deafening. It pierced my heart, the voice so familiar, I would know it anywhere. My flames immediately extinguished as I spun to my friends, to where Cassie was now screaming, her eyes wide, her back arched unnaturally off the ground. Her screams woke up Mallory, who instantly shuffled to her girlfriend. "Cassie?" she asked. "Cassie, baby, what's wrong?" Her voice was confused, her hands hovering over her girlfriend, unsure of what to do. Of how to help. Cassie's body dropped back with a thud, her body convulsing as if hundreds of volts of electricity were coursing through her. Mallory turned to me, her eyes frantic. "What's happening to her?!" she shouted. "Stop this!"

I turned to Set. "I'll do it!" I said. I didn't bother telling him that I'd already tried going into the river, that it had almost killed me before. That I needed an anchor to keep me in this world. Still Cassie's body shook, her screams morphing into a keening wail. Above her, Nero watched with maniacal pleasure. "I said I'll do it!" I screamed. Mercifully, the convulsions quit, Cassie's body relaxing, going limp against the ground. Mallory scooped her up, holding her protectively against her chest. Her eyes were a livid gold, the color cutting through the tears and smudged mascara that stained her face.

Set smiled, the storm clouds in his eyes settling once again. "Good. Then let's begin." I reached down, removing the nude stiletto pumps I'd been wearing. The dress was ridiculous enough, at least my feet wouldn't be killing me anymore. I turned to the two tunnels, the same two I'd seen for months. Set's shadow loomed behind me, filling me with the familiar sense of dread. Standing where I was now, I finally understood what my dreams had been telling me. I was always destined to enter the rivers, always destined to do it with Set at my back.

I paused at the mouth of the first tunnel, the rush of the water beckoning ahead. Set grabbed my shoulder, spinning me around. "Try anything heroic, and I'll let Nero kill your friends. Slowly."

I pulled my shoulder from his grasp and took my first step into the grayness of the tunnel. Just as before, the trip was short, the water waiting not far from the entrance. The sunlight streamed in from above, even more unnatural than the first time, considering I now knew the river was under a building and had no source of outside light.

I dropped into the water, my dress billowing around me like ink. With one final breath, I surrendered myself to the water.

30

I expected the darkness. The blinding abyss that I'd seen the last time I'd entered the water, or maybe the base of Maat's Hollow again, but this time was different. This time I was outside, the sun bright and warm on my skin. I wore the same dress, my bare feet dug into the soft white sand. I turned in place, but no matter where I looked, there was nothing around me. Nothing but endless sand and sunlight. "A child of Aries found in the Inbetween, things are dire indeed," a strong, female voice said. I wheeled around to the source of it, coming face to face with a beautiful woman. Her skin was a deep burnt umber, her eyes the greenest jade, her hair long and jet black. She wore a white chiffon dress, the base of it willowing out behind her on some unseen wind.

"What is this place?" I asked her.

"Nowhere," she responded. "Everywhere. It is a place reserved for those like you, so they may come speak to me, if they wish." Her voice was beautiful, musical almost.

"Who are you?" I asked her. She didn't answer. Instead, she simply smiled, and flashes of images appeared in my mind. A statue of a fierce warrior queen, a hand wrapped around the was-sceptre, a goddess with wings of the brightest colors. "Maat," I whispered.

"I've been waiting for you. Waiting for you to discover the truth of your power so that you might visit me."

"I've tried," I answered. "I was never strong enough."

"You've always had enough strength," she gently corrected. "You just didn't believe you did. You thought you needed others to give you power. It wasn't until you realized the magnitude of your own strength, the truth of what you are capable of, that you were worthy of passing through the river." I dropped to my knees in front of her, relief pouring from me. This was the key. We didn't need the sceptre to put down Set. We didn't have to fight him alone. Maat could help. "No, my child, I cannot," she said, and I didn't know if I'd said the words aloud, or if she'd heard them in my mind.

"Why not?" I demanded. "It's not fair for us to have to fight him alone. We aren't strong enough. You *have* to help us."

She grabbed my hand, raising me to my feet. "My presence on Earth would upset the balance of power too much. Set's return has already done enough. Earth would not survive two ancient beings fighting to the death. It must be you." She held out her hand, and from nowhere, the was-sceptre appeared, the inlaid metal swirling like mercury. I stared at it in awe. "This is what you came for." She held it out to me. "Take it."

"Set will take it from me the moment I return," I contested.

Maat smiled softly, "Take the sceptre and have faith. All is not lost."

I reached out tentatively, my palm touching the wooden handle of the large staff first. The sceptre burned with heat at the touch, hot and yet it didn't burn me. I looked to Maat, but she'd already disappeared. Nothing but empty space and sand where she once stood. I closed my eyes and wrapped my fingers around the sceptre.

When I opened them again, I was back in the cave, lying alongside the river bank. Next to me, the sceptre pulsed with power. I grabbed it, the same power coursing through me that I felt in the Inbetween. I stood up, marching back to the antechamber.

I entered the cavern, Set's eyes lighting up when he saw me. I glared at him, the strength and devastating power of the sceptre coursing through me. We'd had a plan—get the sceptre then use it to trap Set in his cage. But I didn't have the cage. I didn't have Maat to help, or even the Guard. Only I stood between Set and the innocent people of the world. And I had the weapon to take him down.

Set took a step toward me, his hand out to grasp the sceptre. I turned it forward, placing my other hand on the back end, aiming it directly at his heart. He stopped in his tracks. "What is this?"

"I told you, I won't let you have the sceptre," I warned him.

"You use the sceptre, and you're sentencing your friends to death," he said. Logically, I knew he was right. Knew if I used this weapon, Nero would kill Cassie and Mallory. I hesitated, looking to them. To two of my best friends. People I would gladly give my life for.

Mallory stared back, her eyes hard, her arms still wrapped protectively around her girlfriend's limp body. She had been so much to me.

An enemy, a trainer, a comrade, and finally, a friend.

But she wasn't just my friend, she was a warrior. And I knew she would gladly give her life too, if it meant saving everyone else. As if he could feel the silent conversation between the two of us, Nero moved behind her, one hand wrapped in her caramel colored tresses, his blade at her throat. A single tear fell down her face, but she made no move to escape, and I knew she'd made up her mind. As if she could read my thoughts, Mallory gave me the slightest nod. Her permission to fight. To attack Set and finish this, even if it cost her life.

With a numbing resolve, I turned away from my friends and back to the god in front of me. I called to my power, called to the power I could feel burning in the sceptre. I built it up as much as I could. Just as the power hit its breaking point, and I could no longer hold it, the entrance to the cavern exploded.

The concussion of the blast threw me backward, and I lost my grip on the sceptre. It went skittering across the floor, and as I crawled after it, stone and rubble rained down on us, my back getting pelted with debris. From the entrance, soldiers poured in, a mixture of hybrids, Coterie, and Kindred. Everyone was fighting everyone, and it was difficult to tell friend from foe. I was confused until I saw who led the charge. Amina at the helm, the Guard tore down the steps of the temple, descending everything into chaos. Set must have posted Coterie and hybrid guards at the entrance to keep anyone else from getting in. They should have known that wouldn't have stopped them. That nothing could get past the strength of the Guard.

The space filled with the power of my Guardsmen, with the strength and emotion of my Rafiq. I saw him blazing through the enemy, his blade flying, his eyes a molten gold. He cut down the hybrid ahead of him with a mighty roar, his gaze finding mine across the battle, our eyes locking. Behind him, a Coterie soldier raised his sword, intent on bringing it down on Roman's back. I screamed his name, pointing behind him. Roman spun, bringing his blade up at the same time, gutting the man that would've killed him.

My allies fought fiercely, Brynn's purple dress twirling with her as she flew through the air, knocking down a hybrid with his dagger intent on one of Amina's soldiers. Bodies dropped to the cavern floor one by one, and I smiled when I realized who they belonged to. The floor was littered with hybrids and Coterie men. Traitors to the Kindred. There were only a few remaining. Soon all of the enemy would be dead.

We would win.

From behind me, Set let loose a mighty roar, one that shook the entire cavern. I threw my senses out to the Guard, searching for their power, them eagerly grabbing ahold of me as I combined my power with theirs, as they pulled me behind the shield they'd created. I could feel each of them, their strength and bloodlust almost tangible. I pulled on it, took my share as I built a fire within me. I rose to my feet, turning to Set and launching it at him. The flames flew toward him, not just a fireball, but a giant wall of fire that wrapped itself around him, holding him in place.

I scrambled toward where the was-sceptre still laid, no one having been able to reach it yet. I could feel him behind me, the cooling presence of my Rafiq as he ran after me, just ten feet behind. He knew what I was going after. Knew how important it was.

Ahead of me, Nero also saw what I was lunging for. He broke from his location, where he'd been thrown during the blast and sprinted for the sceptre. He was closer, but I was faster. My fingers wrapped around the handle of the sceptre and I turned, throwing it to where I knew he would be.

Not Roman, but Grady.

He caught it, and I screamed to him. "Get it out of here!"

He didn't hesitate, sprinting for the stairs, two of Amina's soldiers flanking him. Set let loose another mighty roar, shaking the cavern again as he thrashed against his fiery prison. The flames faltered but did not break, and Grady disappeared from view, out into the world. To safety.

Searing pain ripped across my back as Nero's blade came

down across my flesh. I screamed, Roman's cry echoing mine. I dropped to a knee just before the crimson pommel of Nero's sword slammed down on my nose, crushing the bones. I fell backward, landing in a groan as blood instantly spewed from my now broken nose. Nero stood above me, his heavy booted foot on my chest, onyx blade poised at my throat.

"I should have killed you the moment you showed up at Ozero Lobaz. Now you've cost me the most prized possession in the world." He raised the sword upward. There was nothing I could do. I was completely at his mercy.

"Nero, no!" I heard Roman yell. "Please, Father, don't! I beg of you!" I turned to look at him, my vision blurry. He staggered to his feet, the bridge of his nose cut, blood dripping from the wound. His chest was heaving with exertion, his tux covered in ash and blood. Behind him, Amina cut down the final enemy. Brynn ran to Mallory and the now awake Cassie, helping them both to their feet.

I could see the moment the realization of what he'd said hit Nero. The moment the word registered in his head. *Father.* Nero turned, his eyes wide in disbelief. "What did you just call me?"

Roman staggered forward, stopping ten feet away from Nero only when he pushed the tip of his blade deeper into the thin flesh of my throat. "It's true. I am your son. I didn't die fifteen years ago, like you thought. The Council saved me and took me in. They lied to you and let you believe I'd been killed along with my sister so they could use me against you one day." Nero hesitated for the slightest moment, his eyes scanning over Roman, and I knew he was seeing what I did. The same set of the jaw, the similar build. Roman was physically so much like his father, that once you knew they were related, you couldn't help but see it.

"Impossible!" Nero protested.

"It's true," I responded, ignoring the bite of his blade. "I've seen the records myself."

"I'm begging you Father, if I ever meant anything to you, please don't kill her," Roman pled. Indecision churned in Nero's eyes as he studied the younger man in front of him. On the opposite end of the cavern, Set ripped free from his fiery cage. His eyes churned as he built his power. No matter Nero's decision, in a matter of moments, Set would kill us all.

"Wait!" I shouted, both to Nero and Set. "Don't kill us! I can get you what you want! I can help you get your revenge on Maat!" I screamed it at the top of my lungs, desperate for Set to hear me and halt his assault. Nero stayed his hand, whether from Roman's confession or my words, I wasn't sure. He looked to his new master. Whatever signal he was given, Nero pushed his foot off me, and my lungs filled with air again.

I rose to my feet, ignoring the pain that radiated from every part of me. "You don't need the sceptre," I said to Set. "I can help you get your revenge, just let them go." I swallowed, my mouth dry and full of dirt.

Set's eyes calmed slightly, the red veins pulling back. It was the best I was going to get. "Take me," I pled. "Take me, and you can use my blood to make more Kindred hybrids. That's what you want, isn't it?" I asked him. "To corrupt her creation. That's what you said."

"No!" Roman objected. I ignored him. I'd been in this situation before. Underground and faced with life or death decisions. This time I wouldn't let others pay while I walked away. This time, I would protect them.

Set turned those red eyes on me. "It is no longer enough." The electricity in the air charged and I knew he was going to let loose his power. He was going to disintegrate all of us.

"I saw her!" I screamed, and the power quieted. I heaved a breath. "I saw Maat. I can get you to her."

"How?" Set sneered.

I stood taller, ignoring the searing pain. "Spare their lives, and I'll tell you."

The chaos god paused, mulling over my words. He looked to Nero. "Take her."

My shoulders slumped in relief. He'd agreed. Nero grabbed ahold of my shoulders, pushing me toward the god.

"Nero, you can't do this!" Roman yelled as he approached the Nomarch. Brynn reached for him, but he shook her off. Roman dropped to his knees, in front of me, in front of Nero, tears in his eyes. "Please, Father. I'm begging you.

As your son." He paused. "I love her." His voice broke. My breath escaped me at the gravity of what he'd said, of what he'd confessed in front of everyone here. In front of Brynn, Cassie, and Mallory. In front of Amina, a Nomarch. He would save me from Set, just to damn us with the Council.

Nero's eyes softened for the slightest of seconds, and I knew he believed what Roman had said. He believed he was his son.

As quickly as they had the first time, his eyes changed again, his lips setting into a hard line. "I have no son."

I wheeled around on Nero, thrashing in his grasp as he pushed me toward Set. He punched me, his fist landing directly in the wound he'd put on my back, dropping me to my knees at Set's feet. Set placed a hand on my shoulder, his other on Nero's.

A tear escaped as I looked at Roman. "I love you," I told him. "I'm sorry."

And then we vanished.

Epilogue

Roman

I leaned over the table to study the map. Again. I surveyed the giant red Xs that dominated the space, their bloody color taunting me.

I'd failed her. Again.

The door opened behind me, a single set of footsteps echoing on the hard floor. I didn't bother turning around. "What's it say?" I asked.

Mallory Saenz stepped up next to me, leaning against the table, her eyes lingering on the map. She tossed a single sheet of paper over the top of it before crossing her arms. "Same thing as the last ten letters." My eyes froze on the simple sheet momentarily before I snatched the red marker and drew another X, this time on the western side of the map.

"Aren't you going to read it?" Mallory asked.

I shook my head stiffly. "I don't need to." I knew exactly

what Daniela's letter said. *Searched the area. No sign of her.* Her responses were always short. No greeting, no signature. I didn't take offense. It was better that way. Daniela was still posted within Amina's forces overseas and she was taking a large risk corresponding with me the way she was. An even bigger risk using her resources and connections to quietly search for Kyndal. Keeping her letters short minimized the risk of exposure if someone were ever to intercept them. "Tell her to move to the east side of the river, just north of the city," I ordered Mallory.

"They've already tried there," she responded.

"Then the south side of the city," I replied immediately.

"Been there."

I scratched the back of my neck, my unusually long hair prickling my skin. "Then tell her to search the Egyptian Museum."

"They've already done that, Roman," she responded, her tone growing testy. "The cave was empty. She's not there."

I slammed my fists down on the table, splintering the dark mahogany. "Tell them to check again!" I roared. The glass doors in front of me blew open, the wind flying through the room, billowing the curtains out wildly. Within the wind, I could smell the salt of the ocean spray, hear the crash of the waves against the cliffs of Awen. It was late, the sky so dark and cloudy, not a single star was visible in the sky. Mallory raised her eyebrows in surprise although she made no effort to move. I closed my eyes, taking a few deep breaths to try and reign myself in. When I was younger, anytime my temper got out of control Sandra had always told me to breathe. Close my eyes and take three deep breaths.

It never worked.

I kept my eyes trained on the table, unfurling my fists finger by finger. The wind left as quickly as it had arrived, leaving behind it nothing but a light breeze. "It's been six months. Six months, and we haven't found a single lead as to where she is. There have been no hybrid sightings, no wraith attacks of note, it's like they dropped off the damn planet."

"We'll find her Roman. She will resurface and the moment she does, we'll get her back."

I pushed off the table, turning to Mallory. She and I had never been very close. Her girlfriend Cassie was one of the closest things I had to family, and over the years Mallory and I had grown to be friendly. But I had never thought of us as friends. It had always been Cassie that connected us. Without her, I always assumed we'd have no reason to talk to one another. But I realized in that moment, it wasn't just Cassie that we had in common. It was Kyndal, too. And Mallory cared about her just as much as I did.

"I can't feel her," I admitted quietly. "The bond. It's gone silent." I hadn't admitted that to anyone. Could barely admit it to myself.

"You've never been this far away from each other before. Maybe it doesn't work over great distances."

I grimaced, feeling defeated. "I tried the magnification spell in the book. Nothing happened."

Mallory pursed her lips, equally frustrated. "Have you thought. . ." she began, cutting herself off quickly. I stared at her expectantly. She began again. "I mean, have you thought about asking for Astrid's help?"

"No," I answered immediately. "No way." I took a few steps back.

Mallory followed. "I'm just saying. Daniela is connected, but she doesn't have nearly the resources Astrid does."

"Why should I ask *her?*"

"You're living in her house. She kept Amina from killing you after you announced you and Kyndal are still involved. Clearly, she has a soft spot for you."

I ground my teeth together, trying to stifle the anger I could feel rising up again. On the surface, Mallory was right. Astrid *had* done a lot recently to keep me alive. It was her influence that kept the Guard intact. If Amina had her way, she would have disbanded the Guard immediately after Cairo and then executed me. While she hadn't been able to do that, she had managed to strip me of almost everything, including what remained of my good reputation and my house. She'd turned the people against me, playing on the fears they already harbored—that I was still a dangerous hybrid. It wasn't safe for me in Awen.

Hence, me living in one of Astrid's several guest rooms.

I knew enough to know that Astrid did not do those things to save me. She did them to gain leverage over me, and over Kyndal. "I don't want Astrid's help. She plans to use Kyndal's blood to lock Set away. She wants to kill her. I won't let that happen. We'll find another way." Mallory took a deep breath in through her nose. I knew she was irritated with me, but I didn't care. All I cared about was getting Kyndal back safely. "Tell Daniela to send people to the Egyptian Museum again. Maybe we missed something," I said. Both an order and a dismissal.

Mallory nodded once, then walked out without another word.

As soon as the door shut, I flopped back on the bed and shut my eyes. I was exhausted, both mentally and physically, but no matter how tired I got, I never fell asleep for long. Even now, as sleep evaded me, I laid there in the quiet and thought about her.

Where was she?

Was she all right, or was she hurt?

I built her in my mind, imagining her somewhere safe. Sitting on her back porch. Running through the Allegheny. Lying in bed next to me, her wild hair fanned out around her.

I must have fallen asleep at some point, because the next thing I realized, sunlight was streaming through the still open balcony doors. I refused to move, instead choosing to stare at the ceiling from atop the comforter. The room was bright, the ornate details of the chandelier above me clear.

From the look of it, I'd slept through the early morning and it was closer to noon. I could feel the heat of the wind off the ocean, the humidity of it sticking to my skin. With a groan, I hoisted myself up, dropping my face in my hands and scruffing my hair. The wind blew in again, this time bringing with it a different heat. A familiar sensation I would recognize anywhere. I jumped to my feet, wheeling toward the balcony.

She stood there, overlooking the ocean, her back to me.

"Kyndal?" Her name tore out of me.

She turned toward me. She was dressed in her fighting gear, her hair pulled back, green eyes fierce.

A warrior.

I knew she wasn't real, that there was no way she could be here in Awen. A part of me understood that I must have fallen asleep and was imagining her.

I didn't care.

Real or not, she was standing right in front of me, so close I could *feel* her magic radiating from her. Almost against my will, I ran toward the balcony, stumbling over my feet. I reached for her, drawn by her warmth. I expected to feel nothing or for my fingers to fall through her skin like mist and prove this was an illusion, but my fingers brushed her arm, and I *felt* her. My eyes wide with shock, I looked up to her face.

"Kyndal?" I said again. I couldn't think of anything else to say.

She smiled, her green eyes twinkling. "Hi, Roman."

About the Author

Whitney Estenson was born and raised in Topeka, Kansas. The daughter of two teachers, she spent her summers swimming at the pool. Through the years she played several sports, including softball, basketball, volleyball, and running track. While traveling to the next tournament, an hour or several states away, Whitney always brought a book. It was on these long trips that she developed a love of supernatural and fantasy stories.

After high school, Whitney attended Washburn University, graduating with a Bachelor of Arts in English Education in 2009. That summer, she married her husband Josh in a seven-minute ceremony on a Jamaican beach. When she returned, she began her teaching career and has been teaching middle school ever since. In 2012, she received a Master of Science in Educational Technology from Pittsburg State University. In 2013, Whitney and Josh welcomed their daughter Avery.

Follow Whitney on Facebook: The Ascendant Series by
Whitney Estenson,
Instagram: the_ascendant_series,
and her website: theascendantseries.com

--A Gift For You--

The first two chapters of Book IV in

The Ascendant Series:

HOUSE OF SCORPIO

Available on Amazon and wherever books are sold.

1

Roman

The city was sleeping.

I leaned against the pillars of Council Chambers, staring upward, watching as a black cloud traveled across the night sky on an unseen wind, revealing behind it hidden stars.

I let the wind fill me and recharge my strength as I stared at the stars. There were four of them. Three clustered together, their lights bright and twinkling, the fourth off to the side. Near the others, and yet separate, not as bright. As quickly as they appeared, they disappeared again, covered by a different cloud. It was strange for the skies above Awen to be hazy. Apart from when we burned a funeral pyre, I couldn't remember a time where I hadn't been able to look up and see the clear sky. When the stars hadn't shone down brightly on the city, illuminating the buildings with their brilliant light. Now, the buildings cast an eerie orange glow, the torch light reflecting off the dense clouds that covered the island.

I scanned the city, my gaze jumping from one building to the next as I marked the areas that still showed signs of battle, that had not yet recovered from the attack late last year. We'd made progress, the various cleanup crews focusing on the most important buildings first. Like the arena, which had suffered the most damage—I'd personally seen to that. Now the walls were repaired, the destroyed dais removed as if it was never crumbled upon the sand. We didn't have enough soldiers to dedicate to the recovery effort, and several of the secondary buildings were still broken and unattended. Glaring reminders of the chaos Set and his hybrids had created.

Chaos *I'd* created.

I pushed away those dark thoughts, instead opening the notebook in my hands and shifting through the pages, trying to find an empty spot. The papers were covered in scribbled notes and roughly drawn sketches, their corners turned down from use and years of wear. I couldn't count how many times I'd opened this thing. How many times I'd wrung it between my hands, frustrated that all it did was raise questions rather than provide answers.

I managed to find an empty corner on one of the back pages. I grabbed the pencil from a hidden pocket in my tactical pants and scribbled down a few words, adding to the growing list.

No weapons.

Healthy.

Sage.

I underlined that last one several times, the tip of my pencil digging into the paper. I'd been recording everything I could remember all day, any chance I got, desperate not to forget anything, just in case it could be the key.

The key to finding her.

Last night, after six months of no leads, six months of silence, I'd seen her. It had only been for the briefest of moments, but she had been real. I had felt her presence as if she were standing next to me. I had no idea how it happened, no idea if I could do it again. All I knew was one moment I was lying in bed, thinking of her, and the next she was there, standing on my balcony.

"Kyndal?" I had said, not believing it was really her. I shook my head at my own stupidity. I'd imagined over and over what I would say to her when I finally held her again. How I would tell her I love her, declare it in front of everyone, shout it from the rooftops if they let me. How I'd promise her that *no one* would ever take her from me again. Ever. But last night, face to face with her, I hadn't remembered any of that. Instead, I bumbled around like a fool, unable to say anything but her name.

I closed my eyes, imagining her smile, remembering the mischief I'd seen dancing in her eyes at my obvious lack of speaking ability. Kyndal always enjoyed poking fun at me whenever given the chance. In fact, she was one of the few who wasn't too afraid to do so. She was fearless. Just one of the reasons I loved her.

One of the many.

I heard them coming from several hundred feet away. No one was walking the city at this time of night. The general population was confined to their housing under Amina's new citywide curfew, so I knew the only people walking the streets were those given special permission to do so. That was a short list that only included her personal sentries and the Guard. After our return from Cairo, Amina cleaned house, eliminating all Council guards and replacing them with soldiers from her own armies. Soldiers loyal only to her, as the Guard was now expected to be. I listened closely to the cadence of the steps. The Guard was on tenuous ground with Amina's sentries. Her soldiers thought they were better than us, and they took every opportunity to lord their assumed power over us, knowing we couldn't afford to step out of line. I was in no mood to deal with them tonight. Luckily, the steps didn't move with the casual arrogance of the sentries, but rather firmly and with purpose, moving directly north toward where I now stood on the top of the Council Chambers stairs. There were three distinct sets. I recognized two of them, the sound and pattern of their gaits familiar to me now. I knew that Grady Dunn was on the right, his heavily-booted foot echoing louder than the quieter steps of his partner, Brynn Hughes. He'd been injured in Cairo, and although he was healed long ago, he still carried a slight limp, favoring his right leg. Most people didn't notice small things like that, but I always did. I learned early in life that tiny details like this could be the difference between victory and defeat in battle.

Quickly, before they could round the corner that would bring me into view, I rolled up my notebook, concealing it in my boot. I straightened my back, standing up tall and shifting my face into a neutral mask. Moments later, they rounded the final turn, bringing them onto the main road that led to the bottom of the steps. They walked exactly as I knew they would, the soldier they were escorting walking a half step ahead of them. This time it was a woman. I didn't recognize her, but I could tell she was a warrior. She was dressed in traditional fighting gear, although her dagger wasn't strapped to her belt. Grady or Brynn would have confiscated that when they arrested her. Her hair was buzzed short on the edge, revealing faint scars along the side of her neck. The original wounds must have been deep to leave a permanent mark such as those. It was difficult to scar a Kindred, but not impossible.

As I studied her, I immediately knew it wasn't going to end well for this soldier. Her back was ramrod straight, her eyes steely and defiant as she looked up at the imposing building before her. Just as she understood why she had been summoned in front of the Council, she must have understood what her fate would be, and she didn't hesitate to approach that first step.

As the trio reached me, the soldier paid me no attention, instead keeping her eyes trained on the ornate front door. I nodded respectfully at Grady and Brynn, each of them returning the gesture. None of us allowed our masks to slip. A short time ago, I never would have believed I would ever show the two of them an ounce of respect, but a lot had changed. I now counted Grady and Brynn among my closest friends. Friendships that had been forged in battle and proven time and again.

This was the first I'd seen of either them since my dream, and I was dying to tell them everything, to tell them I'd seen her and see if they had any idea how I could do it again. But it wasn't safe to tell them. Not here. Not when others could be listening.

Almost as if he could read the tension on my face, Grady raised an eyebrow at me in silent question. I shook my head, blowing him off. Just as quickly as I'd done it, Grady turned back around, back to the task at hand, as if the exchange had never occurred. I pulled open the doors to Council Chambers, escorting the three of them into the marble foyer. The torches inside flickered with the breeze, but I turned from their heat, unable to watch the shadows dance on the walls without thinking of her. Of how my Rafiq made fire seem so alive, and how it held no such life since I'd lost her.

I led them down the silent hallway, our boots thundering across the hard floor the only sound. I didn't stop until I reached the next set of doors at the top of the main chamber. There were sentries stationed on either side, though they neither acknowledged us nor moved to open the doors between them. Nearby, Grady bristled, noticing the slight. I pulled the doors open myself, making sure to glare at the sentries as I revealed the waiting Nomarch Council in the chamber below. Letting them know the insult didn't go unnoticed.

Behind me, there was a sharp intake of breath. It was quick, a show of weakness that the unknown soldier swiftly stifled. *She is brave*, I thought. *Good*. She'd need that strength if she planned to survive the next ten minutes. It was easy to tell what made her nervous. It was rare for the Council to be waiting. Typically, they enjoyed making their subjects sit and squirm before making a grand entrance, but not tonight. Tonight, they wanted each person to feel the full effect of the power waiting for them as they descended into the pit. From our place at the top of the ascending gallery, we could see all the thrones, each carved from a single piece of stone, including the one that still sat empty. For there were no longer twelve Nomarchs.

Now there were only eleven.

The Council hadn't replaced Nero, even though it had been half a year since he'd defected to Set's side, taking his army of Coterie soldiers with him. They hadn't even bothered to pretend like they planned to promote the next in line to the Aries throne. Since Nero wasn't dead, technically his seat still belonged to him, but circumstances as they were, he could be replaced. They'd done it before when Ezekiel betrayed us, replacing him with a new Nomarch at the next full moon. That was when the Council still functioned properly. When each Nomarch had a voice.

It had been a long time since the Council worked the way it was supposed to. Now, the Council was nothing more than a trick, a thinly veiled illusion meant to pacify the masses. Those of us behind the scenes, the ones privy to what happened inside Council Chambers, knew the truth. The Council no longer existed. Instead, we only had one ruler.

Amina.

Former Nomarch of House Scorpio, Amina was now Governor of the Kindred, sole ruler of us all. She had declared herself as such after the battle of Cairo. She'd returned to Awen as the victor with the was-sceptre firmly in her possession, spinning a story to the Council about how *her* soldiers recovered the weapon, and only thanks to *her* leadership did we now have the one weapon that could put Set away for good. She made promises of retribution for the deaths of our warriors and ensured a swift victory for the Kindred, united under her rule. Whether through ignorance or fear, the weaker Nomarchs had been eager to agree with Amina, gifting her immediate executive power of the Kindred, making her Governor of us all.

It was a power she was supposed to relinquish when the war is over, but those of us that knew what she was really like, didn't trust she would. She had played the situation perfectly, capitalizing on the efforts of others to further her own agenda. We knew she would never return the power, and as soon as the war was over, she would eliminate the Council completely.

The entire power shift had taken place behind closed doors, without informing the people, and yet slowly, through those of us that resisted her rule, news of Amina's takeover had spread. The soldiers were outraged, demanding that she relinquish her power and return it to the Council. Others called for a complete overhaul of the Council, demanding instead a free election of our leaders. Their cries fell on deaf ears. Although Amina was widely disliked, she'd gained the favor of enough Nomarchs, controlled enough of the House armies, that the individual voices of the people no longer mattered. As a result, pockets of soldiers had grown restless, agitated. Fights broke out in the streets between the warriors who felt slighted by House Scorpio skipping their turn on the wheel and those who believed in her cause or had gained her favor. Infighting between the Houses increased, until it got so out of hand, not even the Nomarchs could keep the peace anymore. Amina, desperate to hold onto her power, began throwing soldiers in the Hollow just to stop the fighting or shut them up. Eventually, once the others realized that those who went into the Hollow weren't returning, it was enough to scare most of the others into silence.

Once her sentries controlled the city, Amina did her best to keep the focus away from herself, instead finding a new villain in the story—the Guard. She claimed it was our insubordination that almost cost us the battle in Cairo, that it was us the people should be blaming for the soldiers we lost fighting Set. She told the people Kyndal was working with Set and had been a traitor the entire time. A spy sent to rip the Kindred apart. Without Kyndal here to defend herself, many people—those that hadn't left Awen to see for themselves—believed her lies. Amina took it a step further, stripping the Guard of our property and reputation, doing everything she could to demean us, just stopping short of disbanding the Guard completely. Instead, she tightened the reins, forcing us to fulfill her every whim and grounding us to the island.

I knew if she could, she would debrand each of us and cast us out. The only reason she didn't was because of The Book of Breathings. Only the Guard could use it.

Despite Amina's campaign against us, the truth of what happened in Egypt had spread slowly. The soldiers, the ones who had been on the ground in Cairo, knew the truth. They saw through her deceit. They knew it was the Guard, not Amina, that found the sceptre. That it was *Kyndal* that retrieved the weapon. They knew she wasn't a spy. That she traded herself to the Chaos god to keep the rest of us safe.

They knew she had sacrificed herself to protect us.

It was dangerous to support the Guard. Amina was always searching for dissent, always looking for the smallest slight, the weakest excuse to find someone guilty and make an example of them. Another rebel to throw in the Hollow.

That exact reason was what brought me to Council Chambers this evening.

We descended into Council Chambers, Brynn, Grady, and I stopping short of entering the circle of thrones. The soldier continued, marching into the middle, her eyes jumping from one Nomarch to the next. I followed her gaze, my eyes lingering on one Nomarch in particular. A woman with stark white hair that hung over her equally pale shoulders and down to her waist—Astrid of House Cancer.

The closest thing the Guard had to an ally on the Council, Astrid had been quietly undermining Amina from the start. Astrid was ancient, over 1,000 years old if the rumors were to be believed, and as such had plenty of connections and warriors loyal specifically to her. She wielded that loyalty like a sword, using it to protect the Guard as much as possible. What would she think when she learned I'd seen Kyndal?

"State your name for the record," Amina commanded the soldier, bringing my attention to her. From where I stood, just behind her throne, I couldn't see Amina's face, but I could picture it. Her eyes would be stern, her face as tense as the rest of her body. As tightly strung as the hand resting on the edge of her throne. She wore a deep blue pantsuit, the only color I'd seen her wear since assuming her new position. A visual reminder of what House, what element controlled the Kindred.

"Briar," the soldier answered evenly. "From House Taurus."

My eyes cut to Grady, also a member of House Taurus. He stood not two feet away from me, but I saw no flicker of emotion on his face. Idly, I noticed Brynn glance toward Grady as well. Waiting for him to say something. To speak up. We both knew he wouldn't. There was no way he could.

"Although you hail from House Taurus, you serve in my army, do you not?" Amina questioned.

Briar nodded once. "That is correct, Governor. I have been a member of your army for twenty years. I have served you proudly."

"Have you now?" Amina asked, the lilt in her voice making it clear that she thought the exact opposite. "Then why is it that you disobeyed my orders?"

"With all due respect, Governor, I have not betrayed you. You are mistaken."

"But you have," Amina disagreed instantly. "You were overheard in the training ring spewing lies to my soldiers, claiming it was not my warriors that defeated Set, but rather giving credit to the Guard. Do you deny it?"

"Adamantly, Governor." The soldier's—Briar's—voice was like hard granite.

Amina lunged forward from her throne. "Are you calling me a liar?" she spit back at her.

"I didn't say that," Briar answered, her tone sharper than was wise. Completely unfazed by the raging Governor. "What I am adamantly denying is your statement that what I was saying was lies. What your source heard was accurate, but all I did was tell the truth. As you mentioned before, I have served in your army for many years. I was in Cairo, and I *saw* what happened that day." That caught my attention. I didn't recognize her from Cairo, but there had been so many soldiers, it was possible I missed her. Amina sat back slowly, her cold eyes never leaving Briar. To her credit, Briar didn't back down. "I will not allow the sacrifices of our own soldiers to be brushed under the rug, replaced by the unwarranted claim of a false leader."

The room went still, each of us waiting to see what Amina would do. No one had spoken to her so brazenly before. Slowly, with the stillness of the deadly warrior she was, Amina stood from her throne.

"You are a traitor. Your kind can not be allowed to remain among decent warriors, lest your poison spread amongst them like a disease."

Briar cut her off. "Then send me to the Hollow with the countless others you have falsely condemned. I am more free beneath its stone than I am under your rule." Next to me, through the bond that connected me to the Guardsmen,

I felt the smallest tendril of Grady's power stir before he clamped it down.

"I am inclined to oblige you," Amina sneered. Her head snapped to the side, her eyes cutting to us. To her Guard, oblivious to Grady's slip. "Take her to the Hollow," she ordered.

Obediently, the three of us stepped forward, Brynn and Grady grabbing Briar by her arms. She made no move to resist. We turned her toward the exit, even as she twisted to stare at Amina, "You can't throw us all in the Hollow," she shouted over my head. "There are more of us than you realize, and we will only support our true leader." I glanced once at Grady, then past him to Astrid, who was watching Briar with intense interest. "She is born of true blood, and when she returns, she will set us all free. You won't be able to hide from us then."

She. Such a small, simple word, but it rocked me to my core. There could only be one person she was talking about.

"You are a false ruler!" Briar continued as we ascended the gallery, pushing Briar through the same door we'd entered. "When the Descendant returns, we will be delivered!"

The door slammed behind us, cutting off Briar's rant and leaving her alone with the Guard. I took two sharp steps forward, pushing Briar out of Grady and Brynn's tight grips and into the marble wall. Two more steps and I was invading her personal space. Neither of my Guardsmen tried to stop me. "What do you know of Kyndal Davenport?" I hissed in the soldier's face. She couldn't know anything. It was impossible. I'd been searching for her for six months and still had no leads.

Briar smiled smugly. "I know that she lives. And I know that only through me will she return to Awen."

2

Kyndal

The sound of drumbeats echoed off the stone walls.

The vibrations shook the dirty ceiling above me, raining dirt and sand down on my head, yet I hardly noticed. What did it matter? My hair was already greasy, dirty, and tangled, and I'd long since forfeited my vanity. I couldn't even remember the last time I'd been permitted a bath. Sunlight streamed in from the tiny barred window high up in the cell—my only source of light. I wasn't permitted a torch, no fire of any kind. They didn't seem to understand that it didn't matter. I didn't require a fire source in order to create my element. I could create fire in the dead of winter, in the middle of a blizzard, or even under water—although I'd admit I hadn't tried that one.

Yet.

I leaned over the side of the stone bench, a knife in one hand, a flattened stone in the other. Slowly, with a precision that came only from months of practice, I ran the knife over the stone, honing its edge to razor sharpness. I knew what waited for me outside the cell door. In my mind's eye, I could see the sand arena, the high stone walls, and makeshift seats that hovered above the pit. Lined with hunks of stone, broken boards—or less common—a trunk of a tree. I could picture the spectators staring down on the gladiators, throwing stones, food, weapons, whatever they can find at us. Smaller than the one in Awen, this arena was a pale comparison, but its beaten-down appearance only added to the savageness of the pit.

It'd been two days since my last fight. Typically, I was forced to fight every day, sometimes several times in a twenty-four hour period, but the last one had been difficult. I'd taken on two Fire User hybrids at once. Each of them was armed with daggers and I was weaponless. It'd been challenging to defeat them, and while I proved victorious, I was badly injured and had taken longer than normal to recover. The extra day was not a kindness, but rather, necessary. The pits were meant to be a show, entertainment for the hybrid troops who had grown restless during the last few months of inactivity. It simply would not do for me to die a quiet death.

I looked now at the gash in my upper thigh. The bleeding had stopped last night, but the tissue was still bright red and tender to the touch. Truth be told, I could use at least another day to heal it. Leaving it open as it was left me susceptible to infection. But without my element, my healing powers worked slower, and I was left with no choice. I knew Set would not let me rest any longer.

Carefully, I ran the sharpened knife over my forearm, pleased when a thin red line followed the blade. Just as the cut was sealing itself, a small magic, the metal door on the other edge of the cell groaned open. The drumbeats flooded the cell, no longer an echo, but now filling every inch of the tiny space. A large, burly soldier stepped into the doorway, shrouded in shadow. I expected him to be a hybrid, this place was crawling with them, but as he stepped into the faint light of the cell, I realized he wasn't. There were no pulsing dark veins, no serrated teeth. Technically, he was Kindred like me, except I recognized him as a member of the extremist group known as the Coterie. An exclusively male group that renounced Maat and solely worshipped her consort, Thoth. The Coterie soldiers had defected from the Kindred decades ago and now were foot soldiers for Set— following in the footsteps of their commander, Nero.

The soldier stared at me expectantly. I stood slowly, minding my injured leg and faced him. "Tell me something," I began, my voice dripping with disdain. I hated the Coterie soldiers and took any opportunity I could to piss them off. They were traitors, not to mention they had tortured Roman and I just a few short months ago. "The Coterie only worships Thoth, right? You renounce all other gods. . ." I let the sentence drop.

The soldier crossed his arms, his biceps bulging outward. "Yes," he answered. "What's your point?"

I shrugged, sheathing my knife in the belt of my pants. "I just wanted to know what it felt like to be serving the sworn enemy of your deity. I mean, I knew you were all a bunch of heartless bastards, but you must really hate yourself for switching sides. Taking Set's orders. Doing everything he tells you. If you thought serving Maat was bad, I can't even imagine how you look yourself in the mirror." I reached the doorway, but the soldier stepped in front of me, his large frame hovering above my obviously smaller stature. I glared up at him. "What? Did I hurt your feelings?"

He paused, glaring down at me, so close I could feel the power and bloodlust radiating off him. He wanted to hit me. Part of me wished he would. I would welcome the chance to beat on a Coterie soldier. We stared at each other for a moment longer, each of us waiting on the other to make a move, when suddenly the drumbeats stopped. I raised my eyebrows. "Looks like that's my cue."

I pushed past the man, marching out into the corridor. I wound through the makeshift hallway, studying it as I always did, as if it would suddenly divulge new information. Carved from the same stone as my cell, the walls were jagged and awkwardly cut. In some places, giant pieces of the wall were missing, like they'd been blown apart in a battle and never repaired. Every so often, sunlight streamed in from the same type of window as that in my cell, but they were situated at a greater distance, forcing the hallway into alternating blocks of light and dark. The floor was sturdy, clearly formed by rock as well, but the top layer was made of sand. Not the soft kind you would find at a beach, but the irritating type that seems to find its way into your clothes, forcing you to spend the next month pouring it out of your shoes.

The Coterie soldier followed me through the passageway, even though the walk was short and there weren't any turn offs or ways of escape. The corridor from my cell led to one place only.

The pit.

As I rounded the final turn, I felt the pounding of their feet. The audience was already there, the mix of hybrids, wraiths, and Coterie soldiers practically salivating as they waited for the fight to begin. As they waited for blood to spill. I reached the end of the corridor, pausing at the iron bars that blocked my entrance to the arena. There was no natural light in the pit, as such it was the only place that allowed torches. They were bolted to the walls, their strength filling me as I pulled their magic into me, replenishing my depleted power supply.

I unsheathed my knife, gripping it hard with my right hand. The fit wasn't exactly right, not like the cool metal of my Kindred dagger, but it was all I was given. I knew that being given a weapon at all was a sign of how difficult this fight would be. If I was forced to fight two hybrids without a weapon, what would today bring?

I received my answer moments later. Metal scraped against stone as the set of iron bars on the opposite end of the arena opened and my opponents entered the sand. Three wraiths marched out, each with dagger in hand, and I breathed a sigh of relief. Wraiths were easier to kill than hybrids. They burned easily and I didn't have to aim for the heart, but my relief was short lived. For the wraiths were not all that came out of the other gate. They were also followed by two hybrids; a Water User and an Air User.

Five against one.

Behind me, the Coterie soldier snickered. Now I understood why he hadn't taken my bait earlier, why he hadn't attacked me when I provoked him. He knew what I was going against. There was no need for him to hurt me. There was plenty of pain waiting for me in the pit.

Another soldier appeared on the opposite side of my gate, unlocking it and pulling it open. My opponents snarled in anticipation as they waited for me to take the final two steps into the arena. I paused a moment longer and their snarls turned to twisted smiles at my hesitation. They thought I was scared. A normal person would be, but I hadn't felt fear in months. Fear only came from having something to lose, and I'd had everything I cared about stripped away months ago.

There was nothing left that could hurt me.

I called to the power that slept deep inside me, using the torches as fuel to give strength to my limbs and dull the pain of the cut in my leg. My eyes changed from a vivid green to a sharp red, and suddenly everything was clearer. Sharper. I could hear the individual grains of sand grind underneath the boots of the wraiths, smell the metallic tang of old blood that stained the walls. I could feel the power course through my veins, a liquid inferno that sang with the promise of blood. I wanted to fight them, to tear them apart. There may be five of them, but I was a Descendant. The most powerful Kindred that walked the planet, and I would not, could not, be stopped.

I stepped onto the sand.

Immediately, the wraith to my left lunged for me. A stupid, reckless move. I dropped low, his arm sweeping wide over my head, even as I swiped with the blade. It cut across his stomach with razor sharpness. A wound like that made with a Kindred blade would have killed him. With a regular knife, all it did was piss him off. I heard him hiss with anger but I had no time to turn around. The first hybrid was running for me, gold eyes ablaze. He threw his arm out toward me, a burst of air following its path, blasting me into the rock wall. I bounced off the rough surface, swallowing a growl. It wasn't so much the pain that had me growling, but the annoyance of getting hit by an elemental attack. If the other Guard members had been here, I could've shielded myself from it. Alone as I was, I couldn't risk using the necessary strength to uphold the spell.

The hybrid followed his attack, his right hook swinging for my jaw. I raised my arm, blocking the blow, returning with a right of my own, directly in his stomach. He buckled forward, just close enough for me to headbutt him directly in his nose.

A satisfying crunch echoed in my ears, quickly drowned out by the jeers of the crowd. They hated it when I did something well. Over his head, I saw all three wraiths coming for me again. They would be on me in moments. I kicked the hybrid in the back of the knee, bringing him to the ground as I lunged for his Kindred dagger in the loop on his belt. I grabbed it, rolling through to the other side of him, putting more distance between me and the wraiths. Buying me precious seconds. I came up from the roll, blade poised, and threw it as hard as I could at the lead wraith. It buried itself in his abdomen and moments later he was gone. The other two wraiths continued their advance on me, not even blinking as they marched through the dust that had once been their ally. I may have eliminated an enemy, but I also had forfeited my best weapon. Forced to improvise, I reached up and grabbed the scalding handle of the torch, ripping it off the wall. I threw the torch at their feet, spreading the small flames with my power, creating a wall between them and me. They immediately quit moving, hissing at me over the growing flames. I pushed the fire closer to them, the growing flames adding to my power, making me even stronger. They were stupid enough to stand too close and the edges of their pants caught on fire. With one final shove of my power, the flames flew up their bodies, engulfing them in a fiery death.

The crowd roared as the wraiths burned. I knew it wasn't excitement for me, just the thrill of watching someone die. With all my focus on the wraiths, I never saw the other hybrid coming. The Water User barreled in from my right, knocking me onto the ground. My knife flew out of my hand, skittering across the sand and into the flames. The hybrid jumped on top of me, straddling my hips, his knee digging into the wound on my leg, that thanks to him was bleeding again. A sharp left ricocheted off my cheekbone, my face instantly swelling. The hybrid raised his dagger, bringing it down directly toward my face. I barely moved fast enough to get my head out of the way. The dagger embedded itself in the ground, so close it sliced my ear on the way down.

I bucked my hips, trying to get the hybrid off me, but he was too heavy. I lunged up, throwing a hard right. It snapped his head to the side, but he came back just as quickly, hissing in my face, his teeth sharp and serrated. I tried to hit him again, this time with my left, but he grabbed my arm, pinning it to the ground. It took him seconds to do it, but it was all the time I needed. While he'd been focused on controlling my arm, I snuck my right hand in between us. Faster than he could see, I built a fireball and blasted him at point blank range.

Directly through the heart.

He flew backward, his lifeless body smacking against the rock wall before landing in an awkward heap on the floor. The crowd roared with disapproval as I jumped to my feet and ran for the dead hybrid, ripping his dagger out of his belt.

I spun around to face my final opponent. Across the small pit, his dagger firmly in his grasp, was the Air User hybrid. Blood had quit gushing from his nose, but it stained his face, adding to his sinister appearance.

"I'm going to rip you apart," he snarled. I let him talk. Let him detail exactly all the creative ways he was going to kill me, the whole while building my power. I pulled from the sand under my feet, the rock in the walls, the flames in the torches, bringing it into myself until I couldn't hold it anymore. Then, with a scream, I released it all, aimed it directly at the hybrid. Just as I had once done on the streets of Cairo. The hybrid went up in flames, his screams cutting off as he fell to the ground, dead.

The audience went quiet, the wealth of my power stunning them silent. I threw my stolen dagger down on the ground, knowing I wouldn't be allowed to keep it, as I glared back at them.

Victorious.